A Liverpool
Girl

Elizabeth Morton was born and raised in Liverpool, spending much of her formative years either at convent school, or playing her piano accordion in northern working men's clubs. When she was eighteen she trained as an actress at the Guildhall School of Music and Drama and went on to work in TV, film, and theatre. She is known for the Liverpool sitcom, *Watching*, playing Madeleine Bassett in the ITV series, *Jeeves and Wooster*, and performing in Willy Russell's plays, including the role of Linda in *Blood Brothers* in the West End.

She began writing after winning the London Writers' Competition and has written plays as well as episodes of *Doctors*, the Radio 4 drama series *Brief Lives*, Channel 4 series *Coming Up* and CBeebies.

She was shortlisted for the Bath Short Story Award in 2014, the Fish Short Story prize, and in 2015 won prizes in the Exeter Short Story competition, and the Trisha Ashley Most Humorous Short Story. In 2016, she was one of six shortlisted for the CWA Margery Allingham award.

She is married to *All Creatures Great and Small* and *Doctor Who* actor, Peter Davison.

ELIZABETH MORTON

A Liverpool Girl

EBURY
PRESS

First published by Ebury Press in 2019

3 5 7 9 10 8 6 4 2

Ebury Press, an imprint of Ebury Publishing
20 Vauxhall Bridge Road,
London SW1V 2SA

Ebury Press is part of the Penguin Random House group of companies
whose addresses can be found at global.penguinrandomhouse.com

Penguin
Random House
UK

www.penguin.co.uk

A CIP catalogue record for this book is available from the British Library

ISBN 9781529103526

Typeset in 13/16.872 pt Times LT Std
by Integra Software Services Pvt. Ltd, Pondicherry

Printed and bound in Great Britain by Clays Ltd, Elcograf S.p.A.

Penguin Random House is committed to a sustainable future
for our business, our readers and our planet. This book is
made from Forest Stewardship Council® certified paper.

MIX
Paper from
responsible sources
FSC
www.fsc.org   FSC® C018179

For my father

Chapter One

May 1953

They had already started decorating the streets in Liverpool in preparation for the coronation. Union Jack tea towels were hung out of tenement windows, a flag was unfurled and hoisted up a pole outside the Cunard Building. Splashes of red, white, and blue had begun to brighten up the city, crepe paper wound around lamp posts, and streamers threaded through railings. A picture of a smiling, soon-to-be-crowned Queen Elizabeth, stuck amongst towers of treacle and condensed milk, cheered up a corner shop window. Packets of jelly and Spam took their places in bare larders, next to bottles of lemonade and ingredients for Victoria sponge cakes.

Babby Delaney glanced up at the bunting, tied from lamp post to lamp post, already edged in soot and twitching in the breeze. Along the dock road,

1

someone had daubed God Bless the Queen on the end-of-terrace wall. Babby was wearing her old communion dress. She was ten years old, and now it strained at the seams and rode up her thighs, exposing white flesh, but she didn't care. Her mother, Violet, had nipped the dress in at the waist with a red sash, bought blue brocade for a shilling from the raggy shop, and stitched it around the hem.

'Mam, what sarnies you made Da today?' Babby asked.

A milky sun rode high over the Mersey and Babby raised her face to it, feeling the warmth on her cheeks. This heat would bring out more of her freckles, stipple the slope of her nose with them. By instinct, she searched out for her mother's hand and grasped it tightly as they walked together, falling into a steady rhythm.

'Mam ...?'

'The usual,' Violet answered. 'Banana and sugar buttie. But Da won't be eating them. You know what the cheeky beggars do?'

Babby, her eyes bright with curiosity, waited for a moment, then shook her head.

'They put all their carry-outs in a big pile and they choose another fella's to eat. That way they get a different sarnie each day – might even get a bit of boiled beef, if he's lucky.'

'None's as good as yours, Mam,' said Babby, loyally.

'I don't know about that,' replied Violet, laughing.

When they got to the Boot Inn, they found Jack, back early from the morning shift at Graving Dock, leaning against the stone wall outside, sunning himself, the gentle breeze blowing his straw-coloured hair upwards to a peak. He seemed older than his thirty-seven years, but despite the two deep grooves between his eyebrows and the hollow cheeks, he was still a good-looking man, broad-shouldered, calm-featured, with strong, graceful limbs, light-blue eyes, and a lopsided smile that revealed neat white teeth.

'Da!' yelled Babby. She ran towards him and he knelt and opened his arms wide, ready to scoop her up.

'Don't you flaming dare! Babby's coronation dress!' cried Violet.

He looked cleaner than usual, there was no dirt wedged under his fingernails, no soot on his face from handling the carbon off the boats, but she was still relieved to see him wipe his hands on his trousers. He laughed, chucking his daughter under her chin. 'You look a picture, sweetheart. Not often we see you in a dress, is it, love?' he said. 'Them hobnailed boots look a bit queer with it, though. We'll have to get you some fancy shoes.'

Babby laughed and twirled, the dress spinning out at the waist. She didn't see her mother shoot a glance at Jack.

'Brought your butties,' said Babby.

'Ta, love,' he said, taking the newspaper-wrapped parcel.

'We best be off,' Violet said. 'I've left our Hannah sleeping in the pram in the back yard. Pat's minding her, but she'll be waking any minute.'

'Your dress is grand, Babby,' Jack said, placing his palms flat against his daughter's cheeks as he spoke into her face. Her eyes met his with a fixed, level gaze. Then he glanced down, took her hand, turned it over in his.

'What's this stuff all over your fingers?'

She grinned. 'Glue. Mam let me and Pat cut out a picture of Queen Elizabeth from the *Echo*. We got flour and water, mixed it all up in a bowl, and then we stuck the Queen on the back of the tea tray and we've put it up in the window of the front room so everyone can see it when they walk past. It was Mam's idea.'

'Was it, now?' he said, exchanging a smile with Violet. Then he added, 'Can't wait to have a look at that. I'll be back later.'

'You singing in the pub when you've finished work? Can I come back and watch?' Babby asked.

'No, love,' he said.

'*Please*,' she said. She was the exact likeness of her mother, with chestnut brown hair, and deep-brown eyes, Babby gave him a look reserved for daughters and their fathers, and for a moment he almost relented.

'Your Da said no. Didn't you hear him?' said Violet.

'Pubs are no places for kiddies,' he said.

'Why not?'

'Come on, Babby ...' said Violet.

Babby watched her mother turn away impatiently. 'I want to hear Da sing.'

Her father pulled her to him, put his mouth against her ear. She could feel his breath, little puffs of air, as he began a simple song, one of her favourites. ''Twas a Liverpool girl who loved me,' he murmured.

She wriggled in closer to him, luxuriating in the soothing sound of his voice, the flesh on her arms rising up in goose pimples at the sweetness of the tone.

When he reached the end of the verse, Jack stood. 'That's your lot,' he said. 'Now off you go before our Hannah starts screaming blue murder when she finds out you're not there. You know you're the only one who she wants to see when she wakes up.'

Babby nodded, waving back at her father as she set off back home, trailing a stick along the railings, enjoying the clattering sound, with Violet urging her to get a flipping move on.

When they had disappeared around the corner, Jack opened the newspaper that Violet had wrapped the sarnies in. Banana and sugar again. He put the package away. God, the Boot Inn smelled welcoming! He tried to push the thought aside and looked the other way down the street, towards the River Mersey, just visible beyond the silhouettes of the huge ships docked there. In the sunshine, the river looked as if someone had scattered silver pieces over its surface. But then something tugged at him and he turned back to the pub again. Through the open door he could see old Sweaty Sock sitting at the bar. Sweaty Sock had earned that nickname because he was never out of the Boot. Just the one, Jack thought. And then he would come back that evening to play his accordion and sing. He didn't want to end up like Sweaty Sock, so just the one. Then he would tell Violet what the foreman at the docks had said to him earlier that day, when he got home.

'All right?' said Sweaty Sock, raising his head, which was flopped in drunkenness, when Jack approached the bar.

Jack gave a small nod in reply.

'The Mouse passed you over again?' pressed Sweaty Sock.

Still smarting, Jack listened as Sweaty Sock continued, 'There'll always be fewer jobs than the men jostling and shoving to get noticed by the Mouse. The pen can be a cruel place – and the Mouse? Don't be fooled by his name. He might speak in that soft voice because the bronchitis did for him, but he's the toughest foreman these docks have seen. Hard as they come.'

'Aye,' answered Jack, as Elsie, the barmaid, pulled him a pint of brown ale. He lifted it to his lips, licked away the froth from the rim of the glass.

'Stop me if I'm speaking out of turn, but it's only right, Jack. No one is saying that you're not a good and reliable docker. One of the best. But the Mouse has to be fair. There's others that don't have the luxury of earning an extra bob like you do with that squeezebox of yours,' he said.

'I don't do it for money,' replied Jack.

'Why do you do it, then?'

'Reckon I like it. I like singing and the craic.'

'Word is, you're earning a fortune,' said Sweaty Sock, winking and shuffling up along the bar, beside him. 'Folks flock to this pub to hear you singing. Like a lark, they say. I heard you was flush ...'

Jack bristled. He pinked to the tip of his ears and felt a rush of anger, his palms sweating.

He took a swig of his pint. Flush? That was a joke. A man needed an honest day's work to keep his family – singing at the pub would never replace the earnings from dock work and that was the end of it. Perhaps one more pint might take the edge off it. Or two. Or three …

At first, he didn't notice the four men come in through the doors. There was the scraping of chairs and the sound of boots on the floor. One of them, a big, bulky brute of a man with a muscular frame, broken veins like the map of the British Empire purpling over his forehead and cheeks, thumped his fist on the table. Then there was some muttering and snorting. Jack looked over to where they were sitting. Their expressions seemed to be forming into grins. Laughter followed. Was it him they were laughing at, he wondered.

He stood up, felt the ground moving under him slightly. He recognised two of them as dockers who worked in Seaforth, whose jobs were to secure the guy ropes and guide the containers up to the wharf. The third was a younger, newer face, but he was definitely the one who had been chosen over him that morning, and the morning before that.

And then the Mouse walked in, his large overcoat billowing out behind him.

It took Jack a moment to register his presence, but when he did, he placed his pint on the bar. 'Well, that's a bit of luck!' he said, striding over, chest puffed out, meeting him at the door. 'We can have it out now, Mouse. You've not given me a day's work for best part of a week.'

The Mouse sighed. 'Jack, bide your time. There's others in the pen that need it more than you.'

'Who says?'

'*I* say,' said a voice from the group at the table.

Jack spun on his heel.

'What's it to do with you?'

The young man stood, squared up to him, smiled a cocky grin, hands thrust deep into his pockets, jangling change.

'Keep out of it,' said Jack, angrily.

The Mouse put out an arm, placed it between the man and Jack. 'Steady on, Jack.'

The young man thrust out his chin, started to sing, ''Twas a Liverpool girl, who loved me ...'

'Shut up!' said Jack.

'One of yours, in't it? You're the fella with the squeezebox? You singing here tonight?'

'I said keep out of it!' said Jack.

Who threw the first punch, who was to blame for the fight, no one would ever know. The police made enquiries, scratched their heads and went away – and came back none the wiser. The only thing anyone could be certain of was that there was a scuffle, cursing, and fists flailing in the air, a broken bottle, and a good kicking, and then poor Jack crashing to the sawdust, his face distorting into a grimace, blood pooling from the back of his head, spreading to the size of a saucer, then to a dinner plate, before dribbling between the gaps in the floorboards, Elsie screaming like a wild animal and racing around from behind the bar, terrified and panicked, and the Mouse fainting dead away, the dockers looking on with horror at the realisation that what had been a lively joshing had, in a few brief moments, changed all of their lives forever.

'What we going to tell Violet?' said Elsie, tears gathering in her eyes. 'What's going to happen to her and Pat and Babby and little Hannah now?' she wailed.

But the question remained unanswered, left hanging in the air as the sound of bells clanging, screeching whistles, and the squealing of tyres became the bigger distraction to poor Violet's fate.

Chapter Two

1955

'Sod this for a ride on the Bobby Horses,' Violet muttered under her breath. The long queue snaked around the front of the Liver building, stretching almost all the way down to the Pier Head. She took Babby's hand and dragged her off in the direction of Water Street, calling back to her son, who was jigging Hannah up and down in her pushchair, to follow. Surely there had to be better ways to find a job than stand in line with the other poor wretches, waiting for the meagre handout that was the three half days a week secretarial work from the man from Liverpool Assurance? How the gossip got around in this place. One mention of a job in the pub and, before you knew it, there were five hundred sharp elbows pushing and shoving you out of the way.

'Mam? Mam!' complained Babby.

Violet sighed, admonished her with a look, then turned away, rubbing her temples tiredly. The last thing she wanted was to get into an argument with her wilful child, so she counted in her head: one elephant, two elephant, three elephant ... She breathed deeply, then stopped to help Patrick with the push-chair. The wheel was coming off and it had stuck in a groove between the pavement slabs. Patrick, typical of a fourteen-year-old boy, thought a good kick would solve the problem.

'Don't do that. You'll destroy the thing,' cried Violet.

'Where we goin', Mam?' he asked.

'Never you mind,' said Violet. 'Here ... let me sort out the pushchair. You go and get your sister. And no running along top of the walls. I'll crown you two if you start playin' silly beggars. I'm not in the mood.'

Babby glanced over her shoulder, saw her mother shoving her hand in her pocket, took advantage of the pause, and ran on. Violet felt the crumpled envelope containing the letter that she had received that morning, reminding her that the rent was going up by two shillings for the house they lived in at Joseph Street. Three pounds and two shillings! It seemed an absurd amount of money for the end-of-terrace that had somehow lost its neighbours when the street had been bombed out in 1942. How could rent be so expensive? Violet had needed this job, needed it more than she needed the love of a good man, or a decent night's sleep, or food in her belly.

'Where we going, Mam?' whinged her eldest daughter after Patrick had brought her back.

'Oh, do be quiet, Babby!'

Violet marched on ahead, instructing Patrick to push the rusting pushchair and to be careful with the wobbly wheel, whilst she searched in her purse for a scrap of paper. Babby watched her mother squinting up at street signs, and reached into the pushchair for the paper bag of broken biscuits.

'Don't think I can't see you, Babby. Share the brokies with your brother,' said Violet. 'And don't eat them all in one go! I waited an hour outside Jacob's for those.'

Babby didn't reply; instead, she hugged the stale, broken biscuits towards her and wheeled around in a circle, laughing at her brother.

'Little pickers get big knickers,' said Violet.

Patrick laughed back. 'Little pickers get big knickers,' he chanted, his voice rising to a crescendo as he raced after Babby and whooped.

What Violet wouldn't do for her kids to have big knickers; big, huge, gigantic knickers. They were skinny, scrawny things, their thin arms and legs poking through their threadbare jumpers and frayed shorts. On the other hand, Hannah – now a toddler – was chubby, with delicious fat arms and fat legs. Violet loved to blow raspberries on her tummy, but Hannah would go the same way as her brother and sister in time, especially if she inherited the same lively bones.

'Mam, I'm givin' our Pat a custard cream,' said Babby, stopping for breath and shoving a tendril of her curly brown hair out of the way.

'Good girl,' replied Violet. And she couldn't help herself. A smile tugged at the corner of her mouth. Thank God for the kids. 'Wait here,' she added.

She stopped outside a row of shops that were boarded up apart from a pawnbroker and a grocery store. Shading her eyes with her hand, she peered into what looked like a shutdown café. There was a curtain with a faded flower motif that sagged limply on a wire halfway down the plate glass window. Babby and Patrick followed Violet's lead, and yet, despite standing on their toes to get a look, couldn't quite see above the curtain and into the dingy room beyond. Hannah, intrigued, cocked her head, kicked her legs, squirmed and arched her back, and cried 'Mam! Mam!' as she demanded to be unstrapped from the pushchair.

Violet regarded her reflection in the rippling glass. She licked a finger and traced the arch of her brows, then ran a tongue over her lips and pinched her cheeks sharply. Straightening out her skirt, she undid a button on her blouse, then another, and reached inside the neckline.

'What you lost, Mam?' asked Patrick quizzically.

'Go and keep an eye on Hannah,' replied Violet, her bosom now swelling and spilling out over the top of her blouse, pillows of white dewy flesh dazzling in the morning sun. Babby frowned. Violet was fairly sure Pat wasn't sharp enough to make the connection between his mother's breasts and paying the leccy bill. But Babby knew, all right.

Violet was smiling when she came out. She was waving a piece of paper above her head, hopping from one foot to another excitedly.

'I've got a job! I told you your dad is looking after us in heaven, kids!' She knelt to speak into Babby and Pat's faces. 'Uncle Billy has said I can start next week!'

Uncle Billy? thought Babby, frowning. This was a new one. There was an Uncle Matty, an Uncle Charlie, an Uncle Joe, and plenty others besides – and aunts, for that matter, none of whom they were related to. But she had never heard of an Uncle Billy. No doubt this Billy was one of those shadowy figures who came up trumps when the Delaney family needed help.

'Start tomorrow! The Kardomah Café!'

Patrick and Babby's eyes widened. They had seen the pictures, yellowed by the sun, of knickerbocker glories and banana splits in the window, the polished brass rails, the neat tables with bowls of sugar cubes, silver cutlery, even linen napkins, but they had never been inside.

'Eh, Mam!' said Patrick, and hugged her, as she enfolded him in her skirts. 'That's posh, that is.'

'I know, love. Well, we're posh now. We're right posh. Don't let anyone tell you that they're better than us Delaneys. I've got a job at the Kardomah Café!' The way she said it, with her nose in the air, executing a small curtsey, made Babby brim with pride.

Violet saw her smiling and ruffled the top of her hair. And she hoped to God she could stick at it, at least until the end of the month.

They reached 17 Joseph Street. It was hard to imagine it had once been an attractive terrace. Their house stood, ugly and alone, on the rise of Everton hill, consumed by damp and dry rot, with rusting window frames. It had spongy floorboards, small grates which were never lit, and ice on the inside of the windows on cold mornings. But it was home to the Delaneys and, as Violet cooked them supper of the stew and tatties Liverpudlians called Scouse, with the smells of onions and Bovril wafting through the parlour, they felt happy and hopeful.

'Hey, Mam, now you've gorra job, will you be able to fix the leaky roof of the outside lavvy?' said Babby.

'We'll see,' Violet said, with a smile.

The following morning, opening the curtains, the sight of the River Mersey from the upstairs room lifted her spirits as always. In the sunshine, it looked like a long silver sleeve trailing across the ground. Factory chimneys belched smoke and the cranes of the ship yards rose up beyond the ugly tenements, the ships' masts forming an intricate forest.

'Always raise your eyes upwards, rather than down the hill. Might even see your dad up there having a pint in the clouds,' she whispered to Hannah, who was still asleep in the bed. She planted a kiss on her cheek, looked back to the window, and decided there was nothing like the vast Liverpool sky to make her feel better about the world.

Violet left Hannah dozing and made her way down to the parlour. She went over to the black-leaded range and stoked the dying embers of the firebox, put in a few pieces of kindling and a couple of lumps of coal to heat the back boiler and the oven. Despite it being seven in the morning, when she opened the shutters she saw Mr Boughton, the rent collector. He was pestering Phyllis O'Neill who lived opposite, twirling his umbrella, parading about in his ridiculous cape. With his phoney smile she thought he looked like the man in the Lucky Strike advert – a right fool. It annoyed Violet that he loitered in the road, and when she saw him handing out a farthing to her neighbour's daughter, the very picture of a kindly old gentleman, she raised her eyes and tutted.

'He's a one. Doling out coppers like he's the Sheikh of Arabia. But when it comes to fixing the house, or putting the rent up, he's as tight and as miserable as they come,' she said to Pat, who had come down to the scullery to make Hannah's porridge.

But not even wily old Boughton could dampen her spirits. She greeted him with a smile as she came down the front steps.

'I've gorra job, Mr Boughton,' she said.

'Oh really?' he replied.

'Kardomah Café. Start this morning.'

'Kardomah?' he said. And he grinned.

'What?' she asked.

He didn't answer. 'See you Friday, Violet.' he replied. 'You owe me a week's rent.'

Violet didn't respond. She wasn't going to let some mean-spirited moneygrubber spoil her day.

She got the tram into town and, when she reached Mount Pleasant hill, it was the cloud of dust rising above the rooftops from the streets beyond that struck her first. The smell hit the back of her throat. Clutching her handkerchief to her mouth, she choked and winced as the particles of cement and brick stung her eyes. It was as bad as the air raids in the Blitz. An accident, perhaps. You would hear of buildings finally buckling under the strain of weakened foundations. She turned the corner, gathering pace. The roaring sound was deafening and she pressed her hands over her tightening eardrums. Bulldozers. There were two of them, the kind that were used in the war, old army tanks fitted with giant blades and stripped of their armaments, causing havoc. They crawled over the debris like metal cockroaches, flattening everything in their wake, on the square of land where, until the day before, houses and shops had stood. There was a crane, with a huge wrecking ball suspended from the top, which at that very moment, right in front of them, smashed into what remained of the terrace. A crowd had gathered. A cheer went up whilst Violet tried to push her way forward to see what was happening. As the dust settled and the crowd broke out into applause, only one back wall was left standing, three storeys high.

It was an unsettling sight; a kitchen sink suspended in the air by its pipes, the outlines of fireplaces, a picture of the Virgin Mary hanging on a nail, remnants of people's lives and no clue as to where these people had gone.

Violet rushed forward, tried to duck under a piece of rope holding back the crowds.

'What the bloody hell are you doing?' she asked a man in overalls and a tin helmet, soot and dust covering his face.

'I could ask the same of you, love. You're not allowed past the rope. It's dangerous. Not a place for a woman.'

'Please, tell me what's happening?'

'You must have heard, love. Corporation's building a load of new flats. Slum clearance ...'

'But you've got to stop! I've got a job at the Kardomah Café! I'm supposed to start work today! Here ... at the Kardomah!' she shouted plaintively.

'I'll have a cuppa and a sticky bun, then,' he said and laughed.

'Mine's two sugars!' shouted another voice, followed by more guffaws.

She blushed, felt her cheeks reddening, knowing it was of little use, and there was certainly nothing the foreman could do about it.

'Sorry, love. Stand back, please ...'

The wrecking ball swung against the building once again. The Kardomah Café became a heap of rubble and bricks, crashing to the ground as Violet pressed her hands over her ears.

Tears sprang to her eyes and she crumpled to the ground.

The man bent down, went to pick her up. 'Can I get you a cup of tea?' he asked kindly. But Violet was in no mood for tea and he saw the sharp end of her tongue.

'Cup of bloody tea's not going to bring my job back. And you – out of my way! You're as much use as a back pocket on a vest,' she said bitterly. She gathered her skirts and set off to see a fella, who knew a fella, who knew a fella, who might be able to help.

Chapter Three

'I got yer, I shot yer! I got yer, I shot yer!' The cries and chants at break time in Saint Aloysius's playground, underscored with the banging of bin lids, the slapping of skipping ropes, and the clanking of the machinery at the nearby tobacco factory, made Babby's ears throb.

She sat on the rockery with a mossy statue of Our Lady tilted at an odd angle and drew her knees up to her chest. Johnny Gallagher pointed his forefinger at her. 'I got yer, I shot yer!' he chanted.

'No, you haven't. I'm on base,' she said, smiling. 'Anyway, aren't you too grown up for kid's games now?'

'Never too old for cowboys and injuns,' he replied, grinning.

Suddenly, there was a rush of bodies, with three boys piling on top of her.

'Gerroff!' she cried, kicking and wriggling under the scrum.

'Where is it?' said one of them. And before she knew it, the boy lay flat on top of her, dove his hands into the pocket of her skirt, and snatched her lunch ticket. A cheer went up as the boy raced around the playground, waving the ticket above his head.

'Babby's got a nought! Babby's got a nought!'

She felt her heart thump at her chest and her face flushed crimson.

Johnny Gallagher leapt up, chased the boy, and hooked a finger under the bottom of his knitted jumper.

'Give it back!' he said. 'She can't help it if her mam is skint!'

Nobody wanted a nought. If your lunch ticket ended in a nought, it meant that you received free school dinners. The unfortunate opposite of winning a raffle, thought Babby. A nought meant you were poor, and with that came humiliation and embarrassment.

'Leave it, Johnny,' Babby said. 'They're eejits. Anyway, I have to go on a message for Mam to the Co-op at lunchtime and collect the divvies.'

'I'll thump 'em if you want. Give 'em bloody noses.'

'Thanks, Johnny. But you're all right. Will you tell Miss Brody about the message?'

'Aye. You better come back, though. Don't be using it as an excuse to go home and eat jam and sugar butties with your Pat.'

'I'll be back,' she said. 'I love school, me.'

Johnny laughed. Babby hated school and the nuns who ran it; she hated the taunts and the times tables and the toffee-nosed kids who looked down on her because the Delaneys had nothing.

'See you later,' she said.

'Don't be going to play out in the bombsites,' he called after her.

Three hours hour later, when Babby appeared in the parlour, casually slinging her school bag on to the floor, she knew that her brother, Pat, who had just got a job working as a message boy at Cunards, would guess straight away that she hadn't come from school. The timings were all wrong. 'Where've you been? Skiving again?' he asked

She didn't reply, just shrugged and asked her brother, 'You eating the last of the brokies?' Sitting at the kitchen table, she grabbed the plate that was in front of him and began pushing crumbs around it with her finger.

'There was only one left. You been sagging school?' he asked again, standing and brushing crumbs from the biscuit off his lap.

'Course not,' she lied. 'Could have shared it with me.'

'You been playing at the hollas?'

The hollas were the hollowed-out wastegrounds where the bombs had fallen in the war. The gaping wounds in the earth that pockmarked the city made Violet shudder every time she walked past one – she swore on her life that there were ghosts wandering about in there, there were. But Babby loved the hollas where they could roam around, feral and savage, set fires, and play hide-and-seek in the derelict houses. Johnny Gallagher once jumped from the first floor of a house and the windowsill had jumped with him – what a laugh that was.

'Mam'll wallop you if she finds out.'

'She won't find out if you don't tell her.'

'What are you doing, running around on your own out there like a wild thing?' He laughed. 'Look at your knee. Mam will tell you to put iodine on that.'

Babby had fallen on a pile of bricks, but she winced at the thought of iodine which would probably hurt more than the scrape she had got. There was the sound of the door. It was Violet.

'Don't snitch. If you tell her I've been sagging school again, I'm for it,' said Babby.

Patrick raised a teasing eyebrow. Violet went straight down to the cellar to put a shilling in the gas meter so Babby took her chance and jumped up from the table and hid herself in the best room, the front one that her mother rarely went in. It had

a balding chintz sofa and carefully arranged ornaments in a glass cabinet – a Toby jug, a statue of
Jesus displaying his bloodied palms and a painted
coronation mug. She loathed the mug. Union Jacks
always reminded her of the day her father died.

Patrick followed her, lolling against the doorjamb.
'What d'you think our mam'll do next if she doesn't
find another job?' he asked Babby.

Babby gave him a quizzical look. It made her feel
uncomfortable to be dragged into the uncertainty of
an adult's world. She had never felt this when her
dad was alive, especially when he would bring back
the half-crowns that he got from the tips for playing
his piano accordion and singing at the Boot. Though
the ground had fallen from under her when he had
died, with the money from the dockers' widows'
charity, Violet had managed to hold things together
over the past two years. But that was running out
now.

'Dunno,' she answered.

'The money that Mam got from widows' fund,
there's nowt left.'

'Isn't there?' asked Babby.

She sighed. A week had passed since the disaster
with the Kardomah Café. And still no job for Violet.
The seriousness of the situation began to dawn on
Babby.

Violet appeared from the kitchen, carrying a bowl of tripe. Babby didn't know how she could eat the vile stuff and her stomach somersaulted just to look at her mother prodding at it with a fork as it slithered off the end of the knife.

'What's wrong, Mam?' asked Babby, trying to sound casual.

'I've got an announcement,' said Violet, beaming.

Babby and Patrick exchanged a worried look.

'Your Uncle Terry knows a fella who knows a fella—'

'You got a job?' asked Pat.

'I have, love.'

'At the Boot?' asked Babby.

Patrick glanced at his sister, threw her a warning look.

Violet slammed down the bowl and wiped her mouth on her apron.

'Now why would I want to get a job at that godawful place? Since what happened to your dad, you know I'd never set foot in there again. No, it's at the wash house.'

'You going to be washing?' asked Babby.

'Am I heck, as like! Going to be minding the prams.'

Babby's face clouded. The last thing she wanted was her mother working at the wash house. That was *her* place. That's where her gang would 'borrow' the prams from and play steeries with them in the hollas. No harm done, and with a bit of luck, they would replace the prams before the owners came out of the wash house, wondering why the pram's wheels were slightly buckled and there were mucky fingerprints all over it.

'Now, have you thought any more about going to live at your Aunty Pauline's?' asked Violet.

'No!' cried Babby.

Violet sighed and shook her head. 'I just don't know what else to do, love. The wash house job is early hours.'

'I don't like Pauline. She wears those hideous clothes from the raggy shop and she doesn't half love herself. She makes me go to church and pray all the time when I stay with her.'

'And that's just the kind of thing I should be making you do.'

'Pray, you mean? And church? You always said, if there was a God, he wouldn't have taken Dad from us.'

'I never did!'

'That's why you stopped going to Mass. You said those nuns and priests will be clacking their rosary beads all the way to hell! You so did, when you asked them for some money when we were waiting for the widows' fund—'

'I didn't mean it. I wasn't thinking straight. Of course they don't just dole out money; they do other things instead, like – like … like looking after you when you're in trouble. Sister Immaculata explained it to me. I actually like her. She was kind.'

Babby screwed up her eyes. The thought of Sister Immaculata, her bulging, fleshy face staring out from the distinctive starched white wimple she wore, the cowl spreading out from under her neck so it looked as if she was a giant baby wearing a giant bib, made her shudder. The notion of a world where everyone had to go traipsing back and forth to church, to genuflect, or pray for forgiveness, or sacrifice their souls to the Virgin, was appalling to Babby.

'No, she wasn't kind. Otherwise you would have started going to church again.'

There was that familiar hard edge to her mother's voice. 'Oh, do be quiet, Babby. Pauline can look after you. Just till I get back on my feet. Who's going to take care of Hannah if I'm working? You can't. You've got school,' she said. 'God, Babby stop pouting! The wind will change and you'll stick like that. Do I need to shake some sense into you? If only you would behave, love. Always giving cheek, looking for a fight. You'll send me into an early grave, you will. You're bold as a pig, selfish, all at the same time. I can't waste any more time on you. Now. Go and put the hot water bottle on the stove!'

Babby humphed.

'And fetch me the iodine' said Violet. 'How did you do that? Playing steeries again? I don't know, five of you crammed into the pram – not even *in* the pram, *on* the pram – sitting on a couple of wooden planks, pushing it down the hollow; no wonder you get yourself in a mess.'

Babby poked at the graze and a dribble of blood ran from her knee down her shin.

'Don't do that, you daft apeth! You'll make it worse!'

'I wasn't at the hollas. It was Johnny's fault. We were playing,' she lied.

'Kick the can,' whispered Patrick, under his breath.

'What's that, Pat? What did you say?' said Violet.

Babby blushed and her eyes darkened.

'Did you get the message from the Co-op, Babby?' asked Violet.

'I tried. But they kept shoving me to the back of the queue. That Mrs Liddy's got a beak on her like a flamin' tin opener. She could open a tin of beans with that nose.'

'Don't curse. Mrs Liddy's nose is no reason not to get the messages.'

'I don't like the way she looks at me, like they all do at school ...' Babby sighed. She dropped her head and started poking at her knee again. 'Cos we're too poor to have dinner money.'

Violet reached out a sympathetic hand to her daughter's arm. 'Look, love, we can't afford to behave like we've got fancy hats. When your dad was around things were different. Don't forget, when he started off in the pens on the dock road and stood in line, waiting to see if he could get a day's work, sometimes three weeks on the trot he came back with nothing. You come from dust. You end up as dust. We're all the same. It's what happens in between that makes the difference.'

'Should have just stuck to the pens instead of singing at the Boot,' said Pat.

'Yes,' Violet answered sadly.

'I could do that,' piped up Babby. 'Sing. Miss at school says when I sang 'Ave Maria' it made her cry.'

She looked at her mother who was smoothing down her dress, picking off a loose thread from her skirt, and letting it swirl in a shaft of sunlight. Babby knew her singing was the one thing that hurt her mother more than anything else. It should have been a comfort when she sang. Other people said she had a voice that was clear and pure and true, just like her father's. But it pierced her mother's heart to be reminded of her beloved husband and Babby knew that she wished she would save her singing for their infrequent outings to church, or the tin bath on a Friday.

Babby watched Violet stand up to clear the tea things, but panic rose to her mouth when she saw her stop and pick up the pair of battered school shoes by the scullery door, lift them to the light, turn them over and examine the soles.

'Have you not been to school again today? Babby, I've told you!'

'Mam, no! It – it …' Babby stammered. Her mother should get a job as a detective. How was it that a scrape of mud on her shoes would have said so much?

'I don't want to hear!' Violet said. 'Git! Upstairs to your room and don't come out until after supper!'

Later that evening, Violet shut the front door on her sister Kathleen and said goodbye with a sigh, turned off the oil lamp and made her way up the stairs. She stopped outside Babby's bedroom door.

'Love,' she said, twisting the handle, 'are you awake?'

She heard the bedsprings creak. Pushing open the door, she saw the mess of Babby's hair all tangled up in the sheets, her face pressed down into the pillow.

Babby stirred and briefly raised her head, turned and looked towards the direction of the light that was spilling into the room. Violet hesitated. No words were sufficient to describe how much she loved this child. But she was at her wits' end as to what to do with her.

'Just seeing if you were asleep.'

'Well, I was, but I'm not now! Is that why you woke me? To see if I was asleep?'

'No.'

'Then what did you want?' Babby asked, fighting a yawn.

'Nothing,' Violet replied. She went towards the bed and pulled at the eiderdown, tucking it in around the edge of the straw mattress. After pushing a piece of hair behind Babby's ear and planting a warm kiss on her forehead, she left, closing the door with a soft click.

How could she tell Babby that her sister Kathleen had said yes to taking in Hannah and Pat, but had refused to have her? Her aunt had said the same, and she barely knew her because she lived twenty-five miles away in Preston. Only Pauline, now. Babby was a wild one, all right. Violet turned over the letter she had begun to write to Pauline, felt it going damp around the edges in her sweaty hand. She would ask Pauline one more time and hope to God she said yes.

Chapter Four

Thank goodness, the sun was shining. Violet rounded the corner of Bevington Bush, nearly careering into the West Indian man with his gold tooth who was setting up a low table for the wooden dolls. Every day he was there, whatever the weather, dancing and clattering them up and down an old plank in the hope of raising a few pennies to buy himself a glass of his rum tipple. Liquid sunshine, he called it. She smiled as he winked at her and rattled his tin box.

'I haven't got a bean, love,' she said. Never mind. She was determined today was going to be good day. A fresh start. It wasn't much, but it was a new beginning. She had arranged for her sister, Kathleen, to come over and look after the kids this week, so at least that was taken care of. For now.

When she entered the wash house, the noise of the machines was overwhelming but the women's chatter as they washed and scrubbed their laundry in the huge industrial-sized sinks, their laughter and gossip, was lovely. She knew a good few of them and nodded hello to her neighbour, a woman for whom the Temperance Society came knocking at her door. Some arrived carrying bundles on their heads, but most wheeled them in prams. There was genuine pleasure that Violet was going to be minding them.

'Eh, Vi, perhaps you can make a better job of stopping the thieving varmints than the last useless cow,' said a woman, up to her elbows in milky foam as she lathered a slab of carbolic soap. Violet laughed. The woman continued, 'Some of these kids are pure bad. Just like those gangs of nippers who hang around outside the football ground on Saturdays, offering to mind folks' bikes for a penny, even though everyone knows it's them who'd nick them if you didn't come up with the goods. Flaming protection racket, that's what it is. Start 'em early, round here.'

Two women laughed in agreement whilst holding a crisp white cotton sheet at its four edges, walking towards each other, then moving apart – an elaborate dance of folding, flapping, folding, underscored by feet slapping at the tiled floor.

Violet went on. Matron was sitting at her desk in a small office, surrounded by papers stuck on a spike and spread across the table. A rusting mangle was pushed up against the window.

'I'mViolet Delaney …'

'Ah. Well, hello, Violet. You're on prams. Let's see how it goes and then, for a few extra bob, we'll put you on sheets … Sheets was where I started. And look at me now.'

Violet had heard about Matron and how she prided herself on being the only one in Liverpool who knew how to treat the infected sheets when cholera broke out. Violet assured her she could rely on her to prove herself with the prams, that the sheets sounded grand. She took her place on the small stool in the outside yard and lifted her face to the sun, lolling her head back against the wall. The rays felt warm against her cheeks and she rolled up her sleeves, exposing her flesh. Yawning, it occurred to her that the hardest thing about this job would be staying awake. She rubbed her eyes and blinked them open; falling asleep would be a disaster. She was exhausted after being up all night with Hannah who had a nasty chest cough, but she must stay awake. Had to stay … awake …

Jolting upright and leaping off her stool, hearing a squeal, followed by another, she spun on her heels to see a gang of kids yank a pram away around the corner and go racing down the hill. Bleary-eyed, she picked up her skirts and gave chase. Had she fallen asleep? If she had it had only been for a moment or two. But they were gone. Panic gripped her. What if the foreman came out? Or Matron? Her first day and she had failed miserably in the first twenty minutes of the job. She wanted to cry. She had no idea what to do. Would the little devils bring the pram back? That's how it usually went, but she couldn't be sure. Should she risk not saying anything and hope it would be returned before its owner came out with her washing? Good God, how could she have been so stupid and fallen asleep? She felt her cheeks flush crimson, tears stab her eyes.

'You all right, lovey?' said a kind voice. It belonged to a woman who had arrived with three bundles of sheets to be service-washed and ironed.

'Yes,' replied Violet. 'Leave that here. I'm doing the pram minding ...'

The woman reached into her pocket, gave her a threepenny bit.

'Thank you,' she said. 'Take that for your trouble.'

'Oh, it's no trouble. Just doing my job,' replied Violet, feeling sick with nerves, a sharp pain gathering with intensity in her stomach.

At Joseph Street, in the back bedroom, Babby took an intake of breath. She looked at the clock, opened the latch to the window, climbed on to the ottoman and perched her bottom on the sill. From there, she heaved herself out of the window and on to the roof of the privvy. Scrambling down the drainpipe, she left the house without her Aunty Kathleen knowing she had gone. At the end of the road, she went down the passage into Havelock Street, past the hospital, and headed off towards the hollas.

Down by the dock road, with its piers of stone and granite masonry, there were narrow streets lined with small, dingy houses that no amount of scrubbing and sand-stoning their front doorsteps would ever make look clean. Soon she arrived at the waste ground.

'Did you get that from the wash house?' she said, trying to catch her breath. She had found what she had feared – the Kapler gang, Johnny Gallagher and his brothers who lived in Cicero Terrace, and a couple of boys who lived in Kapler Street, with the Irish girl from Tommy White's estate.

'What's the matter with you?' asked Johnny. He had a bottle of ginger beer with him. His friend Dougie was sitting in the pram with his legs dangling over the side. He shook the bottle, put his thumb over the end of it, and let it squirt out like a fire extinguisher into his mouth.

'Give the pram back!' cried Babby. 'Me mam'll lose her job over this!'

'What's it worth?' asked Johnny Gallagher, pulling the pram towards him. He started to laugh.

Babby sighed. 'I haven't got nothing – and neither has me mam!'

'Aye, everyone knows you're brassic, round here. Is that why your dad never had a proper funeral?' said Dougie.

Babby shrugged. She had no idea how to answer that, but guessed he was probably right.

'We'll give it back after one steerie. Gerrin' the pram with Dougie,' he said, pulling at his baggy shorts.

Dougie laughed again, beckoned her over and wriggled his bottom up to the hood.

'Come on lass, gerrin. I don't bite.'

'Stop messin' about!' said Babby.

There was a pause. 'Give us a cuddle, then,' said Johnny.

Babby frowned. A cuddle? These were the boys she was used to hanging out with at playtime in school, playing Kick the Can, or Grandmother's Footsteps, or Knock-Down Ginger. Why would they want a cuddle? The thought of it was unsettling.

'Well, I'd rather do that than gerrin' bloody pram with that soft Olly,' she said, gesturing to Dougie with the stupid grin on his face. At least a cuddle would be over and done with more quickly than a steerie, and she could get the pram back to Violet.

Johnny grinned. 'Come here then, love ...' he said.

Babby went over to him. She stood in front of him, stiff as a board, arms clamped to her sides, not quite knowing what to do. 'But no kissing,' she said. 'I'm not bloody kissing no one.'

'No kissin' ...' said Johnny, laughing.

He pulled her to him, his strong arm snaking around her waist, his hips pressed into hers. The other boys gathered around, gawping and laughing as he bent his head towards the nape of her neck.

'I said no kissing!' she said, slapping his hand away.

'I'm not!' he said, grinning back at the gang.

'What are you doing, then, shoving your face in mine? Having a good sniff of me or summat?'

The boys jeered. This was good fun. A right laugh. Even more fun than playing steeries.

'Now you put your arms around me waist ...' said Johnny.

Babby raised her eyes and did as he asked. With his arms firmly around her now, Johnny began to sway.

'Sing that song, Babby. The one about the sailor. I've heard you sing it before. Famous, you are, round here, for your singing. Like a bell, me mam says. Sing it in me ear, go on.'

Babby raised her face to his. She pushed the tangled web of hair away from Johnny's eye. 'Well, now, me lads be of good cheer, for the Irish coast will soon draw near. Then we'll set a course for old Cape Clear. Oh, Jenny, get your oatcakes done,' she sang softly.

Johnny grinned. It was true her voice was beautiful and for a moment he was enthralled, lulled by the sweet sound of it.

What a flaming fool, she thought. Now's my chance to get the pram back. 'You bloody gobshite!' she cried, and brought her knee up to his crotch, swiftly with one blow that left him reeling, crying out in pain, and falling to the floor.

The crowd erupted with delighted squeals of laughter. This was the funniest thing that had happened to them all week. Maybe all year. Babby, meanwhile, shoved spoon-faced Dougie out of the pram and ran with it, unable to get the thought of Johnny out of her head, his arms around his waist, face close up against hers. And for the life of her, she didn't know what to make of it all.

Violet came back out of the wash house. Miraculously, there it was. In exactly the same place that it had been before she fell asleep. She recognised it straight away, the silver hood and calfskin lining filthy – not that a bit of spit wouldn't remedy that. 'Oh, thanks be to God!' she cried, her hands flying up to her face.

'Thank me, not God,' said Babby, stepping out from the shadow of the horse and cart that the rag and bone man was manoeuvring into place in front of the prams.

'Babby!' she called. 'Babby, I'll bloody swing for you. You should be at school! What are you doing here?'

'Johnny Gallagher and his mates took the pram. I got it back for you – aren't you happy?'

'I don't care, Babby! I'm sending you to your Aunty Pauline's. No, not another word!' she snapped.

Babby gawped at her mother with a mixture of horror and confusion. How bloody unfair! She dropped the stick of larch that she was clutching, in shock. 'What about school?'

'What about it? We'll find you another, we will.'

'Mam, if we need money, I could sing at the Boot Inn. I could learn to play Dad's accordion properly. Please – let me ...' she pleaded.

'No! Put those ideas out of your head. That accordion looks like a cash register and sounds worse. If I could get any money for it, I'd have pawned it long ago. Forget it, Babby. Pauline said perhaps you could move to the convent school near hers. I wanted you to pass your eleven plus and become a teacher. Or a nurse. So this will be like a second chance – if they'll have you.'

Babby paled. 'I'm not going to that prison! I hate the hats they have to wear. They say all those stupid things like you can't wear patent leather shoes because your knickers reflect in them, and you have to sit with a telephone directory on your knee in case a gust of wind blows your skirt up. And I hate those awful navy-blue dresses. Like flippin' sacks, they are. And I hate the girls – I've seen them. Their noses stick up. They're boring and snobby!'

Violet sighed. 'You're being ridiculous.'

Babby reached into her pocket and handed her mother a dog-eared piece of paper.

'What's this?' Violet said, her voice rising in pitch, as she scanned the note. 'From Gladys Worrall? Is this a joke?'

'I can sing. I know I can. I've told Rex and Gladys. And she said I can collect the bottles and sing.'

'Over my dead body! After what happened to your dad? You stay away from that place, you hear?' As she said it, Violet's hand gripped Babby's arm so tightly, she made little crescents of white in Babby's flesh where her nails dug in.

'Gladys had no right saying any of that. Look at you, Babby. You're a child, but already boys are buzzing around you like bees around a honeypot. You haven't noticed, but don't think I haven't seen them. And these are men in the pub. It's no place for a child.' She paused for effect. 'And believe me, I know, love ...'

Chapter Five

The next day was a Saturday. Violet was out with Pat collecting the groceries, and Babby was looking after Hannah who was having an afternoon nap curled up on the battered armchair. She covered her with a crocheted blanket and then mixed a cup of Camp coffee with three sugars stirred into it to disguise the bitter taste. Having drunk it, she went upstairs and into her bedroom, dragged the accordion out from under the bed and opened its case. It was wrapped up in an old moth-eaten man's scarf, patterned with flamboyant green peacock feathers, and with hand-knotted fringes at each end. She remembered her father wearing it, and when she unfurled it she buried her face in it, breathing in the smell of him – cigarettes and camphor oil.

The mother-of-pearl keys caught the light and it looked beautiful. Babby slipped the leather straps over her shoulders and when she pulled out the bellows to prepare to play the first notes, it made a groan as if it was sighing with happiness. The buttons of the Italian Coronado piano accordion felt smooth under her fingertips and she opened the bellows wider, as wide as they could go, stretching the instrument across her chest. Watching herself in the bedroom mirror, co-ordinating the mother-of-pearl black-and-white piano keys in her right hand, with the buttons in her left, the accordion looked like a beautiful giant fish. Its keys became the fish's teeth, and the diamanté inlay looked like its glittering scales, the curving bellows like its fat, striped body. Babby felt for the indented button that told her where to place her fingers, and idly ran her right hand up and down an octave. She was enjoying the cascading notes, chords piling upon chords, enjoying the fact that she seemed to have an instinct for the music that her father used to play.

She began to work out the tune to a sea shanty and, as her fingers skittered across the keys, she thought back to him singing low and sweet into her ear, a kind of musical sorcerer, whose voice made her feel hopeful and happy.

'Come on, Babby, love,' he used to say, as he pulled her to him. 'Wriggle in beside me. Put your hands through the straps. I'll play the keys, you play the chords.' He would rest his chin on the top of the bellows and his long mane of sandy-coloured hair would flop forward as he ran his fingers over the keys. The grate that needed cleaning, the scrubbing of the step, the pop bottles that needed returning, the pots that needed washing – everything would be forgotten and they would spend hours together like that.

She began to sing. As she did so, Hannah's head came around the door, thumb stuck in her mouth. Babby smiled and Hannah grinned.

When she stopped playing, Hannah clasped her hands, and cried, 'Again! Again!'

'Now Delaney had a donkey,' sang Babby, louder, more joyful.

'That everyone admired,' chorused Hannah, with delight. And then Babby laughed, and ruffled her mop of tangled hair, pulled her to her. 'Me ma's chubby, me da's chubby, and I'm chubby,' she said into Hannah's face. It always made her giggle. 'You've got a bum, I've got a cherry,' she said, squeezing her little sister's chin. Hannah let out an explosive yelp of delight and chuckled. But then suddenly Babby heard a noise downstairs, stopped, cocked her head, and listened. It was the clattering of pans, and the whoosh of water from the faucet.

Followed by the chilling sound of Violet's voice: 'Babby!' she called.

Babby, panicked, struggled to shut the bellows. It made a honking sound, like a goose, all the beauty going out of it in an instant. 'Shush, Hannah,' she said.

'What was that sound?' Violet asked Pat, who had followed his mother into the house with a bag of provisions.

'Not sure,' came the stuttered reply from Pat that said nothing but told Babby that he was frightened as to what was coming next. Then she heard Violet's footsteps pounding up the stairs. She pressed her fingers to her lips, indicating to a bewildered Hannah to be silent.

'Babby! Are you up here?' cried Violet, her voice sounding more strident.

When Violet twisted the doorknob and flung open the door, Babby dropped one end of the accordion in shock. It let out another discordant, crashing moan as it flumped open. Babby stood there, trying to read the extent of Violet's anger from her flashing black eyes.

'M-Mam ... I'm s-sorry,' stuttered Babby, grasping for an excuse or explanation.

Violet stood frozen to the spot, watching Babby staggering to the bed, struggling to put away the accordion away in the case.

'How long have you been playing that thing?' Violet said, gasping for breath.

Babby trembled. 'Not long. Found it in the cellar ...'

Violet shuddered.

'How long?!'

For a moment, it was as if Babby had lost the ability to speak.

'Put it away! I don't want ever to see you with that awful instrument again,' said Violet. 'You know how it upsets me,' she continued. 'And it upsets you, love, I know it does, even now, after all this time. Well, just the sight of a Union Jack flag or someone singing "God Save the Queen" upsets you because it reminds you of that dreadful day when your Da died, but that *thing*! Do I have to relive every ... every ...? Oh, Babby,' she murmured, tailing off into a more defeated tone. She paused, knowing that this was a moment that she should take advantage of. 'Now Babby, I need you to go to Pauline's. She's said she will have you until Christmas. You'll like it there, I promise. I-I can't look after you like your dad would want me to, so will you go, love?'

'What about our Pat?'

'He can look after himself. He's fourteen.'

'But Hannah. What will she do without me? Hannah and I, we're more than sisters. I'm like her second mother ...'

'And that's not right. You're only a child yourself. You shouldn't be taking care of a toddler.'

Babby sniffed. 'If I do go, will you promise you will come and get me at Christmas?'

'I promise, love. It's not forever, I promise. I do love you ...'

Babby felt the weight of her mother's solicitude. 'Suppose I could give it a try ... I'll not be eating her revolting dumpling stew, though. Or her mouldy semolina.'

'I'm sure that can be arranged. So that's settled, then?'

And before Babby had time to reply, Violet promptly left the room to write Pauline the letter.

Chapter Six

Two weeks later, when Babby returned home from school, she found her mother kneeling in front of the hearth, leaning over an open suitcase.

'What an earth do you think you're doing, frightening me like that?' said Violet. 'You don't go creeping up on people! Could give me a heart attack and then what would you have done? Here, come and help me with this case. I'm packing it for you, ready for Pauline's.'

The suitcase had a curved handle, a polished silver buckle, a lock with a small silver key, and a mirror when you opened it up, on the inside of the lid. There were little elasticated pockets for lipsticks and powder puffs, and it had stains of make-up on the pale-blue satin lining.

Next to the suitcase there were piles of clothes that Violet had decided Babby should take. They included the coronation dress, far too small now;

elasticated skirts and shorts, three pairs of navy-blue gym knickers, and the baggy, shapeless tunic that Violet had knitted for special occasions.

'You're not making me take that thing!' said Babby.

Violet had used cheap green nylon wool that she found in the bin at Blackler's Department Store. She had threaded blue ribbon around the collar and around the hem and tied it in bows, but it looked ridiculous.

'There's no point, Mam. I'll never wear it. It's itchy and scratchy and brings me out in a rash the minute I put it on. I'm itching just flamin' thinking about it!'

Violet ignored her, folded it, and put it into the case.

'What about this?' asked Violet. She held up a white dress draped over the back of the chair, made from the gown she wore when she had married Jack. She had nipped it in at the waist and shortened the sleeves and raised the hem to just below Babby's knees.

'Still looks like a flippin' wedding dress, all that white stuff.'

'Tulle, it's called.'

'I don't care. If I didn't want to wear it for the Queen of the May procession, why would I want to wear it now?'

'Perhaps Pauline might have better luck with you Babby,' said Violet, with a sigh. 'But you need at least one best dress for church.'

'Church?'

'You can't go to convent school and get away with not going to church.'

'We don't go to church any more, not since Dad died.'

'Yes, well. Perhaps we should start again. The Delaneys need to make some changes.'

Babby curled her lip and watched Violet put the other carefully folded items, the dresses, the navy blue brushed cotton knickers and socks, into the small case. It seemed like an impossible task. The case was straining its sides.

'You need to sit on it,' said Violet. Babby humphed, did what she was instructed to do, but it still didn't close.

'Shove up,' said Violet, and she sat down on the case beside her. Finally, she managed to click it shut and twist the lock. Panting and wiping her forehead she declared, 'There. Thank you, Babby. Teamwork.'

Babby stood and turned to leave.

'Wait. We've not finished yet,' said Violet and she dropped a bundle of navy-blue serge material, a half-finished skirt with elastic threaded around its waist, at her feet.

'Put that on. Stand on that chair so I can get the hem straight. I want to make a good job of this.' Some hope, thought Babby. Her mother was useless at sewing, cooking, or anything else that was vaguely domestic.

'Why do I have to wear this?' asked a reluctant Babby, wriggling into the skirt.

'Stand still,' replied Violet through a mouthful of pins, tugging the skirt one way and then another. 'I just want to get this hem straight ...' Instinctively, Babby backed away as her mother jabbed a pin into her leg.

'Ow!'

'Don't be daft. That didn't hurt.'

Violet sat down at the table. She was reading the instructions on the sleeve of the Simplicity pattern for the skirt, squinting at it and frowning.

Babby sat back down in the chair, tilting back in it and trying to balance as she gripped the table with her fingertips.

'Don't do that, you'll break the chair,' said Violet without raising her eyes.

Babby groaned again. She played with a ribbon, twisted it round and round a purpling finger, then she said, 'What happened to Dad that night at the Boot Inn?'

Violet jerked up her head. 'Why are you asking me that now?' she asked.

'Just something Dougie said the other day. About the funeral. Why wasn't I there?'

Violet tutted. 'Those McLaughlins are trouble-makers. Don't listen to anything Dougie says. You were too young. It would have been upsetting.'

Babby fiddled with a tendril of her hair. 'Do I really have to go to Pauline's?' she asked plaintively. 'She's not even my real aunty.'

'As good as. We agreed. You'll like it. It's near the beach and the sand dunes, Saint Hilda's and the pinewoods. Babby, it's no good you playing out in bomb sites. You need fresh air, get some colour in those cheeks ...'

Babby sighed. She could feel tears stabbing her eyes. She still didn't understand why she had to go to this woman's house, to a town she barely knew – like an evacuee, except there was no war; at least, not one to speak of yet.

Chapter Seven

It was decided that Babby should travel to Pauline's on her own, for reasons she didn't quite understand, but it had something to do with her mother needing to see a man about five bob and a favour. Word had got around that they were selling knock-off nylon stockings at Great Homer Street market and, if it was true, Violet wanted to be the first in line to find out. So after tearful farewells and reassurances that it was perfectly fine making the four-mile journey from Liverpool to the town of Waterloo, Violet walked her to the tram and said goodbye, promising she would come and see her just as soon as she was able to.

The train ride to Pauline's took no longer than an hour but it seemed like a lifetime. First, she took the overhead railway from Huskisson Dock. As she looked out of the window at the Tate and Lyle factory, she drifted off into thought about Johnny

Gallagher's cousin – the one who fell in and drowned in the vat of sugar. She wondered if it was true. When she took the train from Seaforth the noxious smell of damp grain from the breweries was soon behind her and the ships and cranes became indistinguishable. Dilapidated tenements and bomb sites turned into houses with porches and jauntily painted garden gates leading to neat front lawns with lovingly tended rose beds and colourful dahlias. The sooty red-brick buildings of the warehouses and docks became clumps of trees and green fields, and the train rocked onwards on its tracks, with sand dunes on one side towards the sea, and the open marshes on the other.

Waterloo was a bleak and windy coastal town that had seen better days since the slave traders and ship owners had packed up and left. Down by the shore there were wide, tree-lined roads with huge detached eight-bedroomed houses, sand building up in heaps around their gateposts and doorsteps, their bay windows staring mournfully out to the steel-grey sea. Some had been converted into flats, convents, or nursing homes for war casualties. Pauline lived towards the railway line where the houses were much smaller – rows of shabby Edwardian terraces with tiny gardens in the front and narrow lawns at the back that sloped down to the railway track. Babby remembered, from her last visit, that the house had sagging floorboards, mushrooms growing in the kitchen, and squirrels in the loft, all of which she had thought were amusing anecdotes that she had shared with Johnny Gallagher on her return from a day trip. But now she might actually be living here, it filled her with dread. Not only that, the fresh air made her feel queasy. The smell of the sea and the sound of screeching gulls was unfamiliar to Babby and she preferred the city's dust in her lungs and the black soot in her nostrils and under her fingernails.

How long had it been since she had last visited here? Two? Three years? As she approached, the road leading to the house curved into a crescent. She could see the building ahead, dull and squat, with a crumbling chimney. Her heart pounded. The garden was more overgrown, but nothing much had changed as far as she could remember. There was the same lilac bush poking up between the cracks in the neglected paving stones of the front path, the same peeling woodwork, faded red door, broken gate, loose on its hinges. Babby arrived at the house and stood in the porch, with the smell of damp from the sticky slime-laced windowsills and rotting wood. She pressed the broken bell with the heel of her hand, then after waiting a moment or two, rapped gently on the door that had been left ajar.

'Who's that?' called a voice, from beyond. 'Come in ...'

Babby put her hands deep in her pockets to calm herself. The door swung wider on its hinges when she pushed it open gently with her foot.

Pauline appeared with a mop in her hand. She had a thin, pointed nose that stuck out like a little beak from the middle of her face, and when she spoke, she tilted her head from one side to another and thrust her chin back and forth, like a strange, pecking bird.

'Good God, it's you, Babby. I wasn't expecting you so early,' said Pauline.

Babby wondered if she should apologise.

'And here you are, just standing on the doorstep,' said Pauline. Thoughts began to rearrange themselves in Babby's head as Pauline talked in a volley of words about wiping her feet, the electric meter, suitcases, and lights out – all the time underscoring her instructions with lively gesticulations.

Babby stepped further inside the hall. The house smelled of unfamiliar smells and there was a holy water font screwed into the wall, a framed picture of the smiling Pope above that, and a wooden crucifix on a stand. She could see into the room beyond which had a badly made-up bed in it, pushed up against the wall. A couple of cushions had been placed on it, but it did nothing to disguise the bed as a sofa, and she dreaded that this might be where she might be sleeping. There was a smell of antiseptic, Vim, and cigarette smoke and she could hear Pauline's breathing standing this close to her – steady shallow breaths.

'What have you got on?' said Pauline. 'You must be sweltering in that get up.'

Babby fingered the belt on her gabardine mac. She was about to say that her mother told her to wear it, but she didn't. Pauline commented, 'Ooh, it's got Violet all over it! Still, you'll grow into it one day, no doubt. Well,' she concluded with a sigh, 'you better make yourself at home.'

Babby didn't answer.

'So how long will this job at the wash house last?' Pauline asked.

'I don't know,' replied Babby.

'Well, neither do I. No one tells me anything.'

'Nor me,' replied Babby.

Pauline humphed. 'You actually look smaller – can that be possible?' she asked.

'Maybe you've got taller.'

'Unlikely. You've not been eating properly I suspect. Spam fritters and jelly and custard aren't going to do much good to a growing girl.'

I wish. Spam fritters and jelly sounds delicious, thought Babby.

'Well, we'll soon change that,' continued Pauline.

'Mam said I should give you this,' Babby said, taking out a packet of fig biscuits from her pocket and handing it to her.

'Where did she get these from? Jacob's?'

'Yes,' replied Babby. This wasn't the conversation she wanted. She wanted the one about where she would be sleeping, and was it really true that Pauline had persuaded the local convent school to enrol her, taking up one of the charitable places for deprived city girls? Violet had told her she should be grateful but Babby didn't want to be anyone's charity, and everyone knew these places were only an opportunity for the schools to get money to supplement the education of the girls who were paying the fees. She might as well just turn up with a sign over her head saying I AM POOR. Just like when Violet had got the shoemaker to hammer nails into the heels of her shoes to make them last, and they clattered when she walked up the aisle at church and made everyone turn and look at her.

She followed Pauline into the kitchen as she was instructed. Whatever it was that Pauline had been using to clean the floor – Ajax, probably, judging from the traces of white powder around the skirting board and the feeling of grit underfoot – it was making her nose itch and her eyes water. She tried to hold back a sneeze and failed.

'Bless you,' said Pauline, without looking over her shoulder.

The statue on the mantelpiece of a bearded Jesus pointing at his bleeding heart, his eyes rolling back in his head, made her grimace. Why does Jesus always have to have that mopey look on his face? That wouldn't convince anyone to mend their ways. Wet as a haddock's bathing costume, she thought.

'Hang your gabardine on that coat stand ... Can you manage?' asked Pauline.

'Yes,' replied Babby, flatly. The coat stand was groaning with two musty-smelling moth-eaten fur coats, umbrellas with handles carved into birds' heads, a cane, woollen scarves, and it even had a set of rosary beads dangling from it. As she stood on her toes to hook her mac over one of its pegs, it toppled towards her.

'Sorry!' she said, catching it. This house is so full of stupid clutter, Babby wanted to say. Crucifixes, glass fish, ornaments of china dogs and cats. You could hardly move without knocking something over.

'Wait there,' said Pauline, bustling out into the kitchen and coming back with a plate of food. She placed it on the table which was covered with a wine-coloured chenille tablecloth. Babby stared at the meat, potatoes, and vegetables, baked under a crust of pastry. She looked from the plate to Pauline's expectant face and felt desolate. It was so quiet here. She was used to arguments and shouting and laughter. Only the sound of the ticking clock punctuated the awkward and yawning silence.

'Sit down and tuck in,' said Pauline, brightly.

Babby slumped down on the chair Pauline had pulled out for her, stuffed the napkin into her collar, and raised the fork to her mouth. The bits of kidney were disgusting and the meat was so tough she might have been chewing the sole of her shoe; she had to swallow it in lumps. To think she usually moaned about Violet's dumplings that floated in doughy puddles in a sea of greasy gravy – now the memory of it made her feel homesick. She would even have swapped the green potatoes – with shoots growing out of them – and corned beef from rusting tins from the out-of-date bucket at Kerryson's the grocers, for this.

With a forkful of pie hovering between plate and mouth, she felt herself retch. It was a gagging reflex that she had little control over and she mumbled an apology as she took a small tentative bite and felt the gristle between her teeth, the pastry going dry and sour in her mouth.

'You don't have to eat it,' said Pauline. Her voice sounded softer. Babby could see she was trying to be kind.

'I'm just not very hungry,' she said, laying down the fork.

'Leave it, dear,' said Pauline. 'It'll keep until tomorrow,' and she swept the plate away, covering it with a tea towel and putting it in the larder. She returned a moment or two later. 'I've got something to show you,' said Pauline with bustling enthusiasm.

She produced a long, shapeless navy-blue cable knitted cardigan from behind her back. 'It took me three months to finish it! I unravelled an old sweater of mine and re-knitted it, but it's all coat on me.'

'Thank you,' said Babby, struggling to be polite.

'Try it on,' said Pauline, running her finger down her pointy nose.

Babby nodded, slipping her arms through the sleeves. She put it on in a daze. It looked ridiculous.

'It'll be perfect for school. Saint Hilda's has a place for you. You'll like it there,' said Pauline, standing back and admiring her handiwork.

Babby was still trying to grapple with the idea of Saint Hilda's. She was already missing her old school with its muddy sandpit and the smelly toilets at the other side of the playground – freezing in the winter – and taking it in turns with the register and the handbell at dinner time. This cardigan was *enormous*. The sleeves were so long they flapped about the tips of her fingers and the thought of wearing it was appalling. The grey flecks in the wool made it drab and the flat brown buttons were incongruous. Not only that, Pauline had sewn large linen cuffs on the sleeves which made it even more ludicrous.

Yet Pauline was smiling at her hopefully. 'This isn't going to be forever,' she said. 'And I'll be glad of the company.' She leant in to her, and Babby noticed that her steel-coloured hair, all matted and wiry, smelled of the sea.

'Take these up to your room. The one with the door with the broken handle,' Pauline said, handing her two pairs of shoes. One was a sturdy pair of ugly lace-ups, the other pair old-fashioned, with a T-bar and a buckle; both of them looked more like boats than shoes.

'Why do I need two pairs?'

'Indoors and outdoors. Saint Hilda's is very particular.'

'Yes,' said Babby. 'Mam told me.' She cast her eyes down to the floor. She knew that if she looked at Pauline directly, she might either cry or hurl something across the room.

Pauline continued, 'But the nuns are kind. There are a few lay teachers, old birds you know, who were in the WAAF and whatnot who are fond of tweed and sensible shoes.'

'Oh,' said Babby. It sounded horrible.

Pauline licked her finger, rubbed at a mark on the table and added casually, 'Your mother doesn't deserve what some are saying about her. Especially those dreadful gossips at the Boot Inn. Besides, Gladys Worrall, is a right old teapot ...'

What on earth was she talking about? thought Babby. Gladys Worrall? What was *she* saying about Violet?

'... squeaky clean on the outside, filthy on the inside. Don't know how your mother can stand it. Vi made the best of what God gave her, all right, and what's wrong with that?'

And then suddenly, in waves of panic, Babby's lip trembled and her shoulders shook.

'What is the matter?' asked Pauline.

'I w-want to go home,' stammered Babby. She could feel the blood rush to her cheeks.

Pauline frowned but didn't say anything, just patted her shoulder. Then she stood up and opened the sewing basket on the sideboard. 'When I've finished darning these socks for you, I'm going out to the shop for a pound of lard so you go upstairs and unpack.' Then she sighed. 'Your mother will come and get you in time, chicken.'

'I don't want to go to that awful Saint Hilda's school,' said Babby, suddenly. 'I swear, I won't step foot in that place!' She jutted out her chin in defiance.

Pauline didn't even look up from the sock. She had been warned about Babby's temper.

'Don't talk nonsense. Of course, you will.'

'I don't want to. You can't make me!' Shaking, she watched Pauline place the sock and the needle on the table, then very calmly cross her legs and fold her hands in her lap.

'That's certainly true. Babby, you do have a choice. Your mother has asked me to make sure you go to school, but do you know what the alternative is?'

Babby shrugged. 'Go home. Help Mam with our Hannah and Patrick.'

'No. The alternative is Saint Sylvester's orphanage. Now, I could take you straight there myself, but it's full of wayward abandoned girls and boys and I wouldn't wish that on anyone. Neither would you.'

'I thought the wayward girls went to Saint Jude's?' Babby remembered Violet pointing out Saint Jude's Mother and Baby Home when they had gone for a walk to the beach on their last visit. A building that looked as grim and foreboding as the fate of the poor unfortunate girls who ended up there.

'Let's just say that they start off at Saint Sylvester's – but some get to Saint Jude's eventually,' she said ominously.

'I don't care. I'm not going to Saint Hilda's!' shouted Babby, leaping up and slamming a fist on the table. 'Why doesn't Mam want me?' she wailed. 'Why?'

'Because Y's a crooked letter and you can't straighten it,' Pauline answered firmly, trying to end the conversation.

'What are you talking about?'

Pauline reached a hand out across the table but Babby drew hers away sharply.

'Oh, of course your mother wants you,' said Pauline. 'It's just that it's impossible, right now. Impossible. You'll understand in time.'

Babby stamped her foot and kicked at the hearth.

'That's enough now!' cried Pauline. Seeing Babby's furious temper played out before her – all flailing arms and tossing of hair and humphing – was an unsettling sight. Pauline was already beginning to regret taking in the girl, even though she had been told she would be useful, what with her own failing eyes and water on the knee. 'Go to bed right now, Babby!'

Babby blinked away the tears. She didn't want Pauline to see her crying. She didn't want to tell her that she suspected that her mother was hiding something. She had no real evidence, except that at the very moment that her mother had said things would start to get better, they began to fall apart.

Babby lay on her bed, repositioned the small brass lamp with its flickering bulb encased in a metal rose, and read the list Pauline had left on the bed for her. It was a list of the things she was required to bring to school with her the next day: plimsolls, navy shorts, navy gym knickers, plain white cotton vest, navy drawstring bag (clothing and bag embroidered with name in pale-blue chain stitching), apron, compass, ruler, eraser, fountain pen, Bible, service book. Well, Pauline wasn't half optimistic, thought Babby. Violet had packed none of these items and Babby had no reason to think Pauline would provide them. She wondered how well Pauline knew her mother.

Half an hour later, when she heard the front door open and the chink of coins in a tin, Babby crept out of the bedroom, stopped and squatted, hands clenched around the bannisters, peering down at the scene below. The woman with hair like a hat, who stepped into the hall and, with annoying precision, removed her gloves finger by finger, spoke in hushed tones. Pauline took the small red mission box that was on the hall table, tipped out the pennies and a button, and gave the coins to the woman.

'Thank you,' she said. Babby recognised the blue sash she wore over her shoulder – she was one of the Mission collectors who come from the Legion of Mary to collect money for fatherless children. Why couldn't they just give it directly to the Delaney family? thought Babby.

'Is the girl here?' asked the woman, folding up the gloves and carefully putting them in her croco-dile-skin handbag.

'Yes. Best she's away from her mother, what with this latest business,' said Pauline in hushed tones. 'Anyway, the school will be good for the child – she needs routine.' There followed an animated conver-sation about geranium cuttings and gooseberry jam, but soon veered back to fallen girls, like the ones in Saint Jude's, and scarlet women. Unnerved and fear-ful of being noticed, Babby returned to her room and quietly shut the door. Was everyone talking about the Delaney family? What had Violet done that was the cause of this gossip? Why was it best she was kept away from her mother? She felt as though she was going to be sick. Actually sick, all over the bald-ing candlewick bedspread.

She paced the room, tearing around the skin of her thumbnail with her teeth like a wild animal. She could, of course, go home. She could just get on the train and go home. Or she could write to Violet and she would come and get her; surely she would do that if she knew what a terrible mis-take this was? If Violet was in trouble, she needed Babby to help. She couldn't waste time at awful

Saint Hilda's. Saint Hilda's. The words turned bitter in her mouth, like the sour pastry.

That night she wept tears of frustration until the thin bed sheet was sodden. She had heard stories of evacuees being beaten and made to do terrible jobs, like scrub the bedpans or dig in the fields. She could have fought back against that kind of regime, but how could she fight back when everyone was saying that they were only doing the best for her? Didn't they know she was so lonely here that it was making her feel physically sick? She twisted the sheet until she could wring nothing more out of it. And as the night wore on, tears turned to anger. She had seen the way Violet looked at men, doe-eyed, pursing her lips, tilting her head to one side in a show of innocence. Is that why she had been sent here? So her mother could make a fool of herself? It had only been a few years since their father had died. How could she do this to her?

Chapter Eight

Babby woke bleary-eyed, tired before she had even got out of bed. The school uniform was put on in a daze – navy calf-length pinafore and white shirt, the lace-up brown leather shoes, the blue and silver striped tie, the ugly battered hat with a stupid gold badge on it saying Respice Finem. Breakfast of a fried egg, fried black pudding and gristly bacon with lumps of white bone in it was eaten silently, satchel was packed, and all the time Babby was wondering how could this be happening to her.

She headed off to the school bus stop, with directions scribbled on a notepad and instructions to come straight home after lessons.

'Don't go anywhere near the beach,' shouted Pauline from the garden gate, as an afterthought.

Babby stopped. 'Why?' she asked.

'The dunes. They move. Open up and swallow you. And the tides. The currents. It's a dangerous place.'

Intrigued, and deciding Pauline was probably exaggerating, Babby shrugged and nodded. Already the navy velour hat, squashed firmly on her head with the elastic band cutting into the flesh under her chin, was beginning to chafe and scratch. What the gang at the hollas would say if they could see her in this frightful get up, she could only imagine.

There was a crowd of dark-blue blazers waiting for the forty-three bus to arrive. Amongst the claque of hats and hockey sticks, was a cluster of maroon jackets. They belonged to the grammar school boys of Saint Paul's. For a moment, Babby considered sauntering over and striking up a conversation – she had always preferred the rowdy rough and tumble of boys to girls – but faced with the glossy hair, confident smiles, and fat, knotted ties, not the scruffy, rag-tag mob she was used to, her courage faded. And anyway, what boy would want to talk to her? What would she even talk about? The hollas? The Boot Inn? Her mother dumping her here? The tragedy of her new life with Pauline?

Babby said nothing, just twisted a piece of her wiry brown hair round her finger, moving away from the crowd, conveniently allowing a group of boys to separate her from the girls. A green double-decker arrived and started to fill up. She shuffled reluctantly to join the queue. Inside, there were already girls sprawled on the back seat. The braver ones, she noticed, had stuffed their hats into their blazer pockets. One had stretched her long body across three passive twelve-year-olds and banged on the window gesturing for the others to come and join her. Another girl waved a hockey stick and shouted at the boys three seats away to move up. Meanwhile, Babby made her way down the bus and sat, squashed up against the window.

A tall girl with greasy red hair and clothes even shabbier than Babby's – flapping shoes, frayed collar – was coming down the gangway. The bus shuddered when the driver accelerated and the girl was thrown headlong on to the floor; a riotous cheer went up. A penknife and pencils spilled and flipped from her blazer pocket as she landed in an undignified, crumpled heap, navy-blue knickers and milk-bottle thighs on full view.

'All right Frying Pan?' cried a voice from the back.

The girl seemed undeterred, leapt up and started brandishing her hockey stick. 'Call me that to me face!' she yelled in a thick Dublin accent. 'Sure, if you lot had shoved up, I would've been able to sit down and this wouldn't have happened!'

There was another explosion of laughter.

'There was loads of room,' chirped a spotty thirteen-year old. 'Turn sideways and you'd be marked absent, Frying Pan. I've seen more meat on a butcher's pencil!'

Ha ha, so bloody funny, thought Babby. It wasn't the girl's fault she was so skinny. Just didn't have enough food, probably. And also probably couldn't afford shampoo. Just like her.

Babby turned around and looked at the two imperious-looking girls sitting behind her who were sniggering.

'What are you staring at?' asked the first girl. She had sleek blonde hair and an appraising gaze that made Babby feel uncomfortable. 'Are you new? Don't recognise you …'

Babby turned away.

'Cat got your tongue?' said the girl, laughing and poking her between her shoulder blades.

Babby shrugged. 'It wasn't funny, that's all. Stop laughing at her, just because she fell. You're the only ones having the craic here.'

A group of smirking moon-faced boys exchanged looks. Meanwhile, Frying Pan was scrabbling about for the pens that had rolled under seats or lodged in the slatted grooves of the aisle.

'Sorry, I didn't hear you. Did you say something?' the blonde girl asked Babby again. Then turning to her friend, she added, 'What did she say?'

'I said nothing,' mumbled Babby. She busied herself by pulling up her socks which were bagging around her pink, freckled ankles.

'What?'

'Nothing. I—'

'Ooh, it talks,' said the girl as she licked a finger and ran it over her arched eyebrow.

The second girl sniggered. 'Bit of a Moody Margaret this one, don't you think?' she said.

The first girl grinned. 'Probably just got the Curse.'

The second girl cackled. 'Yeah. You're right. Probably got the Red Cabbage. You got your Aunty Mary, love?' She giggled. 'You can tell us. We're your friends here ...'

Frying Pan, stuffing her pens into her ink-stained pockets, hauled herself up and loomed up over them. 'Leave her alone!' she said.

'Thanks,' Babby said to the girl quietly, when she took a seat beside her.

'Me name's Mary, but everyone calls me Frying Pan because of me greasy hair.'

Babby hesitated. 'I'll call you Mary,' she said.

'That's nice,' replied Mary. 'But I don't care. You can call me Frying Pan if you want – I'll not let it get to me. They're all stuck up feckin' eejits here, not worth the bother. What's your name?'

'Babby.'

'Short for Barbara or summat?'

'No.' Babby smiled. 'Though me mam loves Barbara Stanwyck, you know, from the films.'

'Why, then?'

'Because for ages I was the baby and that's what me dad called me. Then our Hannah came along as a kind of mistake, but by then everyone had got used to Babby and my real name, Jeanie, sounded peculiar.'

Saying the name 'Jeanie' out loud seemed strangely unfamiliar.

'Best not let these bitches know about that. Sure, they'd make a right carnival out of it.'

Babby smiled and thought how lovely it would be to have a friend. Maybe Mary would fit the bill, someone to talk to about how she was missing home, how she would never be accepted here. She had noticed that, compared to these girls, her own white blouse was grubby and frayed at the collar, even after Pauline unpicking it and turning inside out and sewing it back on, and her curly hair had already tangled and had clumps of knots on it, and there was dirt under her fingernails. She was more like Mary than the others ...

The bus reached the ornate iron gates of Saint Hilda's convent which was a mile down the road from Pauline's. The building, with its red brick walls, Victorian green gables, and dark windows with bars on it, made her wonder if it really was actually a prison she had been sent to. That's what it felt like. Walking beside Mary, she followed the line of girls trudging through the nuns' garden. She stopped for a moment in front of the statue of Our Lady. The Virgin Mary looked more sorrowful than the one at her old school. It was one of those days when the sky was shrouded in grey mist and it was chucking it down. The air was damp and a raindrop dangled from the statue's chipped nose. If the nuns were hopeful that the girls might be inspired by the holy grotto of Our Lady of Sorrows, Babby decided this crumbling statue, stuck on a dais made of lumps of cement, wasn't going to do the job. Glancing over her shoulder at the statue, Babby was convinced the Virgin's disapproving eyes were following her. She moved away from the line of girls and broke into an uneasy brisk walk which took her up the school drive and through the large wooden double front doors.

Following the others, she found herself in the cloakroom – a small bare room with a row of pegs, a bench, and under the bench, cages to put in outdoor or indoor shoes, presumably depending on which direction you were heading. She hesitated. There was a smell of damp socks, sweaty feet and shoe polish.

'You new?' asked a girl to the right of her, one of the girls that had been on the bus. Babby nodded.

'Violet Delaney your mother? We used to live off Netherfield Road and I remember your family. You lot were the talk of our terrace.'

The girl paused, walked away to the other side of the rack of coat pegs with her friend. The gaberdines, blazers and hats muffled their whispered conversation, but it was loud enough for Babby to hear what they were saying.

'Her dad died, you know. They say her ma's like a library book: take her out once a fortnight and then pass her around,' continued the girl, with a snigger.

'Daddy Gone Delaney,' hissed the second.

When they reappeared from behind the stand, Babby tried to stammer a response, but nothing seemed to come out of her mouth. A small group had gathered and there was a clattering when they took their shoes out of the cages. As they bent to untie laces of outdoor shoes and buckle up their indoor ones, they sensed that something was about to happen and took febrile, anticipatory looks at Babby.

And maybe because of her lack of words, maybe noticing that she was providing some kind of attraction, without thinking Babby shoved the girl who was still smirking, hard in the chest. The girl fell backwards on to the bench.

'What was that for?!' yelled the girl.

'You lot. Making things up. Stuff this lark,' Babby said, seething. She hadn't even started school and she was getting into a fight. How could they say these things about Ma?

Her thoughts lurched back to the dreadful night her father had died. She remembered how Violet had come and found her when she was with the Kapler gang, throwing old bullets they had discovered buried in the hollas on to a huge bonfire they had made, watching them crackle and explode like firecrackers. 'Babby!' Violet had cried. 'For the love of God, come away from that fire before you kill yourself. Something terrible has happened.'

She could pinpoint the beginning of the end for the Delaney family to that moment. And then the awful realisation the following morning that they hadn't dreamed it. Babby remembered her distraught mother coming home, slumping at the table, then leaping up and hurling her father's knapsack across the room, flinging it so hard against the wall it fell open and the song book, penny whistle, a pair of trousers and a box of Swan Vesta matches scattered across the floor.

Jolting back into the present and turning on her heel, she walked straight out of the cloakroom, out into the corridor, through the doors, and down the winding drive. She tore off her hat. Respice Finem, indeed. Look to the end. What an idiotic school motto. Well, she would show them. She would look to the bloody end, all right. And with that thought in her head, she marched off in the direction of the bus stop, taking a last look over her shoulder at the school and its outhouses rearing up behind her, grim and foreboding, against a leaden, gunmetal sky.

The wind in her face as she approached the bus stop was all enveloping. When the forty-three bus drew up, she jumped on and bought a ticket from the conductor who was whistling and walking down the aisle with his ticket machine slung low around his neck. Babby pulled the skirt of her school uniform around her thighs and readjusted the collar of her blazer to disguise the fact she was playing truant. Five stops later she hopped off and marched towards a parade of shops, dodging through straggles of shoppers spilling on to the pavements from the grocery stores, butchers and bakeries. She had been warned by Pauline that she shouldn't go to the beach, so of course, drawn like a moth to a candle, that was where she was heading. Turning off the high street, she began walking towards the shore.

A cloud of flies buzzed about Babby's head and she swatted them away as, head bowed, she planned to take some comfort in the muffled quiet of the pinewoods. The route to the woods took her past the army firing range, then down towards the shore and through the orange mounds of soft granules of the nicotine dump which smelled like used cigarettes and burned her nostrils. 'Damn, damn, damn!' she screamed, her voice disappearing on the wind, though it was loud enough to send wailing seagulls scattering and wheeling above her. All those horrible things they are saying about Mam. And I hate Pauline ...

When she reached the pinewoods, her feet trod softly upon layers and layers of fallen needles. The beach that she could see beyond reminded her of wrinkled-up washing. At least she could breathe here. The rush of wind in her face calmed her, and the spiky black bald pine trees, like giant stick insects with their brittle branches becoming arms and legs, were silhouetted against a watery sun.

The sea was sleek and motionless. It shimmered on the horizon, reflecting a watery sun, but further inland it was sopped up by the marshes. She could see the liquid reflections of the few boats nudging up to each other, perfectly reflected back in a mirror image of themselves. The mud was thick and sludgy and water pooled in its crevices. Birds cawed and jostled and cackled above a shrimping cart and creepers, growing in long green tendrils, meandered across the silty path. Babby sat on a sawn off tree trunk.

'Hell!' she yelled, disturbing a carefully arranged flock of birds that squawked as they rose in the air. 'Hell's bloody teeth!' But what was the point of shouting? No point at all. No one was listening. The words floated away on the air. Setting off once again, further up the shore in her ugly shoes, the Indoors that she shouldn't be wearing as Outdoors, sand began making mounds and pushing up under the soles of her feet. She unbuckled the T-bar strap and slipped the shoes off, then her socks.

Feeling the sand between her toes, she pressed on, not really having a clear idea of where to. The mast of an old shipwreck, stranded and half sunk into the sand, was silhouetted against the sky. She looked beyond that to the right of the horizon and the curve of the shoreline. Blackpool tower was a fuzzy splinter embedded in the sand. Scouring one way and then another, from the docks to the outline of the pinewoods, she trudged back to the dunes, and leaping from one to another, she felt the marram grass whipping her bare shins. From the top of the sand dunes, she looked down towards the beach. A little way on and she wondered if she would reach the asylum that she remembered Violet pointing out to her once on one of the bank holiday trips to Pauline's. She could see the gables peeking out above the tops of the sand hills. Its correct title was St Peter's Home for the Feeble-Minded but no one called it that. The kids called it the loony bin. Violet said it was the funny farm, and that if she and Patrick kept on mithering her, she'd put them both in there one day. Babby had thought she was joking. Now she wasn't so sure.

A shrimping van had been left stranded on the shore. Looking back over her shoulder at it, a picture came into her head, of Johnny Gallagher and the gang, laughing and waving – they would have had some larks here. After trudging up the dune for a little while, the soft powdery sand made it tiring to walk, and her calves began to ache.

Once down the other side of the dune, squinting against the particles of sand that blew into her eyes when she was on the flat beach, she set off to the water's edge. Negotiating tangled fishing nets, old milk crates and a tyre, she then walked out further, and the sand became smoother. Tapping at a jellyfish with a stick, she made it wobble to see if it was alive. Standing bent in half, with the palms of her hands pressed to her knees, she searched out tiny scallop-shaped shells from the sand and put them in her pocket. Finding an old wellington boot, she picked it up and slung it towards the sea. And then she stopped. Watching the waves foaming and tumbling and gushing on, as they had done for uncountable centuries, it all felt hopeless.

This was useless, she decided. Pinpricks of sweat formed on her brow. She was vaguely aware of lights in the distance, perhaps the oil rigs or the gasworks. She screwed her gaze out to the Irish Sea where it joined the mouth of the River Mersey. She could see the lilac smudge of the Welsh hills beyond and, around the bend in the river, she could just make out the ships' containers and the cranes at Liverpool docks sharpening into focus. In the sunshine, a seagull skimmed across the surface of the gently breaking waves. Then a whole flock appeared, swooping and jostling over her head. A ship, the Isle of Man ferry, perhaps, sounded its belching foghorn as it slipped around the headland. The birds were in for rich pickings.

She felt the ripples of the sand under her feet, and then it softened to mud so that her toes sunk in. Paddling into the sea, she shivered with the shock of the cold water. After a minute or so she began to get used to it and she picked up her skirts and waded further, until the water was up to her knees. She paused, thrust the hair out of her eyes and looked to the horizon and the large expanse of sky. She sighed, felt herself twisting into air. She lifted her face, felt the spray wet her cheeks. With the sea swirling about her, and her feet sinking deeper into the sand, her head dizzy, she felt as though she belonged to some other world. There was the sound of the wind wheezing through the pines and sea birds screeching.

Running her tongue over her dry lips, she shivered. A tense pain gathered in a ball in her stomach.

But when she turned around to go back to the shore, she gasped. She could see nothing but the sea, spilling out like a lake. Her pupils dilated with fear. How long had she been standing here? She remembered her father saying, after one the dockers fell overboard from a ship into the Mersey, that when someone drowns it feels like everything stops in the world and all the grief goes into the depths. She shuddered, trying to put the thought out of her head, and squashing down the overwhelming sickening feeling that was coming over her in waves, realising that there was a very real danger of her getting into trouble in the deepening channels if she didn't move now and she tucked her skirts into her knickers and buttoned up her cardigan.

Then a thought occurred to her. Was this actually the answer? To wade out into the sea, and be done with it? To give in to the murky waters? That would show everyone – they would be sorry if she were to drown. Perhaps it would solve everything if she were to put an end to it all.

She hesitated, let the thought take shape in her head – and took some morbid satisfaction as she imagined Violet weeping inconsolably at her funeral.

'Stuff that for a game of bloody soldiers,' she shouted into the wind.

Of course, she wasn't going to do something as stupid as that. She was a fighter; always had been, always would be.

But she was done with this 'we know what's best for you' malarkey.

She would continue to go to school, say nothing, eat Pauline's dreadful meals, drink the undoubtedly sour school milk. She would be like an actor, going through her moves. And then, when the time was right, she was going home.

The nickname Daddy Gone Delaney was beginning to stick. The lessons in spelling, First Aid, mental arithmetic, and Latin, were bad enough, but were made even worse with the seating arrangements that put the brightest girls at the front and, inevitably, left Babby stuck at the back, understanding nothing, unable to read the blackboard, and thus ridiculed for being stupid. She dreaded the Angelus that interrupted classes every day at noon – Sister Bernardette leading the prayer in her office, her disembodied voice floating through an intercom. When a bewildered Babby resorted to mumbling gobble-degook, the whole class snickered.

'Delaney! Are you with us?'

Babby jerked up her head. 'Yes, sister?'

'Then you'll answer the question.'

'Sorry, Sister Ignatius. The question?'

There was the sound of sniggering. Some girls giggled into the crook of their arms. Others made a show of lifting the lid of their desk, sneered and exchanged disdainful glances behind it.

'Name me one of the Romans' greatest achievements?' asked the nun.

There was a pause, interspersed by muffled giggles escaping from the mouths of a few girls sitting in the back.

The nun began performing a mesmerising feat of threading a piece of chalk through her bony fingers. 'The Romans' greatest achievements? I'm waiting?' she said, in studied casualness.

'Learning to speak Latin?' replied Babby.

The piece of chalk dropped from the nun's hands. There was more sniggering and a couple of explosive snorts of laughter. Babby stared ahead, unflinching.

'Such a div, Delaney,' said the girl sitting next to her, in a low voice.

But Babby didn't care. Because the next day she was going home.

The following morning, a miserable day like every other miserable day, she left the house at seven, stuffed her velveteen hat and tie in a convenient privet bush, and waited for the bus to Liverpool. When it arrived, she took her place on the top deck and thrust her hands deep in the pockets of the shapeless gabardine coat which Violet had bought from the thrift shop. There were holes in one pocket and the hem was coming undone. It had passed muster in the dimly lit shop and Violet had been seduced by its cheapness, but it didn't fit, it was old-fashioned – and it was hard to imagine a person on earth who would have chosen it if they had bought it new. Babby felt conspicuous wearing it and hoped it wouldn't give her away.

She arrived at Skelhorne Street bus station in Liverpool. Outside Lime Street station the Hackney carriages were lined up like a row of black beetles. She made her way to the Pier Head where she planned to get the overhead railway back to Joseph Street. The luminous estuary light welcomed her home and she felt a surge of happiness to be back in the city. A child wearing a cowboy hat was executing slow, lazy circles as he danced along the waterfront, waving his arms, and Babby returned his beaming smile, shot back at him when he pointed an imaginary pistol at her and shouted, 'Pow, pow.' The Mersey glittered and dazzled in the sun and the Liver birds, with their outstretched wings, looked down at the scene played out below. Pulling the sleeve of her shirt over the heel of her hand and wiping it across the top of the rail, Babby examined the filthy black mark it made. Some things would never change. And the grime of the city felt comforting to her. But when she arrived at Joseph Street the door was firmly locked with a note from Violet saying that there was no one in, could the coalmen leave the bag of coal in the coalhole and she would be back at six.

Chapter Nine

At the Boot Inn, Gladys Worrall sat nursing a drink at the bar. She had her usual bottle of Mackeson's milk stout and was chasing a pickled egg around a plate with a spoon. The outlandish pink feather boa coiled around her neck seemed incongruous alongside the spit and sawdust. And there was certainly nothing snug about this place. It was draughty, with dim lighting, hard, split plastic seats, and sticky floors and surfaces where dust had congealed. Gladys Worrall's grand idea to bring a touch of glamour to the dock road hadn't worked out quite as she had hoped. She had changed the name to the Tivoli, after the cinema, hoping it would attract a better class of customers. Yet disappointingly for Gladys, the locals still called it the Boot Inn and chose Burton Ales over Cinzano. And despite an unfortunate incident in the past, they still preferred a good brawl to ballroom dancing. They said that the Tivvy would always be a place where they played tick with hatchets and the fleas wore clogs – and with the sailors and dockers still choosing it over the other pubs in the dock road for old time's sake, one thing you could guarantee was a night out to remember.

Elsie joined her at the bar. Both women were laughing together, roaring throaty, dirty laughs. Gladys blotted her crudely painted lips, leaving an impression of them on a handkerchief. 'Get me a glass of Harvey's Bristol cream, Elsie.' She was slightly squiffy, trying to sound her aitches, as if she was the queen. Her Knotty Ash vowels sounded mangled and difficult to place.

At first, they didn't see Babby making her way into the bar, with her head held high, thrusting her chin out. But they noticed her when the pub went quiet, a blanket of hush descending and eyes turning in her direction. Gladys stared at Babby, not knowing what to say.

'That job, collecting the glasses? Johnny Gallagher told me about it. Is it still going?' asked Babby, straightening her skirt.

Gladys's blank expression gave nothing away.

'I said, that job – is it still going?'

Gladys stretched out her legs and crossed one over the other. 'It is if you'll sing for us, love,' she said.

Elsie raised her eyebrows and admonished her with a look. 'Don't be a devil, Glad. She's only twelve! Is she allowed?'

Gladys looked Babby up and down, fascinated by the thrust of her hip, the toss of her hair, the sheer bloody nerve of her. 'Does your mother know you're here?'

'Course,' Babby lied.

'So, if I said, "Violet, your Babby is singing in the pub", she'd be fine with that?'

'Dandy,' replied Babby.

It was as if a new source of courage had taken over Babby's body. She placed a fist on her hip, cocked her head to one side.

Gladys smiled, thinking she'd do anything for a pretty young girl to liven this place up – and even though this one was a tomboy with scuffed knees and ragged clothes, she would scrub up all right.

'Well, I could get you a job at the Tap down the road. Keep your mother happy. Doing the bottle washing and the coal-hole. Or I could get you one singing here.'

'I'd rather here,' said Babby her eyes widening.

'Let's hear you, then.'

'What, now?' asked Babby.

'Why not? There's the stage,' she said gesturing towards the far end of the room.

It's hardly a stage, thought Babby, as she looked over to a couple of upturned packing cases with a few planks laid over the top. She eyed the pub nervously.

There was a man sipping a pint of ale with a bulldog sleeping at his feet and a couple of dockers in their work clothes, faces covered in soot, glanced over in her direction.

Gladys turned to Elsie. 'You ever hear Jack Delaney singing "Liverpool Girl"?'

'Not had the pleasure,' Elsie replied.

'Babby, you know that one?'

Of course she knew it. How could she not? It was the last song that her father had sung to her before he died. A memory flashed into her head of him singing it into her ear, of warm sunshine, her coronation dress, and of red, white, and blue bunting.

'Do it for Elsie,' said Gladys.

Babby felt her knees trembling.

She made her way to the stage, stepped up on to it, and cleared her throat nervously.

''Twas a Liverpool girl who loved me, oh she loved me, my Liverpool girl.'

Her voice was clear and true and even the bulldog pricked up his ears. The dockers paused, their pint glasses held somewhere between table and lips for a moment. Babby grew more confident, sang louder and sweeter – and beamed as Elsie and the customers gave her a round of applause when she finished.

Gladys smiled. 'Come back Saturday and do the same again for us? I'll pay you half a crown.'

Babby was so happy she could have hugged her. 'Thank you, Mrs Worrall. Thank you!' she said.

Gladys Worrall tutted and shook her head.

'Thank you,' she repeated. It was not exactly the job she had come here for. But it was the job that she really wanted. Surely enough time had passed since her father died and as long as she went back to the school on the hill and kept up with her homework, Violet wouldn't object? Would she?

Chapter Ten

Babby turned, ran out of the pub, over the tram lines, through the passage way that led to the piece of wasteland, then back towards Joseph Street. The sharp intakes of breath as she gulped air stabbed her throat as she charged on. It was good to be home. She was certain that, despite Pauline's doubtless fury on discovering she had run away from school, having a job and earning money would change everything for her mother and she would be allowed to come back. The smell of coal and smoke was welcoming. There was the spot where Patrick had smashed his football through next-door's side window and Violet had walloped him for it, the corner where they had been caught by the police with pockets full of apples they had stolen after scrumping at Croxteh Hall, the dent in the door where a game of Kick the Can had become overly exuberant and the can had shot all the way over the road and Pat, as he returned from

Boy's Brigade, had ducked to avoid it and sworn. It was all reassuringly familiar. She knew every nook and cranny of this place, which was why she loved it here. She would tell Violet she was home, that she was going to work hard at school and could also earn her keep. It would make her mother happy to know she had a job; all would be forgiven and, when Violet was happy, it was blissful.

The sounds of the rag-and-bone man calling, 'Any old iron! Any old iron!' for pans with bottoms that needed mending, or old clothes that he would pay a penny for, morphed into a one-syllable guttural cry, and made her heart leap. She thumped the rusting bell with the heel of her hand, knocked on the window and called. There was no reply, but making her way down the side of the house, she saw the back door was ajar. She shoved it open. 'Flaming heck,' she murmured, reaching out to catch a broom propped up behind it. It knocked over an aspidistra in a raffia pot that sat on a wooden plant stand, which upturned itself on to the worn peg rug.

'Mam!' she called. 'Mam, I'm back!' trying to scoop up the plant. There was no reply, but inside the living room, the fire had been made. She made her way into the kitchen and noticed there were dirty cups and saucers in the sink, a frying pan with a single shrivelled piece of blackened bacon coagulating in white lard, and an empty bottle of Vimto on the draining board. It had only been two weeks since she had been here, but as she stood there, looking around the room, it seemed different – a chair moved to the corner, the vase sitting on the sideboard instead of the windowsill, the hat-stand pushed up against the far wall.

She made her way upstairs, taking them two at a time. But then, when she came upon one of Violet's blouses lying crumpled on the landing floor, she hesitated. Consternation rippled through her and panic lodged in her throat. Through the door that was slightly open, she saw, to her horror, the shape of an unfamiliar body lying on the bed face down, saw bare shoulders and a string vest, an expanse of white flesh. Worse than that, as the body shifted, she saw that there was another underneath. Her mother's.

There was movement in the bedroom. Babby stood, frozen. Her feet felt as if they were stuck in cement, claggy and immovable. She watched as the man heaved his legs over the side of the bed, grunted, pulled up his trousers and rose to his feet, braces looping around his thighs. She felt herself trembling. She couldn't see his face, but then she didn't know if she wanted to. The man shifted again. Strands of Violet's hair fanned out on the sheets and, for a second, Babby thought she should just burst in and to hell with the consequences. But even she didn't have the courage for that and she turned to leave. The board on the top stair, the one she should have remembered was loose, creaked loudly as she trod on it and from inside her mother's room she heard coughing and footsteps. Terrified, she slipped into the cupboard on the landing and shut the door.

She waited, open-mouthed, hardly daring to breathe, every hair on her body standing up stiffly as a porcupine's needles. A door squeaked on its hinges and the footsteps were in the hallway now, passing inches away from her, and stopping at the top of the stairs. Babby closed her eyes and prayed. Then there were more footsteps, now going down the stairs, and the man's voice shouting up to her mother, 'See you, Vi', as he walked out of the house, slamming the door behind him.

Meanwhile, Violet wrapped a bed sheet around her body. She had heard the creak on the landing and knew for certain that someone else was in the house. She came out just as Babby was trying to creep down the stairs. 'Bloody Nora. It's you!' she exclaimed.

Babby froze, then turned around, and stuttered a lame hello, but could think of nothing else to say. She gawped at her mother, her hair dishevelled, red about the eyes and mouth, the chafe of a man's beard flushing her cheek.

'What in the name of God are you doing here?'

'Come home,' Babby mumbled, biting her lip to stop herself telling her mother what she had just seen.

'Ridiculous,' said Violet.

'There are lots of things that are ridiculous,' Babby said.

For a moment, Babby considered running straight back out of the front door, but despite the awfulness of the situation, she decided what she wanted to tell her mother was more important. She had come here to announce that she could help look after the family and get a job, so that they could all be together again and be happy. And that was what she was going to do. The fact that she had found her mother 'making the beast with two backs' as Johnny Gallagher put it, wasn't her fault.

'How long were you spying on us?' said Violet.

'I wasn't, Mam! I didn't know that you were ...' What didn't she know? The words stretched away from her. How could her mother do something so disgusting, so abhorrent, to be doing *it,* because that's what it looked like, with a man, out of wedlock? She felt her cheeks burn with shame. The girls at Saint Hilda's were right. Her mother was 'loose'.

Violet went back into her bedroom. Babby was deliberating what to do when she heard Hannah, in the back bedroom, let out a chesty cough. She went into the room. 'Hannah?' she said. Curled up on the low bed wrapped up in an old blanket and Violet's astrakhan coat, Hannah looked up at her. She was wearing the grubby old blue smocked dress that Babby recognised as once having been her own. A tendril of her curly hair was stuck against her wet cheek.

Babby sat beside her on the bed. 'Why aren't you at Aunty Kathleen's?' she murmured as she drew her towards her. She looked around. There were no toys, or children's books. Just a crucifix and an empty gin bottle. There used to be a brightly coloured spinning top on the mantelpiece above the grate, and a mobile hung with fish and ducks that, when the lights came on in the street outside, made strange-shaped patterns across the ceiling. Had Violet been selling things from the house? What was going on? Were they really that poor?

'What's been happening?' she said to Hannah gently.

Hannah didn't reply. She didn't need to. Her glassy eyes just filled with tears.

'Oh, Hannah,' said Babby. 'Don't be sad. I'm not cross with you. Come on, let's get you some fresh clothes and a cup of milk. This is a right godawful show ...'

Hannah nodded seriously. No one was going to argue with that.

When Babby went into the parlour she found Violet pacing, now dressed in an old kimono. She was expecting more tears, perhaps Violet begging for her forgiveness, perhaps an explanation for the horror she had just witnessed. Instead, Violet turned away, presenting an indifferent back, that was hard to read. On the stove, there were tatties cooking in a pan of greasy water. Violet prodded the potatoes with a fork, licked its prongs, and announced quietly that Babby should forget everything that she had just seen, just put it right out of her mind, she couldn't hope to understand.

'Mam, I just want to come back. I hate my new school, the girls are vile to me. It's like a prison. There are actual bars on the windows. Flipping nuns giving me the evil eye. They make me feel like I'm something they've stepped in.'

Violet laid down the fork. 'Love, I'm sorry you don't like your new school, but who likes school? No one. You're not supposed to like school. Running back here complaining won't make any difference to anything at all, you still can't stay.'

Babby threw herself on the chaise longue and groaned.

'For goodness' sake, Babby. Get over yourself. You look like you've knitted your face and dropped a stitch. Go and do the fire and make sure you pull the newspaper.' Babby sighed, wondering if it would be better if she just left, but compliantly she took the shovel and, with a newspaper across it, used it to draw the fire, watching it catch fire and disappear up the chimney.

Violet, awkward, sat down. Then she casually took the mouldy fur off the top of the jam with a knife and scraped it on the side of the plate before spreading a fresh dollop on the heel of a stale loaf.

'There's lots of things you don't understand, Babby.' she said through a mouthful of jam. 'You're too young ...'

'What would Patrick would have to say about it? Does he already know? About your fella?' asked Babby.

Violet took a scent bottle and, pumping the small crocheted ball, started spraying perfume down her cleavage. 'Until you know the truth of the thing, there is no point getting upset or involved in a grown-up's problems, dear.'

In response, Babby stood. She said nothing but banged the dishes in the sink, screwed up her eyes, and fixed her mother with a look.

'I came home because I thought you needed me,' sighed Babby.

'I need you to do what I tell you for once,' replied Violet.

There was a pause. Violet softened. She came over to Babby who had now slumped into a chair. 'Love ...' she said. But Babby shoved her away, slung her legs over the side of the armchair, stood up and announced she was going off into the back yard for a breath of fresh air.

'Bring in the coal bucket,' called Violet after her.

The following morning, Violet knelt at the hearth, using the bellows to help the fresh coal catch fire. 'About yesterday. I'm sorry you had to see that, love,' she said to Babby, finding it difficult to meet her eyes. 'But it's not only about you, you know. The world doesn't revolve around you.'

'But I hate Pauline – and Saint Hilda's! And I miss Dad and Hannah and Pat – and even Johnny!' said Babby. Violet listened and sighed, and nodded. 'I miss this place an' all, Mam.'

'I understand all of that, but you have to trust me to know what is best for you, and whilst I will love you forever, right until this hair turns white, I can't have you just jumping on a bus home when you feel like it. Maybe Saint Hilda's was a mistake.'

'What d'you mean?'

'Pauline always said it would be. I was the one who persuaded her it might work. But the fact is she spoke to me a week ago about you wanting to leave Saint Hilda's and advised me to make alternative arrangements. So, this time, as long as the priest at Saint Patrick's still agrees, you will be going to Holy Island in Anglesey, to one of the homes that the sister's run. They need a girl.'

'A home? Like *Saint Jude's?*'

'Of course not like Saint Jude's. That's for unmarried mothers, you silly girl. God forbid you ever end up there. In fact, that's precisely why I'm doing this. To tame you, Babby. To keep you out of that place. It's for your own good. No, this is somewhere for children whose families can't look after them. The nuns teach the children and when they are old enough they work on the farm. You can stay for five weeks or five years, depending on your circumstances.'

'No!'

'Yes, Babby.'

'I'm only staying until Christmas.'

'Then what? No, I'm afraid, this time it will be for good. Or at least until you finish your schooling.'

Babby opened her eyes wide with fury.

'Anglesey? I don't even know where Anglesey is!'

'North Wales. Across the water. It's an island. Pauline says it's lovely.'

'No! Pauline's lying!'

Violet, despite everything, feeling sorry for her, tried to placate her by placing a calming hand on her chestnut brown curls, but Babby sprang back as if she was on a coil, and asked, 'What about Hannah and Pat?'

'What about them? Pat will go into lodgings, Hannah will go to Kathleen's.'

And you will carry on with your fancy man! thought Babby, deciding that, actually, the last place she wanted to be was Joseph Street.

'You might like it,' said Violet. 'It's very green.'

'I'll only go if I can take Dad's accordion.'

Violet sucked in air. 'Why would you want to drag that old thing all the way there?'

'It would remind me of home. Of Dad.'

Violet sighed. 'We'll see,' she said.

It really was a hopeless situation.

Chapter Eleven

'I worry about Hannah. She'll be so confused and sad,' said a fretful Violet, when she told her sister, Kathleen, about sending Babby to Anglesey. 'I know it's for the best, but Hannah will miss Babby so much. Those two are joined at the hip. She's nearly three years old, but she follows Babby everywhere, she's like a limpet. I feel sick at the thought of separating them for longer than a few days. It was bad enough whilst Babby was at Pauline's. Hannah is such a fragile little poppet.'

'I certainly can't be looking after them both,' Kathleen replied, unmoved, bustling around the kitchen, rinsing out dirty teacups and sticky glasses.

'Pauline has also said I will have to drag myself off to Mass. And to confession. Apparently, I have to say to the priest that I'm sorry for turning my back on the church and then we can all start afresh. That's if I want them to sort Babby out for me. Angelsey, I mean.' She sighed. 'I swore I was done with all this God stuff after Jack died.'

'Sounds a good idea. Father O'Casey always seems to know what to say. They have an instinct about these things.'

Violet wasn't convinced. She suspected Kathleen was more worried about her ongoing love affair with Spanish brandy and what that was doing to them all, than the business with Babby. God knows what she would have had to say if she had had walked in on her as Babby had done the week before. Kathleen had wanted her to go to talk to the priests and the nuns since Jack died.

'But it's been so long since I've been anywhere near a church. What will Father O'Casey say to me? Will he even remember me?'

'I don't think he'll ever forget you, Violet.'

'It's all very well, Pauline made it sound so simple, but they might take a very dim view. The last time I had a proper conversation with Father O'Casey was at Jack's funeral – and that ended badly.'

'Yes, well you shouldn't have blamed him for the Mouse turning up. Father had nothing to do with the trouble at the Boot and you dragged him into it by asking him to tell the Mouse he couldn't come to Jack's funeral. Poor man. Of course he wasn't going to do that. You shouldn't have made such a fuss.

I still haven't got over you falling drunk into the christening font and telling him that, if God was up to scratch, he wouldn't have taken your Jack away. You should feel lucky they're thinking about giving you a second chance.'

'Lucky?' said Violet, gloomily. 'I hardly think so. Desperate, more like.'

For a day and a half Violet opened kitchen drawers and straightened cutlery, then sideboard drawers and bedside drawers and wandered from room to room, rearranging furniture, repinning the lace antimacassars and, finally, checking the aspidistra plant to see if the soil was dry, and all the time wondering what she should do about Babby. Finally, she decided she had no choice but to take Pauline and Kathleen's advice and go to see Father O'Casey at Saint Patrick's. The priests and nuns would know what to do about her daughter. If there was any place that might help her, it would be there, she thought.

Trudging down the path to the church, with the gravestones like snaggled teeth sticking out from the grass, she almost turned back.

The large double doors were open but inside it was nearly empty, just a few old ladies kneeling in the side altars as they threaded rosary beads through their fingers and murmured Hail Marys, a young woman lighting a candle, and an altar server sorting through hymnals. It was quiet. Violet walked up the aisle and took a seat in one of the pews. She took some comfort in the sweet, heady smell of incense and the beautiful Jesus, with his strong and graceful limbs, nailed to a huge wooden crucifix suspended above the altar on steel wires. Were it not for the fact that her head had been full of Jack and the kids and not having enough money – or time – to even think, she might have come here more often.

Candlelight from the hundred or so melting votives threw off heat and flickered across the faces of the stone statues of the twelve apostles. Violet could have sworn they shot curious glances in her direction. Is this completely ridiculous? she wondered. To go in there and say sorry and then hope they will just wipe the slate clean and help me with what's happening to my daughter?

She waited in the pew until the altar boy told her she was next. Opening the creaking, ornate door of the confessional with its carving of Jesus buckling under the weight of a crucifix, then kneeling in front of the grill, she gagged. Feeling claustrophobic, the sentimental thoughts that she had been having about this place flew away in an instant. The pungent aromatic smell that she couldn't quite identify, mixed with the smells of damp and furniture polish, triggered other, uncomfortable, memories. She had never bothered much with Jesus. Collections for the poor, helping with the flower arranging, sewing and embroidering communion banners – all that had been for other more pious people – better people – than her. So why should Jesus bother with her now? The grill, the dark, and the musty curtains that muffled her voice, the panels pricked with woodworm, the cracked leather kneeler, frightened her. There was a short dry cough from behind the iron mesh.

'Bless me, Father, for I have sinned. It has been, oh … a-a few weeks … maybe a month … no, a year, actually, since my last confession.'

There was a sigh, a pause. Violet really couldn't think what to say next. So, for a second she just sat there, taking shallow breaths, gripped by a terrible fear that the faceless, shadowy figure behind the grill might follow her out and start shouting at her in front of everyone.

'Are you still there?' asked the priest.

'Yes, sorry,' she replied. 'I-I am, Father,' she stammered.

'Speak up.'

'Sorry, yes …' She sensed the blurred shape behind the grill was becoming impatient and she could feel her palms sweating.

'I wanted to confess. For not coming to church.'

A rustle of starched linen and heavy breathing. It was becoming unbearable. She had been squeezing her interlocking fingers so tightly together she had given herself pins and needles. The priest was waiting for her to say something. She was sure he would smell the sin seeping from her pores. He cleared his throat again to tell her that he was waiting. And in a rush of words she said, 'And also the thing is Father. I need your help – the church's help – with my daughter. I'm sorry that I turned away from God and I beg forgiveness for that, but I believe you are looking for a girl to help with the nuns in Angelsey. Farm work, I think?'

'Child, if you are ready to repent, God will look on you with mercy ...Tell me about your daughter,' said the disembodied voice.

And though the tone was firm and censorious it gave her hope, and it was as if a burden had miraculously floated from her shoulders. She felt a cleansing energy coursing through her veins. Maybe, just maybe, she could try to start to be good again.

'I can't look after her any more. And I've heard – I've heard that you might be able to assist me ...'

'Sister Immaculata will talk to you to see if we can make the necessary arrangements if, indeed, that's appropriate, but now an Act of Contrition.'

'O my God, I am heartily sorry for having offended Thee, and I detest all my sins, because I dread the loss of Heaven and the pains of Hell, but most of all because they offend Thee, my God, Who art all-good and deserving of all my love. I firmly resolve, with the help of Thy grace to confess my sins, to do penance and to amend my life. Amen.'

'Penance, Two hundred Hail Marys and a Rosary each day for three months ...'

She would try her best. It seemed like a reasonable exchange.

She noticed Sister Immaculata, a vague and cobwebby figure in the church porch, on her way out.

'Violet. Come with me.'

They went into the presbytery and the housekeeper, a nun with strands of salt-and-pepper hair escaping from under her veil, knocked and entered the room they sat in, pushing a stainless steel hostess trolley with tea and Garibaldi biscuits. The rattling of the china cups and the flip, flop, of the nun's slippers as they hit the soles of her feet when she crossed the parquet floor, were the only sounds in a chasm of silence.

'How can I help you?' said Sister Immaculata, clearing a chair of a pile of prayer books so Violet could sit down.

'Well, I believe you know that my Babby has run back home from S-Saint Hilda's,' she stuttered. 'Pauline said you might have her for the job of farm help for some of your sisters in Anglesey.' Violet wiped her glistening brow with the back of her hand. She expected the nun to laugh, and tell her Pauline had got it all wrong, taking in rebellious girls like Babby wasn't the kind of thing they did at all, but she nodded kindly.

'We certainly do need an extra pair of hands. As you know, Pauline has already been in touch through the Legion of Mary and your daughter sounds an excellent candidate. We're here to help you, Violet, so don't look so worried. This is all part of God's plan. She'll have a good education from us in return for working at the farm, which is owned by the convent. You know what the Jesuits say about giving us the child and we'll give you back the man?'

Violet knew all right. She just wasn't sure what she felt about it. It felt a tendentious contract at its best.

'We'll take care of her, Violet, and we'll make you proud of her. We wouldn't want her ending up somewhere like Saint Judes, would we? Every mother's nightmare, so it is.'

Violet brushed away a tear as the nun gently placed a calming hand on her trembling knee.

'My dear,' she said. 'You really have nothing to cry about. Have faith in God, and in us, and she'll return home as innocent as she left you – and a good deal better besides. Come now. What mother would find fault in that?'

Chapter Twelve

A week passed, the conversations were exhausted, and Babby finally agreed to go – a combination of being allowed to take the accordion and Violet becoming so bad tempered, what with worrying about so many other things, like Hannah, and keeping her new job at the glove factory, that it seemed pointless to try to put it off any longer.

'Cheer up,' Violet said to her. 'Pauline has said you'll love it, and you'll feel a lot better when we get there.'

The boat went from the Pier Head. Violet was anxious they were going to be late. There was a great deal of shouting to get a move on and complaining about hauling the accordion all the way to Anglesey, and whether it was really a good idea, but they finally set off in Kathleen's car as she'd offered to drive them. In an attempt to lift the mood, Kathleen suddenly burst out with a verse of 'We're off, we're off! We're off in a motor car, sixty bobbies are after us, an' we don't know where we are!' and urged everyone to join in. But they got no further than Scottie Road before they lost heart, and everyone went quiet.

As they drove down the dock road, Violet told Kathleen to put her foot down. 'Step on the gas!' she cried.

'Better to be Mrs Delaney, late, rather than the late Mrs Delaney,' Kathleen said and Babby felt a tinge of sadness: the last time she had heard this expression was when her father had spoken it.

Despite it being ten in the morning, the pubs were opening. 'Knocking shops,' said Violet. 'Look at those two fellas with that woman. They're coming out from the night before ...'

'She's a prozzie, I bet,' said Babby.

'What's a prozzie?' asked Hannah, and they all shrieked when Kathleen took her hands off the steering wheel to turn around and tut and the car swerved across the road.

The crossing from the Pier Head was clear. There was sunshine and white peaks of foam. Standing on the top deck, Babby turned to face the smudge on the horizon that was Anglesey. The lighthouse came into view first, then the fields became patches of green, and soon the houses and cottages in the harbour that fuzzed and wobbled in the heat took shape.

Hannah, who had come along because she refused to be parted from Babby until the very last moment, clung to Babby's skirts all the way. Babby drew her to her. How was she going to bear this? Pentraeth Farm, this strange place run by the nuns, full of waifs and strays, was to be her home and nobody would tell her exactly for how long. As the steamer tucked and tossed, as the engines sent vibrations through their fragile bodies, as they sailed towards the headland, Babby felt her stomach lurch, and the promises of trips home and visits from the family became ever more unlikely.

When they arrived in the small harbour – Babby lugging her trunk along and Violet using her teetering heels as an excuse not to help – they were met by a smiling nun standing beside a battered Morris 1000.

Behind her was another middle-aged, wide-hipped woman, wearing muddy wellington boots. This was Mrs Reilly, stout, ruddy and fair-haired, who looked like she was from farming stock, the kind of woman who had crescent moons of dirt permanently under her fingernails and matted hair. She was the owner of Pentraeth Farm, and it was she who first introduced herself as she stuck out a hand, beaming.

'Don't mind Threepence,' she said, as a sniffing dog bounded around Babby's feet, then jumped up and stuck its nose up her skirts.

When they got back to the farmhouse after a bumpy ride, the car phutting and spluttering as it negotiated the potholes and sharp bends in the winding road, they were led into a squat, stubby building with gables and moss on the roof and a huge wisteria vine climbing up the gutters and strangling the crumbling chimney.

'Oh Babby!' sighed Violet. 'I wish I was coming here.'

'Me too,' said Hannah, mournfully.

Babby, feeling the strength of her sister's sadness, pointed at the goat tethered to a long rope munching a clump of nettles on the gone-to-seed front lawn. 'Look at the goat, Hannah. They'll eat anything. Even Mum's rock cakes, I bet,' she said, trying to eke a smile out of her as they followed Mrs Reilly inside.

'That's the twins,' said Mrs Reilly as two red-haired children, raced past them, to go outside. 'Just here for a few months.'

'Who else lives here?' asked Violet. 'Anyone Babby's age?'

Babby fixed her mother with a measuring gaze. Does she mean boys? she wondered. Please God, she doesn't.

'People come and go. At the moment, we have three teenagers from Manchester, all impoverished children from orphanages or broken homes, mostly of northern cities. But they're good kids. Amazing what fresh air can do for a child. The only problem we have is that they're always complaining that they're starving.'

'Where will Babby sleep?' asked Violet.

'In the attic. It's a lot better than it sounds. Bit musty, but it's clean ... And you'll have it all to yourself.'

Violet smiled. 'See, Babby, it's not so bad. You've never had your own room, have you?'

Babby shook her head.

Two young men, about twenty and twenty-two, arrived wiping their boots, ducking their heads as they came in through the low door frame. Boys. But not like the Kapler Gang. Instead of sallow, pock-marked skin, they had colour in their rosy cheeks and glossy hair. Babby followed them with her eyes.

'You'll stay for supper, won't you? asked Mrs Riley.

'That would be lovely,' replied Violet.

'Do we have to go to church every day?' asked Babby, suddenly. There was a silence. Violet looked to Mrs Riley, apologetically.

'Of course not,' she replied, with a smile. 'This isn't like your convent school. The nuns do an awful lot of praying up there in the house on the hill – that's where they live, they just come here to teach, but I make the rules around here,' she said with a wink.

Babby was relieved to hear that she was obviously the one who ran things, and the nuns largely kept out of the way.

'We do have a chapel, though. I'll show you,' said Mrs Reilly.

She took them outside and down to the bottom of the garden where there was a small outhouse with a stone crucifix cemented into the top of the gable.

'This has been here for years. They say that priests used to hide in it, that there's a passage that goes all the way under it and into the house. Not that anyone has found it. Sometimes, if it all gets too much, it's a good place to just sit and think. Would you like to see inside?'

Babby really didn't want to, but she could see Violet looking at her, willing her to answer politely.

'Yes,' said Babby. Mrs Reilly linked her arm and opened the door.

The chapel smelled of damp. There was a chipped and peeling statue of the Sacred Heart that looked as though his bright carmine lips had been repainted and someone had stippled a beard on his chin, and gory paintings of the Stations of the Cross in murky colours, and pews with threadbare velvet kneelers and battered hymn books at each end. A beam of sunlight lit up glittering particles of dust. They stood there for a moment in the silence, with just the cawing of a bird in the distance.

'Come on,' said Mrs Reilly, seeing Babby's nose wrinkle up with the smell. 'You'll like it here, I promise.'

They could hear the sound of the dinner bell across the field. In the dining room, a large airy space with flaking whitewashed walls, trestle tables and benches running down either side, there was food waiting – fish paste sandwiches, crusty rolls spread with thick butter, creamy butterfly cakes, and steaming pots of tea.

'Mrs Reilly can do magical things with butter and eggs and sugar,' said the nun who was pouring out the tea into the pots from an urn on the sideboard. She introduced herself as Sister Benedict, one of the nuns who would be teaching Babby.

Violet nudged Babby and said, 'See? it might not be so awful after all.'

It was only Hannah, a cake stuffed in her mouth, who looked at Babby, doleful and sad, her big eyes pools of worry.

'Don't worry,' said Babby. 'I made a promise to Dad and I will be back to take care of you. You have my word.' Putting an arm around her sister's shoulders, she felt a terrible sense of sadness. Stooping to pull up a sock drooping around Hannah's ankle, she said, 'I'll miss you.'

A tear rolled down Hannah's jam-smeared cheek, a single tear, but it was enough.

'Chin up, Babby. You'll have a grand time,' said Violet. 'Time for us to go, now.'

Babby's eyes filled with tears and anxiety washed over her in waves. Violet, turning quickly away, said, 'Ta ra. We'll see you soon, love.'

'Mam ...' said Babby.

'What love?'

'Nothing,' she replied.

Some things were just too big to talk about.

Chapter Thirteen

1960

'Happy Birthday to you! *Blow,* Babby! Come on!'

Babby stooped to blow out the seventeen candles. The flames flickered and bent with the rush of wind that came in through the door.

'Speech!' cried Albie.

'Speech?' said Babby. 'I'm not making any speeches.'

'You do it, Mrs Reilly,' said Albie.

Mrs Reilly tapped the glass of elderflower wine she was holding with a teaspoon.

The twins, holding hands, hoped from foot to foot, excitedly.

'When Babby came here she was a slip of a girl, weren't you, love? And now you're seventeen.'

One of the boys shoved two fingers in his mouth and whistled and everyone laughed.

It was true; Babby had curves now, a pert nose, and hair that fell in waves down her back. And it showed in her face that she was happy and untroubled. She had even suggested the Union Jack bunting tied from the dresser to the curtain pole. That was something she had never thought possible, so vivid were the memories of her father's death, forever threaded through with images of red, white and blue flags and the coronation.

'Babby's as good as any of them movie stars on me cigarette cards,' said Albie. And everyone laughed again.

'Shall I cut the cake?' asked Babby, and a cry went up. She put the knife into the sponge and cream and jam oozed from its middle.

'Wait! I haven't finished yet,' said Mrs Reilly. 'So, like I said, Babby, when you came here, you had only one thing on your mind – and that was getting out of this place. But gradually you got to like us, and gradually we decided that perhaps you weren't so bad after all. So, we stopped bolting the doors.' Everyone laughed, though some found it funnier than others.

'Thank you, Mrs Reilly. I know I gave you a headache or two.'

'Headache! It were more than that, love,' she said smiling. 'Only joking. We'll miss you when you go back to Liverpool in the autumn. You've worked hard for us. You've been like a second mother to some of these kiddies.'

It was only Sister Scholastica, whose face remained a blank canvas, who was the dissenter. I won't miss her, trouble still runs through that girl like the word Blackpool in a stick of rock, her expression said. She had often complained to Sister Benedict and Mrs Reilly that Babby had long outstayed her welcome. She would be the first to grudgingly admit that the few older teenagers that stayed on to work after they had finished their education provided a useful pair of hands, but if it hadn't been for Violet Delaney finding one excuse after another as to why she couldn't take Babby back home – the younger daughter, her nerves, the house rotting away – she would have sent her back years ago. And she didn't really believe Mrs Reilly thought any different.

'Anyone want food?' said Albie, offering round a plate of curling sandwiches. 'They taste flipping delicious,' he said, through a mouthful of bread and raspberry jam. Mrs Reilly had produced a strawberry tart that she had made, and one of the twins hadn't been able to resist sticking a finger in and scooping out the fruit. When everyone gasped to see the hole in the middle, she tried to hide her red-stained fingers.

'Come on, birthday girl,' said Mrs Reilly, 'let's go and get the rest of the goodies.'

'Can I come?' asked one of the twins, as they all dove upon the cake, the children's eyes desperately searching this way and that, hoping not to be the one who got a smaller piece than the other. The feeling of what it was like to be hungry would never leave them.

'No, this is a birthday treat.'

'Not fair,' came the response.

'Life's not fair,' said Sister Scholastica, but no one in this room needed to be told that. They just didn't want to be reminded of it.

'Will you bring back some Golden Syrup?' said one of the boys.

'And cans of Carnation evaporated milk and conny-onny and demerara sugar?' asked another.

'Not sure if demerara sugar is off the rations yet,' laughed Mrs Reilly. Rationing had finished years ago, but it was her favourite joke. 'We'll see. It's Babby's choice, anyway. When it's your birthday you can make the provisions list.'

'Put some cinder toffee on the list,' whined the girl twin.

'If they have some, I'll get some,' replied Babby.

'Sherbet dib dabs! Flying saucers! What about you make us a wet Nelly and knickerbocker glories, Mrs Reilly?' chorused the boys.

'Get me that stuff that grows on trees. All pink and fluffy, like a bird's nest. Candyfloss, in't it?' said one of the twins.

And Sister Benedict, who had just arrived to see what the commotion was, tutted, and cuffed him about the head. 'Now then, did you fall out of the stupid tree and hit every branch on the way down, Colin?' she asked.

Half an hour later, as the sun burst through the clouds, Babby looked out at the glittering Irish sea. Feet planted apart, one fist on a hip, a hand shielding her eyes, she sighed a sigh of relief seeing the grocery store in the distance, a small square stone building, stuck out on a limb at the end of a gentle slope by the beach.

'Nearly there, Mrs Reilly,' cried Babby. Her mouth was watering, not for the staples of flour and salt and cooking lard, but for the treats on the birthday list.

'Come on. Let's go before the store shuts for dinner time,' said Mrs Reilly.

Babby's right shoe had begun to leak and she could feel a blister on her left foot, so she was relieved to see the store.

The sea stretched away from them for miles, seabirds wheeling above. 'Isn't that beautiful! God's work!' Mrs Reilly cried And it *was* beautiful, especially when the day was clear like this and they had views all the way across to the Wicklow Mountains in Ireland. On the way, Mrs Reilly chatted animatedly about the feast they would have when they got back. Babby's mouth watered at the thought of the taste of home-made strawberry jam that they would make together later.

'Babby, come back!' cried Mrs Reilly, as Babby ran on ahead. This is my favourite part, Babby said to herself, picking her way through the stony path, then running through the fields and leaping alongside the grazing sheep and goats, imagining she was Heidi. She was racing through the lush green grass, running and running, until the field suddenly sloped, and the gathering speed meant she couldn't stop, and her knees gave way and she landed with a thump on her bottom. She could see the beach through a tangled copse with a root-latticed path and she stood up, ducking her head and racing through the pine trees, pushing branches away, until she came out on the other side, and then on to the sea where the tide shrank bank to expose fresh, unspoiled sand studded with pink and white shells. Mrs Reilly, out of breath, was jogging towards her, a doughnut of flesh wobbling around her neck.

'Babby!' she called. 'Come back here!'

Babby hoiked up her skirts, took off her shoes and socks, and paddled out into the water, yelping as the cold water swirled around her ankles.

'Come on now. Let's collect the provisions! We haven't time for this. We want to be back in time for lunch.'

Babby cantered back over the gently breaking waves to Mrs Reilly, picked up a shell shaped like the end of an ice-cream cone and wrote her name in the sand, stood back and looked at it.

Mrs Reilly placed a hand on the small of her back and led her away, back towards the slope that led up towards the headland and the store.

The bell tinkled as they entered.

'Well, happy birthday!' said Daffyd, smiling, hands shoved deep into his apron. He took down one of the sweet jars and unscrewed the lid. 'Have a couple of these.'

Babby thrust her hand deep into the jar of pear drops and soon the sweet bulged in her mouth and she felt it prickle against her tongue.

Plonking down bags of flour, sugar, tins of pine-apple slices and pears in syrup, he licked the end of a pencil and totalled up the messages. Meanwhile, Babby helped Mrs Reilly load the lighter items into string bags that she had produced from her pocket.

'Leave the heavy stuff for Callum,' said Mrs Reilly. 'He'll pick them up in the motor car.'

'Who's Callum?' asked Babby, putting a second pear drop in her mouth.

'A boy from the mainland. Aintree. His father has sent him over for the summer. We agreed to let him work for a few weeks. Driving the Morris Thou, doing the hay wagon, all this lifting. Fresh air for his lungs.'

Babby was intrigued. She wanted to ask Mrs Reilly again about Callum, but she decided to wait and see for herself.

When they arrived at Pentraeth Farm after the bracing walk back, they went into the small stone outhouse in the corner of the grounds where they unloaded the groceries: buttermilk, that would be made into slabs of cheese by the nuns, bacon that would be fried and cooked with omelettes, tea that would be drunk by the gallon.

They went down to the pantry and, whilst Mrs Reilly wasn't looking, Babby screwed off the top of the malt extract and took a huge, delicious-tasting spoonful of it. Just one more and it would get her through the Mass that was being held that evening in the small chapel at the bottom of the back garden.

'Babby! Put that away!' cried Mrs Reilly when she came back in and discovered Babby licking the spoon.

'Sorry, Mrs Reilly,' she replied. And with equal relish, sucked a finger that was smeared in the stuff.

'You only needed to have asked,' said Mrs Reilly.

They sat at the table with the other waifs and strays. How many other children had passed through these doors? As many as the deep grooves on the table, as many as there were coffee rings on the surface, or scuffs on the wooden floors? Mrs Reilly widened her eyes and darted an expression, which reminded everyone they hadn't said grace yet. They all joined their hands and bowed their heads, Babby eyeing the jar of Lyle's golden syrup greedily. *Out of the strong came forth sweetness*, she read on the label, fascinated by the picture of the bees surrounding the dead lion.

'It's from the Bible,' said Mrs Reilly when they finished saying grace. 'Samson and the bees.' But when a curious Babby reached out to have a closer look, the tin fell off the table as she lurched forward. As it tumbled to the floor, Babby jumped up and pushed her chair out from underneath her to catch it, but as she did so, someone barged into her from behind.

'Mind out!' Babby cried. 'You flippin' eejit!' she yelled, before she had time to turn and see who her temper had been directed at. But then, as she got down and bent to mop up the liquid seeping on to the stone tiles and between the cracks with a napkin, on lifting her head, she found herself nose to nose with a boy. The first thing she noticed about him was his black hair, which was so glossy it looked almost as if it was navy-blue, and startling dark-brown eyes.

'Sorry,' said the boy, grinning, mopping up the sticky goo with his handkerchief. He was not much older than Babby, broad-shouldered and lithe. One of those silly Teddy Boy types, Violet would have described him as, even though it was only his jeans and lick of hair falling into his eyes that made him so. Mrs Reilly appeared with a broom and a cloth.

'Let me do that, Callum,' she said. She looked at Babby. And seeing the way Callum was just standing staring at Babby, it occurred to her that Babby was no longer a skinny thing: she had developed a figure. She was a young woman now, taller, with curves where they should be, long flowing hair, deep-brown eyes and skin that had the benefit of fresh air. A real head-turner.

'This is Callum, Babby. Did you settle into your room all right, Cal?'

'Aye, thank you Mrs Reilly,' he said. His voice had Liverpool vowels, but was sweet and low; Babby felt the hairs on her neck stand up stiffly.

'We'll be happy to have you here, Cal,' said Mrs Reilly. Callum nodded. 'Won't we, Babby?'

'Babby?' He swilled her name around his mouth. 'That's an unusual name,' he said, rolling the sticky handkerchief into a ball and placing it on a saucer.

Babby felt herself blushing to the tips of her ears. The boy stood with his hands deep in the pockets of his trousers which were slung low across his hips and his black hair was greased into a quiff that rose from his strong forehead like Eddie Fisher's. His eyes really were like coals. With his rolled-up shirt sleeves, you could see that his arms were strong and muscular. To Babby he looked as if he had been sculpted, not born.

'I'm about to drive the van to the village to do the errands. Anybody want anything bringing back? So Babby – is that what I call you?' he said.

'Yes,' she answered, and when she tried to explain her real name was Jeanie, that Babby was short for baby, her mouth just shaped itself into a small o, and nothing at all came out.

Chapter Fourteen

An hour later, she sat on the windowsill of her room, nursing a cup of tea against her glowing cheek.

'Callum ...' she murmured to herself, as if she was tasting his name in her mouth, chewing it over. That morning she had promised to go fruit picking with some of the younger children, to pluck the gooseberries from the hedgerows, and later boil them up and mix in the sugar to make delicious jam. She heard Mrs Reilly calling up the stairs to her, but burrowing her head under the greying lace curtains, she pressed her face up to the window. With a hand shading her eyes she squinted into the sunlight and watched Sister Benedict fussing across the street, her nun's wimple making it look as if a huge pelican, with flapping wings outstretched, had landed on her head.

'Get a move on, slowcoaches,' the sister said, shooing the twins along the lane.

Babby's warm breath blotted the pane of glass. She pulled the cuff of her shirt over the heel of her hand and wiped the window clean. She was hoping she might catch Callum on his way back before she left.

She opened the latch to the small window, and perched her bottom on the sill. And then she heard what she had been listening out for. The coughing and spluttering of the Morris Thou, rattling along as though there was something loose inside the engine, signalling the arrival of Callum. It came down the cobbled road and pulled up outside the shed opposite. A door opened downstairs and one of the nuns appeared at the side of the van. Callum got out, slammed the door, flicked back his black hair, then leant back on the bonnet. For a moment, he squinted back across the cornfield and then he turned his head and stared directly up at Babby, right up at the window. He waved at her, gave her the thumbs-up sign, crossed one leg over the other. Babby waved back, smiled nervously. In his tight drainpipe jeans, he looked as though he was from another world, a world of cowboys and American milkshakes, jangling guitars and Elvis singing 'Love Me Tender'. He could have been moulded to perfection and poured into his leather boots. Those boots, she thought, with their fashionable shaped heels and pointed toes. Impossibly glamorous.

Finger hooked into the collar of his jacket slung over one shoulder, he just smiled, flashed his eyes again. He remained there, grinning. And he called, 'That all right, Mrs Reilly? If I take Babby with me?'

Babby saw Mrs Reilly come out into the street. 'Babby!' she shouted up to the window. 'Do you want to go with Callum? You can show him where the store is. I'll take the kids down the lanes for the fruit picking.'

'Come on, love!' he shouted.

Forgetting to breathe, Babby raced downstairs, her heart thumping at her chest, and she flushed red to the tips of her ears. She went outside.

'Hello,' she said. She hoped she was not a disappointment. She fiddled with the button on the woollen cardigan, embroidered with roses, that she was wearing.

'Hello, love.'

She could have sworn he winked at her. It was as if he couldn't smile without winking.

Twirling a strand of hair around her finger, with her left hip jutted out to one side, she asked, 'is that OK? If I come with you to the store?'

'Be glad of the company, love,' he said. He seemed older than his seventeen years.

She noticed his eyes take an inventory of her, the shape of her, her high-waisted skirt that hugged her hips, her sweet blouse with Scottie dog motifs, under the cardigan. She knew she was prettier now than five years ago, that she had changed. She had always been the one with the upturned nose – ski slope, was one of the names she was called at Saint Hilda's, but now her nose was retroussé, like Doris Day from the movies, and she had proper curves. That's what Mrs Reilly said, and she hoped Callum would think the same.

He climbed into the driver's seat, started up the engine. Babby got into the seat on the passenger side and tucked her hands under her thighs as they got ready to drive off.

She could feel herself sweating. What if he did something? He looked the type. Any minute he could start holding her hand, slip his arm around her waist, or even start kissing her full on the lips! An image of him sticking his tongue into her mouth, pushing it between her neat teeth, flashed into her head. Would she bite it off? Or kiss him back? The thought of it made her feel dizzy with excitement. But no. She wasn't going to be like Violet. She was a good girl. She was going to be a lady. And a lady didn't start imagining things like kissing, and snogging – necking, Johnny Gallagher called it, or tonsil tennis – with virtual strangers.

She fiddled with the seatbelt. But she was only doing it so she didn't have to look at him in case he saw that she was blushing, such was the effect of his tight jeans and the boots, the leather jacket with silver zip and studs sloping over the shoulders. Glancing up at him, mesmerised by his olive skin, which was as smooth as treacle, and his teeth, perfectly formed and white, she thought she was going to faint. Then Callum pulled the van over with a swerve and they roared down the winding country lanes.

'So, what d'you like, Miss Babby?' he said, raising his voice to be heard over the sound of the engine.

'What d'you mean?'

'What is it you like? I like pop music, and Manchester United, and the picture house, and lemonade powder, and staying up later than I ought to, and newly cut grass, and cold beer, and chocolate milkshakes, and Makintosh Golden Cup bars.'

There was a pause.

'I like singing,' she said. 'And playing the accordion.'

'The accordion?' he said and laughed. 'That's pretty unusual. Do you have one?'

'I do. Well, it's my da's ...'

'Let's hear you sing?'

'No,' she answered.

'Shy?' he asked, and she blushed deeper. 'D'you like it here? At the farm?'

Babby shrugged. 'It's all right. We get treats like rice pudding with nutmeg toffee on the top, egg custard, peeled oranges dipped in sugar on a saucer.'

'Tell me what you're not so keen on.'

'Well, I'm here as a sister's help. Which is a kind of job, except you don't get paid. So, I have to milk the cows that are kept in the shippen – which don't half pong – and then wait for the man to collect the cans to take to the dairy. I have to take delivery of the ice blocks which freezes my hands so much that I get blisters.'

'Let's see,' he said.

She upturned her palms to him and he took one hand off the steering wheel and ran a finger over the hard ridges of flesh.

'Watch out!' she cried, as the car swerved again. Grinning, he steadied the car. Embarrassed, she drew her hand away. 'I also have to count the coal sacks to make sure the coalmen aren't diddling them out of bags and my least favourite chore is to kill and pluck the chickens, but I've got used to it. Anything is better than the classroom and Sister Scholastica reminding me daily that God is watching me, that a pure soul is a precious soul and the grace that is in my heart is not infinite – and woe betide I do anything bad as I would never get to heaven. I hate lessons, always have. Oh, apart from the music and reading. I've read tons of books, now – Shakespeare, Jane Austen, some in Latin even – and I can name you any musical instrument in an orchestra. Sousaphone, trombone, tuba, trumpet – tell me when to stop,' she said, laughing.

'I like it when you talk,' he said, grinning. 'Keep talking.'

'Only if you watch where we're going. You drive like a lunatic.'

He grinned. 'That better?' he said, firmly placing his hands on the wheel.

She nodded.

'But you like it here?'

'Mostly. I know I'm the unpaid help and sometimes me back nearly breaks because of the chores, but I try to do them without complaining. What choice do I have?' she continued.

'You could say no.'

'Ha ha. Well, if dumb were dirt you could cover an acre.'

'What's that mean?'

'Means that's ridiculous. I could never say no!' she said, laughing and nudging him playfully.

He smiled. 'Where d'you learn to talk like that?'

'My mother, I reckon.'

He pulled the car over, switched off the engine.

'Truth is,' she said. 'I look after rag-taggle kids who come here and that's what gets me up in the morning. That's the best of it. We go on hikes and bake, go fruit picking and scrumping. Mrs Reilly is mostly kind and even the nuns who make a bit of a living out of selling cheese, jam, and butter, are tolerable – apart from Benny, that's Sister Benedict.'

'And what about your mam? Dad?'

Babby blushed. 'Me dad died. Mam comes and visits occasionally. With my brother and sister. Christmases. Easter. I used to cry when they left, every time, especially saying goodbye to our Hannah, but you get used to it. The journey's not so bad – boat from Pier Head over to Anglesey – and they all like a day out at the seaside to go crab fishing and winkle picking, and eat ice cream sitting on the harbour wall.' She tailed off into silence, thinking about the times when she'd asked Violet why she couldn't go back home with her. 'It's complicated,' Violet had once said, puffing on a cigarette and gazing into the distance mysteriously.

'Mrs Reilly like your mam now?'

Babby thought for a moment. 'Well, I suppose in a way she is.'

'You like her, then?'

'Yes. My mam would never ask me to curl up with a mug of Ovaltine and a copy of *Woman's Own* like she would. She's kind to me.'

'Your mam different, then?'

'She'd be too busy telling me to do the step, or the coal-hole, or look after my sister, to have time for that stuff. But she's still my mam ...'

Babby hesitated before going on. She thought about the fact that, lately, Violet had begun to complain about Mrs Reilly. Even though at the outset Violet was the one who said she couldn't look after headstrong Babby and she was the one who sent her daughter away, she blamed Pauline for taking that decision. She blamed everyone. She blamed her husband for leaving her in such a mess because he died on her, and so it followed she had started to blame Mrs Reilly.

'What about you?' she asked, pushing the thought aside.

'Oh, me mam's dead. And me dad ... well, me dad ...You ever played Split the Kipper?' he asked, and that was the end of the matter.

When they got back and Callum had left to help Farmer Parry with the haymaking, Babby went upstairs and took out the little red book with a flower embedded on the front in gold that Mrs Reilly had given her for Christmas. She began to write. 'Someone arrived today at the farm for the summer. His name is Callum. We did the errands together. He is good with the lifting, bringing the coal bags up from the coal-hole, lugging sacks around. He told me a joke about a man called Doug with a spade on his head. He likes pop music, especially Dean Martin, and a song called "That's Amore" which he couldn't help singing, not that well but rather loudly, and a whole load of people like Billy Fury, Marty Wilde and Chuck Berry that I had never heard of. He asked me what I liked and I told him I liked singing and I played the piano accordion and he laughed. He asked me to sing but I refused. He's not like the boys in the Kapler Gang. I wonder what Johnny Gallagher is like now? I don't like to compare them, but if I have to, I would say they are like chalk and cheese. I swear, if Callum asked me to kiss him like Johnny did, I would let him. Callum has a sheath knife and we played Split the Kipper where you see if you can get it to stick in the ground in between your feet, and I won.'

Her eyelids felt heavy and soon she was falling asleep. For so long she had been counting the days until Violet would have her back, and now, in the space of twenty-four hours, she couldn't think of anything worse. There were too many thoughts crowding her head, tumbling around her brain so much that it hurt. She would finish the diary in the morning.

Chapter Fifteen

There was no electricity at Pentraeth Farm, apart from in the main building, just oil lamps that were burning constantly, and Babby made her way downstairs to stoke the huge, roaring fire that heated the range and provided hot water. She heard the soft click of the latch and Callum stood there in wellington boots and an Aran jumper. He raked his hands back through his brylcreemed hair. He looked like a gypsy with his beginning of sideburns and dark eyes. *Brylcreem, a little dab will do yer, but watch out the gals will pursue yer.* The words stitched in and out of her thoughts and she worried she might start singing it out loud in an unguarded moment.

'Right, Babby. You ever done this before?'

She shook her head. They had spent the previous four days working around the farm together, riding the hay cart, stacking the bales, collecting the messages, cutting down the thistles, counting the sheep and moving them from the top field to the bottom field. It had been unusual to have company her own age and she found him beguiling and roguish; every time he so much as touched her, an electric shock had jolted through her body and her nerve endings had felt on fire. She wondered how long she could keep pretending she just happened to be rounding the corner to find him there, free to help him on the errands, asking if he could help her with the coal sacks when she had been perfectly able to cope on her own before. Today was different. He genuinely did need Babby's help.

Callum took off his jumper, tied it around his waist, and rolled up his shirt sleeves. The pig was sweating. He opened the pen gate with his foot as he was carrying a churn of water to pour into the troughs. She could hear the sound of the grunting and he sloshed about in his galoshes, ankle deep in mud and pigswill. The stench was awful. Babby pinched her nose with her fingers and when she spoke she sounded comical.

'You really want me to come in there?' she asked.

'Yep. Mind its legs. We need to get her into the lean-to.'

She stepped aside, trying to avoid the pointed hooves as the sow began kicking and squirming.

'Put some welly into it, Babby!' he said, laughing. 'Many hands make light work!'

She stopped, wiped her brow. She would show him. She slapped the pig's backside and pulled and pushed it back towards the lean-to.

'Bloody marvellous!' he yelled, as they closed the door, and then the pen gate.

She laughed back. Her boots were caked in mud.

They sat on a low drystone wall, lifting their sweating faces to the sun. He took out an Embassy cigarette, lit it, and, lifting it to his lips, began to smoke it, the ash curling like a worm from the end of it.

'Give us one,' Babby said.

Callum raised an eyebrow but passed her the cigarette, saying she would have to share as it was his last one. He laughed again as she sucked on it, taking a drag, then spluttered and coughed, exhaling smoke, tears gathering in her eyes.

She offered it back to him. There was a pause whilst he inhaled through puckered lips. Babby watched him as he blew smoke rings, his jaw clicking each time he expelled a quivering blue circle.

And then he laughed again, reached out his hand and placed it on her knee. His touch was like a live current shooting through her body.

'Tell your da I saved your life,' she said, shrieking with laughter as she thumped him in the chest and pushed him back off the wall, then pulled him towards her with her other free hand, to catch him. Trying to regain his balance, his hand reached out and gripped her thigh.

'Bloody loopy, you are! Fruit loop, loopy Lou, loop the flippin' loop!' said Callum. His hand remained there, her skirt riding up her leg, exposing bare thigh.

'Look at us,' he said, and winked at her. She looked down at the hand, flesh on flesh, thigh against thigh.

'What?' she said. And there was a moment when Babby wanted to say, don't stop, don't stop, don't stop, as she felt his hand going hot on her skin as it moved another inch up her leg. But she didn't. And she was glad. For now.

The following day, when Mrs Reilly said she should stay at the farmhouse and wait for the grocery delivery whilst Callum off doing his chores, she asked casually when he would be coming back. Mrs Reilly replied that he had gone to the store again, to collect the stone jars of sarsaparilla and he would return later that morning. Babby decided she would waft around and position herself beautifully, smoking the cigarettes she had secretly bought from Dafydd so she could practice blowing the smoke outside the windows, hoping that Callum might come back soon and find her. She would pick wildflowers and make them into chains to thread through her hair, drain elderflowers through muslin nets and stir the mixture into buckets of syrup and lemon, and later spike the sugary cordial with sloe gin and offer him some on his return.

Meanwhile, she opened the diary and began to write.

'Callum put his hand on my leg. I didn't want him to stop. He is so handsome, like Johnny Halliday and Eddie Fisher rolled into one and he makes my stomach go into knots just to look at him. He's like one of those Teddy Boys, and wears a leather jacket. He has a knife that's really a comb and he gave me a pink coral necklace that he got from Daffyd and a thimble he found in his bedside drawer. When Johnny Gallagher made me kiss him, I didn't want to and I never would have done. This is different. I would let Callum do anything to me. I know it's wrong, and that makes me a terrible person, not a good girl at all, but that's the way it is.'

Callum arrived back early and suggested they go and ride the hay cart and help with the stacking.

'Look what I've got,' he said, grinning. He went into the barn and appeared wheeling the order bike that was used to make deliveries from the farm. It had a large back wheel and a small front one and a huge sturdy basket mounted on the frame under the handlebars. 'Get in,' he said.

'What?' she replied.

'Sit in the basket. It's strong. I'll cycle and we'll get to the fields quicker.'

'Mrs Reilly'll kill us.'

'How's she to know?' he said, laughing.

Putting his arms under her shoulders he hoiked her up and guffawed as he plonked her bottom in the basket with her lags dangling over the sides.

'Callum Lynch, you're mad!' she said as he got on the saddle and, with one push, set off down the lanes. They screamed and yelped and felt the wind fanning their hair out from their faces; and as she looked at him as he tossed back his shivering black locks, something tugged at Babby. Happiness? Is that what she was feeling?

Later, as they bundled the bales at the top end of the field into one huge pile, he asked her to sing.

'Sing for me, Babby. I'd love to hear you.'

They sat together, their backs against the stone wall, gasping for breath. It was hard work, hay baling, but they had put all the energy they could muster into the job, and they would be rewarded. Callum chewed a piece of straw and, as he twirled it in his fingers, he winked at her. When he took her hand and traced patterns in her palm with the straw, she noticed the lines in his palms were etched out with dirt and his fingernails were black from digging in the fields. This close, she also noticed the veins pulsating under his clear olive skin

'Go on, sing for me,' he said again.

She refused at first, but with a little cajoling and persuasion, she cleared her throat and began haltingly at first, but grew in confidence when she saw his rapt expression.

'In Dublin's fair city, where the girls are so pretty, I first set my eyes on sweet Molly Malone ...'

He began tracing more patterns, now slipping up her skirt an inch or two, so he could do it on her bare thighs with a piece of grass. She thought that, for a teenager, he had beautiful strong hands.

'Oh God, that was gorgeous. Sing it again, Babby,' he said. 'Sing it again ...You're making me go strange in me legs ...'

She did. But she only got halfway through one verse before he kissed her gently, leaving her gasping for breath and wondering what on earth had taken him so long and how she had never wanted anything more in her life than this boy.

'Callum ... Cal,' she said, pushing away the hand that was creeping up towards her breast.

'Jesus, I love you,' he said. 'I bloody love you Babby ...'

He sighed and enclosed her with his arm. Beneath his shirt she could feel his ribcage rising and falling as his breathing grew heavier. She looked back into his decisively boned face, symmetrical and engaging, and his black eyes with eyelashes like brushes.

'What?' he asked. 'You looked like you were going to say something.'

'Not really ...' she said.

And then, without warning, he kissed her, long and hard and passionate.

The next day she woke early. She padded down to his room, knocked gently on his door. He answered the door in his pyjamas, scratching his tousled head.

'Shh!' she said, a finger to his lips. 'Mrs Reilly'll kill us if she knows I'm here.'

He grinned, reached out and planted a firm kiss on her lips. 'Let's go,' he said.

'Hold your horses,' she said, pushing him away. 'It's my turn to give you a job this morning. Never mind the pigs, I can beat that any day,' she said, laughing. 'Meet me on the top field in half an hour and bring a bucket – there's spades down there. And wear old clothes.'

He grinned and made a saluting gesture. Half an hour later he found her sitting on the gate of the field, smiling, her legs hooked around the bars, the bucket dangling between her knees.

'Where's your bucket?' she asked, thinking how tall and strong and handsome he looked, with his black hair blowing off his face.

'Couldn't find one.'

She raised her eyes, hit him playfully. 'Good job I brought you one, then.' She laughed, produced one from behind the low wall. 'Right. Here you go.'

'I don't think I can stand the suspense. What are we doing?'

'Collecting the cowpats,' she said. 'We collect as many as we can, then we mix them in barrels with rainwater and Mrs Reilly uses the stuff to spread on the tomatoes.'

'You're bloody joking! The cowpats? But there's cows in there!' he said, pointing towards the field where cows were mooing and snorting and eyeing them suspiciously.

'They don't mind,' Babby said and laughed. 'Come on!'

She jumped off the gate and handed him a spade. 'Last one to fill their bucket is a big girl's blouse!' she yelled.

Callum followed her with a smile on his face. She was a good sport, this girl, he thought, as she ran on ahead, arms and legs flailing, knee-deep in cowpats, skirting in and out of the cows with their swishing tails from the top to the bottom of the field, whooping all the way, screaming with delight, then returning, triumphant, with a bucket of manure and a splash of muck on her face.

'Race you back to the farm,' he said laughing.

After they wiped the soil away from their hands, then washed them under a pump, they dumped the buckets of cowpats in the barrel of rainwater and gave it a good stir with an old broom handle. They were exhausted.

'I'll clean myself up properly and meet you in the shippen. We stink to high heaven, Babby!'

'Right y'are,' she answered. 'It's a good smell though, isn't it? And it's worth it to taste those tomatoes, any road.'

Half an hour later, washed and wearing a pretty print tea dress, unwrapping the squashed squares of jam sandwiches that Mrs Reilly had prepared for them, she looked up and saw him standing in the shippen. His brows were knitted together and a worried smile creased around his mouth, so she knew something was wrong. He was panting, trying to catch his breath.

'Mrs Reilly says you have to go back to Liverpool.' Babby went pale. 'Someone's died.'

'Mam?' She could feel herself trembling.

'No. Your aunt. I'm sorry.'

She had so many aunts, only one of whom was real.

'Which one? Kathleen?' she asked.

Mrs Reilly bustled in. 'You told her, Callum?'

'Is it true?' asked Babby.

'Yes,' replied Mrs Reilly. 'I'm afraid it is. But it's not your Aunty Kathleen. It's Pauline. Heart attack, they think. One minute she was in a chair, peg rugging, then she was dead.'

Babby could picture that, all right. Pauline, cutting up strips of old clothes and sewing them on to a hessian sack to make a hearthrug. Make do and mend had always been her motto. It seemed fitting that, whatever it was that had killed her, peg rugging might have played its part.

Mrs Reilly continued, 'Must be a bit of a shock. And your mother would like you on the boat this afternoon.'

'Oh.' A rush of emotions surged through Babby. She didn't want to go back to Joseph Street and she felt guilty for being annoyed with Pauline for the timing, and angry at Violet for ruining everything once again.

'You need to get ready now.'

Liverpool. Back home. She felt happiness slipping through her fingers like grains of sand.

'You'll be here when I get back?' she asked Callum.

She watched him fiddling with a button on the cuff of his shirt. 'Of course I will. Funerals don't take more than a few days and there's plenty more work to be done here to keep me busy,' he said, taking her hands and looking into her frightened pale face. 'I'll wait for you Babby ... Write to me?' he said.

She nodded, then he added, 'And if you don't come back to Anglesey, I'll follow you.'

'I will, don't you worry,' she said. 'One more thing: me dad's accordion. It's under my bed. Look after it will you, Cal?'

'Yes, love, I'll do that. I promise,' he said, and he kissed her fingertips.

She smiled anxiously, reassured by his words, but fearful of what was to happen next.

Chapter Sixteen

An hour later, from the deck of the small steamer, she watched the Three Graces of the Liver Building grow in size, with the Liver Bird, that at first looked like a tiny bird that might take flight, becoming a huge bronze statue perched on the dome, held there by steel cables. Babby felt a pang of longing. She remembered taking the trip from the Pier Head to New Brighton Fair with her father. 'See the Liver Bird looking out to sea, Babby? She's waiting for the sailors to come home. See the other one? He's looking the other way to see if the pubs are open!'

Would the Kapler Gang have forgotten her? Hannah, most likely, would barely recognise her. Patrick, nineteen now, had a job with Cunard Steamship company in Water Street and had taken lodgings in Seaforth. There was even talk of he and his girl, Doris, saving up to get married.

Babby turned her attention away from thoughts of her brother and sister and Joseph Street, the hollas and her beloved father. The boat slid into its moorings and a woman with open-toed sandals, a camel coat, overalls, and wearing a paisley cotton turban on her head, was standing on the landing stage gesticulating wildly and grinning and thanking God for Babby's safe arrival. 'Yoo hoo!' she called. Babby recognised her voice, the Liverpool accent, the shrill tones. It was her Aunty Kathleen. Had Violet not even bothered to come and meet her?

But then, from behind the small crowd waiting to board the boat after the passengers alighted, Violet appeared, pushing people out of the way. Babby was shocked when she saw her. She was waving as if she was pleased to see her, but she looked detached, unsteady on her feet, her dress bagged around her waist, as if it had lost a belt somewhere and her hair, held up by a diamante clasp, looked unkempt and unwashed. Babby made her way down the gangplank to her mother who had barged her way through to the front.

'Babby!' cried Violet, arms outstretched. 'Darlin' You're home!'

Babby noticed that her nails were bitten to the quick as she grasped her daughter's arms and spoke close into her face. She smelled of cigarettes and stout.

'Just for the funeral,' said Babby. 'Then I'm going back.'

'We'll talk about that later. Oh, how I've missed you, love,' said Violet. 'Seventeen! Can't believe it, sweetheart.'

Babby reeled. Over the past five years she had returned to Liverpool maybe four, five times – for Hannah's First Holy Communion and birthdays, a party for Patrick's eighteenth, and a couple of Christmas's but she had always been sent back to Anglesey the next day and everyone had agreed that it was all for the best. She was a different girl since Anglesey, they said. Good-tempered, responsible, sweet natured, her Liverpool nasal vowels softened to more country tones, but they were always glad to see her return to the island. What had changed now?

'What do you mean? Talk later?' she asked.

Violet stopped, opened her handbag, rummaged inside, and plucked a cigarette from a packet of Players. After making a show of stuffing the cigarette into a long gold holder, she found a box of matches, lit one and held it to the cigarette. Taking a drag and grimacing with the huge effort of it all, a plume of smoke crawled from her lips.

'We'll talk about it later, that's what I mean. Happy to be home, love?' she asked.

Babby shrugged.

Why had Pauline gone and died just as she had met the boy? she was thinking. Callum. Strong, wild, sinewy and handsome – and waiting for her in Anglesey. Why did this lot have to ruin it all?

When they got back to Joseph Street, Babby gasped as they entered the house. Violet had gone downstairs to bring up coal for the fire in the back room.

'Pat! What on earth …? This place is a tip,' she said to her brother who had arrived, opening the curtains, trying to bring light into the shadow-filled room. The tone of her voice showed how shocked she was. The house was filthy dirty – piles of crumpled clothes in chairs, dishes in the sink, overflowing ashtrays, a half-eaten Eccles cake poking out from under the battered chaise longue, and a mug of something unrecognisable, Cocoa maybe, with furring green mould covering its surface.

'Mam is not in any kind of a state to be left alone with Hannah,' he said, scooping up the Eccles cake from the floor. The cake crumbled in his hand.

'Is that what everyone thinks?' asked Babby quickly. She spoke in a low voice. She didn't want Violet to hear and she could see her now, moving about behind the blurred stippled glass of the pantry. 'We'll just have to give this place a good scrub. That's all. It will be fine,' she said. Her thoughts leapt back to Callum, to a picture of him, in the pigsty, laughing and winking at her. She would die if she had to stay here a moment longer than she needed.

'Kathleen has had enough. But Mam is not good. Things have taken a turn for the worse lately. As you can see ...'

Good God! How did it get so bad? Babby wanted to cry. Pat used Cunards as an excuse to stay away, but she knew from Violet's complaining that it was his sweetheart, Doris, that kept him from Joseph Street. Doris worked on the make-up counter at George Henry Lees and demanded new stockings and nights out at the Majestic in Birkenhead, dancing to groups like Bill Haley and the Comets, and lemonade shandies at the Philharmonic pub, and Pat had no room in his life for Violet.

At first, they didn't see little Hannah standing at the door.

'Hannah! she cried.

Hannah ran over to Babby, hugged her, and wheeled around in excited circles.

'You're enormous!' cried Babby, lifting her off the ground and kissing her full on the lips. 'A giant!' She couldn't help noticing that Hannah looked grubby. Her hair had been cut into a bob but was a tangled clump. Her socks bagged around her ankles and her shoes were scuffed, their seams spilt at the back.

'I'm the smallest in my class.'

'No!'

'Yes! And the skinniest. They call me Beetle and Squit.'

Babby looked at Hannah for a moment too long without saying anything and touched her hair, pushed a piece of it behind her ear.

'Do you mind?'

'Not much …' Then she paused. 'Babby, have you seen Aunty Pauline?' she asked, gravely.

'What d'you mean, have I seen Aunty Pauline?' replied Babby.

Hannah's eyes widened. 'They brought her here last night. She's in the front room. Dead as a door-nail. She's wearing Mam's old best hat and pink lipstick from Blacklers and she's holding a lily and she's even got sandals on. Silver ones. And Mam has painted her toenails. Lift up the sheet. You'll see.'

Babby gasped. So that was why the mirror in the hall had been turned around to face the wall. Because Pauline was in her coffin in the front room. And yes, Violet was superstitious, one of those who believed that when someone died their spirit, if it saw its reflection, would either remain trapped on earth, or if still lurking around the house, its image would be reflected permanently. Such nonsense! Violet's renewed friendship with Father O'Casey and the nuns probably had something to do with it. The mirror by the hearth was covered with one of Violet's old moth-eaten silk gowns – Babby had noticed that on the way in – and the second mirror in the hall had been taken off the wall and propped up against the cellar door. She had swept past the front room with the shut door, but the mirrors should have been a clue as to what lay behind.

'Oh no.'

'Oh yes. The priest is coming tonight to see her, Aunty Pauline, I mean. They're holding a vigil. You have to sit with the dead body until she goes to the church. We all have to take turns. Father O'Casey. Pat. And the girl from the raggy shop. And Johnny Gallagher's parents.' Hannah lowered her voice even more. 'Kathleen is worried Mam might start getting upset about Dad.'

'Dad? I mean, what happened at the Boot Inn?' she hissed.

Hannah sighed. 'Mam keeps talking about it all the time. Again.'

'Still blaming the Mouse. Saying he got off scot-free and he should be in prison for what he did. Only no one wants to hear,' said Pat, lounging against the doorjamb, folding his arms and sighing. 'Now, about Hannah ... Are you going to stay here for a few more weeks, Babby?'

Hannah stared at Babby, round-eyed and hopeful.

Babby's heart lurched. Is this what Violet wanted to talk to her about?

'Will you? Please?' asked Hannah. Babby didn't have the heart to say no.

Pauline's funeral was at Saint Patrick's. Would you like an extra Mass for her? The choir? A special blessing? a letter from the priest had said. That sounds lovely, was Violet's reply. Until she found out she would have to pay for the pleasure, so she politely declined as she wanted to save the money for the wake. The Gallaghers were coming. And Doris. And Kathleen. And Phyllis O'Neill. For a moment, Babby wondered if she should ask her mother if Callum could come.

'Mam, do I really have to stay here another three weeks?' she asked.

'Yes, love. The world doesn't revolve around you, you know.'

'Mam, if ... if ... I was wondering if one of my friends from the farm could come and stay ...'

'Friends? You have friends?' her mother said, looking down her aquiline nose.

'Doesn't matter,' said Babby. And in the end, the sour expression on her mother's face meant she was glad she hadn't told her about Callum.

It was a funeral without much fuss. The coffin sat on the carriage drawn by a carthorse and the four Delaneys followed on foot behind, walking steadily and in rhythm, down the hill in a sombre procession, with people peering out from behind their curtains and some standing on their steps making the sign of the cross as they passed.

'Why they doing that, Mam?' asked Hannah.

'Showing their respects. And now you show yours and be quiet,' replied Violet.

There was a cheap coffin from Coyne Under-takers, a bunch of flowers from Geraghty's florists, white lilies and carnations. When they got to the church it was draughty and cold and they barely filled two pews; a woman that Babby recognised as the one who'd came to collect the Mission box from Pauline, and one other person, made the mourners up to no more than a dozen. The burial, in the church ground, on a bleak hill overlooking the city, was a sad, sorry affair with dirt chucked on the coffin turning to mud in the peltering rain, and the priest rattling through prayers that were lost on the wind. A halting 'The Lord is My Shepherd', and a lisping 'Eternal Rest, Grant unto Them O Lord' and it was all over and done with in the time it took to get out handkerchiefs and dab their eyes. 'Guide Me, O Thou Great Redeemer' was sung as they walked back through the cemetery – it was Pauline's favourite and everyone knew the words – and it was announced there would be drink afterwards and grub, in the front room of Joseph Street. 'Back home for boiled beef sarnies and beer,' said Violet, and Hannah yelped with delight, clapped her hands excitedly and asked if there would be piccalilli with the sarnies, and they all told her to shush, anyone would think they were happy Pauline was dead.

'It's a funeral, not a flamin' knees up,' said Pat. Though when Violet started on the sherry, that's exactly what it turned out to be.

'You're a long time looking at the lid,' she announced, woozily. 'Let's have a good time whilst we can.' And she hiccuped and tried to swallow down a burp but it escaped from her lips and everyone giggled when she said, 'Oops! Pardon me for being rude, it was not me, it was booze and food. It just popped up to say hello, and now it's gone back down below ...'

After that Hannah led them in a conga up the stairs with Doris and Kathleen and the Gallaghers laughing and jostling up against one another, then a sing-song in the parlour and finally the room falling silent with Violet's rendition of 'I'll Take You Home Again, Kathleen'. Exhausted, they all fell asleep in chairs, on sofas, and on the stairs.

Half an hour later, Babby, taking her chance of escape, left the house with a handful of Butterkist, and a notion that getting the hell out of there was probably very wise.

Chapter Seventeen

Johnny Gallagher trailed a stick along the railings and the clattering pierced the night.

'Babby! Is that you?' he called.

She turned, a mouthful of the Butterkist bulging her cheek. He came up to her, put his arm around her waist. 'How's my little firecracker?' Babby slapped his hand away. He rammed his shirt into his waistband, ran a finger up and down his nose. Then he threw back his head and laughed. 'Look at you!'

'Johnny Gallagher, you haven't changed! Your mum and dad were at our house.'

'I saw you with the funeral carriage – you looked corking in your black frock, them gloves, and with that lacy thing on your head. '

She smiled. 'It's called a mantilla. You still smashing a football around the hollas?' she asked. 'Still pretending you're Stanley Matthews, or Billy Wright? Or the Busby Babes? What a bloody laugh!'

'Not a bloody laugh! Mind your mouth.'

'Nearest you'd get to those fellas is ogling them at the Regal picture house every Saturday, or the footie ground.'

Johnny laughed. 'Regal has gone. Like the overhead railway. Anyway, we was kids, then. We've got jobs now. Mickey has joined the bizzies.'

'He never has! He's a copper? He could send himself to the court house he's nicked that many prams. He led me mam a dance when she was working there.'

'How is your mam?'

'Round the bloody bend. Me mam has gone mad. And I think she's got a fella but she won't say who.'

Johnny raised his eyes.

'Worse thing is though, she won't let me go back to Anglesey for another three weeks. She wants me to stay in the Pool but I'm biding my time – and as soon as I can, soon as Hannah gets back to Kathleen's, I'm going back.'

'Why d'you want to go back there? Thought them places were terrible. Up to your knees in pig shit all day. Like prisons, I heard.'

'I like it. Like the fresh air and farm work.' She tailed off. She wasn't going to tell him that Callum was the reason she wanted to return.

'How do you know Violet won't change her mind? How do you know she won't say you can't go back at all? Seems you're more good to her here now.'

'Dunno. I'll just have to figure it out myself, find my own way of doing what I want, not what she decides for me.'

'You still singing? Gladys is asking after you, every time I walk in the Boot – still can't get used to calling it the Tivoli. She's given it a fresh lick of paint, new tables and chairs and there's fancy drinks like Cinzano and snowballs. Trying for a fresh start.'

Babby cocked her head. 'Is she really?' she asked.

'Aye. And if she could see you now! You still got your dad's old accordion? She'd pay you double. Much better than what she pays for washing the glasses and doing the slops.'

'Would she?' Babby said, brightening. 'Me mam'd kill me, though. Pub's bad enough. Any old pub, never mind the Boot, even with its new name. But playing me dad's accordion? I could never do that.'

'Why?'

'Mam hates it. She hates it that I love singing. And the music. But it's in my blood, Johnny. Like me dad ...'

'She's worried, I suppose.'

'Aye. Even though she doesn't know much about anything at the moment, she still doesn't want me anywhere near the Boot Inn, and in any case, I left the accordion in Anglesey because I'm going back there.'

'Right enough. But every pub's got an old squeezebox.'

'No, pub's not the place for a girl,' she said.

'But you're not much of a girl, are you? Always been more like one of the lads.'

Babby wavered. A smile played across her lips.

'Ah, Babby. Come on, say you'll play at the Tiv. Your mam don't need to know.'

'Well ...'

He grinned, his eyes widened. 'Say yes, Babby.'

'Suppose it won't do any harm ...' she answered.

'Course not. It'd be grand.'

'I'm a bloody fool to let you talk me around, that's what I am ...' She paused. 'But what does me mam expect? She wants me to stay here for another three weeks? Well, I can't sit round doing nowt. To hell with her – I'll be going back soon. Tell Gladys I'll play just the once, just for the craic.'

'Still the same old Babby,' he said and laughed, thinking she might have curled her hair and be wearing stockings, not ragged jeans, but she was still wilful and headstrong, ready to grasp life by the hands and shake it. Thankfully, some things would never change.

Chapter Eighteen

Babby opened the latch. Quietly, she padded through to the front room. Pat was fast asleep in a chair. Doris was dozing in another. Hannah and Kathleen were top and tailing on the old chaise longue. Violet would be upstairs sleeping off the bottles of stout and sherry that she had drunk, probably until mid-morning. Deciding that it was too late to tell anyone she was back, Babby stood for a moment in the doorway and watched them snoring, bodies tangled up in eiderdowns, blankets, and old coats. And as she did so, it occurred to her that these were the people that she loved – and these were the people relying on her to help with Hannah. With that thought, she went into the back room, took out a pen and notepaper from the drawer, and began to write.

Dear Callum,

I know I've only been away a few days but I miss you so much. I'll come straight to the point. I'm afraid I have some bad news. I have to stay here longer than I thought I would. The thing is, Hannah, my little sister, is not doing so well. Or rather, my mother is not doing so well looking after her. My brother Pat says it's not right to leave Mam in the lurch and Hannah has got nowhere to stay as my Aunty Kathleen, who usually looks after her, is bad with her knees at the moment. There was talk of Hannah coming back with me to Anglesey, but it turns out that's not practical as there's no room for her. So, for now, three weeks Mam says, I'm stuck in Liverpool. I hope you're not too disappointed. I hope you won't forget me!

I'm wearing the thimble you gave me around my neck. I've tied a ribbon around it and it looks quite pretty. I'm also wearing the coral necklace. Nobody has asked about either of them. If they did, I would tell them you gave me them, and they're the most precious things I have. And Callum, when I go to bed at night and I press my face into the pillow and hold my breath, it makes me dream about you so vividly it's like I'm still in Anglesey, actually with you. The other night I dreamed about us in the shippen and when I woke, I swear I could smell the cows in my bedroom.

Nothing has changed here, except that things have just got a little bit worse, when they should have got a little bit better. That's here at home, Joseph Street, but it's the same for Liverpool too. More steam-rollers have gone in to the bomb sites and smashed the remaining houses to the ground. It's almost completely flattened, apart from a few left round our way, which will go any day. I feel sorry for the kids. We had such a laugh playing steeries and cowboy and Indians – and now if you were to play hide-and-seek, I swear it wouldn't work at all well, as you'd have nowhere to hide. They say it's because they want to make the place safer but I think they just want to stop people having fun. Whole streets have just gone. Apparently, they're going to build new houses with running water and lavvies inside, which sounds grand, but I'm not so sure, and for now there's nothing round here.

Towards Lime Street Station, it's a little better. I must admit, there are pockets where the city is still beautiful: the Liver Buildings, and the columns at Saint George's, and of course the docks. But without you here, it just seems pretty grey.

I wish I knew what to do about mother. It's like she loves me and hates me all at the same time. Probably you know what would be the best thing to say to her. Like the other day. That was a humdinger of a row. Hannah has taken to threading the silver tops of milk bottles on to a piece of string and sitting on the step and selling them as necklaces for a halfpenny. I thought that was a lovely thing to do, but Mam shouted at her and said it was ridiculous, we didn't want the whole world thinking we were beggars. In the commotion, Hannah spilled a bottle of milk and you'd think she had started World War Three. Mam did a lot of shouting and Hannah did a lot of crying – and I worried about what's going to become of us. We're all in a complete and utter mess.

Anyway, I hope this doesn't all sound too desperate. I can't wait to get back to you at the end of the month. How are the twins? Still getting into trouble? Still stealing the butter? And Mrs Reilly? Have you had to do any more mucking out? I better go now. I can hear footsteps on the stairs. You are the first and last thing I think of every day. And the best moments in my life, so far, are the ones I can't tell anyone about.

All my love, Babby.

PS. Guess what? I am going to sing at the Tivoli pub. Mam will kill me if she finds out, but I've decided I don't care. It's the only thing that will keep me from going crazy.

Chapter Ninteen

Babby and Johnny found Gladys cleaning the glasses and the squeak, squeak, of the coronation tea towel as she shoved her fist into the beer glass and twisted it round and round was the only sound for a minute. Babby couldn't help squinting at Gladys' quivering hair. The lacquer had dried in droplets that clung to the peroxide blonde castle and Babby decided they could easily be mistaken for nits' eggs.

'So, sweetheart. You'll play here tonight?'

'Yes.'

'How old are you now?'

Babby hesitated, mesmerised by the glinting bunches of glass grapes that dangled from slits in Gladys' elongated ear lobes; they swung gently as she spoke and tilted her head from side to side.

'Eighteen,' lied Johnny.

'And you'll play the accordion? Like your dad? Johnny tells me you are a devil at it. I've got one

in the back that your da used to play when he forgot his.'

'I'll have a go,' answered Babby.

'Good. It'll bring in the punters. Always did.' She
patted her immaculately sprayed head, took a pink
cigarette with a gold tip from a pearlised case, tapped
it on the bar, and stuck it in her mouth. 'You'll do
some of your dad's sea shanties? I could sell you as
Jack's lass. And some of this new stuff in hit parade?'

'Some of the modern stuff sounds funny on the
accordion, but I'll have a go.'

'You know best; I'll leave it up to you to decide.
We still get quite a crowd and I've even opened up
a ladies bar. I'm hoping you might bring in a better
class of person to the Tivoli.'

'Lovely,' said Babby, beaming. 'But I thought
Johnny told you this were a one-off? I'm only in
Liverpool for a few weeks.'

'Best laid plans ...' said Gladys, ominously. 'And
Babby, love. Just a warning. We might have fancy
new curtains and a new sign outside the door, but
Friday nights can still be like hell's gate. Especially
when the boats come into the docks. You've seen it,
haven't you, Johnny?'

'Yes, Mrs Worrall.'

'Good luck. Give 'em hell, dearie.'

Babby sat in a grubby back room, no more than a cupboard, with plastic daffodils in a vase, overflowing ashtrays on the windowsill, and, written in lipstick on a cracked mirror, *Rita loves Frank Sinatra*. Johnny perched on a rickety table beside her. The room smelled of Brylcreem, stale cigarettes and cheap liquor. The bare lightbulb flickered intermittently, hanging on grimly for dear life as it gave off a sickly yellow glow. The sounds of the pub were getting louder beyond the door.

'You look right nice in that sticky-out skirt. You're like just like Doris Day, except with brown hair and freckles,' said Johnny.

Babby smoothed the poodle skirt – the 'something girlish' that Gladys had insisted she wear. She nervously tucked in the white blouse that cascaded in ruffles over her shoulders. The lipstick Gladys had also given her, fuchsia pink, was much brighter than she was used to wearing, and it tasted like Parma Violets.

She thought what Violet might say if she could see her.

'Just off to see if there are any crates for firewood left over at Paddy's Market before they pack up,' she had lied to her as she walked out of the door of Joseph Street.

'Do you need Pat to help?' Violet had asked.

'No. And I might pop into the Gallagher's on my way back,' she had added, thankful that Violet was on her second glass of Makesons and the fuzzy veil of drink was beginning to take its effects.

There was a knock on the door of the dressing room – actually, more of a cupboard with brooms and buckets. A small, sweaty, barrel of a man wearing a bow tie poked his head round the door.

'You all right, treacle?' he asked. He was as Scouse as the Mersey Tunnel but friendly.

She did some sucking in of breath through her teeth and told herself, once again, that it would be fine; Violet would never find out because she would never step foot in the place, so Babby was going to enjoy this. The fat man asked her if he should make an announcement, saying she was Jack Delaney's girl. He said it was probably better to do that now, get it over and done with, rather than keep the audience guessing. She could hear the voices swelling in the bar beyond, like a low grumble. She could even hear women's voices. They must have let them in from the ladies bar, to the main bar. A rare thing, indeed. Something to do with Gladys' idea about smartening the place up.

'Do you have to mention me dad?' she asked, worried that her singing tonight might get back to Violet.

'Well, that's why they're here, love,' he said. 'We've already put it around.'

He left. Babby was breathless with nerves. She could hear him speaking from the bar. 'One. Two. You know what to do ... Now let's 'ave a bit of 'ush for our next act, a lovely little girl and her accordion – Babby Delaney! And what a smashing chip off the old block she is – she's Jack Delaney's girl. So give her a big 'and!'

Babby made her way on to the small raised dais. There was faint-hearted applause. Waiting behind a moth-eaten red velvet curtain, letting her fingers run scales over the keys of the old squeezebox that Gladys had dug out, and finding the dent in the middle C button, whispering Tweedledee, Tweedledum as she pushed it in and out, she heard the compere make a joke about his mother-in-law being unusally fat. She felt sick – partly nerves, partly because of the large glass of cherryade she had gulped down. The musky smelling curtains jerked open, the right one only halfway, leaving Babby hidden from view apart from her shoes poking out from underneath the gold braid fringe. Eventually the man ran on stage and yanked back the curtain, nodding at her to begin, worrying that she appeared so startled, like a rabbit caught in car headlights.

'Ready, queen?' he hissed. As she came blinking into the harsh lights of a follow spot, the smell of beer and cigarettes made her gag. Smoke swirled in the beam of light. With her old-fashioned blended musical tones, glossy hair tied in a neat girlish ponytail, she felt out of place. But she knew some of the audience would be pleased to see Jack's girl – the spitting image of him, with her glittering eyes and obdurate chin, and beautiful lyrical voice.

Johnny, leaning against the bar with pint of pale ale in his hand, winked and gurned, and gestured wildly for Babby to smile, which she did. But catching the expressions on the faces of the people sitting at the tables whose skin had turned an eerie shade of yellow and pink from the lights, she faltered. The women nudging their men to be quiet and the men, who when they stopped talking and raised their eyes from staring with love into pints of Tetley, threw glances between each other. Seeing the expectant faces, Babby became sallow with fright. This was nothing like playing 'Second Hand Rose' for Hannah in her bedroom. The accordion keys felt strange under her fingers and the bellows were stiff when she pressed the button to fill it with air. She noticed a few more raise their eyes from their pork scratchings and pints of Guinness, lean in to one another and whisper behind raised hands. Gladys called out, 'Bag o' shush, Bag o' shush!'

Babby's brows knitted together in a frown. 'Go on love,' mouthed Johnny, palms sweating. She could hear the pub becoming rowdier. She darted a look at Johnny as he gave her the thumbs up. She could see him smiling hopefully now, picking nervously at the skin around his thumbnail, willing her to drive herself on. Gladys, taking her place beside Johnny, swivelled around on the high bar stool and smiled at her as well. It gave her the courage she needed. Something about the sound of the accordion, even though it wasn't hers, as she played the first part of a tune, brought back a memory of her father, but there was no time for that now, so she pushed it aside, took a deep breath and began to sing.

After the first few notes, she saw that Johnny was beginning to relax. He took out another cigarette and lit it from Gladys'. Babby began to sing louder under the swell of the borrowed accordion and the pub went quieter; her voice rang out sweetly, clear as glass and true.

'Farewell to Princes' landing stage, River Mersey fare thee well ...' she sang, losing herself in the song, and the words.

'Gladys!' said Rex to his sister, when he walked into the bar, as Babby, flushed with success, took her bow. 'That's Babby Delaney! Who said she could play here?'

'I did, Rex. It's my pub, in case you had forgotten. Look around you. They're loving it. What have you got against it? It's good for business. What's the harm?'

'I don't like it,' said Rex. 'You know what her mother would say. I want nothing to do with this.'

'You seem more worried about Violet Delancy than the kid.'

Rex bridled. 'Don't start, Glad.'

Gladys snorted and replied that money was tight – and if Babby brought in the punters, that was all that should concern him. It was her pub, and if he didn't like it, he could lump it.

'Keep your nose out, Rex. When you pay the bills, you can have an opinion,' said Gladys flatly, at the end of her speech.

Babby and Johnny ran all the way to the tram stop. 'Come on,' he said. 'Run!' They had ten minutes before they missed the last tram.

Grasping her hand as they raced around the corner, and without pausing for breath, he dragged her on to an oncoming Green Goddess that slowed in front of them outside bombed-out dance hall. He pulled her after him as they made their way upstairs to the top deck where they sat on the platform.

'Babby, I were so proud of you,' he said. He moved closer to her, went to casually place his arm around her shoulders, as the tramcar clattered away on its tracks and the small yellow light bulbs rattled in their sockets. Instinctively, she shrank away and scooted along the warm seat, fixing her eyes on the road ahead. He tried again, and this time she felt the arm rest firmly about her. Should she say something or do something? Tell him that, even though he was her very best friend, she didn't like him in that way and then politely ask him to remove his arm. Or should she just shove it away or wriggle out from under it and hope he got the message. Who had heard of anyone who had been friends with someone for years like they had, kicking around in the hollas, playing merry hell with the steeries, suddenly wanting to start kissing each other? Is that what he was planning to do?

'Ta for coming tonight, Johnny.'

Her eyes met his then slid away. He laughed. Babby sucked on a piece of her hair. Taking it out of her mouth, she surveyed its sharp point, then went back to chewing it.

'You shouldn't do that. I've heard stories of girls dying and when they were cut open had matted balls of hair as big and as round as grapefruits rotting inside their stomachs,' he said, smiling, shuffling up to her closer, his arm still draped across her shoulders, pulling her to him, and she felt as uncomfortable as if it were a dead cat lying there.

'We've been friends forever, haven't we? I mean since we were nippers,' she said, in a volley of words. She looked at him, looked at his face, and mentally flipped through the consequence of what she was about to say.

'Aye ...' he replied.

'But Johnny ...' she said, sighing. Would this be something she might regret? She took a deep breath. 'I'm glad that we've met up again, and hope that we can remain friends always, but that's the way I want it to stay. You're a grand fella. Top rate. I know you'd walk the end of the earth for me. And me for you. But no – well, you know – hanky-panky funny business – love and stuff ...' She tried to lighten the mood, gave him a playful nudge. 'Bit of the other, how's your father. That's not for you and me, Johnny.'

'You don't mean that.'

'I certainly do,' she said, shoving his arm away. He grinned. He liked the way her eyes flashed with annoyance, bringing out the coppery tones in her hair, but he didn't want to accept that she was saying that this must go no further.

'So why did you ask me to come with you?' he said, trying to sound reasonable.

The knot of frustration in her stomach grew tighter. She pulled the sleeves of her jacket over her hands.

'Babby,' he said, and went to put an arm around her shoulders again. She winced slightly and recoiled, not knowing what she should do.

Then the clippie came down the tram.

'Two halves,' said Johnny.

'You're never a half,' replied the conductor. His hand rested on the register.

'He is,' said Babby, lying.

The conductor raised his eyes, twisted the handle and gave them two tickets.

'D'you want a ciggie, Babby?' asked Johnny.

'You know I don't smoke,' said Babby. She wasn't going to tell him about her attempts to impress Callum.

He rummaged around in his jacket pocket and took out a packet of Swan Vesta matches.

'Right, my stop,' said Babby, and got up out of her seat, which was not easy to do as the tram swerved and swayed along the curved steel tracks.

'Babby,' he said as he moved down the tram to catch up with her. 'What's the problem?'

She sighed and looked into the distance.

'I *have* a fella,' she said. 'Didn't I tell you?'

'Have we finished, then?' he asked, in a small voice.

'Did we even start?' she replied, puzzled. 'His name is Callum and you could never be my sweetheart, Johnny.'

'Why?' he asked.

'Why?' she said, genuinely bewildered by the question. 'Oh, Johnny, I'm so sorry,' she added, going down the stairs and jumping off the tram and heading off in the direction of home.

'Where have you been?' asked Violet when she got in.

'Been with Johnny Gallagher to see about doing some washing glasses at the Crow's Nest,' she said falteringly.

'That won't pay much, only coppers.'

'And doing the coal. They say I could help with the delivery bags.'

'Never heard such a thing!' Violet snorted. 'You?' she said, her eyes big and round and accusatory.

'Why not? I'd work hard at it.'

Violet harrumphed. 'You're a girl! You shouldn't be lugging bags of coal. Why can't you work at Blacklers on the hosiery counter? Or do secretarial? Liverpool Assurance are taking on girls. Or what about I get you a job as a seamstress? Doesn't take more than two weeks to train you up on the machines.'

'Pub is grand. Anyway, I only need short term. I can't do any of those jobs if I'm only here a few weeks, can I?'

'Pub is no place for you.'

Babby sucked in air.

'You only ever want to do what you want, Babby. You have to think of the rest of us,' said Violet.

'You're a fine one to talk,' Babby muttered under her breath.

Violet either didn't hear, or didn't have the energy to challenge her, and continued with, 'You could sew gloves like I do. You can do that at home. Any time you like, as long as you have them ready for the fella who comes to collect them on the weekend,' said Violet.

Babby grimaced.

'I need you around the house, Babby. Not running off all the time. You can do the ironing. Setting the table and washing after tea. Cleaning the grate ...' Violet added.

'Stop going on, Mam, I can do that an' all, but the coal and glasses is good.'

'If you had stayed at Saint Hilda's you could have been a nurse. Or a teacher even. Waste of a good brain ...' said Violet, wistfully.

'But I want something more, Mam. I have a talent. I can sing. I want to be like, like—'

'Do *not* say your dad!' said Violet.

Chapter Twenty

The Reccy was a small square of barren land over-looking a tyre factory. There was the smell of rubber and the sound of bulldozers on the nearby building site. In one corner there was a slide, in another, a squeaky see-saw with rotting wooden seats with splinters that scratched your bare legs, and a pair of swings – one that you would put a toddler in that resembled a small, square-shaped basket, and another, with a flat plastic seat. Babby, was watching Hannah on the latter.

'A few more pushes and I can see over the roof of the sweet shop and across the hollas and towards the river ... I can see the Infirmary, Babby. I can see the clock! I can see the big warehouses at the docks! I can see those new high-rise flats they're building!' Hannah cried.

'You'll be late for school. Violet will kill us if she finds out we've stopped here.' Hannah shrugged her shoulders in an 'as if I care' gesture, as she swung herself higher, and higher. Then, without warning, she pushed herself off, leapt forward as far as she could, back arching, yelling 'Geronimo!' and flumping feet first into the sandpit. An alarmed Babby ran over to her and scooped her up.

'Don't leave us,' said Hannah when she had caught her breath, clutching her big sister. 'I need you to play French Elastic. I'm sick of doing it with a chair instead of a person. The chairs keep falling in on themselves whenever I land on the elastic and it takes the fun out of it, not having you there. Will you stay at Joseph Street? We could all be together again.'

Babby looked into Hannah's clear blue eyes, bluer than blue. 'Well, we are together for now … Come on, you're going to be late for school.'

'But I don't want you to go. Mam won't play with me. Please, please say you won't go back to that farm place. Will you say stay here?' She started scraping her muddy heels against the kerb, her mouth turned down at the corners.

'Fancy coming with me to the sweet shop?' said Babby, sidestepping the question. 'Come on,' she said, kneeling so that she spoke directly into Hannah's face.

In the shop, the display of the chocolate bars, the Fry's Chocolate Cream, the Milky Bars, and the sweets, all lined up on the shelves in jars, the rustle of the paper bags, the metal scoops dusted with sugar, and the twist of the lid and rattling of pear drops and orange bonbons, made Hannah shiver with excitement.

'You got money?' she asked.

Babby pulled the shilling that Gladys had given her out of her pocket.

'Can we buy some of those Swizzells? Or liquorice shoelaces? Or Refreshers?'

'Whatever you want, Hannah.'

Hannah sighed. 'Babby, when you say my name it sounds right in your mouth, not like Mam.'

'Whatever do you mean by that?'

'Nothing,' she said, turning the conversation back to lemon bonbons and cinder toffee and pear drops, halfpenny chews, and sugar mice, and the sound of the school handbell clanging in the distance.

As she arrived home after taking Hannah to school, Babby imagined her mother meeting her at the door and saying, 'A letter has come for you from Anglesey', but when she got there, she found the curtains were drawn and, disappointingly, there was still no envelope on the mat, and no word from Callum. She had written to him three times now in the past two weeks, and nothing.

Her heart lurched. 'Mam?' she called. She had never quite got over the time when she had come home and found Violet with her 'fancy man'. There had been no mention of him since, and there had been no sign of him, either, but she still dreaded the prospect of revisiting that awful moment, finding someone making love to her mother, or rather, 'getting his leg over' – which would be a better way of describing it.

When she went into the parlour, Violet was sitting alone in the dimly lit kitchen, in a wheelback chair, her hair looking greyer, her skin more papery and sallow.

'You frightened me,' said Babby. 'Just sitting there with the curtains drawn in the middle of the morning ...'

Violet smoothed her hands over the piece of material she was hemming. 'What's the matter? You look like you've got something to ask me,' she said, with intended precision, making Babby feel anxious about what was coming next.

Babby shifted from foot to foot. 'Has a letter arrived for me?'

'For you?' asked Violet. 'Why would a letter come for you? Are you expecting something?'

'N-no,' stuttered Babby.

'So why mention it?'

'Nothing.'

'Who is it from?'

'No one. Please stop asking.'

'I'm your mother. You shouldn't have secrets from me, love.'

Why can't you just leave me alone?! Babby wanted to cry.

'Did you get Hannah to school on time?' asked Violet.

'Yes,' lied Babby. 'Sorry. I'm tired ...' She pretended to yawn, but she lost heart halfway through. Turning to go, she intended to leave quietly and without fuss, but she'd only taken two steps towards the door when Violet's words held her back.

'Hannah says she likes her new school. Much better than the one at Kathleen's. Sister Immaculata helped me find it,' said Violet, as she bent to shut her sewing basket. Babby knew that her words weren't so much of a passing comment, more of a statement designed for some kind of a reaction. 'Now Babby, you've hardly done any of the chores that I asked you to. Yesterday you promised you would do the dusting and you've given this place no more than a cat's lick, love.' She stood, ran her finger over the sideboard, showed her the black smudge on the tip, and sighed.

'Do we have to go into this now?' Babby said, sulkily. She wanted to ask her mother what had brought this sudden change, since they had been living in near squalor for months now, according to Patrick – dust turning to grime, fingerprints on every surface and wall – and Violet hadn't seemed to care, or indeed notice.

'Why not? Now is a good as time as any.' Taking off the beautiful carved casing with the wire mesh from the wireless and heaving it on to the floor, she started complaining about how the battery had run out, and how they needed to exchange the wet battery for a fresh one.

'I asked you to take this radio battery to O'Connor's three days ago, Babby. Now it's conked.'

'What about the accumulator man? Couldn't he come and top it up? I thought they usually come around.'

'I can't afford the accy man. I want you to do it. Just don't spill the acid out of the battery like last time.'

That had been a disaster, Babby spilling the burning acid on to her shoe when the shopping bag handles broke and Violet calling her stupid, when it was clear it had been far too heavy for her to carry in the first place.

'Get Pat to do it, Mam.'

'No, *you* can do it. You'll just have to be more careful this time ...'

Babby sighed. She knew this was more about Violet venting her frustration over bigger things than her missing tomorrow's episode of *Mrs Dale's Diary* or the one Babby hated, stupid *Educating Archie*, where a ventriloquist performed on the wireless. She looked at her, and was about to argue back, but in an instant, Violet had suddenly just drifted off. What was it that she was thinking?

'Mam,' said Babby, bringing Violet back to life with a jolt, dragging her back to the present.

'Sorry, what?' she said, in a flat distracted voice.

'You drifted off. What were you thinking?'

'About you, Babby. About this letter you are expecting.'

The sentence hung in the air, laden with suspicion.

If it wasn't for Pat appearing at the door, wearing a Mackintosh, belted at the waist, and his blue and white football scarf, a full-blown argument would have erupted.

'Raining dick docks out there,' he said, shaking out the raindrops from an umbrella. 'Blues won three nil. Tremendous game. Jimmy Harris smashed it into the onion bag. One, two, three,' he said, miming kicking a football.

'Where were you last night?' Violet asked him, lifting her eyes to the window and seeing that the pavements were slopping with puddles.

'Dancing. At the Locarno. With Doris.'

Violet got up and poured herself a sweet sherry. She held the glass in one hand and an Embassy cigarette in the other.

Pat looked away, busied himself with the fire.

'Isn't it a bit early for sherry?' said Babby, shocked.

'Not at all. Just a quick one before I leave for church,' she said. 'Mass.'

'Church?' said Babby.

'Why not? You should come with me. Stop you getting crazy ideas.'

'I don't have crazy ideas.'

'Yes, you do. All teenagers do. Mooning about with your head in the clouds. These teenage boys prowling about in motorcycle jackets and slicked-back hair, they're the ruination of good girls like you.'

'For goodness' sake, Mam!'

'Pop music. You shouldn't be listening to it. I've heard you singing around the house. 'That's Amore'. Ridiculous. It does strange things to people your age. Makes them ... No, I'm not going to say it, Babby.'

'Say what?'

'Do I have to spell it out?' she said.

'Yes.'

'And jeans ... Blue jeans. Saturday morning at the picture house ... I've heard all about what goes on in the back seats ... youngsters getting carried away in the heat of the moment. One minute they're heavy petting in the back row, the next they're washing other folks' mucky drawers and bed linen at Saint Jude's. Father O'Casey says it's disgusting. Teenagers!' Violet swirled the word around in her mouth, enjoying the sound of it.

Babby snorted. Was this her mother speaking?! Since when had she thought like this? Wasn't this all a little late? What had happened to her? They had never been regular churchgoers. What a hypocrite. Had she forgotten about the incident with the 'man'? The one that had led to Violet sending Babby packing to Anglesey in the first place.

'Your story ends before it begins, Babby. We'll make a beautiful young woman out of you yet ... I've only got your best interests at heart, you know.' Violet reached out to grasp Babby's hand. 'I'm so glad you're back, love. Are you happy to be home?' she said.

Babby winced. This close, Violet smelled of damp socks and something sweet and sickly, the same smell as when she passed the brewery in Cable Street – hops, maybe.

Was she already drunk?

Chapter Twenty-one

She read what she'd written – *Dear Callum, this will be my last letter, for now* – and crossed it out. Why would it be her last letter? Maybe her letters hadn't arrived at all. Perhaps Callum had been so busy he hadn't time to reply. Perhaps the last two she had written had sounded too desperate, too needy, and he had decided that writing back was not a good idea for now. Or ever?

She began again.

Dear Callum,

I hope you are all right and you are enjoying the farm.

I'm missing you and I do wish I was with you, as now my mum really has gone bananas! The first sign that things were not normal was when she started going to church again, which is strange because she has always hated the nuns and priests. She's called them names and says how would a priest know what it's like to bring up a family, why should Father so and so or Sister whatever think they can tell a mother how to behave? Before they criticise they should walk a mile in her shoes, she used to say. She got especially cross after the incident when she was told she couldn't take communion because Sister Immaculata had seen her eating a meat pie on a Friday outside the Locarno. But Mam didn't have any money and the meat pies were cheaper than fish and chips, special offer as they were on the turn, so what else was she supposed to do? She was only trying to do the best for us.

Anyway, this seems to have all been forgotten. But I'm worried because she seems to have brought Hannah back home permanently. I'm dreading that she is going to say I have to stay here even longer. Everything hints at this. Pat, my brother, is trying to make me feel bad about not offering to help with Hannah. But what am I to do? Mam sent me away. Now she wants me back. She keeps asking questions. She also seems to be obsessed with teenagers. Talked the other day about me getting 'carried away in the heat of the moment' which rather made me think the heat of the moment sounds like something I'd like to find out about myself.

I've told Gladys I will do another night at the Tivoli. It lifts my spirits – but Violet is sure to find out any day soon. I miss you. Write soon.

Reading it back she decided that Callum should really hear none of this. It would only alarm him. Instead, she wrote.

Dear Callum,

Have you been receiving my letters?

Love Babby.

Then she sealed it, put a stamp on it, and posted it on the way to the Tivvy.

Gladys Worrall was standing outside the pub, having a cigarette. She had been arguing with her brother, Rex, and needed some air. Customers were beginning to arrive from the docks and their shifts with Tate and Lyle. A tugboat on the Mersey had run aground, pulling a floating crane, and there was constant chatter about it from the men who were turning up for their pints of bitter on their way home.

'Babby, come and say hello to my friend,' said Gladys, meeting her at the door.

She took her inside. One of the sailors was sitting at the back of the pub. His legs were splayed, white bell-bottomed trousers tenting at his crotch. He was Danish or Swedish, with tattoos of fish and a woman with a garter rippling up his forearms. Gladys beckoned him over. He cocked his sailor hat, grinned, then got up and walked to Babby and Gladys.

'Olaf watched you playing the other night. He wanted to meet you.'

'Did he?' replied Babby, shrinking away.

'You want me to leave you two alone?' asked Gladys.

Babby flinched. 'Why would I want you to do that?' she asked.

'Just thought you two might like a bit of privacy? Olaf could buy you a drink. You could have a chat?'

'Chat? With this lump of herring? He can't speak a word of English. Can you, dopey?' The sailor, stood there grinning, a smile stretching around the back of his head. 'You like that? You big soft Olly?' she said, and poked him in the ribs, flipping his sailor hat so that it tipped to the back of his head. He laughed, and so did she. 'You great pudding ...' she said.

'Just have a drink with him after you've sung,' said Gladys. 'What harm will it do?'

'I will not!' said Babby.

The barman watched what Gladys was doing. It's not right, he thought. Babby was only a lassie.

'Why? He's a good customer. Big ship, *The Norwegian Viking*. I want to keep my customers happy ...' said Gladys.

Babby laughed. She stared at the sailor, who was smiling at her, plonked herself down in front of him and ruffled his hair. 'Look at you, sitting there like the Dumb Man of Manchester!' she said. Seeing the sailor's floppy blonde fringe bouncing as he smiled wider and nodded and tapped his feet in time to the song being played on the Wurlitzer jukebox, a jangling version of 'Que Sera Sera', she said, 'Sorry, chucky, I'm already going steady with someone ...'

She jumped up and walked down the corridor. She knew what Gladys was up to, all right, wanting her to flirt with the customers, pretend that she was interested in them for the craic, and then snare them for a few more bob to put behind the bar. 'As if I bloody would,' she murmured to herself out loud.

Ten minutes later she took her place on the dais and the pub went quiet; all talk of grain machines and cargo and cranes sinking to the river bed, diminished to a hush as she began to sing.

'Perfect order ... She brings perfect order to this place,' murmured Gladys. 'I'll be sad to see her go.'

Chapter Twenty-two

A young man approached the green cabmen's shelter on the corner of Joseph Street as the woman inside took the kettle off the stove, put away the plate of bread and butter squashed into triangles, and began locking up for the night. The young man was no more than eighteen, with clear skin, and clean clothes. He wore polished brogue shoes and he had an accordion slung over his shoulder.

The woman wondered if he was lost.

'You're not from around these parts, are you?'

'Am I anywhere near the Tivoli, missus?' he said.

'Aye. Top of next street along – turn left …'

The boy nodded.

'Can I help you with anything?'

'I'm looking for a lass called Babby Delancy,' he said.

'Are you now?' She paused for effect. 'Well, as it happens, I know her. Tivoli pub, you say? Walk down Havelock Street. Look out for John Bagot hospital. Mind you don't take too many deep breaths. It's the hospital for tropical medicine and infectious diseases. Never know what you might catch,' she said, laughing. 'And then past the hollas. You can't miss the hollas. Great big hole in the ground. Then you walk straight down the hill from there, then down Gordon Street, wiggle around the back roads to Regent Road – that's the dock road – and you'll see the Tivoli pub.'

'Ta,' said the young man, jogging in the direction that she was pointing.

Following her instructions, with the clock face on the hospital building shining like the moon and lighting up the way, he reached the dock road.

The Tivoli pub stood at one end. When he got there, he went to the window and shaded his hand to peer inside.

Just then, Gladys came out with a sweeping brush.

'This the Tivvy pub?' he asked her.

'Who's asking, love?' she said, leaning on her brush, and lighting up a cigarette, the ash slowly curling from the end as she smoked it.

'It doesn't matter. Is this the Tivvy?'

Gladys Worrall paused, nodded upwards to the sign up above her, gestured at it with her brush. In elaborate gold swirling letters it read 'The Tivoli

Pub'. Removing the wilting fag from her mouth, she blotted her crudely painted lips on a handkerchief, leaving traces of a red feathery cupid's bow, appearing more interested in that than the boy as he pushed open the doors of the Tivoli and was greeted by a blast of warm air, the smell of beer, and the welcoming sounds of chatter and laughter.

'I'm looking for Babby Delaney,' he said to Elsie, the barmaid, who was emptying ashtrays.

Babby stopped dead in her tracks, the ice in the drink that she had just accepted from Olaf clinking against the glass. Oh, that voice! The slight catch, the soft Northern burr, the flat vowels. Her heart rose to her throat as she spun around.

She gulped air, excitement welling up from the pit of her stomach.

'What the 'eckers are you doing here, Cal?' she said.

Seeing him grinning at her like an excited schoolboy, it felt that the time apart had fallen away to nothing in an instant.

He paused, as if he was going to tell her something. Something urgent, something important. But then he smiled. 'Couldn't keep away,' he said, laughing, as she put on her coat. *'That's Amore,'* he sang, taking her hand and swinging her arm.

'I don't believe it!' said Babby.

'And I thought you might need this,' he said, indicating her accordion, slung over his shoulder.

'Oh, God, Cal!'

He seemed so happy to see her, with his hand pushing his black hair over the top of his head nervously. He was trying hard to look relaxed, but failing, grinning from ear to ear. 'It's good to see you, love,' he said.

'Thank you! Thank you, for bringing the accordion. The one I play here is *terrible*.'

He smiled again.

'Let's go outside,' said Babby, taking his hand. She noticed that he had tried to look respectable, no jeans and denim jacket, but wearing a tie and ill-fitting demob jacket. It made him look slightly out of place, standing amongst the rubbish and discarded newspapers that people had chucked on the pavement after buying their penny worth of chips from the Acropolis chippie.

He drew deeply on his cigarette which glowed in the indigo black of the night. The leaves whirled around his feet. How different he looked, here, in the city, instead of in the fields, thought Babby. He flicked his cigarette end on to the pavement, and grinding it with his heel, he said, 'I missed you, Babby ...' and came towards her suddenly, pulling her to him with an arm around her waist, and kissed her. With every breath she took, she felt a swelling in her breast and her pulse racing.

'Oh, Callum! I can't believe it! Me too!' she said. 'But why didn't you answer my letters?'

'Letters?'

'I wrote to you so many times …'

'Don't know what you mean. But I could ask the same of you.'

'What?'

'I wrote to you an' all. You didn't reply and I thought I had the wrong address.'

Babby's face clouded. Mam, she thought. 'You don't think anyone has been interfering?' she asked.

'Why would they do that? *Who* would do that?'

Babby couldn't answer, but her expression seemed to say she had a good idea who. Almost certainly her mother. Is that why she had been acting so strangely? She had thought it was the drink, but now she wasn't so sure.

'Who cares? I'm here now. And Mrs Reilly doesn't know I've left. She's gone with one of the sisters for two days to a retreat in Wales. I'm supposed to be looking after pigs but I've got one of the lads to do me errands.'

'You cheeky bugger,' said Babby.

'I was going to go to your house to find you, but thought I'd try the pub first. You told me about it …'

Babby hesitated. Just as well she thought; if Violet had been the one sabotaging them because of the letters, he would have got short shrift at Joseph Street.

'The woman at the cab shelter told me she knew you.'

'Peggy? Been there for years, giving out teas to the cabbies, collecting the gossip ...'

'I'm glad I asked her.'

'So am I,' she replied. 'What now, then?' she asked.

'Can I walk you home?' he said.

'Long bloody way to come, just to walk me home, but yes, you may.'

None of it made sense. But as they linked arms and walked on towards the hollas, it dawned on her, as they walked up Gordon Street, that there were many stories that she had been told that didn't add up. Perhaps the time had come for her to make some stories of her own that did. This was as good a time as any.

They could barely contain themselves. Words tumbled over words, sentences crashed into one another, laughter punctuated every pause for breath. When he asked her what she was doing at the pub, she told him she was singing, and how it was a good way to make a few bob, just for the few weeks that she had to stay on in Liverpool, but that she'd rather do that than clean folks' steps or work in a typing pool – she'd hated those lessons at school though her nimble fingers had made her the best in the class. She also told him that Violet had said that the pub wasn't the place for a lady.

'Surely she'll find out?' asked Cal.

'Probably.'

'Not sure I like you at a pub, either,' said Cal. 'Pretty grim ...'

'You sound just like me mam! God, she hates it. But the truth is she just doesn't like me singing. It can be awkward, with all the sailors watching and wolfwhistling and catcalling. But I can handle meself,' she said and laughed. 'You mustn't worry.'

They walked on, dizzy with the familiar scent of each other, and drunk on the heady chatter that ricocheted between them – about when Babby was coming back to the farm, of how there was nothing here for her in the city apart from singing at the pub.

'And your Hannah?' he said.

'Ah, Hannah. She's the only thing for me in Liverpool,' she responded.

'Jesus, I've missed you,' he said, as they walked in step, exhilarated by the perfect rhythm of their feet treading the pavements, stepping out harmoniously, excitedly, together again at last.

'This the famous hollas?' asked Callum when they reached the bottom of the hill.

'Aye,' replied Babby. 'Come and have a look. Not much left of it, but there's still one derelict old house standing.'

There was a pause as they caught their breath after climbing in through a door off its hinges. 'What now?' asked Callum, as they looked around at the empty room, at the rubble, a ripped fluttering curtain, an upturned kettle on the floor.

Babby, laughing, picked up the curtain, wrapped it around her. 'I'm the Queen of Sheba ...'

He grinned and led Babby to the darkest corner of the empty bombed-out terrace house, picking their way through bricks and cement, split floorboards and mangled bedsteads and a rusting stove. He opened her coat and put his arms around her waist. Her heart was beating so loudly she was sure he'd make a comment about it.

'I thought I'd never see you again,' she said, breathlessly. 'I'll bloody kill me mother.'

'Nowt to worry about on that score, so stop frettin'' he replied.

And as he kissed her, she did exactly that. She stopped worrying. Stopped worrying about Violet. And Hannah. And Pat. She didn't even worry about his hand tugging away at her blouse, trying to free it from her waistband. She just let him, and gasped as his fingers touched her bare back.

'What about your mam? Will she be waiting up?' he asked, withdrawing for a moment.

'I left a note, said I'd be back at eleven and let meself in. Anyway, if she has been interfering, with the letters and stuff, I don't owe her anything now.'

'Well, I'm glad you did a runner. What's for us now? Gretna Green? Eloping?'

'Not bloody likely! I barely know you,' she said and laughed.

'I know I love you, Babby ...'

'Don't be stupid.'

'I mean it! So does anything else matter?'

'I suppose not,' she murmured, enjoying the sensation of the feel of his warmth breath on her cheek.

'Babby,' he said, 'you know I start National Service next September? Though they're saying they'll finish that soon, so I may be lucky ...' His little hot puffs of breath hung on cold air. He slipped his right hand under her shirt. Not content with the barrier provided by her clothing, he was making for the hooks and eyes of her bra. 'I just wanted to tell you,' he whispered as he undid the strap, 'I think you're a grand girl ... the best ... Can you really not come back to the farm tomorrow?'

'I'll follow you,' she gasped, breathless. 'As soon as I've got money and sorted out me mam.'

'I can't bear it. That this might be the last time I'll see you for ages. Hey, tell your mam you're going to go to another lassie's tonight, a friend maybe, and come to mine instead. I'm staying at a boarding house in Canning Street. It's a right dive, but I could sneak you in.'

'I don't have any friends like that. Only Johnny Gallagher.'

He made a face.

'Who's he?'

'One of the Kapler Gang. Just a boy. Trouble. But he looks out for me.'

Babby could hear a train in the distance, the gentle sound of hiss, chuff, chuff, hiss, as it went along the overhead railway. Two dogs that were running about in the street began to howl. Looking over her shoulder through the smashed window, she could see them racing in circles and sniffing the air. He kissed her again. It was a kiss that was deep and throaty and with a tongue counting every tooth, twisting and winding around hers, as if he could eat her whole if she would let him. She gasped. And as he continued to kiss her, it felt so good, and sweet, and right, that everything that mattered so much, seemed like nothing much to worry about at all.

'Cal ...' she said finally, when she came up for air. But the sound of the engine and the screeching of the wheels on tracks was so loud, he didn't hear. When she gazed into his face, he looked so hopeful. He began to pull up her skirt, yanking a button off its thread. Fear gave way to a new energy with the feel of his hands on her skin. She let herself enjoy the smell of cigarettes on his breath and the feel of his tongue dipping and diving in her mouth and his whispering in her ear, 'God, Babby, I've missed you something rotten. You do strange things to me, all right.' *If you can't be good be careful*, were the words Violet had often sung out to Pat as he left the house to see Doris. Would Cal's mother have called out the same to him if she'd lived, she wondered?

She placed her hand gently on his arm to stop for a moment. He didn't. So, she pinched, quite hard, her nails making clean white crescents in his skin. He peeled his upper body away from hers.

'What is it?'

'You'll never leave me, Cal?'

He smiled, pushed a strand of hair away from her eyes. 'Never,' he replied. 'Like I said, I love you.'

He began to kiss her again and she kissed him back. This girl could kiss so hard, she made his lips sore, he thought. Then he paused. 'Are you OK with this?' he asked. 'I don't want to make you do anything you don't want to. You must tell me when to stop.'

'I'm fine,' she answered. She just wanted to look at him for a minute, trace the line of his forehead with her fingertip, kiss his brows, one, then the other.

'Lie down, then,' he said. He took the Queen of Sheba curtain, shook out the dust, and placed it on the floor. He sat and took her hand, drew her to him. They wriggled up to each other, lay down side by side, looking up at the inky sky through a gaping hole in the roof. The cold air, laced with hops from the nearby brewery, made her dizzy, feel drunk with anticipation of what was to come.

He turned to her, kissed her again. His right hand was pressing her left shoulder gently into the floor and the other hand spread across her thigh; when he withdrew it, she caught him glancing down to see the imprint of his long fingers on her white skin.

'Sorry, Babby. You really OK?' he said, in between short urgent breaths. 'Just want you so much.'

'I'm so happy,' she answered, whispering close into his ear. She touched his cheek, his lips, his neck. 'Carry on ... please don't stop ...'

Was this 'the heat of the moment' that her mother talked of? wondered Babby. She certainly felt as if she was in the eye of the storm. And, allowing his hands to wander over her body, it occurred to her that they should at least be courting, or married, to be doing what they were doing right now. Getting carried away. But this felt so different. Like they were running out of time. He going back to Anglesey, she had Violet to contend with. And then he kissed her again, more forcibly than he had ever kissed her before.

'You feel grand – and you taste delicious,' he said. His voice sounded different, modulating sweetly to a lower, more seductive tone. He rolled on top of her.

'Babby ...?'

'What?'

She could feel the full weight of his body on hers. Exhilaration sharpened her senses.

'Please ... please ... Can I?'

She was searching for a reply which of course was 'no'. This was what had been drummed into her by nuns, aunties, Violet. If he really was planning to do to her what she thought he wanted to – well, this should be her wedding night. This should be about making babies. At the very least, this should be the man she wanted to marry, or was going steady with. But she hardly knew Callum. And what with God right there, looking down on her, horrified, no doubt ... It was just, well, the truth was she liked it ... more than liked it. She was excited by it, excited by the way it felt when he kissed her, and the way it made her forget all those things about her father and Violet and being poor and having to sneak off to sing at the Tivvy, and feeling guilty about abandoning Hannah.

The growing sensation within her filled her with a boldness that allowed her to summon up the courage to whisper in his ear, '*Do it.*' And shocked that she wasn't telling him to stop, when he did, she shuddered, jerked, and cried out with vivid and surprised pleasure. Finally, as he rolled off her with a long exhaling of breath, he kissed her gently on the nape of her salty neck. 'Are you really all right?' he asked.

'Yes,' she replied, smiling and trembling. She had no idea what had just happened, but knew that, whatever it was, it felt good and kind – and true.

They tidied up their clothes and sat, side by side, staring at each other, her head nestled into the hollow of his damp armpit. He peeled a wet strand of hair off her cheek.

'I really, really, love you,' he said.

They lay there in the dark, unmoving, with the moon shining in. And they both knew that this guilt-laced encounter, in someone else's bombed-out old house, had changed them forever.

'Me an' all. Love you, I mean ...' she answered. Watching the moving shapes that a cloud passing over the moon was making on the ceiling, Babby could hear the shrill sound of a bird cawing and the swish of the tall grass that had grown up in clumps through the floorboards. She was bursting to talk to him – about the farm, his plans, her plans, his parents, Pat and Hannah, Violet's betrayal.

The thought of that sent a shiver down her spine. She had never defied her mother before like this, surely the biggest act of defiance that was possible. But Babby wasn't able to think about the consequences of anything much now. Because, with Cal, she had been prepared to risk everything. Because this was being alive, wasn't it? The very best of life, she thought.

She felt him move away from her and thrust his hand in his pocket then produce a packet of sweets.

'Ever had one of these?' he asked. 'Spangles?'

Babby shook her head as he unwrapped one and popped one first into her mouth, and then his own.

'Suck it,' he said. 'Suck it really hard ... Stick your tongue in the middle. Feel it making a hole?'

After a few minutes, he took the sweet out of his mouth. It had done just that.

'Give me your hand,' he said, and slipped the sweet on her finger as if it were a diamond ring.

'Oh Cal, I'll wear this forever.'

He smiled. 'Come on. I'll walk you home. Can I come and see you in the morning?'

She wavered. 'I'm not sure. About Mam …'

'Well, I've got to see you before me boat at six.'

Sounds lisped in the shadows and the trees and Babby hoiked the accordion over one shoulder. She hesitated.

'I'm doing the lunchtime shift at the Boot Inn. I mean the Tivvy. You could come and see me after, when I'm done,' she said.

'The Boot Inn?' asked Callum.

'It used to be called that. Changed its name to go posh. After the trouble there.' Babby lapsed into silence.

'What trouble?' said Callum.

She faltered. 'A fight. My dad played his accordion there and he was mixed up in it. Badly.' The words seemed to echo in her head.

'How badly?' he asked, his voice little more than a whisper.

'I was ten. It was so long ago …' She realised it had been years since she had talked to anyone about what had happened and though she wanted to tell Callum her father had died in the fight, she couldn't. Not now. She just couldn't.

Callum said nothing, and she turned to him, leaning up on her elbow.

'What's the matter, Cal? You look as though you've seen a ghost. Are you all right?'

'Aye,' he said. 'Aye,' he said again, drifting into silence before they gathered themselves up and walked on towards Joseph Street.

Chapter Twenty-three

After they had said goodbye and Callum had kissed her on the front step, he didn't walk towards Canning Street where he had told Babby that the boarding house was. He walked the other way, back to the pub. Last orders had been called but there were a couple of stragglers still at the bar. He came through the door, out of breath and ashen-faced.

'Any of you know a fella called Delaney? Used to play his squeezebox here?' he asked a thickset docker who was draining his pint.

'Why?'

'Nowt much.'

'Aye. What's it to you?'

'Someone I know liked to drink here.'

'Terrible business. Jack Delaney died, got tangled up in a brawl with someone he should have kept clear of.'

'Did they call this fella the Mouse?'

'They did. Know of him?'

Callum felt a chill wrap around his neck with icy fingers.

'Aye. He is, *was,* me Da,' he said. So quiet, so low, so troubled, he was uncertain that anyone even heard.

Before he had time to say any more, Gladys appeared at the door. 'Locking up for the night, son,' she said. 'Come back tomorrow when we open.'

'Right y'are,' he said. 'Ta very much.'

And he turned up his collar to the wind and walked off into the night towards the new flats rising up from the hollas, similar and ugly against a black velvet sky.

Chapter Twenty-four

Violet would be sleeping. That was all she ever did, nowadays, thought Babby, when she got back home, flushed with happiness, but still angry about the mystery of the letters. Quietly she went upstairs, put the accordion back under the bed, pushed open the door and saw Violet lying sprawled out on the bed, sheets all rumpled up beneath her, nightdress gaping, snoring loudly. She was spark out, all right. Creeping back downstairs, she made her way into the back room.

She opened up the top drawer of the dresser. Reaching into the back of it, she trembled. From upstairs, she heard a noise, someone coughing, the creaking of bedsprings. Shoving her hands into the depths of the drawer, she retrieved sheaves of papers, rolls of ribbon, bias binding, hemming tape, safety pins, then she found a fat envelope tucked into the far corner, lodged under more papers and the rent book and an old ration book. She grasped it and pulled it out.

Feeling it around the edges, she discovered it contained two letters. She went over to the range and found the matches, struck one and lit a candle that was in a metal holder, placed it on the table and allowed the flickering flame to illuminate the first letter. '*Dear Babby*,' she read under her breath.

She squinted at the words again, repositioned the candleholder, to make sense of them, for here was the proof that Violet had intercepted Callum's letters; probably the nuns in Anglesey were doing the same with her letters to Callum.

Dear Babby,

God I miss you. You can't believe how hot it is here. Absolutely sweltering. I went swimming in the sea yesterday so perhaps you and I could do the same when you get back. I took the twins and the girls wore knitted costumes and they looked a sight when they bagged up and got sopping wet. You know what skinny dipping is? When you come back I'll show you ...

So it really was true. Violet *had* been hiding the letters. Babby staggered backwards and slumped into a chair. She looked again at the sheet of notepaper, turned it over, and as she did so, gathered up her skirts and scrunched and twisted them into a knot in her lap. '*Come back soon, love Cal*' it ended.

The truth of what had been happening over the past two weeks was there in black and white.

She stood, reeled, paced around the room as she clutched the letter to her breast, stumbled, and rifled through the papers again. It was so upsetting that, for a moment, she forgot how to breathe, seemed to temporarily lose her sight and the use of her legs.

And then, suddenly, Violet was standing there, white luminous face smeared in cold cream, nightgown billowing out behind her.

Babby flicked on the light switch and turned so that Violet got the full force of her anger. 'You hid my letters from Callum! Didn't you?'

Violet shrugged.

'You're drunk,' Babby said.

'No, I'm not drunk ... just a glass or two helps, that's all.'

'Mam ...'

'Oh, do be nice to me ... I had to hide those letters ... Sister Benedict told me to.' She sighed. 'The truth is ...' She faltered. 'Are you sure you want to hear this?'

'What?'

'The nuns warned me about this boy. They said he's a bad lot. Don't think you're the first to fall for his charms.'

Babby moved forward, jabbed a finger at her mother. 'What rubbish,' she said.

'It's not rubbish. Why d'you think he's there in the first place? Because he's a saint? No, because his family can't look after him – because he's out of control. Just like you.'

Her words struck at the very core of Babby.

'He's just the kind of boy who could get a girl like you into trouble. It's just a silly crush, you have. Do you want to end up in Saint Jude's?' said Violet.

'How can you say that?' cried Babby, feeling her bones tensing and separating.

Violet dragged a chair across the linoleum, sat down. Babby pressed her lips together, held herself stock-still, without moving a muscle, as if she had been frozen in time.

'I'm so disappointed in you, love,' said Violet.

Babby noticed her mother was slurring her words.

Violet continued, 'Your dad, I had a dream about him last night. He was standing right at the end of the bed. He looked like a blurry Jesus without the beard, and with those huge hands of his. He said, "Keep an eye on Babby. She's a wild one ... Keep her away from Anglesey. God forbid she'll end up at Saint Jude's."'

'What cobblers! You should never have read our letters. That's evil! Anyway, why is everyone so worried about what will happen to me? Why are you always going on about Saint Jude's?'

'Oh, darlin', darlin', I worry, that's all. You've seen how easily that happens. I know several girls who've gone there and never been seen again. So tragic,' she said mysteriously.

'Who?'

'Never mind. All I'm saying is that I'm allowed to worry. That's my job. I'm sorry I didn't pass the letters on from your lover boy, but I was only trying to protect you.'

Something, a sense of someone listening to their conversation, made them both turn and look towards the door. Hannah was standing there in her night-dress, holding her peg doll. The little girl associated Violet's drinking with laughter and gaiety and waltz-ing around the parlour to the wireless – and she was sure that she was drunk right now, so she hoped that her mother would jump up and start dancing around the table.

'Tell me about Daddy in the dream,' said Hannah.

Babby wondered how long little sister had been standing there, how much had heard.

Violet sighed. 'Never you mind. Get back up those wooden hills.'

'Did he sing that song about the bald mouse?' asked Hannah. She moved to her sister, tugged at her skirt. 'You sing it, Babby, I love it when you sing, we all do. They say you sound like Dad ... but I don't remember him. Did he look like a blurry Jesus in real life?'

Babby shot a look at her to tell her that this was serious but she didn't understand.

'I won't be singing, Hannah.'

'Will you sing it then, Mam?'

'Of course I will, chicken.' She pulled Hannah on to her knee and they began to sing it together, falteringly at first, then louder, as Babby looked on, aghast.

'Daddy was looking better than ever in the dream,' Violet said when they'd finished, brushing her hair out of her eyes. 'Full of life. Those gorgeous rosy cheeks of his ...' She rearranged herself, clipping pins into a tightly wound bun she had scraped off her face. Cooing and stroking Hannah's hair, rearranging her nightdress, she said, 'You, me, Babby and Pat. We must all stick together – that's our only hope.'

She stood up, swayed unsteadily on her feet. 'And another thing, Babby,' Violet said. 'That accordion. When it comes back from Anglesey, I'm taking it to the Rotunda and selling it. It's what your dad would have wanted. He mentioned it to me many times, that – that he wanted rid of the thing. It's brought bad luck to this family.'

Babby could feel a rush of tears well in her eyes.

'That's not true!' she said.

Violet's words built to a crescendo with a flurry of sighs and moans. 'Yes, it is!'

'Have you told her, Mam?' asked Hannah, wanting to bring the arguing to an end.

Violet plonked herself down on the chair in front of the range, turned around in it, patted the hair on her head.

'Not yet.'

'Told me what?' asked Babby.

'Tell her now. You promised,' said Hannah.

Violet sighed. Her body folded into itself as she sat and then shifted in the chair.

'Go on, Mam,' urged Hannah.

'Babby, I've been a bad mother. I should never have sent you away. I've decided, we all have, that we don't need you to stay for just a few more weeks. I've decided you're coming back ... For good.'

Babby could feel herself trembling, her whole body shaking.

'I want us all to be together again, us Delaneys. This boy is no good for you and Hannah is not going back to Kathleen's.'

But I've grown used to my new life! Babby wanted to scream. I like the fresh air and the country and Mrs Reilly I even like the skinny, grubby kids that spend the summers with us ... and I thought I could stay until I was eighteen!

Instead, in shock, tears springing to her eyes, she just said, 'I'm going out to get some air.'

'No one is going anywhere,' said Violet, rebuking Babby with a stare. She nodded at Hannah to shut the kitchen door. She laid a flat hand over the checked tablecloth, folded creases into the corners, and sighed one of her sighs. 'Sit down, Babby,' she said, simply and gravely. 'Those letters were shocking.'

Babby felt that strange, twisting thing in her stomach and her palms go sticky and hot with the dread of what was to come, and refused to sit.

'I want to stay in Anglesey until I'm eighteen. You promised.'

'I want you back. I've missed you and I want us all to turn over a new leaf,' Violet said.

'I thought I was just coming back for Pauline's funeral.'

She could see Hannah sucking on the sleeve of her nightdress nervously, with a look of panic on her face.

'Mam said you were coming to look after us. That everything was going to be different now you were a big girl ... seventeen, ain't you?'

Violet reached for the bottle glinting on the table.

'Mam, stop it! Don't you think you've had enough?' Babby asked Violet, trying to snatch the bottle from her. Violet wrestled it back from her and Babby could do nothing but watch as she poured herself another Harvey's Bristol Cream sweet sherry. Violet's recent drinking was not something that anyone talked much about, but there was no escaping it tonight. Hannah was still too little to understand. She called Violet's drink Ma's happy juice. But everyone knew there had long since been anything to celebrate. It used to mean sing-songs, and dancing around the table, and kisses. It meant the Boot Inn, Jack's accordion, and wild protestations of love. But now it meant raised voices, frustration, and, with the business of sending Babby away to Anglesey, spitefulness.

'That's that decided, then,' Violet said, to bring the conversation to an end.

Had she actually gone mad? wondered Babby.

'Are we excited about Babby coming home?' The way Violet said it, chin thrust out, and with a toss back of her hair, was infuriating to Babby. 'Are we?'

Hannah nodded and gave Babby a desperate smile.

If only her father were still here, thought Babby. He would know what to do. He would make everything all right. She missed his footsteps leaving reassuring muddy imprints on the brown hall carpet so they would know he was home from the docks or the Boot Inn. She missed him bringing home sherbet dib dabs, and chocolate to melt on a plate in the fire and smear on the brokies. She missed the money, which meant they could afford the gas bills and half-decent cuts of meat instead of the scrag ends, and shoes that didn't have to be shod with metal caps. But most of all she missed his calming influence on Violet, which meant she didn't make such vindictive decisions, like this latest announcement.

'Please let me go back to Anglesey? Just for the summer?' asked Babby, her big eyes pleading.

'Do I have to tell you again? Quite apart from Hannah needing you, those letters were deeply troubling,' said Violet.

'You shouldn't have read them ...'

'I'm glad I did. I have spoken to Sister Immaculata at Saint Patrick's about what's been going on between you and the boy, and Sister Benedict and Sister Scholastica and Mrs Reilly as well, they all agree you shouldn't go back.'

'No! Benny read them as well?'

How could Benny have done this?! Now Violet had produced an envelope from her pocket, took out the letter that was inside and unfolded it.

'We're all worried about you, Babby, that's all. Worried about you going off the rails. I sent you away so that wouldn't happen. You've always been a problem child, ever since you were little. Read this – it will explain everything. There's no hiding from the Lord. Or at least, the bride of the Lord. Sister Benedict.'

The paper Violet thrust at her was headed, with a crucifix, and a picture of the Virgin Mary. At the top Babby read the address clearly, Sisters of Pity, Saint Coloma's. This was a bad sign.

Violet crossed her legs, her bottle at her side. She held the letter between thumb and finger as if it were a dead mouse as she handed it to Babby who began to read, '*Dear Mrs Delaney, We think it unwise to have Babby staying with us at the farm, at least for the foreseeable future. She is developing an unhealthy relationship with one of our summer children. A boy. Callum Lynch is his name. This will only end in unhappiness. I am enclosing a written extract of her diary to give you a measure of the problem.*'

Babby screwed the letter up savagely and threw it at her mother.

'Read the rest of it out,' said Violet.

'I won't,' said Babby.

'Then I will.'

Violet picked up the note, smoothed it out on her lap and began to read, enunciating each word slowly and deliberately, snorting at the end of each sentence, clutching the glass full of sherry, the veins on the back of her white knuckled hands standing out like knotted ropes.

'*Callum put his hand on my leg*' she read. '*I didn't want him to stop. He is so handsome, like Johnny Halliday and Eddie Fisher rolled into one, he makes my stomach go into knots just to look at him. When Johnny Gallagher made me kiss him, I didn't want to, and I never would have done. This is different. I would let Callum do anything to me. I know it's wrong, and that makes me a terrible person, not a good girl at all, but that's the way it is.*'

She put the glass down on the worn pink chenille tablecloth for emphasis, took a slug, sighed, put the glass back on the table.

Babby took a deep breath. Then, snatching the letter from Violet, she scoured the words across the page again, read another couple of sentences. Such a betrayal! It couldn't be Mrs Reilly. It must be the nuns. They were all the same, Saint Hilda's, the farm, Saint Jude's. She glared at her mother sitting at the table.

'Well. That was embarrassing, wasn't it? *I would let Callum do anything to me*? No wonder the nuns are terrified. Perhaps they should just go ahead and warm the bed for you at Saint Jude's? What have you got to say for yourself?' asked Violet.

Babby shouted a reply. 'I'm not staying here. I *am* going back. You said I would stay there until I was eighteen. I'm not eighteen. I'm going back. I have to. Mrs Reilly will have me back.'

'No, all this nonsense! I've tried so hard with you Babby. It's pointless—'

'Mam, I'm going back to Pentraeth Farm!' she cried.

'Didn't you listen? They don't want you!' shouted Violet.

'Yes, they do! I'm going back! You sodding watch me!' she cried.

'Oh, aren't you the clever one? With a mouth on you like the Mersey Tunnel. You're impossible!'

'You can't stop me!' Babby slammed a fist on the table, making the cups and dishes rattle.

'Don't be ridiculous. You're not going anywhere.'

Shiny tears gathered in Babby's eyes. The very act of breathing became difficult.

Violet softened. 'We want you here – we do actually love you, Babby,' she said, hoping it would all be forgotten about in the morning, and with that, she scrunched up Callum's letters and Sister Benedict's and threw them into the range, where they curled, first at the corners, and then towards the centre, until they floated like gossamer, up into the chimney, and there was nothing left but ash.

'I'm going,' said Babby. She grabbed her coat and left, slamming the door behind her so that it made the windows rattle. She ran all the way to Canning Street, hurtling along with a westerly wind blowing in from the Mersey filling the air with a sweet smell. Hartley's Jam Factory, most likely, she thought. It cheered her spirits and felt like a good omen. If Callum's boat was sailing at six, she didn't care about Violet's disapproval: she was going to spend every precious last minute of the day and night with him.

Chapter Twenty-five

The door of the boarding house was shuttered. She looked up at the building. Twenty-one Canning Street, Callum had said, she was sure of it. Finally, a face appeared at the window. It was a woman with a hairnet covering her head, wearing an old housecoat. No Blacks, No Irish, No Dogs, said the cardboard notice, propped up on the windowsill downstairs.

The woman pushed up the sash window, asked Babby what she wanted at this time of night.

'I'm looking for Callum, my friend,' called Babby, up at the window.

'No Callum here,' replied the woman, irritated that Babby had dragged her out of bed.

'But this was the address he gave me,' said Babby.

'No one by the name of Callum here,' the woman repeated.

Had he given a false name? wondered Babby. She hesitated.

'Git,' said the woman, before closing the window with a bang.

'Very nice,' said Babby, shouting up at the window. Her voice echoed around the streets. Perhaps she should wait.

She sat on the step, her back to the railings. The stone soon became like ice and numbed her bottom. Her coat, threadbare and old, did nothing to keep the bitter cold from seeping up through her bones.

Suddenly there was a vicious flash of lightning. She waited for the growl of thunder to pass. But then the growl exploded into a volley of crackling gunfire. She turned up her collar. It was summer, but this was Liverpool; the rain began lashing down, and with it a cold wind rushed about her that sounded like the wailing of banshees. She would go home, meet Callum at the Tivvy the next day as they had planned, and hope all would be explained.

The following day, at half past twelve, she walked up to the pub. She saw Gladys through the stippled glass window, with a feather duster. Taking a deep breath, she went in.

'Babby? Are you all right? You look a bit queer ...'
'I'm fine.'

'Come and help me with the sweeping,' said Rex, wiping his hands on a cloth. 'If you do a good job, you'll find a shilling under some of the table legs – I've hidden them for you.'

Sure enough, after ten minutes, she found a silver coin. It did nothing to raise her spirits, but she appreciated Rex's kind gesture and apologised for feeling so glum.

She made herself a brew, changed into her gingham frock, with the full tulle underskirt that she had soaked in sugar and water to make it stick out stiffly, and when the punters began to drift in, she took her place on the tiny dais. She tried to lose herself in the music. It normally worked, but this afternoon she was finding it difficult to think of anything apart from Callum and where he had gone.

'I'll gather lilacs in the morning,' she sang, with the sounds of the accordion accompanying her with a doleful melody and lingering on the minor chords. Halfway into the second verse, Gladys slid up behind Babby, grabbed her by the elbow, and whispered, 'Eyes and teeth, love. You're going to put them off. What's the matter? You look like a wet weekend in New Brighton.'

Rex saw her brows knit together in a frown. 'Is there something wrong, love?' he asked.

She shook her head, then whispered, 'If anyone comes here looking for me, a boy by the name of Callum, and I'm in the back, tell him to wait for me ...'

She had been waiting all morning, hoping he might come by the house after all. She had sat staring out of the window, supposedly sewing one of Violet's linings for the glove man, but desperately hoping Callum might appear. That's not what they had arranged. But she thought he might have changed his mind. Only he hadn't. The boarding house, when she had headed there again on her way to the Tivoli, had been locked up.

Babby took heart from Rex promising that he would keep an eye on who was coming through the door. As long as she did what she had come here to do and put on a good show for the punters, Gladys had said.

She nodded back at him as he gave her the thumbs up. After a faltering start, she became aware that the people in the pub were now really listening. There were a couple of Danish sailors, a group of dockers who had come straight from the pen – fellas who had been given the knock back by the new foreman and were drowning their sorrows – a couple of West Indian dockers who'd been talking about unloading crates of rubber, gesturing expansively as they described one of the crates splitting open as it came off the boat and the rubber wriggling like snakes all over the deck. One of the West Indians, without warning, when she finished the last chorus of 'Liverpool Lullaby', leapt on to the stage. 'Any requests?' he shouted.

His friend started singing, 'Day-o! Day-O! Daylight come and me wan' go home!'

The dockers chorused, 'Oh Danny boy! The pipes, the pipes are calling ...'

A drunken fella raised his glass and shouted, 'The Fields of Athenry!' They began banging their glasses on the table, thumping their feet. This is what she was supposed to be good at. *You hum it. I'll play it.* Years of watching her dad working out songs.

But today she was finding it impossible. One of the men called out to her, gestured at the side of his head. 'Love, it's up there for thinking, down there for dancing. Give us a tune.' And he jumped up, pushed a table back and started to whirl a woman around the pub.

Babby started haltingly. 'Now gather round you sailor boys and listen to my plea ...'

The words stuck in her throat, lodged there like a plum stone but a roar of approval went up around the pub and people started to clap in rhythm.

She continued to sing. 'And when you've heard my tale, you'll pity me ...'

When she played a chord of b-flat by mistake, nobody appeared to notice. Whether it was because no one was listening, or they were all too drunk to notice, was difficult to tell.

Then, after a few more songs, she took her bow and left the stage.

'What's all this about?' said Pat, when Babby came out of her dressing room in her jacket. He was leaning against the bar.

'How did you know I was here?' asked a shocked Babby, packing away the accordion.

'Word gets around. Breaking our mam's heart, you are,' he asked, glugging back a glass of beer. 'Come on home. Mam is waiting for you,' he said, moodily. He removed the cigarette from his mouth, ground it into the ashtray. He and Doris would have already set off for the Majestic dance club, looking forward to kicking up a storm with Johnny and the Rockets on the jukebox, if Violet hadn't asked him to find Babby. He was irritated that he had had to change his plans.

'I shan't come,' protested Babby.

'You'll do what I say!'

'No, I won't!'

'Balls and bloody brick dust, you won't! We'll see about that!' And with that he strode over and lifted Babby up in his arms. He carried her her outside, kicking and shouting, and plonked her on the pavement.

'Gerroff! I don't need you interfering! Why would I need that?' she said, kicking and thumping his back with her fist. 'I don't want to go with you.' Her eyes grew large and round and he took her hand. She could feel his grip tighten. 'Gerroff me,' she said, wriggling away from him.

Then, springing back, she took a run at him. 'I'll decide when I'm leaving. Doing the dirty work for Mam. Always thought you were on my side of the argument, Pat!'

'I am! But you're my little sister, Babby. And I worry about you. You're out of your depth here. Look around you. You should be at home. This is a right dive,' he said.

Gladys, who had come out to watch the show, snorted. 'I'll have you know, me and Rex are very proud of the Tivoli. I'm not best pleased to hear you shouting your mouth off in my bar. The only time when this place was in the mire was when your bloody father dragged us into it.'

Pat momentarily faltered. But then he let the thought go. He knew where that would lead.

'Babby, get your things. We're off. This ends now,' he said. It was upsetting the way he said it. She wasn't used to Pat talking to her like this. Short, sharp angry words.

'There's someone I was waiting for ... I can't leave now!'

'Who?' he asked.

'A boy ...'

Then a thought occurred to him. 'Wait a minute. You're not waiting for this Callum character? Right Jack the Lad, Mam says. He's not in Liverpool? He the type to make you do something you don't want to, love? Has he been hanging around this pub? Because if – if—'

'Everything I have done with him, I wanted to! *Everything!* I love him, Pat!' she snarled, then, the minute she had said them, wished she could take the words back. She flushed red.

'I should forget him, Babby. Besides, there's always Johnny Gallagher. He's a nice boy and he would make a good husband. His dad has the dairy which will come to him. I can put in a word with his Ma ...'

Babby, her face full of freckles, glared at him and narrowed her eyes. At times, she had a look that knew no boundaries.

'Dairy? Bloody cows! No, Pat! I'm in love with Callum.'

'Love? Now look, you're not thinking right. You have no bloody choice. Who do you think you are?'

The two years difference in age that had always made Pat seem so wise, now incensed her. How dare he!

'I don't love Johnny Gallagher. I don't love him at all. He is my friend. We play kick the can in the hollas and he grabs me like a boy. He's not like Callum ...'

She felt herself swaying backwards.

'What's wrong with Johnny?' asked Pat. He looked genuinely bewildered. 'He's a good boy and his dad has the business. And he is fond of you Babby.'

Babby's nostrils flared. 'Fond of me? I want more than "fond of me".'

They walked home in silence, Babby dragging her feet and Pat pulling her along, prodding and shoving her to get a move on.

When they got back, she paused momentarily before she put the key into the lock. The house felt colder inside than out. The damp always seeped through the walls with the vaguest hint of rain. She shivered and pulled her jacket around herself for warmth.

'Go and sleep, Babby. I won't tell Mam what you've been up to at the Tivvy, if you go and sleep ...'

She nodded, ragged with exhaustion and disappointment, too tired to argue, too tired to sleep. Maybe tomorrow Callum would arrive ...

But though she waited, and waited, Callum did not arrive. Not at the Tivoli. Not at Joseph Street.

Not that day. Or the day after. Or the day after that.

Chapter Twenty-six

The empty promenade near Seaforth docks had been built out of the headland in a half-hearted attempt to attract weekenders and holidaymakers. It hadn't worked. The stretch of coast was a barren place, no ice-cream vans, or winkle stalls, or slot machines. There was just strangely undulating tarmac, a couple of shrimping carts and a man with a bucket, sticking a rod into the marshy sand and into the crevices of the mud-flats, looking for worms. None of this was of any concern to Babby. She had come here to be alone, to think about the letter she had received that morning from Callum, delivered to Gladys at the pub and handed to her when she had gone to tell her that she wouldn't be coming back to sing, at least for now. When she had read it, it was as if all life had been breathed out of her, the blood whooshed out of her body.

Clouds were bulking the sky, the greyness relieved here and there with blue patches, and seagulls were screeching. She made her way to a neglected Victorian bus shelter. Sitting down, she took the letter out of her pocket, turned it over in her hands. She opened it on her knee, and smoothed out the creases.

'Oh Callum.' She said his name out loud and when she did the picture of him in her head sharpened into focus. She could conjure up his smile, the way his hair fell over his eyes in a tangled web, and exactly what he was wearing when he turned up at the Tivvy. There he was, in her head, standing outside the hollas, under the street lamp, promising her he would be back the next day, winking and waving and blowing a kiss at her as he walked backwards around the corner, she running back to hug him again, he lifting her in his arms and swinging her around and around. And then he was gone, as though he had just spun away into air.

With tremulous fingers, she took the letter from the envelope. She stared at it, ran a finger around the edges.

And then another memory came, of the back field at Pentraeth Farm, a place where time could not be hurried, Callum crouched behind the leafy branches of the sweet-smelling elderflower tree at the bottom of the field, smiling or squinting, she couldn't be sure, but holding his arms out to her, his large, black wide-apart eyes full of longing and love. She remembered how he had bent down and moved a piece of hair out of her face, plucked a single strand of it and tied it to a nail on the cowshed and said it was to stay there to remind her how much he loved her. How only he would see it, and only he would know, it would be invisible, but in time the world would know all right. He would shout it from the roof of the barn, and it would sail all across the river Mersey to Liverpool.

Turning up her collar to the wind, she could feel the sand blowing off the beach stinging her eyes. She moved to the corner of the bus shelter, out of the wind, and continued to read. She noticed the letter was becoming blotted, going damp around the edges from the fine drizzle there was no escape from, the thin, indecisive kind of rain that soaks you through without you noticing. The ink was blurring in some parts. But she had read it so many times today she knew it by memory now.

Dear Babby,

I'm sorry I had to leave so suddenly. I got word from Mrs Reilly that I had to go to Italy. Rome. I hear you have been trying to get in touch with me. I am afraid I will be away for a while. God knows when I'll be back. Please don't wait for me. You will always remain in my heart, but I would suggest the only thing for it is for you to move on with your life. It's hard, but there you are. That's just the way it is. I would keep away from the Tivoli. I'd say Violet was right. It wasn't the place for a lady. I wish you good luck for the future, and happiness.

Yours Sincerely
Callum.

Her heart kicked at her ribs. There was something peculiar about this letter. It just didn't sound like him. And why didn't it have a Roman stamp on it? It should have confirmed all her fears, but it did the opposite. Was this Violet's work? Or Patrick's? There was something more going on. She had begun to think he had had only one reason for coming to find her in Liverpool, but now she wondered if there was more to it. How could he have changed from being so completely in love with her, to this? It didn't make sense. And if Violet had lied once, maybe she could lie again? Or Pat? If only Violet hadn't thrown the letters from Callum on the fire she could have compared the handwriting. There was something familiar about it, but how could she be sure it was his? He would probably have written with a meandering scrawl at best, not this graceful sloping script. No, this letter was not from Callum. He would never have said these things. Callum loved her. And that was the end of it.

Still smarting, she put the letter away. She would tell no one.

She fixed her eyes on the pale-green peeling wrought-iron work that curved up the sides of the shelter as she squirrelled the letter away. It was so disconcerting, this matter of Italy. Good God, what if I never see him again? What then? How could I go on? she asked herself. But then she stopped, determined to bring this sorry matter to a different conclusion to the obvious one. The tears began to pool in her eyes.

The sun, she noticed, was trying its best to break through the dead mist. Tiring of it all, of the whole sorry business, her gaze lifted towards the sea, then up to the grey sludge of sky. Fortune favours the brave, she murmured under her breath.

You'll come back, Callum. I don't believe you don't want me. You'll come back and find me. You will ...

When she got further down the hill, the fresh air, laced with hops from the nearby brewery, made her dizzy. Walking the length of the anonymous slab of concrete wall with broken bottles cemented into the top of it, she finally reached Joseph Street. Thoughts still raged through her head. The last thing she was going to do was look backwards instead of forward, run into the arms of some Johnny Gallagher, instead of marching on to happiness with Callum.

'Still no word? So where is he, then, this boy who loves you and wants to be with you forever?' called Violet as Babby put the key into the latch.

'Mam, stop!'

'He only wanted one thing. Teenage boys only want one thing – go and ask those poor, miserable girls at Saint Jude's,' Violet said. And she snorted, unbuttoned her cardigan, buttoned it again, and muttered something about making sure the door was on the latch, and went upstairs.

Babby watched her disappear. She felt rage seeping from every pore of her body. She could feel it now, igniting a spark, blood rushing savagely to her brain and bursting into flames, a conductor of resentment and bitterness, and she called after her mother, 'Why d'you have to ruin everything?'

Chapter Twenty-seven

Two months later

Perhaps her mother and Pat had been right, she thought. Weeks had passed and she had stayed away from the Tivvy and got a job at Linacre's Haberdashers store around the corner from TJ Hughes, but still she had had no word from Callum. And every night she would go to sleep and wake with dark shadows under her eyes, pale and drawn, a fist kneading her stomach, sadness gnawing at her, trying so hard to build a shell around herself – and failing. Mrs Reilly had confirmed to her mother that Callum was in Italy, yet she still didn't believe it. And it wasn't even the despair. She could cope with the despair. It was the hope that she couldn't cope with. That was so much worse. The hope that she still might find him and he would tell her it had all been a terrible mistake and he had come back to marry her and that they would live together forever. And it was this hope, this desperate hope, that was more important than ever. Because time was running out.

She woke with a start, her nightdress soaked in sweat and her hands twisting the pillowcase. The truth of what had been happening to her body over the past weeks seeped into her consciousness. She felt a tearing sensation and panic rise to her throat. It was the third time that week she had had this nightmare where she was sitting in the back field of the farm and was overtaken by a curious urge to run and run until, finally, she raced down to the beach and saw Callum, facing out to the sea. But when he turned, it was Johnny Gallagher who held his arms out to her and caught her as she sobbed. In her dream, she'd spun away from him, struggled to break free from his grasp, and then she awoke with a start, with the light bursting through the smeared pane of glass of the bedroom. A single tear rolled down her cheek. The dream always ended with Callum calling her name.

She lay still in the half-light. Hannah was still fast asleep on the small single put-you-up. Raising her head and squinting, she saw that dawn was breaking. Oh God, please let me go back to sleep, she prayed. It had been weeks since Callum had disappeared, her last image of him silhouetted against the white face of the Infirmary clock as he walked down the hill, and she had not heard from him since. She had written letters to Mrs Reilly, to pass on to him, but they had always been returned with the same note. *I'm afraid Callum had to go away to Italy unexpect-edly, I believe he has relatives there, but we have no forwarding address at present.*

She turned on to her right side and scrunched her knees up into her chest but that lasted only for a minute before she decided lying flat on her stomach might be better. Left leg bent? No, straight was more comfortable. Maybe it would be best if she were to lie on her back? Good idea. But now she didn't know where to put her arms. Fold them? It felt strange. What about rolling on to her right side to face the wall instead of the window? Now turn the pillow over to its cooler side. After a moment, it felt hot again, as though her cheek and hair might ignite. She bent her knees and put her head under tented sheets until she felt moisture dribbling from her armpits and down the side of her nose. Another look outside. Must be five o'clock. Oh God, oh God, oh God. Nothing worked. Not even singing or reciting the Rosary. And feeling exhausted but wide awake, she gave in to another hour of staring at the ceiling, listening to the pigeons and worrying that she might be pregnant. Really, she should have known better.

She had been told about the sanctity of marriage and communion with God, and husbands. The one thing that Sister Scholastica had taught her in biology lessons spent studying badly drawn diagrams, and on one occasion the pinned open and split carcass of a rabbit, was the intricacies of the reproductive organs. It had been weeks now since she had the Curse.

With her hands pressed on her stomach, desperately hoping for some twinge to signal that God had decided to answer her prayers, she tried to concentrate on the sensations, willing that sick feeling, or that of a huge hand rudely groping around in her belly, intermittently gripping, tearing and twisting bits of her knotted insides, pulling and dragging them downwards. Never had she wanted more the griping stomach pains, the backache. What was that? Something coming alive inside her, she thought, alert with hope. But it was only a tummy rumble and, much as she tried to convince herself it had a greater significance, the gurgle that followed suggested otherwise. No, this was certainly a feeling of life. But it was another kind of life. The sore and fulsome breasts, trying to hide the sound of retching from her mother every morning – this was a child growing inside her.

Half past six. The sun sneaked in a thin line of light from between the gap in the curtains. She got out of bed and padded her way to the outside lavatory. Just as she had done for the last three mornings, she knelt down, rested her elbows on the lavatory seat and prayed.

'Dear Jesus, I am so sorry about Callum. Please forgive me. Please don't punish me in this way. I promise I will never speak to Callum again. People would blame him and he's a good person, I'm sure. And what about everyone else who would get hurt? Please God, I know you work in mysterious ways but not this time, please. I will make it up to you. I swear on Mam's life ...' And screwing up her face with angst, she beat a fist against her heart and chanted rhythmically, 'Mea culpa, mea culpa, mea maxima culpa ...' until she became dizzy with the smell of the damp in the room and her own sweat. 'Oh God,' she cried softly, 'do something – won't you please do something?'

If only I could be practical about this, she thought, on the walk to her work at the haberdashers. She looked up at the huge poster on a wall. 'Bovril for All Meat Eaters' it said in five-foot tall letters with a picture of a roast chicken and a plume of hot steam rising from it. There was something disconcerting about it, but she didn't know what. Perhaps it was to do with her general state of mind, her nerves, or the collywobbles she was having, as Violet would describe them. Each time she thought about telling someone that she might be having a baby – anyone, Pat, maybe, or her Aunt Kathleen – she would gulp down air and her heart seemed to jump to her throat. Callum was the only one she wanted to tell; he would know what to do, surely? But perhaps it had been better that she hadn't seen him whilst she had got used to the idea herself. She needed to have her mind free of distractions, and the missing him feeling, a sort of permanent dull ache, had now been overtaken by a heightened anxiety.

She walked over the railway bridge that was a good mile away from Joseph Street as a train passed underneath. Enveloped in a cloud of steam, there was the smell of coal and grease and the sound of metal clanking and squealing wheels. She went down the other side of the road and on past the parade of shops that included a grocer, where she and Pat used to buy 'fades' – fruit that was on the turn but still perfectly edible – a butcher's that sold pig's trotters and liver, the pawnshop, a blacksmith's. There were a couple of shops that were beyond repair and boarded up because of the clearances, and a chemist's. Stopping outside a café, she caught sight of herself reflected in the shop's plate glass window and for a moment thought she saw a bulge just below the waistband of her dirndl skirt. In a panic, she smoothed her hands over her stomach. But she was too early on, of course she wasn't showing, it was only her blouse, bunched up and stuffed into the top of her underwear.

She remembered Johnny Gallagher talking about his cousin, Carmel. The same thing had happened with her, sixteen and in the club, and he had said it had broken her mother's heart. Carmel and her bog boy were married at nine o'clock at night, Carmel in her black mantilla, her mother's old navy-blue coat hiding her huge belly, with no one there to see. Shuffling in to Saint Mary the Virgin – that's a laugh, Johnny had said – the sounds of the church mice scuttling across the marble floor, embarrassed, because even they were that ashamed. Babby certainly didn't want that for her baby. The shame, the pointing and the laughing, and the 'Oh, Mrs Delaney, we're awful sorry what's happened to your Babby.'

Violet was going out tonight, going to Kathleen's for a stout and a gossip. The chemist shop's bell tinkled as Babby entered and she felt her cheeks stinging with embarrassment moments later as she asked in a quiet voice for a bottle of Epsom salts. The bottle of gin – mother's ruin – she didn't need to buy, as Violet had one already, sitting on the mantelpiece. She had heard horror stories of knitting needles and bent coat hangers, but she knew she didn't have it in her to go that far. She thrust the bottle into her hand-bag and carried on to work.

Creeping into the house that evening, she was sure Violet wouldn't be back until ten and Hannah, who had gone with her, would stay there until the morning. Patrick was going out dancing with Doris and he wouldn't be coming by tonight, so that was grand. It was her only chance to try this whilst the house was empty, and it was a chance that she was going to take. She took off her coat and hung it over the back of the chair. The light sloping in from out-side through a gap in the curtains fell across her cheek and she noticed, in the mirror above the man-telpiece, blotted by rust and time though it was, that the exhaustion of the huge effort of it all was begin-ning to show on her face. How could this happen to me? she said silently to herself, turning the words around in her mouth, repeating them, whilst hoping to God this was going to work.

On the stove, Babby placed two rusting pots and a kettle, to bring them to the boil. Soon the room was full of steam, with condensation running down the windows, and she began to sweat. She had placed the tin bath in front of the range. She wiped away the moisture on her top lip and dabbed at the necklace of perspiration that had appeared around her throat in glistening beads of sweat. Carefully, using a tea towel wrapped around the pan handle, she lifted the first pan off the stove and poured it into the tin bath, then did the same with the kettle. There was the bottle of gin, glinting in the flickering light of the fire. She had heard you had to drink the gin at the same time as you sat in the bath water as hot as you could bear it, but she decided to take a glug now for good measure. She poured in the second pan of water. It hissed and splashed as it gushed out and caused her to jump backwards and yelp.

She poured in the whole bottle of Epsom salts in one go and they fizzed as they hit the water. Probably it was the Epsom Salts, that was making her nose itch, and she found herself stifling a sneeze as she knelt at the side of the bath and stirred the water with a wooden spoon, waiting for it to cool sufficiently so that she could get into it. I'm terrified, she thought, and yet this is all I can think of right now. I can't sleep, and I'm constantly worrying: what will people think, will this hurt, will people somehow notice, what if this doesn't work? She had heard that if you punched yourself violently in the stomach, that worked as well, but she had tried and all it had done was make her feel sick. She took off her clothes and stood shivering on the linoleum floor. With the bottle of gin and a glass in hand, she dipped her toe in. The water was painfully hot, but there was no use in doing these things by half. It needed to burn like hell. She needed to 'shock the body into some kind of acute stress, causing a violent reaction in order to expel the baby'. She had read that somewhere, couldn't remember where, but the words were imprinted on her brain. Baby. She couldn't, *mustn't*, think of it as a baby. That way disaster lay. And yet … And yet … She had found herself thinking of names. Jennifer for a girl. Teddy for a boy. The gin made her feel woozy but she took another mouthful, then another, winced at the taste of it, slugging it down, straight out of the bottle.

Jesus, Mary, and Joseph save me … She climbed in, sank down slowly into the water with small screams, saw her pink flesh reddening, shivered with pain. The gin helped. She glugged down most of the rest of the bottle, making sure she had left just enough in the hope Violet wouldn't notice, wrapped the Epsom salts in her blouse to chuck away later, and lowered herself in further, pulled her knees to her chest. The Epsom salts felt gritty under her bare bottom. Shapes moved around the room and very quickly she became lightheaded. But within minutes the scalding hot feeling abated and she stretched out her legs, lolled back her head, and felt swathed in a warm liquid embrace. She was drunk, and soon overtaken by an overwhelming feeling of not caring about anything. Jennifer or Teddy, her baby, was still growing inside her, and no one was going to take that away from her. She was now actually enjoying it. Luxuriating in the warmth, instead of shivering in the grey, lukewarm second-hand sludge that she was used to. Clean, warm water. A sense that everything was going to be all right after all.

All she had to do now was find her Callum.

The following morning, Babby woke early.

'No.' The way Violet said it with a gleam in her eye, made Babby's knees buckle.

'Please,' said Babby. Violet was in the back yard pulling up weeds from the cracks in between the stone slabs. Babby regarded Violet's hunched back, watched her mother with her bare hands and a spoon, digging out the stinging nettles that had grown in a clump. Violet was not going to interrupt what she was doing for anybody. Babby yelped.

'I have to go. I have to go and see Mrs Reilly. I have to see the sisters. They still have some of my things.'

'Things?'

'My clothes. The vanity case. Stuff. I can get the boat to Anglesey and be back this evening.'

'Don't be so stupid. You can't go. You went to bed last night and left me to empty the bath. How lazy.

I'm furious, Babby. No. You're not going anywhere.'
The way she said it, so forcefully, as she yanked up
a thistle, made Babby let out the sound of a small,
wounded animal.

Try and stop me, she thought, I need to find out if
it's true that Callum is no longer at Pentraeth Farm.
And she quietly slipped outside into the street as
Violet sighed and called after her, 'You'll be back,
Babby!'

An hour later, Babby was walking towards the landing stage with her coat over her arm. She bought a
bottle of fizzy pop from a kiosk, wiped the top of it,
and took a glug. There was a calmness about her as
she fixed her eyes on the *Mersey Princess* coming in
to dock. She was scared but part of her had never felt
so determined in all her life. She could actually feel
the end of her nerves tingling. She watched as two
men on board threw ropes on to the landing stage,
which were caught by a younger man and wound
around the cleats. The passengers got off the boat
and, clutching her ticket, she walked down the gangway, briefly turning to look back at the Pier Head.
With the wind fanning her hair to reveal her high
forehead, it gave her a sharp thrill in the pit of her
stomach knowing she was going back to the farm.
She made her way on board and as the engines started

up, there was a humming and vibrating and rattling, of glasses and bottles, cups and saucers. She looked at the bleached-out photographs of cheerful sailors and elegant ocean liners hanging on the walls.

Then there was a hand under her elbow, the swish of cloth, and the flapping of swathes of black material coming upon her like a huge black crow. The glancing touch felt cold, unfeeling. The nun, wearing polished wooden rosary beads about her waist and with a set of keys that she jangled in her deep pocket, gave her a supercilious stare.

'You must be Babby,' she said, with a brief, smug smile. Babby's mouth gaped open. It was as if every muscle in her body had ceased to function, as if she was unable to summon up the energy in order to utter a single word.

The nun's eyes were small, triumphant puddles staring out from her face, encircled in the white coif and veil.

'Come with me, dear,' she said. 'The boat won't leave until you come with me ...'

Babby trembled. She shrank back against the wall, frozen, without a clue what to do next. The nun stepped forward, reached out, clutched her hand with her bony fingers – and Babby felt terrified. Despite what the nun was saying about wanting to help her, she felt sick with fear, and her thoughts

lurched to the refrain she had heard all her life. *Saint
Jude's. Saint Jude's. You'll end up in Saint Jude's,
Babby, you will, Babby.* Had she followed her? Had
she actually spied on her and followed her all the
way from her house? The nun's face grew knotty,
red and cross.

'All these people – you're holding them up,' she
said with a humph. 'Your mother said you would
make things difficult.'

The nun gripped her arm.

'Where are you taking me?' asked Babby. She
squirmed away, and stamped a foot. 'I won't go to
Saint Jude's!' she said suddenly, but then, as if all
the energy drained from her body, she let her arms
fall to her side. There was a silence. Babby wanted
to say something about how the nun couldn't make
her do anything she didn't want to, and Violet was
a coward for sending her instead of coming herself.
But she just couldn't. Couldn't find the strength to
get the words out.

'Saint Jude's? Don't be silly. I'm taking you home
to your mother.'

The air was heavy with an oppressive quiet. A
cold chill crept up her spine and, with it, a kind of
sickness rose to Babby's throat as her legs wobbled
underneath her. She gulped down great gasps of
breath and trembled with shock.

'No!' she cried.

'Don't make a fuss, dear,' said the nun. 'Violet said you would make a fuss, but it won't help anything.'

The nun walked over to one of the men who had thrown the rope from the boat. She murmured something in his ear. He nodded. It was as if Babby's frightened pale face was invisible to them all as the nun then took a minute to chat to him about the inclement weather and the swell of the tide. Finally, she went back to Babby.

'May God bless you and love you even in the overwhelming darkness,' the nun whispered in her ear, grasping her am tightly.

Babby felt her body go limp. She turned wearily, to see another nun, smiling and waving at her on the landing stage. A dull ache formed in her chest. Letting the sister take her by her sagging arm, her cheeks burned as every pair of eyes followed her down the gangway, on to the landing stage, and off towards the direction of home.

Chapter Twenty-eight

Babby stood in the doorway, her eyes red-rimmed and swollen with tears as she gnawed at the skin around her thumbnail.

Violet was sitting in the parlour, pushing and pulling a needle through a piece of linen.

'Don't say a single word,' Violet said, raising the palm of her hand to Babby when she came a step further into the room. 'I know everything. I know about the baby. How far gone are you? And who's the father? I'm assuming it's the boy Callum?' She leaped to her feet, threw down the needle and thread, and banged a fist on the table. 'Oh God, Babby, how could you have been so stupid? I'm glad your da is not here to see this. The shame of it!'

Babby could feel herself shaking.

'What have you got to say for yourself?'

'I don't know,' snivelled Babby. 'I don't know.' She felt sobs rising to her throat. 'If I could only find Callum—'

'Callum isn't going to get you out of this mess. He's gone,' said Violet sharply.

'Why did you send the sisters to find me? Why did you tell them?' She sounded in actual physical pain.

'I knew you wouldn't come back if I went after you,' said Violet. 'You don't listen to a word I say.'

'I don't believe you!'

Violet didn't reply. Instead, she stomped around the table and into the kitchen, reappearing with a bottle of cherry brandy.

'It's my nerves, Babby. Some days I can hardly drag myself out of bed. The sisters, they've got your best interests at heart. They seem so – so organised. Like they know what to do. About the situation. I can't think straight. I have no idea ...'

Babby took off her coat and slumped on to the chair.

Violet banged the bottle onto the kitchen table, and then threw her hands into the air exasperatedly. 'Look at you. You're so young. And so beautiful. You could have had anyone. But now? Pregnant!'

'How did you know?' Babby asked, defeated.

'I've probably known for weeks,' replied Violet. 'Look at you, your *bust*,' she said, waving a hand in her direction and turning down the corners of her mouth. 'No one else would know, but I'm your mother. And all the time drinking fizzy pop, cream soda bottles suddenly appearing from nowhere. And when I found the Epsom salts packet wrapped up in your blouse, the gin bottle nearly empty, the bath left with all the water in it ... It only confirmed what I'd dreaded along. But I just prayed it had worked so I didn't ask you about it. Oh Babby, who's going to have you now?'

'I only want Callum,' Babby said and sobbed, her knees buckling under her.

'That's not going to happen, sweetheart,' said Violet, softening. She patted the threadbare chaise longue. Babby collapsed on to it, crying. Violet allowed her to put her head into her lap, stroked her hair, pushed a piece of it behind her ear. 'Have a good cry, love,' she said.

'I'm sorry, Mam,' said Babby in between heaving sighs. 'I'm so sorry. I don't know how it happened ...'

'Well, I would have thought that would be obvious,' said Violet, dryly.

'Cal did – *does* love me!' she replied. How could she tell her mother that it was just that. Love. That's what had got her in this mess. Violet could never understand how exciting – and in turn, how desperate – that love had felt. When Callum had taken her in his arms that night at the hollas, there was nothing she could have done about it. She had felt so helpless. It was a wicked, wicked thing to do, a dreadful mistake, but the love had felt like iron manacles clasping her heart and that was all there was to it. She had *wanted* to make love to him, as much as he had to her.

'Oh, you stupid girl. Stupid stupid, girl. I love you. And we'll get through this together. But it's not going to be easy – we haven't got a carrot – so thank God for Johnny Gallagher.'

Babby started. 'Not him again. What's he got to do with anything? I'll not have anything to do with him—'

'Pat said he would have a word with his mum and dad.'

'*No*,' replied Babby, obdurate and immovable.

Violet sighed. 'Then it's only the nuns that can save you, love,' she said, with a look that Babby had never seen before, but recognised all that it contained.

Babby was desperate. She dropped to her knees. 'Mam,' she said, 'I just need to find Callum and everything will be OK ...'

Violet who was holding Babby's hands, her fingertips blue with fear, released them. 'This Callum isn't the answer. Don't be ridiculous,' replied Violet. 'Really, love, do I need to get a brick to knock some sense into you? Babby, do you have any idea what this is going to be like, bringing a baby into the world without a father? *I* know. I know what it's like to have mouths to feed, children with no shoes – and that's with them having a father. If suits were a penny, I couldn't afford a sleeve. Your dad standing there like all the other miserable wretches in the pen. Being passed over, another day of no work. I don't want that for you. And I certainly don't want that for your baby!'

'Callum's not like the men in the pens. Or them that drink at the Boot.'

At which point Violet's eyes flashed. 'I will not have that place mentioned in this house again. Do you know how much it hurts me, the thought of you standing there with your father's accordion, all those men leering at you, and catcalling?'

'Don't know what you're talking about.'

'Of course you do. You knew what you were doing all right. Probably playing up to it, just like your dad used to, running his hands through his hair and winking and flashing that grin. Doing the same, were you, Babby? You wouldn't be in this mess now if you hadn't gone sniffing around the Boot Inn.'

'Callum has got nothing to do with all that! I met him at the place you sent me away to so I'd be *safe*. Safe from what?'

Violet paused. It was as if she was going to say something, but couldn't.

'From myself?' asked Babby.

'Oh, don't be absurd. Sit up,' said Violet, her tone hardening. 'Stop feeling sorry for yourself now and stop sniffling. We have to be practical about this. I knew you would say no to Johnny Gallagher. But do you know what the alternative is?'

'Find Callum.'

'No! Isn't he in another country? How do you think you'll find him? No, the alternative is Saint Jude's.'

Babby's mouth fell open in horror.

'Saint Jude's?'

'Yes. The mother and baby home.'

'I know what Saint Jude's is! You've spent your whole life telling me about how awful it is! How cruel the nuns are. How some girls never even come home, just end up working there forever, or mad and alone probably, at the bottom of the road in the asylum. You'd really want me to go there?'

'I only said those things to keep you out of the wretched place. I'm sure it's not that bad. Now, I've organised for Father O'Casey to come here and talk to you. The priests and the nuns know how to manage these things because I'm damn sure I can't think what else to do ...' She exhaled a long breath, snapped angrily, 'I've tried so hard with you, Babby, but it's pointless. You never listen to me, you just charge on regardless, turning everything upside down, upsetting us all. And now look at the mess you're in.'

The thought of Father O'Casey and Sister Immaculata telling Babby what she should do with her baby, organising her life, just taking over as though she and, for that matter, Callum, had nothing to do with any of this, made her feel sick. With burning tears spilling on to her cheeks, she asked, 'What has any of this got to do with them?'

Violet struggled to her feet, thinking that if this Callum was here she would have clocked him one around the head. She steeled herself. 'I understand that this is your decision. And I know you're so young. But you've an old head on young shoulders so you ought to know that this is your only alternative.'

Babby listened as Violet talked on with humphs, and sighs, and wild hand gestures, saying how, even if they were to find Callum, even if he were to marry her, how would she know she would be happy?'

Babby couldn't make much sense of any of what she was saying. She suspected Violet could make no sense of it herself.

There was a long, protracted silence.

When Violet joined her on the sofa, Babby shuffled up to the other end.

'There are no other choices. You'll go to the home until you have the child. We're too poor to invent the European tour – no one would believe it. We'll just say you have a job in service.'

'European Tour? What's that?'

'Like Pauline did. Oh dear. Well, there's another secret out of the closet. The tour was about inventing a trip to Europe to explain why you've gone away so no one would know you were pregnant. Listen Babby, don't be naïve, you know as well as I do that having a child whilst you are unmarried would bring disgrace to us all. It would be such a shocking and awful thing to bring an illegitimate child into our family, none of us would ever recover from it ...'

'What about if I have the baby and you say it's yours?'

'Oh, love.'

'I can say the baby is my sister?'

In an instant, and judging by the look on Violet's face, she realised this was as absurd as a European tour. Violet was not a coper at the best of times and, of course, she wasn't married either. Babby drew in her breath as though she was about to say something more, but said nothing. Raising her thumb to her mouth and biting around the base of her nail, she shrank back into herself. Her mother had sadness etched out in every single line of her face, as though they had reached a conclusion on the matter and there was nothing more to discuss. But in Babby's mind there was one other choice.

She would go to the home. Have the child. And then she would run away and find Callum. One desperate notion ricocheted around her head after another. I have a baby growing inside me, she thought. And when he finds that out, he'll come and find me. And we will go back to Anglesey where we can live on a farm and grow fat tomatoes and keep chickens and ducks. And he will cherish the baby and me, and we will have six children and make a life together working in the sunshine. And when we have our family, and our lovely home, all this sadness will be forgotten, and we will refuse to feel shame, because our future will be built on love, and Mam will be proud of us. Surely this was possible? Wasn't it?

Chapter Twenty-nine

The next two weeks passed in a blur. It was decided that Saint Jude's – or Saint Jude's Home for Fallen Women, which was its grim moniker – was the best place for Babby, at least until she had her baby. It wasn't due for another six months, but she couldn't be trusted to stay at home without running off and the nuns often had girls who came to the home this early, as they were useful. 'You don't get anything for nothing, Babby. We should be grateful. What's a few months' work? That's what they said.'

A date was set and Violet trailed around after her as the day approached, as if she knew Babby would bolt if she let her out of her sight and she might never see her again. Babby cried until she had no tears left, but it was Callum she was crying for, as well as her baby.

'Thank goodness we have found a solution to the little problem,' Babby heard old Father

O'Casey say through the crack in the door of the best room.

'Well, Father, it's like a weight lifting off my shoulders ...' said Violet.

Babby shuddered. Why was he making it sound so easy? As if she would just go away to Saint Jude's and the lovely nuns would take care of her until she had the wee one and then she would come back home and that would be grand. And the baby would go to a nice family and a gorgeous woman who had been crying for years. Johnny might even still want her back, you know, if it was all taken care of. But I don't want Johnny, Babby wailed silently. It's Callum I want!

The night before it was arranged they would go to the home, as the sun set over the Mersey and the vast sky turned pink to purple, Violet put her to bed early with a hot toddy and a glass of warm milk and told her she loved her. It wasn't what Babby expected. She'd expected more recriminations, tension, probably a beating around the head.

For the past couple of days, what Violet mostly looked was sad. And disappointed. During the night Babby was sure she had heard the sound of Violet crying through the walls, but when she got up she found her mother had tidied herself up, done her make-up to disguise her puffy eyes, dressed herself in a paisley frock with a wide yellow patent leather belt, and was smoking a Players N°6 at the kitchen table.

So then, thought Babby as she watched her sucking on the cigarette, now they had to concentrate on what would happen next, rather than fret about what had gone on before. There was no big plan. But at least, she thought, it might buy her some time with finding Callum and keep Violet happy. At least at Saint Jude's she might be able to think what to do.

She followed her mother down the path, and they ducked under the gap in the fence that now surrounded the hollas and, taking the short cut to the tram, clambering through the hole and across the piece of wasteland, they made their way to Sandhills station. Babby was still an expert at dodging ticket collectors, on how to jump off the train and dart into the waiting room or hide in the ladies loo in order to get through the barrier without having to buy a ticket, but no such nonsense would be happening this morning, Violet said.

When they got on to the train they sat silently, staring out of the window, lulled by the somnambulant rhythm as it rocked on its tracks. It was hard to think of what to say to one another. They were lucky enough to find an empty compartment with two rows of seats, the material on the bald covers rising up in tufts. Babby fixed her gaze on the leather loops of the ceiling straps swinging in tandem as the train chuffed on. After a short while, without thinking, Babby took the opportunity to put her feet on the seats, though Violet told her not to, slapped her shins, and said she was leaving dusty footprints all over the place. 'Besides, the last thing we want to do is draw attention to ourselves,' she said. Babby grumpily complied, squashing up beside her mother and pulling down the window, letting the air rush into the carriage.

'Babby ...' said Violet.

Babby, with legs slung over the armrest of the seat and chewing a thumbnail, sighed. 'What?'

'The more I think about it, the more I think you are doing the right thing,' her mother said.

'Why's that, then?' said Babby.

'I want you to have a life. The truth is, I don't want you to marry someone you hardly know, not even Johnny. I really don't. Or to be a mother, a child, Babby, struggling on your own. I want you to have a future.'

'Oh, I see. So, you're sending me here so I can be happy?' said Babby, caustically.

'In a way, yes,' answered Violet. 'Eventually, I mean ... I know it's hard for you to see that now. Oh, love. Don't you think you can make a fist of it?'

Babby took out the handkerchief that she had stuffed into her pocket, and dabbed her eyes. 'No, Mam, I can't *make a fist of it*. You know why? Because there's guilt and there's shame, isn't there? With shame, you need the world in order to tell you to curl up and die. That's when you want the ground to open up and swallow you, but if the world isn't there to watch you do the terrible thing, you can't have shame, can you? If I give away this baby, who would even know?'

'Oh Babby ...'

'Not even Hannah knows. But Mam, what if I feel *guilty*? Guilt is when your conscience tells you not to do something because in your heart you know it's wrong. And I will have that forever. Maybe not the shame. But I will have guilt and I think the guilt is worse. Sod it! I – I ...'

'Don't curse!' cried Violet.

'Sod it,' repeated Babby. She liked the sound of the swear word. You could tell by the way she spat it out and looked at Violet with her chin jutting out, as if challenging her to tell her to stop. She didn't care who might hear in the next compartment and she tutted when Violet grabbed the metal frame of the window and pushed it shut.

'Babby!'

'I'm not sure I will stand it,' wailed Babby. 'I don't think they are being kind and I don't like what's happening to me.' She punched her fist in her stomach and Violet gasped. 'But I don't want them to have my baby.'

'Babby ...' Violet said, appalled that her daughter might be about to change her mind and jump off the train right that minute.

'You're ashamed of me,' said Babby. 'That's all ...' Pressing her fists in her eyes to stem the flow of tears, she let out a low moan.

'I don't want you to go through what I've been through. These last years without your father have been the hardest years of my life. Bringing up a child on your own is so difficult ... you can't imagine how lonely it is, love, and so hard without a proper wage coming into the house, pin money is just not enough to raise a family. I'm not ashamed of you, I never will be, but the world will turn its back on you and I don't want that for you,' said Violet, reaching out a hand and placing it on Babby's knee.

Babby tutted, then pleaded, 'But I won't be on my own if I find Callum. I've got to find him. Can't we just wait until we find him? We need to know it's true that he's not coming back before we do anything. If we don't find him, then we can properly investigate. Get a detective, maybe. Do they have detectives for these things?'

'Ridiculous notion,' said Violet prompting a groan from Babby. 'Of course, we're not going to get a detective.'

'Sod this,' said Babby.

Violet gasped. 'You can't keep saying that! And on a train!'

'I just did,' replied Babby.

'What if people in the next compartment heard you? Or the ticket collector might walk past?'

'There's no one on this train except us. Pat might know how to find Callum.'

'Even if he did, how exactly do you think that would help things? He knows nothing about this ... situation. It would just make him upset,' Violet said. Her fingers flickered over Babby's for a moment before she committed herself to the gesture and squeezed lightly.

Babby pursed her lips and snatched her hand away. 'Or he might do something to help us. And I don't mean marrying me off to Johnny Gallagher.'

'Please stop going on about your brother ... he's worried about you. You're his sister. Brothers always think they know what's best.'

There was a silence. 'You look nice,' Violet said, changing the subject suddenly. Babby tutted. She regretted the outfit, but it was the only thing she had been able to find that fitted her, an old flounced tea dress of Violet's made from a Butterick pattern that she had discovered in the bottom of the wardrobe under a layer of tissue paper. The frilled bodice disguised her full breasts, but her curves made it ride up her smooth thighs and she thought she looked like one of the dock road prozzies. She didn't respond and Violet grew angry again. 'Look Babby, like I said. This is the only place for you for now—'

'And Callum? Finding him.'

'How on earth are we going to find Callum? It's impossible – *you're* impossible. Even if we did know, would we just walk up to his house, knock on the door and ask him, come home? Marry Babby? You read his letters.'

Babby sighed. 'We can go to the port. I bet they have a list of all the English people who boarded ships bound for Italy. I bet they have names and everything. Great big books of names. I could ring them. Tell them I'm coming.'

'No!' Violet shouted. 'Stop talking so daft. What's wrong with you?' she asked, putting her head in her hands and pressing her temples.

'*What's wrong with me?*' echoed Babby, thinking that she had no real idea where Callum was, that she hated it that Violet didn't seem to be able to stop drinking despite her sporadic announcements of abstinence, that she felt sick all the time – and her mother was asking what was wrong with her. It was laughable.

Babby sighed again. She saw the desolation in her mother's face and Violet, in turn, saw Babby desperately hoping that finding Callum and having this baby might be the answer to all her problems. She went into her pocket and brought out a handkerchief, offered it to Babby who had begun to sniffle again.

'Babby, I only want what is the best for you. I always have,' she said.

But Babby decided that, given the present circumstances, Violet was not to be trusted.

Finally, after passing three stations adorned with hanging basket flower arrangements – that was when you knew you had truly left the city of Liverpool behind – then chugging on through the sand dunes stretching towards the stick-like pinewoods, past the rifle range and the gun site with the sound of shots popping in the distance, past the Victorian red-brick power station looming out of the marshes, beyond the sewage works with the pungent smells that forced themselves even through the closed windows, they reached Waterloo and then Freshdale. Remembering Pauline's little house and Saint Hilda's, Babby thought back wistfully to a less eventful time in her life. How unhappy she thought she had been then. And now this. They had reached their stop. Not even the ticket collectors bothered to turn up here, it was so quiet.

'Come on, love. You must just see this as part of life's journey.'

'But I want the baby and Callum to be part of the journey.'

A sob rose to her throat.

Violet put down her bag. She hugged her, pushed a piece of hair behind Babby's ear, allowed her hand to rest on her cheek.

Babby continued, 'And if I give the baby away to the nuns? Will I never see it ... him, her ... again?'

'That's generally how it works.'

Babby began to tremble. Clacking their rosary beads all the way to hell, she thought. Her mother had said this once, and she knew now that she was right.

Violet took her hand and Babby heard her swallow in her throat. 'I don't want people talking about you, love. Your bump will begin to show soon and I don't want them talking the way they talk about me – oh, I know they do. People can be cruel. I want them to think of you as a good girl. We can make this problem go away. We should be grateful for the sisters who have said they will help. It's best Callum doesn't know.'

Babby shifted from one foot to another.

'You're different to me. You're talented and bright as a button. You can be better than me. Is that too much for a mother to ask? Isn't that would any mother would want?' said Violet.

The train disappeared, towards where it would eventually reach the end of the line at Southport with its beaches that never saw the tide come in and the pier stranded ignominiously on its spindly seaweed- and barnacle-encrusted legs, from where the train would then head back towards Liverpool and the docks. A forlorn Violet and Babby stood for a moment, gazing up and down the platform aimlessly. Babby was carrying a heavy carpet bag which contained a few changes of clothes, a nightdress, spare shoes, and a toothbrush.

They looked at the scrawled map that Babby had made before they left and set off down Virgin's Lane – that's a joke, thought Babby, darkly – walking as fast as they could past the mansions and nursing homes, past Saint Sylvester's orphanage – Saint Sillys as it was known, though there was nothing silly about that place – and eventually reaching the building looming up out of the scraggly pinewoods at the bottom of a potholed road that led to the beach. Saint Jude's – a draughty, leaky Edwardian mansion, with its mock Gothic turrets, gables, and vaulted windows. A thought came to Babby that she puzzled over. She had a memory once of coming here with her Aunty Pauline and her father, delivering wilting flowers and teddy bears from a child's funeral to the nuns. Babby said nothing to her mother but she wondered, what would her father have thought of this? Kathleen? Pat? How big a secret was it? It occurred to her, had Violet lied earlier on the train when she said he knew nothing about this? Did he have any part in sending her here? She was certain her brother loved her, just as she did him, but did he really think this was for the best? Surely not if he could see this place. She kept the thought to herself.

All this was running through her mind as they approached the building that was set off the road with a rose garden laid out in circular beds, a large pram in the front porch, and a red-painted door with a brass knocker. Babby clutched her mother's hand and Violet, for once, looked scared.

'I want to go home. Please don't leave me here, Mam,' Babby hissed, as the gate clanged behind her. She worried that the noise may have alerted the nuns to their arrival. 'Please don't.'

'Oh love, chin up ...'

'I don't like it here!' said Babby, grabbing on to Violet's sleeve. She felt she was going to cry. Then suddenly, she gasped. 'Look,' she said, hopping from foot to foot. Beyond the hollyhocks which grew in clumps on the edges of the front lawn, she pointed past the low wall, past the stone fountain, past the cement crucifix. None of these registered. She was pointing at the statue of Saint Theresa of Lisieux, stuck into the ground at an angle, a stone bench beside it. It was exactly the same one as at Saint Hilda's. A tremor jolted through Babby's body like electricity. She yanked Violet towards her.

'Please don't make me! That's a bad sign. It's the same statue as Saint Hilda's and the nuns at Saint Hilda's were *horrible*.' She was twisting the belt of her dress, winding it tightly around a purpling finger.

'What do you mean? I can't see a statue.'

'Behind the hollyhocks. You can't miss her. She's got a stump for a hand ...'

'Don't be foolish,' said Violet.

Babby couldn't stop herself from walking across the lawn towards it. She stood before it and shuddered. That settled it. Saint Jude's was a bad idea. And she had to think of a plan.

Chapter Thirty

An hour later, they were sitting in Sister Agnes's office drinking weak tea with grey sludge on the surface and clinging to the sides of the cup, and trying to avoid staring at the small carving of Jesus whose legs were buckling under the weight of a crucifix, next to the plate of garibaldi biscuits. Babby cast her eyes round, glancing into the corridor through a door that had been left slightly ajar, darting from the Child of Prague on the mantelpiece to another of Jesus proudly displaying his weeping wounds in an alcove; from the obligatory framed print of the Last Supper on the wall, to an empty holy water font nailed beside the door. Violet tried to settle into an old suite made of brown corduroy, hidden by loose covers of flowery stretch nylon, some of which had slipped off at the corners and curled up around the edges, showing frayed brown patches underneath. There was a three-bar electric fire with moulded plastic logs and living-flame effect provided by an orange light bulb, quite the modern thing, a nest of teak tables, a chrome drinks trolley with an empty bottle of milk on it, two more small crucifixes and a tatty bookcase groaning with hymnals, Bibles, prayer books, and copies of the *National Geographic* magazine. An ornate wooden wireless was tucked away into the corner.

'Now, child, there's no need for you to tell us why you're here. We have been through this with your mother. You understand what will happen? We will take care of you and you will help us with the domestic chores until your time, and we will arrange for your baby to be adopted. Despite what you might have heard, the babies from Saint Jude's go to loving homes and will have a much better future than you can offer. You understand that, child?'

Father O'Casey, who was also present, had already come to the house and talked and talked about God looking after Babby and cherishing her child, saying that this was a gift and her burden would leave her exalted, so she didn't want to go into that again, and she just nodded briefly. Violet gave a tight, worried smile.

'So, all we need you to do is sign these forms.' Sister Agnes pushed papers and a pen across the table to her. Babby hesitated, looked to her mother for reassurance.

'Go on, love,' said Violet. 'It's just a formality.'

Babby took the pen with a quivering hand, considered flinging it across the room, but instead wrote with spidery, sloping words, her name, age, and address. Sister Agnes told Violet, gently, that she should probably leave. She said that there should be no contact for three weeks so that Babby could get herself into some kind of routine. When Violet began to cry and blame herself for what had happened, Sister Agnes told her that, as so often in these case, she felt that the fault lay at the door of the young man and that Violet was being too hard on herself; she wasn't to blame for this and should direct her rage at this Callum boy. It didn't help much. Violet sat there weeping, mumbling that if it hadn't been for Jack's death this wouldn't have happened. The nun asked, 'Who's Jack?' but Violet just shook her head and cried some more.

'Now, now,' said the nun. 'We know how lively Babby is, bit of a flibbertygibbet.' And Father O'Casey smiled and said that was about right, and Violet added again that if Jack had been here they wouldn't be in this mess. He would have known what to do. Violet sniffed and decided Sister Agnes was a good woman. From where she was standing, anyhow. Babby, though, was angry and frightened and longing for Violet to take her home.

Violet exchanged a tearful goodbye with Babby and promised she would visit her in three weeks. Everyone agreed it was for the best. Biscuits had been eaten, tea drunk – at least by the sister and Father O'Casey – and now it was up to Babby to make the best of it.

'We need you to take off your clothes and wash in the bathroom down the corridor. Follow me,' said a nun, who came into the room the minute Violet left.

'Yes, Sister,' replied Babby.

They set off up a flight of stairs and along a corridor. The nun opened a door at the end of it. There was a sink and a bath full of cold, used water with a skein of grease on it. Babby shivered at the thought of it clinging to her skin and getting under her nails and between her toes. More alarmingly, the bath had a lid on it, a wooden board with hinges in the middle. It was folded back in half but the nun told her she should fold it over so it covered her, with just her head and shoulders poking out from the end, presumably so no one could see her naked when she washed, or indeed so she wouldn't see herself, and be distracted by lustful or narcissistic thoughts. Babby, however, suspected some of those nuns liked a good look – and by the way the nun lingered at the door and watched her undress, she was probably right.

Ten minutes later, when she had lowered herself into the cold bath, the door was flung open and Sister Agnes stood there with a freezing pail of water, ready to pour it over her head.

'Deep breath,' she said. She came towards her and Babby felt the ice-cold water splashing against her back as the nun tipped the bucket. It was so cold it felt like shards of glass sticking into her flesh.

'Don't make a fuss, dear,' said the nun. 'Now, out you get.'

She stood against the door and watched Babby as she got out of the bath, water dripping from her body as she stood on the stone floor.

'Here,' she said, giving her a shift dress, and told her to dry herself with a thin piece of fraying linen, and dress.

After that she was led to the dining room, where she sat on her own at the end of a long table, and had soup which was also grey and cold, like the bathwater, and bread that was stale and tinged blue around the edges. From there the nun took her down yet another long corridor, but not before she took her into an alcove and made her get on her knees in front of the statue of Our Lady and pray for forgiveness. 'Mea culpa, mea culpa, mea maxima culpa,' she said, instructing Babby to beat her chest, watching over her and wondering why she wasn't crying for her sins.

Father O'Casey might have been kind, Sister Agnes stern, but Sister Benigna had cold fish eyes and a mean mouth, and a look so fierce it seemed she could strike the fear of God into you with one glance.

'What's your name?' she asked, joining Sister Agnes at the alcove.

'Babby.'

'What kind of a name is that? That's not one of God's names. Where in the Holy Bible is Saint Babby? Anyway, in here we don't use real names. You will be called Marie until you leave.'

From a door at the end of the corridor that squeaked open, she heard one of the girls that she hadn't yet met, but knew were in the dormitories where she would be sleeping that night, sniggering. Were they laughing at her?

'Babby's not my real name,' she said. She was sure that the nun could sense the waves of fear that shuddered through her body.

'Not my real name, *Sister.* Show some respect, girl. Now, Saint Ursula. One of the Holy Virgins. She bore the world's sin on her shoulders and she never complained. Indeed, she got her head chopped off for it. That's the thanks she got.

Wasn't going to let any filthy man's hands stain her virgin soul.'

'Yes, sister.'

'If we could all be like Saint Ursula ... You know, Saint Ursula was mortal. But she resisted the temptations of the flesh. You're not born a saint, you become one, do you understand?'

'You mean I could become a saint?'

'Don't be idiotic, girl. *You!* You're a little whore!'

Babby flinched at the word. It was hurtful and cruel and she knew then it would always sadden her to hear it because she would remember this moment. That was the first time Sister Benigna cursed her. And Babby, hard and determined, decided it would be the last.

The dormitories were long, draughty rooms with about twenty beds in each. Some of the girls were heavily pregnant, some not showing, like Babby. Their hunched bodies were covered with thin sheets. There was a skylight, and windows that had ill-fitting frames and rattled when the wind blew. The noise was terrible. Groaning, coughing, but mostly sighing and sniffling. Feeling as alone as she had ever been in her life, Babby fell asleep that night at nine thirty, mostly because she was exhausted. But an hour later, at ten thirty, she was woken by a clanging bell.

'Chapel,' said the girl in the bed next to hers.

'At this time?' asked Babby. 'I'm half asleep.'

The girl turned. A slice of light fell on her and it was the long red curtains of limp hair that Baby recognised first. She gasped. 'Frying Pan!'

'Oh my God! Is it Babby? From Saint Hilda's?'

'Yes! What are you doing here?' asked Babby.

'Same as you, most likely,' said Frying Pan.

Babby smiled. Frying Pan was grinning. 'Couple of eejits, us two. Getting knocked up,' she said, indicating her heavily pregnant stomach.

Babby nodded.

'What happened to your fella? Couldn't get him to marry you?'

'Something like that,' answered Babby, sadly. 'And you? When did you get married?' she said, indicating the ring on Frying Pan's finger.

'This, love? This is from Woolies. The nuns make us wear wedding rings. They might give you a curtain ring if there's not enough to go round. No, my fella was married already. Though he does still love me and we will get married one day. Just the bloody baby that's the problem. Don't get me wrong, sure and I would love this baby – just me and Declan have a bigger love. The Cause. Ireland. One Ireland. You know what I mean, Babby?'

'Yes,' replied Babby, not quite sure, but supposing it was something to do with her being Irish.

'Bloody hell hole, this place. Makes Hilda's seem like a holiday camp. It's the praying that gets you down. Not only prayers at the beginning and end of each chore, the laundry, peeling the potatoes, the coal sacks – and there are at least ten chores a day, so that makes twenty novenas, plus the Angelus and grace and Holy Intentions. But the list goes on if it's say also the month of the Sacred Heart. And there are so many feast days and saints days – Saint Anthony of Padua, Saint Boniface, the First Martyrs of the See of Rome – and any excuse to get us pure means these Masses seem to take place every week. It's a wonder we don't all top ourselves.'

'Frying Pan, what's your real name?' asked Babby. 'You told me once, but I can't remember.'

'Mary,' she replied. 'But the nuns said I had to use me confirmation name. You'll have to have a new name an' all. In here, I'm Theresa.'

'I'll call you Mary. I'm supposed to be Marie.'

'Well, I'll call you Babby, so I will.'

Babby would find out later that night about Mary's big love – and her lover. In the meantime, she put her feet into her slippers and followed another girl out. Collette was her name, she told her, and they walked in file to the small chapel off the corridor with statues of Jesus pointing at his bleeding heart, genuflecting at each of the Virgin Mary images in the alcoves. When they entered the chapel, the warmth hit Babby – a carefully designed conceit to make the place seem more welcoming than the draughty dormitories and cold corridors. In one of the pews an old nun sat weaving a pair of rosary beads through her fingers. Babby was told to sit next to her and she could hear her lisping her Hail Marys. 'Blessed is the fruit of thy womb, Jesus. Holy Mary, Mother of God ...' There was a general shuffling and shoving and sniffling as they took their places in the pews.

She knelt to receive communion at the altar rail. Saint Jude's chapel was gloomily painted with the same pre-war cream hospital gloss paint as the dormitories. Maybe a miracle will happen, thought Babby. But, like a cloud blotting out the sun, she sank into gloomy despair again and realised she would have to do without the help of miracles. Copying the other girls by joining her hands and resting her elbows on the polished brass altar rail, after a short poke in the ribs by the girl next to her telling her she had to take communion, she screwed up her eyes and wondered how on earth she was going to get out of this place. With her bare knees going numb against the cold marble slab, she noticed how pregnant some of the other girls were. How long had they been here? Three months? Two months? Did they ever leave? One of them had a strange tic: it seemed she was measuring and re-measuring the hem of her shift dress, making sure it was touching the floor, just how the nuns liked it.

'What's the matter with her?' Babby asked Mary.

'Been here too long,' she whispered. 'They took her baby away. Babies, actually. Twins. Now she's gone round the bend and they don't know what to do with her. Her mam and dad won't have her back, but she's good for the laundry here. Probably she'll end up down the road in the loony bin.'

'The Body of Christ,' said Father Dwyer, who was saying Mass. When he placed the host on Babby's pink tongue, poking out between her white teeth, she looked up at him with doleful brown eyes. He put his hand on her head, said nothing. She tried to swallow the wafer-thin host, but found it had glued itself to the roof of her mouth, forcing her to try and peel it off with the tip of her tongue. Eating the consecrated bread had always panicked her. She had often wondered whether Jesus would feel little stabs of pain if she were to grind it between her teeth. Was this why the nuns at Saint Hilda's had told them it was a sin to chew holy communion? Trying to concentrate on good things: Callum's kisses and the way his black hair fell into his eyes when he laughed; Hannah; her piano accordion; the way it felt when the blood rushed through her body and breath filled her lungs when she sang – all this came flashing into her head and yet she still hadn't managed to swallow the Corpus Christi. In the moment that should have been reserved most for God, her thoughts had leapt to worldly matters. If Jesus had hidden depths, I have hidden shallows, she said to herself. Trying to put all this aside, she decided to plot how she would escape from this place. And it wouldn't be a moment too soon.

'Saint Jude. Let him pray for us,' said Father Dwyer. The patron Saint of Lost Causes must be getting an awful lot of intentions from these girls, thought Babby, darkly.

After Mass, they trooped out. Following on behind, Sister Benigna, clutching her rosary beads to her chest, had one of her mean looks on her face – a look so sharp that you could have cut ice with it. Meanwhile, the organ, played by a small birdlike nun, started up, a droning, miserable version of 'Praise to the Holiest'. Babby looked around at the glum faces. Well, at least this was one thing she could do something about; and with a burst of renewed energy, she lifted her face and began to sing her heart out. If there was one thing she could do, it was use her voice to try and drown out all the snivelling and sadness that lashed at this place.

'Praise to The Holiest in the Heights!' she sang gustily, beaming. The sister's head turned, a frown etched into her face. Babby's voice was loud and clear and pure.

'Sure, you sing like an angel, Babby,' said Collette, lying in the bed next to her, later that night. She had curly red hair like snakes wriggling down her back, and skin so white you could see her blue veins. 'Know any songs from the hit parade?'

'How about this?' replied Babby. She started singing. 'Zigger Zagger, Zigger Zagger, Ooh ooh ooh, what you do to me when I'm feelin' blue, Zigger Zagger, Zigger Zagger, hold me tight, baby I love you.'

'Louder, Babby,' said another voice in the dark.

Babby sang out, her voice loud and full of happiness. She clicked her fingers in time.

'Sure, that'll stop us girls crying, if you could do that every night Babby ...' said Collette. She began to sing along and then the girl beside her joined in, then the one in the opposite bed, and then a few others until they were all singing with her, clicking fingers, rapping the bed frames, together in the dark.

The door opened. And then Benigna came in, standing there, her hand on the doorjamb, foot in the room, body out. 'Did I hear singing?' she asked.

'Yes, sister …' replied Babby. 'Hymns. Raisin' our voices in prayer, that's all.'

The door closed. A guffaw erupted.

'Three cheers for Babby!' shouted Mary. 'Hip, hip, hooray!' And their voices echoed around the dormitory and ricocheted off the walls in a chorus of defiance, united in their love, clinging to a raft of hope. 'Hip, hip, hooray!'

Finally, after a day of exhaustion from the praying, the laundry, the tears, the sheer sleep-sapping energy drain that came with most of them being at least five months pregnant, an hour later most were asleep. There were occasional sounds of the sniffling in the dark, but mostly it had become quiet.

Babby was trying to nod off. She and Mary talked long into the night about Saint Hilda's, about Callum and their mothers. Babby's bed was pushed up against the wall and there was a window above her. Suddenly there was a noise, and then, through the small window above, a pair of feet appeared. Then legs. Big, hairy man legs.

'Jesus Mary and Joseph!' cried Babby.

The man wriggled his body through the gap, then jumped down, stood beside her bed, put his hand over her mouth. 'Not a word if you want to help the cause,' he said in a thick Irish accent.

Babby could smell him. A man smell, dirty boots, beer, and cigarettes. Terrified, she lay with her eyes bulging out of their sockets, trembling.

'Shush,' said Mary. 'Be quiet and I'll explain later.'

Babby watched as the man went over to Mary's bed. They were talking. Plotting. You could hear it in their whispers. He made a salute to her, held up his fist, then he lay on top of her, hands straight up her nightie, kissed her, with Babby gaping and the other girls, those who were still half awake and used to it, probably, turning their heads away from him. And then he got under the covers and kissed Mary again, right there in the dormitory, Mary moaning and him groaning. With Sister Agnes padding up the corridor saying her novenas for their sinful souls and the starving in Africa. God knows what was going on between the two of them, but whatever it was, it was all over in five minutes. And he was back through the window, saluting as he went. 'One Ireland, one cause.'

'This is life,' whispered Mary. 'The very best and the very worst of it.'

And Babby had to agree with her.

The following day, on the way to chapel yet again, Babby met Collette properly. She told Babby she had three kids.

'I'm one of the homeless girls who get to keep their bairns because no one wanted them,' she explained. 'They were too old, see. Snotty-nosed toddlers and boys and lasses that kick and curse and scream like the devil. They only want fresh pink babbies. Me and my pals are in a different dormitory but they moved me here because I'm near my time.'

Apparently, if it were possible, the other dormitory was worse than Babby's.

'The nuns send us out at seven in the morning to find jobs, with our kiddies, can you believe it? We're not allowed back to the Mother and Baby Home until five thirty at night ... When we get back, they leave us outside, little 'uns as well. Doesn't matter if it's freezing cold or pelting it down, they won't let us in a minute earlier than half past. Even stare at us from the windows, checking their watches before they open the gates!'

'You're joking?' said a wide-eyed Babby.

'I am not. All day I'm tramping the streets of Southport looking for food, or shelter, or a job – it's a crime, so it is.'

That afternoon, when Collette had left with her kids, Babby was called by Sister Benigna and sent to the dormitory to change the sheets on the beds. She was handed a pile of lovely clean crisp white sheets that smelled of fresh air. Collette and the girls would be delighted, she thought, when they came back. But then, two hours later when Babby was peeling potatoes, she was called again by Sister Benigna.

'Monsignor's gone. He's done the dormitory rounds. Take the sheets off that you just put on.'

'You mean I have to put the filthy ripped rags back on the beds?'

'Yours is not to question why.'

When Collette returned, Babby said to her it wasn't right. None of it was.

'What can you do?' replied Colette, with a shrug of the shoulders and a sigh.

'Tell Agnes that she's wrong to treat you like this,' replied Babby.

'I can't do that!' said Collette.

'Why not?'

'Why not? Look Babby, you have to understand how this works. When they say they only have our best interests at heart, they're lying. You know how we know they're lying? Because their lips are moving. We all know this, knew it from the minute we stepped in this place. Just like you. But we have no choice because they are the only ones who will have us. They'll either take your baby, like you, and then you'll be free to live your life. Or they'll give you a roof over your head, like me, whilst I get back on me feet. Who would have me and my kiddies? Me mam has chucked me out, won't have anything to do with me since I got knocked up by Charlie, the fella who brings the coal. But why wouldn't I have had Charlie? My husband used to beat me black and blue. Charlie brought me some comfort. But now? Well, it's only the sisters who'll give me a bed. I hate them. I really, really *hate* them, and they're going to take this kiddie when I have him. I know that. But what else can I do?'

'Oh God, Collette. We're on this track and we can't get off. There has to be another way.'

'See this?' said Collette. She took a ring from her pocket. 'Curtain ring. Not even a ring from Woolies. The nuns make me put it on when I go out. In case anyone notices that I'm showing. And they make us wear these awful duffle coats to hide our bumps, horrible shapeless things. Even in the summer. It's hideous.'

'That settles it,' said Babby. 'The next chance I have, I'm going to say something to the old batey-faced witch, you see if I don't.'

And three days later, she did.

'Yes, girl. What is it?' asked the nun, when she answered the door of her office to Babby.

Someone should have warned Babby. As she stepped into the room, she couldn't take her eyes off the walls. They were covered with giant insects. Varnished beetles, huge colourful butterflies, scorpions, and ants with legs as big as a boy's fingers. Some were in glass frames, others were pinned on to velvet-covered jewellery pads. Babby supposed the first time you saw them was a kind of a test. The first time must always come as a bit of a shock.

'The sisters brought them back from the Missions in Malaysia – bet you've never seen a spider as big as that hairy ugly beggar, have you? Don't be scared,' she said and laughed. 'The girls like them. They fight to come into my office and have a look.'

'It's wrong what you're doing here, with the girls!'

Sister Benigna's mouth gaped open. The cheek of the little slut!

'Who says? You? What would you know about right or wrong? You don't deserve that thing in your belly! Not another word. Go. You're nothing but trouble. We know about the music. The singing. The pop music. Zigger Zagger. You little Jezebel! Singing and mooning around with the devil's tunes. Just like a *Delaney*. And, you know, you're supposed to go to chapel each morning and each evening. Don't think we haven't noticed you have barely been at

all. And why aren't you wearing a wedding ring?!'
She pulled open the drawer of her desk, rooted
about, and slammed a tarnished Woolworth's ring
on the table. 'Put that on. Now get out of my sight.
Fifty Hail Marys and confession. I'll deal with your
proper punishment tomorrow.'

Chapter Thirty-one

She was leaving Saint Jude's Mother and Baby Home. She had decided. And she was never going back. That's what she told herself as she shook Mary awake. Mary stirred, rolled on to her back with her arm covering her face. 'Jaysus, I'm asleep. Trying to get some kip before chapel.'

'Wake up, Fry – Mary. I'm leaving and I need to give you this,' said Babby, tugging at the bedclothes.

Mary could feel air as Babby waved something under her nose. She lifted her head off the pillow, propped herself up on her elbow. 'What is it?'

'Give this letter to the sisters when they realise I've gone,' answered Babby.

'I heard what you said last night to Benigna. Good on you girl. This letter about that?' she said, yawning, pushing away her tangle of red hair from her eyes.

Babby nodded.

'Go,' said Mary. 'Go to the King's Arms in Garston. Say I sent you,' she said, kissing her cheek.

'The King's Arms? I know it!' exclaimed Babby. 'I've been there with my father.'

'Even better. There's a job goin' there, helping out and singing. With a room.' And Mary hugged her tightly.

Babby handed her the piece of paper she'd been waving under her nose. 'Read it,' she said. On it Babby had written:

Dear Sister Agnes,

Babby has returned home and with my blessing. I have agreed to keep her here for the foreseeable future. We are making our own private arrangements for the child. Please respect our wishes and give us time to decide what we will do about Babby. I know it is a wicked, wicked thing that Babby has done, but we want the best for her and her child. Thank you for your kindness and charity.

Love and God Bless.
Violet Delaney.

'You crafty sod!' said Mary, smiling. 'But if you think that will be an end to it with those witches, you're wrong Babby.'

Babby shrugged, pulled the carpet bag that she had packed out from underneath her bed. 'What choice do I have?' she said, slinging it over her shoulder.

'Bugger all else I can think of,' said Mary. 'Except ... here ... wait a minute ...'

She took a piece of paper from her pocket, scribbled on it, and pressed it into her hand. Then she whispered in her ear, 'There's always this ... Do you have money?'

Babby looked at the paper. 'Just my bits of wages.'

'You were kind to me and there's a woman I know in Lydiate. See this as your last resort. Your *very* last resort. But if you need it, call the number. Say Mary gave it to you.'

'Thank you,' she said. 'Thank you, Mary.' Not quite knowing what to make of it, but grateful all the same.

And with that, Babby hugged her again. When she raised her head, she saw figures in their nightdresses standing by the dormitory door. It was Collette and a few of the other girls who guessed what she was up to, having seen her dress. Collette put her fingers to her lips and waved with her other hand, signalling that Sister Benigna was prowling the corridor. Babby blew them all a kiss and climbed up and out of the window, on to the ledge below, chucked down the bag, then leaped and dropped on to the ground, landing with a thump, before picking up her belongings, brushing herself down and running like the wind until she was just a silhouette, then merely a patch of a shadow, then a nothing.

It was getting late, so she set off walking along Virgin's Lane, into the village, past the church and the school, and then, from the green with its memorial cross, she took a bus to Litherland. Finally, exhausted from walking the last mile, the bag becoming heavier with each step she took and feeling she had arms two inches longer, she approached the pub in Speke Road. It stood alone and defiant, as though it existed on its own island, part of the crater that was once the Bryant and May match factory, now a bomb site. She remembered the stories of Hitler's Luftwaffe dropping fifty bombs on the factory, and the sky lighting up blood red from the fires, and the devastation that it caused.

Her fingers were blue with cold but the pub would be warm and it would smell sweet, although it was no place for young woman. And a young woman with a baby on the way. But it was her only hope. Anything was better than the Mother and Baby Home. She slipped off the Woolies ring that was still on her finger, put it in her pocket, dusted herself off and straightened herself down and tried to make the best of a bad job. Her hair felt like a hat, it was so matted and flat, but she used her fingers to rake through it and soon sorted herself out. The yellow gaslights from inside gave off a dim glow, the light pooling on to the pavement in buttery arcs. The sounds of a piano, someone singing, seeped out into the cold night air. Babby recognised the song immediately. It was a song about a donkey – one of her dad's favourites. She could hear the sound of women's high-pitched laughter which cut through the night. It was a place that her dad had taken her and Pat many years ago, and they would sit outside, waiting for him, with a packet of Walker's crisps and a bottle of pop. She and Pat would find and unwrap the blue folded paper and empty the salt from it, sprinkling it over the crisps, and it was a comforting memory.

She remembered the Mouse, who manned the pen and was disliked by many because of that, who'd been befriended by her father who always had a soft spot for the unloved, the waifs and strays. Jack would drink here with the Mouse who also ran the bingo, and Babby would sneak in and give him the bingo cards she and Pat had filled in. She liked the way the Mouse would call 'Two fat ladies, clickety click; key to the door, number four. Bit of order, please!' The only time you were allowed to make a noise was when he said 'Legs eleven' and then everyone would wolf whistle and whoop and the whole room would start tapping their pennies against their beer glasses. Then it would all go quiet except for the sound of the barmaid coughing like a miner as she chain-smoked behind the bar. And then there would be singing. And Jack would pull the bellows of his accordion in and out, and that's when the real fun would start.

She didn't know what she was going to do, but she knew that this was a place that would welcome her. She could sing. It was the one thing that brought her some comfort. She could lose herself in the words and the music, and she couldn't describe it, but she supposed it was a sense of belonging.

'Mother went to get a fork to stick in donkey's ass, but stuck it into father's head, and out went the gas ...' She heard the lewd and beery strains of a chorus coming through the doors and people were clapping along, some banging their glasses in rhythm on the table. Thrusting her hands deep into her pockets amongst the lint and penny wrappers, she drank in the sound of it. Pulling her coat around her for courage, she took a deep breath and pushed open the swing door, pressing hard on the brass handles. And it hit her. A tide of warmth and welcome, the fear disappearing in a moment as heads turned and looked at her – and smiled.

'My God! It's Jack Delaney's girl, isn't it?' a woman's voice said. 'Come in, love.'

The roaring fire. The ceiling with chamber pots hanging from it – there must have been three dozen of the things at least. The woman who'd spoken – Florrie, that was her name, Babby remembered – was standing on a three-legged stool, reaching up, trying to keep her balance, with a feather duster in her hand, carefully dusting them one by one.

'Is it Jack's girl? My, you've grown, haven't you? And how is Violet?' she said.

Babby nodded. 'Well,' she answered, and felt she had passed her first test. She could feel the warmth, the heat from the flames prickling her cheeks and reddening her face. She heard the squawk of a parrot in its cage behind the bar. Florrie had been trying to teach the old bird to mimic the customers when they asked for a pint of beer. Trying to be casual, Babby walked towards her. Men, nursing pint glasses of brown ale, stood aside like the parting of the red sea.

'Mary's told me about your singing,' said the landlady, kindly. 'Take your coat off, love.'

'No, I'm fine,' answered Babby. 'Thank you.'

She knew it was unlikely that Florrie could solve her problems, but she was far enough away from the part of Liverpool that Violet would be searching to try and find her and bring her back when news got out of her running away from Saint Jude's Mother and Baby Home. 'I'm looking for a job – and I can sing,' she said.

'You sung before?' asked Florrie.

'The Boot Inn – well, the Tivoli, as it now is,' she answered.

'How are Rex and Gladys?'

'Grand,' she answered. 'Grand ...'

'Well, we'll always welcome one of Jack's ...'

Babby hesitated. 'How did you know I was Jack's girl?'

'Same eyes, love. Same smile. Terrible thing what happened to your dad ...'

Babby nodded. 'I've heard a room goes with the job,' she said.

'Aye, a room. It's no palace, but the sheets are clean – and apart from the pub sounds coming up from under the floorboards, it's grand ... There's even a sink. I need someone to wash the glasses, and the singing would be a rare treat. If you could do a few Irish tunes like "Mountains of Mourne" and "Whiskey in the Jar", it would remind me of home and that would be even better.'

'I-I have a stage name,' she stuttered, thinking it might buy her time before Violet tracked her down.

'That's nice. What is it?'

'Coral,' Babby answered. She touched the coral necklace around her neck that Callum had given her.

'Well, Coral. You're very welcome. Any friend of Mary's is a friend of mine. As long as you keep your hand out of the till and a smile on your face for my customers, we're going to get along just fine.'

Later, in the room upstairs, she lay on the bed and stroked her belly. She would have done anything to feel the griping pain that came each month, but she had given up on that long ago. Her stomach was a tiny rise now, still able to be disguised, but the inevitability of what that would become was as certain as night would follow day.

Florrie had left her a Valor stove which Babby had lit. Now she took comfort in the warm glow it gave off, the patterns on the ceiling made by the grill with small holes, the low hiss of the gas, and the heady smell of fumes. Violet had one in the small outside lavatory at Joseph Street and for a moment she had a pang of feeling homesick, for her sister, for Pat, even for Violet.

But then a picture came into Babby's head. Of herself, in a cream shift dress, lined up with the twenty other girls, barefoot, on the landing outside the dormitories, waiting to be inspected by the nuns before chapel. She knew that she would recall that day with vividness for the rest of her life, the feeling of tender swollen breasts, the knowledge of what was in her belly. But as she drifted off to sleep, her heart juddering at the thought that she had no idea what she was going to do in the future, not the slightest notion, she took heart in the fact that tonight she had a bed and a job to go to tomorrow. And, for now, that was enough.

Chapter Thirty-two

No doubt word was going to get around pretty quickly, but she reckoned she had at least a week to think. The nuns and Violet might even believe she had done something ridiculous like set off to Italy. The night before Florrie had listened to her sing – just to be sure she could – and told her she would cook her a breakfast of porridge on weekdays and, at the weekend, salt fish. In return, every morning, she would collect the glasses, clean up the slops, help drag up the crates of beer. In the evening she would sing for the customers when it was getting close to chucking-out time. She'd nodded gratefully. The work sounded hard, but nothing like the Mother and Baby Home, no crucifixes waved at her, or freezing baths, or being woken for chapel at five thirty. The customers would love to see her face full of freckles and her chestnut-coloured hair – and they would love the sound of her voice. They liked the old Irish songs, almost as much as Florrie did, and that was saying something.

That first morning, when Babby had dressed, she was greeted by a knock at the door and a steaming cup of Ovaltine, two oatcakes and a slice of orange on a tray. Florrie smiled. 'Here get this inside you, lovey.' She sat on the edge of the bed. 'And how do you know Mary, then?' she said. Babby hesitated.

'School.'

'You went to school with her?'

'Yes,' she answered. 'Saint Hilda's.'

'Ah yes,' answered Florrie. 'And how is Mary? Still got those ideas in her head? Fighting for the cause?'

Babby nodded.

'She's got fire in her belly, that one,' said Florrie. 'Sometimes I wonder where it's going to get her,' she added, nodding sagely.

Happy to sip at the cup of Ovaltine and nursing the mug against her cheek, Babby decided she had never tasted a hot drink as good as this. 'Thank you,' she said, as she stirred in a huge heaped teaspoonful of sugar and cupped her hands around it for warmth.

Florrie ran through a list of other duties that she should be expected to do at the King's Arms.

'You should answer the door to the coalmen. Then show them where the coal-hole is. Take away the food leftovers from the tables and always make sure the ashtrays are empty and the bottles removed when they're finished. You should wash the glasses ready for the first customers to arrive and sweep under the tables. Dust the chamber pots – you'll have to get up on a ladder for that one, but that needs to be done early, mind, for we don't want customers to come in and find a young lady like you perched on top of it. I shouldn't wonder if a good few of them might try to get a sneaky eyeful where the sun don't shine,' she added with a laugh. 'You also need to help behind the bar, always with a smile and a pleasant tongue. And no cursing or flirting with the customers. But now we come to the important bit, the reason why you're here.'

Babby felt herself jolt. Getting ready with an apology or an excuse with a mouthful of Ovaltine, she stammered, 'W-why I'm here?' Did Florrie know about her 'condition'?

'The singing,' said Florrie. 'We lost Molly, our piano player, and though there are plenty who will give it a try – I've even had a go at it myself – there's nothing like an accordion.' She waited for a response. 'I hear you play one.'

'Yes,' replied Babby. 'But I don't have it with me.'

'Never mind about that,' Florrie said. 'We can get you one right now. Christie's father works at the Rotunda on Scotty Road. Do you know it?'

Of course, Babby knew it. Everyone knew it. The Rotunda was the pawnshop where people took their watches, silver and pearl necklaces, wedding dresses, all items with a story or two behind them. It was where Violet had threatened to sell her Da's accordion.

'That will be grand,' said Babby. 'I've learned how to sing loud enough so my voice reaches over the top of it. And really, I've been practising all my life.'

'That's settled, then; I'll call Christie. You can start with the squeezebox tonight?'

Babby smiled and nodded agreement. How, in just twenty-four hours, she could go from feeling so dreadful, to this hopeful, she couldn't quite comprehend.

After a day of Florrie teaching her how to pull a pint, how to smooth the cream off a Guinness with her finger, how to flip the top off a bottle of beer, and how to use the optic measures for spirits. Christie Murphy arrived that evening looking quite the romantic hero, with dimples in his cheeks, a tangle of red hair, and soft downy blond hairs on the back of his hands. He had a bag with him and the accordion slung over his shoulder. He was a big man and as he stood in the doorway, blocking out the light, his shoulders could barely fit the frame. Florrie called him over and he smiled warmly and laughed.

'You didn't tell me it were a lassie you wanted this for. Who's this?' he asked Florrie.

'Me name's Babby. I have a tongue – you can ask me,' she said. She was mesmerised by his broad shoulders, ruddy cheeks, and hands as big as hams.

'You going to be able to play this beast, love?' he asked.

'What's that supposed to mean? I can play as good as any man. I had the best teacher,' she replied.

He grinned. 'Oh aye? And who was that then?' he asked.

Babby glanced away. 'Just someone I knew. From a long time ago.' The sentence hung in the air and Florrie and Christie shared a look.

'You're a bit of a wild one, I can see that,' he said, grinning.

'She sings as well,' said Florrie. 'Ask her to sing.'

'Any requests?' Babby asked.

'"A Sweet Old-Fashioned Girl",' he said, laughing.

'Get on with you, cheeky beggar,' replied Babby.

He offered her a cigarette and she took it. She wanted to seem brave, as though she had met his type before, show that she wasn't going to be impressed by his bulk, nor by his wide grin and twinkling eyes.

'You know "The Rose of Tralee"? Come here, sit on me knee and sing it.'

'Get away with you,' she said, and he laughed. 'I'll sing it later – maybe!'

When Florrie said it was time for Babby to sing, Christie, sitting on a bar stool, sucking on a cigarette, with one foot resting on his knee, allowed another broad grin to spread across his face. Let's see what the little girl can do, he thought.

'Go on love, show us how it's done!' he cried, as Babby took her place and slipped her arms through the straps. Two customers, staring with love into their pale ales, raised their heads. It had been decided by Florrie it would be a good idea for Babby to stand on a crate of beer so her head could be seen above the punters. She planted her feet firmly apart on the small, three-foot square crate – not that anyone wouldn't have noticed her mass of curls shivering over the top of cloth caps, head scarves and coiffured hairdos. 'Give us a tune, Queen. One of the old ones. "Liverpool Lullaby" or "Maggie May".'

'Aye, lovely, we need a bit of sunshine in our lives,' said another.

She pulled out the bellows and the accordion hissed a long sigh. It was heavier than she was used to, more difficult to negotiate, with more keys, and differently textured buttons. But as she closed her eyes, like a blind man, she felt her way around the instrument which was more responsive with each new touch of her nimble fingers. She began to sing and she had barely reached the end of the first chorus when someone began to hum, others shuffled up their seats, another hugged his partner towards him, and women sighed and swayed in time to the music. At the end, as she bowed her head, there was applause, and voices calling out requests, saying how much they loved this tune, or that. And happy that she was home, if home was her accordion, despite the maelstrom of her worries whirling around her, she felt something close to calm. Meanwhile, Christie raised his glass, sat through every one of her songs, cheered for more, and told the pub to be quiet every time someone so much as muttered. 'Hush thy mouths!' he yelled. He really had never heard anything like it, he told Florrie.

'Me too an' all,' said Florrie. 'But you keep your hands off her, Christie. I feel responsible for this girl. I don't know why, something to do with poor Jack, probably. And that's an end to it.'

When he appeared the following night like a force of nature, barrelling into the pub and bringing in leaves and a blast of cold air, Christie smiled at Babby, and she smiled back at him.

'Come here, sit on me knee and sing wi' me,' he said.

'Stuff that for a game of soldiers,' she said, and he laughed.

That evening he took his boot off, banged it on the bar when she began singing, and once again yelled, 'Hush thy mouths!' When it was over and people began to drift out, back to their homes, back to their wives and children who no doubt would be complaining that they had drunk away their week's wages and left the food to go cold, he called her to him.

'Where do you think you're going, Babby?' he asked her.

'To do the bottle washing,' she replied. He laughed and grabbed her roughly, pulled her to him. She sat down on his knee, arms folded over her stomach to hide the tiny bump, fearful of her secret, and felt his thigh move up between her legs. It was hard as granite, as though he wasn't made of flesh, but carved out of rock.

'That's better,' he said. 'I'll tame yer.' He smelled warm and sweet, the cigarettes and beer all mixed up and in his hair and seeping out of the pores of his skin. And she liked it, the feel of another person's touch, if only to remind her that she wasn't completely alone. No, she didn't mind it. Not at all. Of course she wished it was Callum, not Christie, but Christie would do for now.

Two weeks passed and Babby was thoroughly surprised that Violet hadn't tracked her down yet. She knew it was only a matter of time, but she was taking each day as it came, and she had earned ten shillings in tips and nearly fourteen pounds in wages, which was grand. How was she to know that Violet still thought she was safely under the care of the nuns? Babby had no idea when her lie would be found out and so each day was a bonus. And each day she had grown closer to Christie. Christie was a laugh. A right laugh. He would produce pennies from behind her ear and teach the parrot to say 'Babby's nicking shillings'. And he knew what he wanted. He thought he'd break her in time, Babby knew that, but she also knew that he didn't reckon on her spirit. He'd sit back and watch as the customers jeered and clapped and urged her to get up on the tables and sing some more. He liked pop songs but also the old ones. She would start with a few Elvis and Perry Como numbers – but she always ended with 'The Old Rugged Cross' and people started coming for the singing.

She would have a drink with Christie after hours and sing for him in the lock-ins, with the windows steaming up and the curtains drawn shut. She even let him take her to the Luxe picture house to see *Let's Make Love* and he fancied himself as Yves Montand and she was prepared to flatter him as he swung around a lamp post and mimicked a French accent whilst telling her 'Time ees money, and I don't like to waste either, Babby.'

But all the time the baby in her belly was growing – and she hadn't the faintest clue what she was going to do about it. Christie still had no idea, but then he didn't know the skinny, lithe Babby of four months ago. He thought her curves had always been a part of her.

'Whatever your wicked plan is, good girls like me stay virgins until we are married ...' she said, when he pressed up against her, and she felt his ribcage almost crushing her chest. 'I love Our Lady with a deep, deep, passion, and that's why you never can have me,' she lied, wriggling away from him.

It was the only way she could think of and it worked for a time; he stopped going after her. Then one day she was singing, 'Oh, Mary this London's a wonderful sight,' when Christie appeared and spoke into her ear. 'I'm falling for you something rotten,' he said. 'Why won't you let me near you?'

She shrugged him off, but he followed her out of the pub, stood with his arm blocking her way in the corridor outside. 'Where are you off to, Babby?' he asked.

'I have to do the slops.' she said. 'And wash the bottles.'

'Florrie expects more than she's a right to,' he said.

'Not really,' answered Babby. 'She's been good to me.'

'Aye. She has. Now it's your turn to be good to me.'

And leaning in to her, he pushed her up against the wall and started to kiss her.

'No!' she cried. But not before he took her breasts in his hands. And she knew from his face when she winced and shoved him away because they were swollen and tender, that he understood why.

'You're having a babby? Our Babby is having a babby? You're in the bloody club?'

'N-no,' she stuttered. 'No, I'm not – i-it's just …'

He stood back and looked at her, with a mixture of shock and amusement.

'Whatever you say, love, secret's safe with me,' he said, tapping the side of his nose, and winking.

'Leave me alone!' she cried. 'Bloody leave me alone!'

Chapter Thirty-three

Violet was on her way to town. She had a new job on the cheese and meat counter at Grassington's grocers and hated it. Her hair smelled of cheese and her fingers of meat and the worst thing she had to do was wash the bacon slicer at the end of the week. Today, she had decided to make a start on it but there was a queue of customers already building up when she arrived. It was there that Sister Agnes found her, deep in bacon fat and sweat breaking out on her forehead. The fat made her feel a little nauseous just to look at it, but not as nauseous as she felt when she saw the nun standing there, brows knitted together in a frown.

'Mrs Delaney, I'm afraid I have some bad news,' said a flustered Sister Agnes.

'What, Sister?' She felt that sinking feeling, a dull ache weighing heavily on her chest. She knew it must be something to do with Babby.

'There has been a misunderstanding. Your daughter
…'

'Yes?'

'Your daughter has … well, we thought you had
given her permission to leave Saint Jude's. She's
gone. I'm sorry …'

'What?'

'One of our girls, Collette O'Brien, told us today
that it was your daughter who wrote the letter sent to
us saying she had decided to keep her child, not you.
Never underestimate what girls like these will do if
they think it will win them a favour as it has Collette
– she's been allowed to visit her sister and no doubt is
having a grand time in Blundellsands. But if it's any
consolation, the other girl responsible for colluding
with your daughter has been severely reprimanded.'

'What?' Violet exclaimed, aware of the queue-
ing customers. Why couldn't you have told me this
at my house? she wanted to ask. Had she deliberately come here to embarrass her so she couldn't
rail at their incompetence? 'Where is Babby?' she
demanded to know.

'I'm sorry. We thought that she would come back.
They usually do. Usually they go back to their lov-
ers, then return with their tails between their legs
when they realise they really have no other choice to
make. These chaps … Married, was he? The father?'

Violet could feel her skin pricking. She was fuming. She herself could say what she liked about her daughter, but one thing she wasn't going to put up with was someone else blackening Babby's name in public. She was aware the people in the queue were stirring. They had the whiff of a bit of gossip in their nostrils, something they could take back to tell their friends and husbands to liven up their day. Ooh, you should have been there. Violet Delaney being torn to shreds by some nun. Her daughter has only gone and got herself knocked up. Well, what would you expect from the Delaneys? You heard what happened at the Boot Inn as was?

'So how long has she been missing?'

The nun shrugged.

'How long?' repeated Violet, undoing her pinafore ties, pulling it over her head. A man in the queue shouted a complaint. They'd been waiting for half an hour and now what were they supposed to do? 'Climb over the counter and help our bloody sens?'

Violet turned to the queue and apologised. 'Sorry, my daughter's in trouble,' she muttered. And the woman standing behind the angry man told her to hush his mouth, couldn't she see Violet was upset? The nun looked like she wasn't to be trusted, muttered the woman, and the man agreed that that was about right.

'Two weeks. We assumed she had gone back to you. It said so in the letter.'

'What exactly did Babby say?' asked a trembling Violet. 'And how did she get out?'

'She just left, Mrs Delaney – we're not a prison. She has chosen the path she wants to walk and we can't do much about that, I'm afraid. God loves a sinner, but your daughter is trying the Almighty. And she was a bad influence on the other girls with her pop music and preposterous notions about love.'

'Move out of my way,' said Violet. 'MOVE out of my bloody way!'

The nun humphed. Violet was in no mood for an argument, especially with half the store gawping and seemingly enjoying the spectacle of a woman in distress and a nun sneering at her. Violet, in a fluster of skirts and tossing back of hair, ran to get the girl on the fish counter to step in for an hour then swept away and left. When she found herself sobbing outside George Henry Lees, leaning on the plate glass window, looking behind it at a bed with a mink cover for sale for two hundred pounds, she thought how ridiculous the world had become to pay two hundred pounds for a bed ... and wondered what on earth she was going to do now.

Chapter Thirty-four

The sun rose as if it had a hangover. Seven more days had passed and Babby had asked Florrie if she could have a day off. She tearfully counted out the money that she had been keeping in a small jar beside her bead. Exactly twenty-one pounds. She slipped it into her pocket in a tissue. The woman's anonymous voice at the end of the phone in Lydiate that she had called three days earlier had been practical but unfeeling. The last resort, Mary had said. And it really was the last resort, she thought, as her legs shook and a lump rose to her throat, and the voice answered yes, they could fit her in, she should meet the car outside Lewis's department store, and don't forget the money – the ten pounds. Babby wished she could have afforded to do this properly. There had been talk amongst the girls at Saint Jude's that if you had a hundred and twenty pounds, you could go to a doctor who would sign a paper saying you were mentally unstable, unsuited to have a baby, then to a second who would say the same. It was safer and half-legal. But they had all agreed a hundred and twenty pounds was an absurd amount of money. So for Babby, it would have to be Mary's last resort.

Babby got off the double decker bus that pulled into Skelhorne Street bus station and made her way past the black cabs lined up in rows along the pavement, the drivers casually glancing up at her as she passed, her cheeks burning with shame each time it happened. She stood outside a café, trying to nonchalantly gaze at the Kit Kats arranged in a pyramid on a dusty coronation plate, whilst surreptitiously checking the time. Eleven o'clock. Down past the Adelphi Hotel and underneath the statue of the naked man outside Lewis's, then she should find the alleyway.

Her stomach was somersaulting and tying itself in knots at the thought of what she was about to do. Normally the twenty-foot high bronze figure of a man proudly stepping out in all his glorious nakedness would have made her smile, but today she fixed her eyes to the cracks in the paving slabs.

'Are you looking for gold down there?' a passer-by said. 'You won't find any, sweetheart.'

'Sorry?' she answered, startled.

'Are you looking for gold ...? Never mind.' The passer-by could sense something was wrong and felt a twinge of sympathy for this girl, who seemed to be spinning into dust in front of his eyes.

She turned away and didn't answer. Raise your face to the sun, she thought.

That's what her Da always said. She was almost glad he wasn't here to see this mess she had got herself into. But that was a terrible thought and she pushed it away. She pulled her coat around her. What if someone she knew was to see her? Even those who had never set eyes on her before could probably tell by the look on her face where she was heading.

The shame. That was the worst. Perhaps worse than the act itself. Bloody Christie – she'd hated him, teasing her like that. But as the moment approached, with Mary's bit of paper turning damp in her sweating palm, she started to think about her baby. Being in the club, or having a bun in the oven, or up the duff – those phrases bore no resemblance to the thing itself, her actual baby growing inside her. She tried to push these thoughts out of her mind. When she passed a woman and her infant child, the faint sound of mewling coming from inside the beautiful Silver Cross pram squeaking on its springs and with its chrome glinting in sunlight, she felt a pang of sorrow for what she was about to do. Was it wrong? Of course it was. But what choice did she have? And Mary's piece of scrunched-up paper? Well, this at least would give her a choice. And the money she had worked so hard to save. Was that so bad? To choose which direction her life would take?

But yet again the thought of this child crowded her head – not a pregnancy, but a baby, a toddler now wheeling around in circles, like the one bowling towards her, tugging his mother's coat – and now taking shape as a small boy of her own, or like the children she had passed earlier with their paper boats made out of newspapers, floating them across the pond in the gardens behind Saint George's Hall. And then not a child any more, but a young man at school, wearing a back-to-front cap and a blazer and tie, weighed down by his schoolbags. Would her child have hated school as much as she had? Would he speak out of turn like she did? Would he be the kind that would be caught stealing crab apples and scrumping from Croxteth Hall, sneaking in over the wall after dark like her brother did, and her father and his father before that? And then the child became a man in her imaginings, like the two men with the *Liverpool Echo* under their arms, who stepped aside on the pavement to allow her to pass, heads bent in studied concentration. Her young man ... She imagined him carrying the coal scuttle for her, then later, returning home with his sweetheart like the couple holding hands as they came through Lewis's revolving doors, happy and in love, and laughing and excitedly discussing their new pop-up toaster. Finally, as the old man at the flower stall offered her roses, she imagined herself old too, with her boy planting a tender kiss on her greying head. All the possibilities of what this child could become came flooding into her head, crowding her thoughts in vivid technicolor. If only ... if only ...

She snapped back into the present. On the opposite corner of Lewis's she saw a man pause from cleaning the plate glass window and glance in her direction. Was it so obvious? She shivered in her coat and turned up the collar, and she could feel her legs trembling. How had this happened? It wasn't fair. But life wasn't fair. Violet had drilled that into her since the day she was born.

And so she stood under the naked statue at the foot of the alley running down the side of the Lewis's building, in pestering rain, and waited for a black Morris Oxford.

The car pulled up exactly at eleven fifteen. She saw an image of herself, a fat liquid reflection on

the bonnet, and it was as if she was looking at someone else. The man sitting in the driver's seat got out,
opened the rear door, and indicated to Babby to get
in. He handed her a red spotted cravat. 'You need to
let me tie this around your eyes,' the man said. 'Got
that? Have you brought the money?'

'Yes,' she replied.

She handed him the tissue and he counted the
notes and coins carefully. Then he leant over and
tied the cravat around her head.

'That's a good girl. Now, put your head down,
don't draw attention to yourself,' he said as they
pulled away from the kerb. She could feel the backs
of her knees, sweaty and sticky, flesh prickling
against the cracked leather seat.

He hadn't quite tied the blindfold tightly enough
and she twisted it slightly, hoping to get an idea of
where they were going. She was sure they were driving north, uphill, past the hospital and the university;
she heard the rattle of a tram and the hiss of a steam
train, children chanting a skipping rhyme and boot-
ing a football against a wall, probably a school, then
after about twenty minutes, out towards the coun-
tryside, where the fresh air heightened her senses.
Finally, she decided they were probably heading to
Lydiate, an area where she had once been strawberry
picking, where there were fields and ditches, isolated

farms, and rows of squat cottages. Wherever they were going, she was certain that she would remember this place forever. She was also certain she would remember the smell of the man's aftershave, thick and musky and, right now, making her feel she was going to be sick, actually vomit in the car.

Pulling outside a small house with a plume of lilac smoke coming from the chimney, the man said, 'Take the blindfold off. Now get out and follow me, but keep looking at the ground.'

As they got out of the car, she noticed he was glancing back over his shoulder, presumably worried that he was being followed.

She stood for a moment, gazed at the dark-blue door of the cottage at the side of this road that had no name, the number six painted on the gatepost. There was a pigeon pecking about in the gutter, a small hole in the roof. There was absolutely no sign to indicate what went on inside. She wondered if it was just known as 'the house with the blue door'. Did people gossip about what went on behind the closed, moth-eaten curtains and the occasional nervous young woman going up the step to ring the bell?

The man pressed it, hard, with the heel of his hand. The door was opened by a thin woman wearing a paisley-patterned housecoat with pencilled-on arched eyebrows that made her face look like an exclamation mark and her hair in rollers under a chiffon headscarf. She led Babby into a poorly lit, cheerless kitchen. It smelled of cabbage and damp. It was stuffy and there was condensation on the inside of the grime-laced window, and Babby undid the top button of her shirt in order to breathe. The man who had driven her came in, finished a cigarette, then disappeared. The woman directed her through a low doorway to a smaller, airless, room. It was a kind of an outhouse, with whitewashed walls and a linoleum floor; a curtain patterned with pink flamingos was on a wire that curved around what looked like a gurney with wheels, pushed up against the wall.

'Take your coat off, love, and go behind the curtain and slip your knickers off, there's a good girl.' Babby did just that and stuffed them in her pocket. She stood waiting, watching the shapes move on the other side of the curtain, listening to a tap running, a bowl being filled with water, hugging her arms around her for comfort, nudging up against a table with a metal band running around the edge of it and legs that stuck out at a slight angle.

'You've no need to be frightened,' said the woman, pulling back the curtain.

A second woman came in. She wore half-moon spectacles that sloped upwards like cat's eyes.

'Jeanie Delaney?' she asked, peering at Babby over the top of her glasses. Babby nodded and swallowed hard. 'Mary sent you?' the woman asked. Babby nodded again. 'Come with me, dear.'

When she went into the next room, she felt a rip tide of worry. The first thing that struck her was that it was full of steam and heavy streams of condensation ran down the sweating walls. This room had faded wallpaper, with a Chinese pattern of bamboo shoots. Some parts of it were peeling, curling up at the skirting boards and the corners. On a sideboard was a stainless-steel kettle and she caught sight of herself in it, her distorted face grimacing back at her. The woman gave her a sheet of paper and a pen and asked her to sign something that said she was agreeing to the 'procedure' with no recourse to action. Her hand shook as she scrawled her name on the dotted line. The letters undulated as she tried to focus on the smaller print on the other side of the page. There was a sink, a table covered with an old red chenille cloth draped over it, a towel on top of that, and a bed with no headboard. The woman told her to lie down, pull up her skirt. She laid her hands flat on Babby's stomach. She was kind, told her it wouldn't hurt. Well, only a bit. She measured her belly. 'Four months, looks like,' she said. 'Shame you haven't time on your side. One day – and let's hope soon – this will be legal. Parliament are close to passing a new law. Amazing, really. You'll be walking in through the front door of a hospital or a clinic and no one can say a thing.'

Babby didn't really know what she was talking about, but she thought she meant that this was about as bad as it would ever be. The metal-pointed instrument lying on the table caught the light of the oil lamp and flashed as the woman moved it aside. 'You've tried the mother's ruin and the hot baths?'

'Mother's ruin? Oh, you mean gin?'

'Yes. Never works. Unless you take it with a dash of quinine – and then you'd most likely end up dead, like some girls I know of. Desperate. We'll sort you out, chicken ...' Chicken. The word turned strange in Babby's mouth. She felt sick; partly nerves, partly because of the large glass of Jameson's Irish whiskey she had gulped down before she left the pub.

The woman saw her looking at the instrument. 'Don't worry. We won't use that unless it's necessary. We'll use the soap and the syringe ... Now, take this pill first and you'll drift off. Lie there for a minute and keep yourself calm – we need you to feel as relaxed as you can ...'

Babby covered herself with the blanket the woman gave her. She began to feel woozy and wondered what the pill was that she had just taken. She could hear a tap being turned on in the kitchen and there was the sound of gurgling pipes, a car engine fading away. Her eyelids became heavy and, as she closed her eyes, she had an image of the needle going in to her. Stab, stab, stab. Fainting with tiredness, a shape began to form in her head. She saw someone. Someone blurry, opalescent in the light, soft around the edges. It was her father. And then Violet. And then the statue of Our Lady at Saint Hilda's smiling at her. She guessed Christie would be waiting. And Mary had made her promise to send her the news. She saw the headline in the evening paper. 'Republican march ends in violence'. A great big brawl, petrol bombs, bonfires reaching the sky. Mary and her man would be celebrating that night. She would be dancing around the flames singing songs for her beloved Ireland, and causing merry hell with the rest of them. Thoughts rearranged themselves in her head. Sister Agnes was looking into a mirror and the mirror shattered into a thousand pieces. Violet again, now; she was drinking gin, thumping the glass on the kitchen table to the music of the accordion, but then the door slammed open and she cried out for Babby and begged forgiveness, blamed her husband for the lump of sadness in her heart. Callum, he wasn't sleeping either, in her dreams. The bedclothes slid from his limbs, no matter how hard he tugged at them, and she was looking down on him as he was left shivering on the bed, with the faint sounds of singing in his ears – 'That's Amore'.

A minute later she jolted awake from the dream and found herself lying on the table with the cover on the floor. Panic tore through her. The woman was standing beside her with a bowl of steaming hot water and a greying towel draped over her forearm.

'You haven't done it?' said Babby.

'What's the matter, chicken?'

She began to plead. 'Please … you haven't …?'

'Not yet. You drifted off. The pill. It does that,' said the woman. She was rearranging the cover over her body. Babby sat up.

'What's the matter?'

Babby began to shake. 'How could I have been so stupid?!' she murmured to herself, pushing her fists into her eye sockets, swinging her legs over the table. She felt a terrible sense of sadness, as if part of her had been ripped from her body. Tears like giant pendants spilled on to her cheeks and dropped silently into her lap, forming a puddle in the scrunched mess of the cotton skirt. Her shoulders folded into herself and her head dropped into her chest.

'You've changed your mind, then?' asked the woman. 'We can't give you your money back ... This has taken a lot to arrange.'

'I can't do this without Callum. He needs to be told what I'm going to do! Then, if ... I need to go,' gasped Babby. She leaped up, pushed her arms through the sleeves of her coat, and barged her way past the woman, stumbling, falling into the cold air, the sound of a cow mooing in a field behind her and the rattle of the trains on the nearby tracks.

She got back in the evening, after two buses and a train ride, drained of all energy. As she stood for a moment under the creaking pub sign as it swung back and forth, her thoughts turned to Callum and Anglesey. She thought back to when they had lain on the hay bale together. The smell of him. How from the very first time she had met him, he had made her see things differently, the smell of newly mown grass, her love for Hannah and Pat – and even Violet. She sighed and went inside.

Florrie could see straight away something was wrong from the way Babby sighed as she began to go about her chores, but she knew not to start questioning her now. The pub was quiet and when the customers suspected that Babby wasn't going to be in any fit state to sing – they could tell from her face

as she made her way behind the bar and poured herself a glass of water – they put on their coats and
began to leave.

'Sorry,' she said, barely looking up, as the door
swung open, 'we're shutting up.'

The man didn't move. 'Babby,' he said.

'Callum!' she cried and felt her legs buckle
beneath her as an electric shock jolted through her
body.

'Oh, Jesus, Babby! I've found you, love!'

'Cal! I've missed you!' she yelped, steadying herself on the brass rail, her whole body shaking. How
many times had she told herself that the minute she
saw him again she would tell him everything about
the baby, had gone over and over it in her head, but
now panic gripped her. How could she possibly take
even one single step from behind the bar? Other people might not have noticed, but surely Callum would
see instantly she was having a baby. She reached out
and grasped his hands over the countertop, kissed
him full on the lips, all the time thinking: how do
you tell someone you're pregnant? What if he ques-
tioned her as to whether it was his? God, how she
wanted to feel his bones against hers, his warm body
pressing firmly against her chest, wanted to throw
her arms around his waist, wanted to cling on to him
like he was a raft. But she daren't. The thought of

what he might say made her physically ill. She could have cried. She did cry. And he, twisting his cap in his hands as if he were wringing it out, had tears spilling on to his cheeks.

Florrie, looking in, shouted to the barman sweeping up in the back room, to get a whisky sour for Callum and a sweet sherry for Babby who had instinctively pushed her hands over her belly. She thought Callum seemed taller – could he really have grown two inches in such a short time? Or had she become smaller as well as fatter?

She hoped the dim lighting might disguise the tiny bump below her belt, her full skirts cascading in waterfalls of folds, skilfully designed to cover any sign of her pregnancy. What was impossible to disguise however were her breasts. Full now, against her ruched neckline, the way as Violet used to arrange her cleavage when trying to show herself to her best advantage.

'When are you going to come out from behind that flipping bar?' Callum asked.

She could feel herself panicking again, fear coming in waves. And there was a silence. Babby wanted to say something, but she still couldn't. She just didn't have it in her. She would like to blurt it all out, about Saint Jude's, and the man in the Morris Oxford car, and the child growing inside her, but she just couldn't. She shivered, because of the fear of where this might all lead. Please don't cry again, she told herself. Please don't cry.

'Well, if you won't I'll just have to come back there myself.' And with that, he vaulted right over the bar. 'Hold me,' he said, enfolding her with his arms and pulling her to him. 'I've got you now.'

Her bottom lip quivered, as she squirmed away from him.

'I can't.'

'Why ever not?'

She felt herself blush. 'God, Callum, I'm so sorry. I'm so, so sorry. Forgive me, Callum ... Will you hate me if I tell you what trouble I'm in?'

He didn't answer, but he pushed her against the bar, and grasped her tightly, let his hands move over the slight swell of her belly, up to her breasts. And then he kissed her. The feel of him, the smell of him, so familiar, so comforting, brought more tears to her eyes.

He put a reassuring hand on her shoulder, pushed a strand of hair out of her eyes.

'Don't worry, love. I'm here. Because I love you. And I don't care about the baby. Because I'm going to marry you – you see if I don't.'

Babby looked at him in shock. 'Baby! How did you know?' she asked.

'Look at you, Babby.' His gaze moved down over her body.

'Is it that obvious?'

'It was obvious the minute I walked in here,' he said, brushing the tangled web of hair from her eyes. 'Look at the clothes you're wearing. The way you were hiding behind that bar and wouldn't let me near you.'

'Oh God, Callum. I'm sorry ...'

'Hey, there's nothing to be sorry about. Stop blubbing like this ...'

'What a mess I must be. Do I look awful?'

'No, you look beautiful. Completely beautiful.'

'And you don't hate me for – for it?'

'Why would I? You couldn't make a baby on your own, could you?'

Her heart felt as if it would burst. It was like a tremendous weight lifting off her shoulders. Gently, she placed his hand on her stomach. Gently he kissed her, excited with the possibility of what this new life might bring. To hell with what the world might think. He had lost so many people in his family, he wasn't going to pass over the chance to make one of his own. He loved this Liverpool girl.

'I'm never ever going to let you out of my sight again. If you knew the trouble I've had finding you, Babby! You really are happy to see me?'

'Oh Cal. Of course I am. Say that all again, Cal,' she said, thinking he looked a little more tired, a little older, but still so handsome. 'And tell me everything. But start with the part about never letting me out of your sight again. Will you?'

'I never will, that's for sure. And I can tell you that my heart has been breaking. Tell you that I've been looking for you for weeks. Tell you that your family has been stopping me at every turn. And Babby, I know that I did wrong when I didn't go back and find you the next day. But I couldn't help myself. I had to find out for myself about ... about ...'

The sentence petered to silence. He couldn't say it, the truth of why he'd left, and he stumbled on. 'I had to go back and help Mrs Reilly with the pigs.'

'The pigs?' she said, bewildered.

He was ashen. 'She was short-handed and I knew she would find out if I wasn't there to help. You mean you didn't get my note?' he added quickly.

'What note?'

'The note where I said I would be back to find you once I had ... had ...' His words tailed off again

'The only note I received was the one saying you were going to Italy.'

'Italy? I've been trying to find you for weeks now. I even took a job at Liverpool Assurance in the sorting offices and I've got digs in Upper Parly Street. A boarding house. Clean and warm and the grub's all right. But every time I turned up at Joseph Street I was told by your Mam and your Pat to forget you, give up all hope, that you weren't interested in me. Pat seemed as though he felt sorry for me, he was kind, but firm. Your Mam was spitting nails. But I couldn't rest until I found you, Babby. I had to hear it from you. But they said that you didn't want to see me. Over and over.'

She reeled, clutched on to the back of a chair for support. 'I never said any such thing! Why on earth would anyone do something like that?' Callum frowned. 'Oh God, someone's been lying! Someone's been lying to both of us and I'm sure I know who it is.'

At first it was just a rush of words that she couldn't make sense of. Why would her mother not want them to marry? The shame, not to be made an honest woman of, would be awful. But wasn't Callum offering to make her his wife? They could do it easily, late in the evening, no one would need know. Surely it was better than giving the baby to those vile nuns? Why would Violet want her to do that instead of marry him? She had heard they had been sending some of the babies to Australia. That's what Collette had told her. Would Violet have wanted that if she knew he was offering to make her his wife?

'I knew something was up when a fella came in, asking for me at the office,' said Callum, 'asking about you. Mrs Reilly knew where I was working so she must have told him where I was.'

'What did he look like?'

'Tall. Ruddy face. Shock of silvery black hair.'

'Rex?' she said, as an image came into her head of the man that once sat on her mother's bed, with grey creeping into his coarse black hair, and a pair of braces looping around his thighs. 'It sounds like Rex. I'm sure something is going on between Mam and Rex. Makes it all the more galling that Mam is on her high horse about you and me, Cal.'

'I put two and two together and I knew something was wrong from what he said about you being too far gone to be helped. Violet knows nothing about this pub, does she?'

'She sent me to the awful Saint Jude's. One of those homes ... you know?' She could barely bring herself to say it. 'But I couldn't stand it. And the one thing I had was my singing to give me time to get out of this mess. At least until I found you. Florrie has been so kind.'

'Jesus. An unmarried mother's home?'

'Yes,' she said. Shame burned her cheeks.

'What if ...?'

She put out a hand to reassure him.

'Never. I would have walked over hot coals to keep this baby,' she said.

'*Our* baby.'

'Our baby,' she said, and smiled a quivering smile.

'Everything will be fine, so dry your eyes. I'll deal with your mother. And hey, Babby. A baby! We're having a baby! There's no one going to let me feel bad about this.'

Florrie, entering the room, could see that this was no ordinary visitor for Babby. She could tell by the way they looked into each other's eyes, their whole bodies oscillating in the candlelight. What was that? Was it love? It looked like they might be made out of gossamer. So young, so inexperienced, but with such desire, a love that was so intense it might burn if you were to reach out and touch either of them.

Babby smiled at Callum, the big wide grin that, lately, Florrie had begun to worry had gone forever. 'I knew you would come back for me – I knew it. Just to think I might have—'

The words left her mouth and her hand flew up to her face as if to push them back in.

'Might have what?' he asked.

But she didn't give him an answer. She just folded the ugly experience neatly away. And decided she would never speak of it again.

Chapter Thirty-five

The following morning, which was a Saturday, so no Liverpool Assurance, Callum had said he would take Babby out for the day. They had so much to talk about: the child, where they would live, what to say to Violet and when. Babby had tossed and turned, going over how Callum told her it was Rex who had heard Babby had been playing at the King's Arms, that Violet didn't have a clue and it was best to keep it that way for now. 'You probably wonder why I'm telling you?' Rex had asked Callum. 'Well I'm a man who's not done much of anything in my life apart from an awful lot of running, but this is my chance to do something right.' He would deal with Violet later.

Now, after taking the ferry out of the city across the Mersey, they arrived in New Brighton where they sat cross-legged on the harbour wall. The sea was crystal blue. Green feathery weeds under the surface swayed in concert, and small silver flecks of fish darted about between them. You could see right down to the bottom of the seabed. Babby said, 'Drop this crust in ...' and produced the corner of the heel of a loaf. 'If we're lucky, fish will begin to circle when they get a whiff of it, so look out for the rings on the surface. There's one! Did you see it?'

He kissed her cheek, they got up, and he put his arm under her elbow and steered her towards the promenade and the Tower Ballroom. 'One day I'll take you dancing there,' he said, breaking loose and skipping along the high wall in leaps and bounds, as if he was Fred Astaire, with Babby shrieking and urging him to come down before he killed himself.

New Brighton might have seen better days, with its peeling pink and lime-green plastered walls and its shuttered graffitied arcades, but there were still a few slot machines on the promenade, the big wheel, the caterpillar ride, and stalls with candyfloss bobbing in plastic bags, selling sticks of rock and periwinkles. Callum and Babby were an arresting sight, their heads thrown back, their feet in rhythm, revelling in the secret of each new curve and abundance of her body. People smiled when they saw them, but didn't know why; perhaps something about the girl's dewy complexion, and the boy's expression of sheer joy?

Callum took her into the Milk Bar café where a bell tinkled as the door opened and a waitress, wearing a white starched apron, winked at him as he led Babby to a table. The fringes on the orange lamp-shades hung low over each table, and the banquette seats were red plastic, the splits in them prickling the backs of Babby's knees. Callum took his cap off and laid it on the table amongst the cheap paper napkins and cutlery. He slipped a sugar cube from the porcelain floral bowl in the middle of the table into Babby's mouth whilst they waited to order. She smiled at the sweetness of it, and of him, taking the melting sugar cube out of her mouth, looking at it, then popping it back in.

They made swift work of banana splits sprinkled with almonds and then, running a finger under his collar, he undid the top button, leaned back in the seat, licked the spoon and let it tinkle into the glass dish smeared with ice cream.

Babby propped her elbows on the table, twirled her spoon, and sighed.

'So what happens next?' she said. 'And what about your da?'

Callum shrugged. Now was the time for him to tell her. Tell her that the Mouse was his father, the one who had been in the fight that led to her father's death – and the real reason he had left her that night after the hollas and stayed away for so long, too long, was because he was in such shock, such panic and turmoil, that he couldn't face her. How do you say it? My father was responsible for your father's death?

He couldn't, he just couldn't. Not then – and not now when she looked so happy.

They went outside. A screeching seagull wheeled overhead in circles. Babby blinked against the brightness and screwed her gaze to the horizon that wobbled and shimmied where the sun met the sea.

He took a deep breath, tried again. 'Babby,' he said, gravely, putting a hand on her arm.

She turned to meet his eyes. And she looked so hopeful.

'What? What is it?

'Nothing,' he replied. Whose secret was worse? he wondered. Babby having a baby, or his? Which was the bigger crime? No, he refused to see this child as something to be ashamed of, so there was the answer.

She laughed. 'Then what? What's the matter? You've not changed your mind about marrying me?'

'Of course not!'

'Then what's wrong? You look as if someone has just walked over your grave.'

'Babby, I haven't told you the whole story.' There, I've said it, he thought.

She stopped in her tracks. 'What d'you mean?'

'Me mam's dead. Scarlet Fever. She were twenty and I never knew her. But me dad ... He's, well, he's still alive. Just good as dead.'

'Oh Cal, I'm sorry. Did he cut you off?'

He paused, allowed the version of the story in Babby's head to take shape. 'Got into trouble ... Too much drink, as usual ... Same old story. You don't hate me for it?'

Go on, he thought. Say it, tell her now. But again, he faltered.

'Why would I?'

'I'm ashamed of him. Of what he did. Supposed I wanted to impress you, that's the truth of it.'

'I don't hate you for it. Of course not. I love you.'

'Brawling never ends well. A kid would have known better.'

She was silent. Like her own dad? she thought. But this was too much to speak about right now. The daylight was disappearing, the air was growing colder and everywhere was beginning to be engulfed in a blanket of mist that made the big wheel of the fair and the pier look like they had been woven in mohair. She didn't want to waste the rest of their time together talking about things that made her heart stop.

They made their way through the Pleasure Gardens, holding hands, fingers entwined, occasionally stopping to kiss when no one was about. Years of perfecting the art of pushing distressing thoughts aside in an instant meant they smiled when they saw a boy standing at a fairground stall throwing a ping-pong ball into a jam jar, win a goldfish, and punch his fist in the air. The wind picked up. Piles of deck-chairs covered in billowing tarpaulin looked as if they might take off at any moment and Chinese lanterns squeaked on unoiled hinges. As they walked over a bridge that crossed a lake, she noticed one of the love boats had escaped its moorings and was drifting forlornly on the choppy water. It had begun to drizzle. Seaside drizzle, thin and indecisive, and yet it would soak them through before they even noticed it was raining.

'Everything will be fine,' said Callum, as the fairy lights along the promenade swung away into nothing. 'Come on, weather has turned.'

'I'm not sure it will be fine,' Babby said, squinting out to sea.

Callum slowed his pace. 'Why? What's that supposed to mean?' he asked.

She hesitated, wavered. 'Well, because. Because …' she replied. She wanted to say that she was worried he was keeping something from her. She wanted to say that if he thought he could charm her mother into coming around to the idea of them marrying, he clearly didn't know her. But when he pinked around the ears and turned away again, with hard-to-read eyes and a troubling sigh, she knew she would have to wait.

They got back an hour later and went up to Babby's room. The sea air and the long walk along the promenade had exhausted them both and Callum fell asleep on the bed. After half an hour or so of listening to his breathing, she got up and crept out of the room. She would have stayed with him longer, but she had to get up and do the slops. For a short time, she felt a kind of peace, knowing that Callum was sleeping. Later, finally seeing him waking, his eyes blinking against the light and a huge yawn breaking into a smile, something tugged at her. Happiness. Was that what she was feeling? And yet – and yet …

She had prepared boiled eggs and toast, laid it out on a tray for him.

'Ssh,' she said, putting a finger on his lips. 'I'm fine. I'm going downstairs to let the coalmen in and then I have to sing.'

He nodded, and smiling, let his head fall back on the pillow.

'I love you, Babby,' he said, grasping her skirts, and pulling her back towards the bed. 'Told you I'd follow you to Liverpool.'

'I love you, too,' she replied, twisting to him. 'But what's the matter?' she asked.

Can you love someone and keep a secret from them? he wondered.

'Nothing, love. Nothing at all ...' he replied.

Two hours later, Callum had left to return to his lodgings and the pub was filling up. Christie had arrived and was lining up his ale and his whiskey chaser on the bar. He was ready for getting drunk – she knew that when he snaked his arm around her thickening waist. She brushed him off, darted away from him. She was glad that Callum had left, and though she had nothing to hide with Christie, she still felt anxious.

The music on the jukebox was playing 'Love Is a Many-Splendored Thing'. A couple bent over it, deciding on their next tune, moved aside when they saw Babby.

'Hey, love, you going to sing for us? Save meself a bob on jukebox, don't mind if I do,' said the man. He turned to his girl. 'You're in for a treat. This one has the voice of a songbird and you wait until you hear her play that thing. Only she could make it sound like it's the music of the angels.'

Babby nodded a smile. She opened the bellows and began to play, gently at first, notes cascading, chords building up a heady accompaniment.

'Told you,' said the man when she started to sing 'Ellan Vannin' and the woman smiled and agreed she really had never heard anything as gorgeous as that sound in all her life.

But then everything stopped. It was the voice at first. That voice that struck fear in Babby's soul, the sound that made her halt dead in her tracks. She looked up and saw her mother, cupping her hand around her mouth and shouting 'Babby, will you get down off that stage there, you stupid, stupid girl!' Rage was the overwhelming emotion that ran through Violet's veins and, in a fury, she marched over and pulled Babby by the hair. 'I'm walking blind into an early grave. Have you any idea what you're doing? You! Get down now! You're coming home with me.'

The accordion, which she had dropped one end of in shock, let out a discordant, crashing moan, flumping open on an appropriate minor chord. Babby just stood there. Christie, with his finger hooked into the collar of his jacket which was slung over one shoulder, just smiled, flashing his eyes and tossing back his head. He remained at the bar, standing there, grinning.

Florrie came rushing out from the back room. 'You're taking her nowhere, Violet Delaney!'

'Oh, really? And are you going to look after her, then?' Violet's voice, sharper than glass as she hissed the question, caused the pub to become silent, as though a blanket of hush had been thrown over everyone's heads. Violet's face. Babby had never seen a face like it.

'Leave the wee girl alone,' Florrie said. 'She knows what she's doing.'

Babby stared at the floor.

'The wee girl? Thinks she knows what she's doing? That's a laugh,' said Violet.

Babby could feel her knees trembling. Tears welled up in her eyes and the mass of expectant faces in the pub was intimidating. She had nowhere to hide.

Florrie said once again, 'Leave her alone, Violet.'

'She's coming home with me,' she replied. And she began to shout at the onlookers, the two-shilling Johnny sailors and the dockers, 'You lot. I know your type. You and your mates peltin' our boys with stones, taking work from them that wait in line in the pens ...' She scoured the room, looked at all of them, her chin jutting out, as if challenging them to tell her to stop, her eyes resting on Christie.

'Go away, old woman,' he said. Which only made it worse.

'And who are you to tell me what I should do?' she said.

Christie came over, put an arm around Babby's shoulders.

'Get your hands off my daughter!' said Violet.

And someone in the pub, one of the Orange lads, started singing, 'Billy Boys, Billy Boys, make some noise, for the Billy Boys! We'll wash our hands with your Fenian blood! Sing, Billy Boys, Billy Boys!'

Any excuse for a bust up; the Catholics in the pub, leapt to their feet and started roaring, the Protestants, raised their glasses and cheered. Meanwhile Violet started shouting. She was taking on the whole pub now, with Babby looking on, appalled. She wished the ground would swallow her whole. Christie barely knew what Violet was on about. Something to do with what happened to her husband. But it was clear to everyone, that she hated him. Hated them all. Their *ways*.

'Come on, Babby. Come on home now. Hannah is missing you something dreadful and you should have told me you had run away from the home,' she yelled at Babby.

Babby trembled. 'How could I have told you? How could I? You would think it was such an awful thing to turn my back on the sisters.'

'And it is. Such a stupid, idiotic thing,' said Violet.

'No, it's not,' Babby replied. 'Tell me why?' she asked, challenging and obdurate.

She listened as Violet, quieter now, told her with humphs and sighs and frantic hand gestures that this pub was no place for her daughter, and what did she think she was going to do now? Had she any idea of the shame that she would bring on the Delaney family? Her father would be weeping tears in his grave, she hissed, at the thought of a young lady behaving the way she had.

'But I'm not a lady!' Babby yelled.

'That's one thing we know for sure. In the club at seventeen. The shame, Babby. How can you have let this happen to us?'

A grin spread across Christie's face. 'Well, this is a rum turnout,' he said, then his eyes grew cold and powerful. 'Come with me,' he said, gripping Babby's arm. 'Come outside, love ...'

'I don't want to,' she replied.

'I can help you,' he said, under his breath.

'Help me? How?'

'Well, you can back come to my house wi' me for a start ...'

'No, I'm fine here,' she answered.

He moved in closer to her. She could smell cigarettes on his breath and his arm snaked across her shoulders. She could feel his hand circling her neck, feel his grip tighten.

'I'm offering to help you.'

'I don't want your help!' she replied.

'What d'you mean, you don't want my help? You'd rather stay here? Or go wi' the old woman? Your ma? She going to bring it up?'

'She's not old. Just had an awful lot of sadness in her life. Makes you tired.'

'I'm offerin' to save you, Babby. *And* the child, if that's what you want. Come. With. Me!' It was frightening the way he said it. There was cruelty in the way his face twisted into a knot of anger and his beer breath made her gag.

'Christie, I don't look at a man and think: tell me what I should do now. I can figure it out myself,' she blurted out in a rush of words.

Anger flashed in his eyes.

'Oh, aren't you the clever one? In the club and think you know it all!'

'Get over yourself,' she shouted. And as he reached forward, causing her to spin on her heel and spring away from him, she found her mother standing there, incandescent with fury.

At a loss as to what she should do next, Babby could think of nothing but to give in. Florrie watched helplessly as Violet gripped Babby's arm, and steered her off.

'Don't even dare think of following us!' Violet shouted over her shoulder. 'Any of you!'

They walked back to the house in silence, Babby's face streaming with tears.

A shiny wet Hillman Imp car, parked under a street lamp, reflected macabre, distorted images of them on the bonnet. Fitting, thought Babby, in the light of what had just happened. Violet opened the door when they got home and Babby pushed past her and headed for the stairs.

'Where d'you think you're going, young lady?' Violet called after her.

'Up to my room.'

With that, Violet whipped around her, putting her arm out, blocking her way through. She said nothing, just raised an eyebrow. Babby stood for a moment, looking at her mother, waiting to see what would happen next.

'Let me past,' she said, her hand coming away sticky from the bannister, the same way as her feet came away sticky on the linoleum as she shifted from foot to foot. She stomped into the parlour and went and sat, not at the table, but in the shabby armchair pushed against one of the damp walls, folding her arms in a gesture of defiance.

'What the hell do you think you are doing, Babby?' said Violet. Babby shrugged and Violet thumped her fist on the dresser. 'You'd better start explaining herself.'

'Not now. I said I'm going upstairs,' she retorted, standing.

'Like heck you are. Come back here,' said Violet, following her around the table.

Babby stopped and turned. 'What?'

Violet jabbed her chest and said, 'What about me? Did you give me a single thought in all this?'

'You? Is that what you're angry about? How *you* feel?'

Violet's face clouded with ferocious indignation. 'Don't give me that cheek. You're not too old to feel the back of my hand!' She was furious at the way Babby was curling her lip at her, enraged about this baby, the shame, Jack dying on her, and this boy, Callum, ruining her daughter's life. But most of all, enraged that she hadn't had the courage to tell Babby the truth of it all from the beginning. She was so enraged that, when Babby said she didn't care what she thought – Violet could whack her about the head with an iron crowbar for all she liked – it wouldn't make her change her mind about Callum and keeping the baby, Violet spun around and snatched up a kitchen knife from the drawer. Babby looked on with horror.

'Mam!' cried Babby, as Violet tore away from her. 'Where are you going?'

Violet disappeared upstairs, then moments later reappeared on the landing with Jack's accordion, gasping and breathless.

'What the hell?' cried Babby.

'Thought you'd left this bloody thing in Anglesey – someone bring it to you, did they?'

And she stood there, shaking with fury, and stabbed the knife, one, two, three, into the bellows of Babby's accordion.

'Mam, no!' cried Babby, running up the stairs

Violet waved the knife, stuck it out in her daughter's direction. The blade flashed and when Violet lurched and stumbled forward, Babby thought she was about to plunge it right into her.

Instead, Violet stabbed the accordion again and ripped into the pleated layers of cloth and cardboard, hacking at the metal casing, slicing and chopping out all the goodness and joy and love Babby had in her heart, until it felt as if she was dead inside, as if Violet had cut her body and soul into a thousand tiny pieces with the knife.

'Mam, don't! I can't stand it! Why are you doing this?! Please, please stop! If you don't stop, I'll ... I'll ...'

'You'll what?'

And Babby just shook her head defeatedly and watched Violet staggering around, in danger of slipping and falling down the stairs if she made one wrong-footed move.

'P-pl-please stop! Stop it, Mam!' stammered Babby.

But Violet didn't stop. It was as if a blind rage had swept through her like a fire, and she continued to saw at the accordion, rip right into it.

Babby just watched, inconsolable, a tsunami of tears brimming up, then rolling down her face. The knife swished, made sounds in the air, and Babby's body jerked and twitched. She felt as if her mother had stuck the knife not only into the bellows of the accordion, but deep into her daughter's stomach and twisted.

She was shaking. And then a tearful Hannah appeared around the bedroom door, begging Violet, who barely noticed her terrified little face and quivering lip, to stop, but still she continued to cut and slice, and poke and prod and stab at the accordion with the knife, rearing up and lunging at it, over and over again, yelling at Hannah to get back in her room, until, finally exhausted with rage and the sheer effort of it all, she wiped her brow and dropped it.

'Bringing shame on the family! Go, leave right now, and take this bloody thing with you,' she said, jutting out her chin and waving an arm with a flourish.

What's the point? thought Babby; it was useless now. Yelping, trying to stuff the sound she made back into her mouth with her hand as Violet finally pushed it down the stairs, she just watched as it tossed and tumbled, one stair after another, until it honked and fell to the ground in a mangled heap and she walked sadly down to it.

Meanwhile, a sobbing Hannah had come out of her room again. She sank to her knees on the landing, clutched the bannisters so tightly her knuckles were white, and begged Violet to stop. Pat, who had just come into the house with Doris, looked on in horror.

'Good God, Mother, what have you done?' he cried. He saw the accordion lying on the floor just as the bellows let out a final sigh, as though it was taking its dying breath.

Babby turned to him. 'It's OK, Pat,' she said, as Violet slumped to her knees. She saw her future, the future she had imagined with Callum, in one of those tiny houses by the seaside in New Brighton, or a farm on Holy Island, or even a small terrace like Pauline's in Waterloo, becoming a meaningless nothing. She saw her past also – the first time she remembered hearing her father play, the first time she remembered being truly happy, when music and colour and light first filled her heart, when she danced around the kitchen to the sound of his singing, when the beautiful, beautiful accordion was the only way into a world where she had hope and dreams of what life could be without having to work in mindless dead-end jobs.

And then Violet struggled to her feet, tossed back her head and marched down the stairs. 'Enough of the theatricals,' she said without a hint of irony. 'Get over yourself, love. Turn off the bloody waterworks. Now.' And then she announced she had something to say. Something that would change everything.

'Babby,' she said. 'I'm going to tell you something. I'm going to tell you why you must *never ever* see that boy again!'

'I feel sick,' said Hannah, in a small voice.

'There's nothing wrong with you,' snapped Violet.

'Go to your room,' said Babby.

Hannah gave a round-eyed doleful look and left.

Babby shook her head. 'You know nothing,' she muttered.

'That's a funny thing to say to your mother,' said Violet. 'Don't you think?'

'You're mad,' she riposted. She looked mad, Babby thought. A bottle sitting empty on the table caught the light. Was it any wonder, after so many gins and bottles of stout, she was crazy?

Violet's eyes widened. 'What did you say?' she asked.

'You're *mad*, Ma!' said Babby, loudly.

And then Violet slapped Babby hard across the face. Babby raised her hand to the red mark and then Hannah was downstairs, yelling, 'Mammy, don't!'

'Get back to bed!' Violet shouted, spinning around on her heel and glaring fiercely at Hannah.

Babby's cheek hurt. She pressed her palm against her reddening face, willing the pain to stop. Hannah, still loitering, started to whimper when she saw white fingerprints across Babby's cheeks when she removed her hand.

'Go, Hannah!' Violet cried, and stuck out a wavering finger, pointing. 'Go to your room and don't come out until I say so!'

Hannah went, closing her bedroom door behind her. 'Please stop shouting,' she called from behind it.

'How could you, Babby?' said Violet, banging a fist on the table again, as if to emphasise the strength of her feelings. 'You've always been trouble! But this? I never imagined this would happen! How could you?!'

'Steady on, Mother,' said Pat to Violet. 'What's all this about?'

'How could I what, Ma?' shouted Babby.

'How could you even think to have a child with that boy Callum Lynch?'

Pat was ashen. He looked to his mother, then back to his sister, gawping in shock as he listened to this frantic exchange of words.

'Callum Lynch? *Lynch?* Danny Lynch's son?' he asked.

'Yes. The Mouse,' Violet replied, flatly. 'The one who killed your father.'

Babby paled. Her legs buckled and she sank into a chair in shock. Dry-mouthed, Babby looked at her mother with horror. 'Callum's father killed Dad? Wait ... are you sure?' asked Babby.

'As good as,' said Violet.

Babby could barely understand what her mother was accusing Callum's father of. The room was heavy with an oppressive quiet. Her heart felt like it might explode and a sickness rose to her throat as her legs wobbled underneath her.

'Daniel Lynch took your father's life over a pittance and his hurt pride. So think on. Whilst he's living a life of Reilly, your father is in his grave. Whilst Callum still has a father, someone to take care of him, to share life's troubles and celebrate the good times, you and our Pat and Hannah have no father at all, not for any of that. So how does that feel?'

'Is it really true?' She felt her legs wobbling and buckling again. She didn't know what to say if it was true. But even if it weren't, Violet thought it was, and that explained everything. It explained why Violet hated Callum so much, why even the mere mention of his name sent her into the blackest of moods. And why she didn't want her to marry him, even though he could have brought her respectability which would have saved her from the sorry mess she found herself in now. Wasn't marrying the father of one's child the conclusion that everyone in her situation would want? But no, Violet wanted her to be as far away from this boy as she could. So far away she would have had her give away her child to the nuns to send to Australia, if it had been her decision.

'Mam, answer me,' she said, her eyes glassy and wet with tears.

'Yes, of course it's bloody true!' said Violet.

She was even angrier now, grabbed both of Babby's arms in a ferocious grip, pinching her flesh with her fingers. There were white moon crescents where her nails dug in and she came nose to nose with her and spat through her teeth. 'It's true! And that boy knew it from the day he first set eyes on you!'

And then seizing a plate from the dresser, she threw it against the wall, with a scream of frustration. It smashed into tiny pieces. But as she looked at the shattered china, she realised that the act had had the opposite, not the desired effect. It only made her feel worse – so what else was there to do but collapse and cry unselfconsciously in an outpouring of self-loathing, clutching at Babby, begging her never to see the boy again, insisting that the pain of losing Jack would be nothing to the pain of having to look into the eyes of his killer's son every day.

She gulped down breath and trembled with shock.

Babby stared at her, wanting to fling the bottle on the table – the bottle that she held responsible for all this – across the room, and scream and collapse to the floor and remain there in a crumpled ball of despair. But what would be the point? Instead, she brushed away a tear that had spilled over her eye and was rolling down her cheek, and said nothing.

Violet, meanwhile, with a renewed burst of energy, placed a fist on her hip and slammed her palm flat on to the table.

'You choose, Babby. It's Callum Lynch – or me. But if you decide to marry him, understand this: you will never be part of this family again.'

Chapter Thirty-six

'Is it true?' asked Babby. 'Your dad is the Mouse?'

Callum was sitting outside the King's Arms on a low wall, clasping a bottle of beer tightly with both hands. He raised it to his lips. With his face reflected in the glass of the window, the lights of the Luxe picture palace opposite shimmied over his forehead. He bowed his head and got off the wall, and shuffled from one foot to another silently. He shrugged sadly, spoke in a whisper.

'Yes.'

Her blood went cold. This was too much to take in. Why would he not have told her? She could see no reason. Apart from the one Violet had told her.

He faltered, thrust his hands deep into the pockets of his jacket. 'That's why I had to leave when I found out. I was never going to come back, Babby. I really was going to go to Italy. But I couldn't stay away, I missed you ... Oh Babby, despite what my father did to your dad, I couldn't just leave you. I suppose Violet is furious?'

'She doesn't want us to have anything to do with each other. Says looking into my eyes would be like looking into the eyes of her husband's killer – or some such tommyrot.'

'None of us know what happened that night,' said Callum, 'Not even the police. No one was arrested. I only know this: your dad, he was a docker. And a proud one at that. He used to handle the cargo and he was a devil with the guy ropes and well liked. He'd go down to the pen, wait with the others. My da, he was the foreman, used to pick them that would work each day. And it was a hard job. But he tried to be fair.'

'Why did they call him the Mouse?' she asked.

'Because he spoke so soft, like. But he was still stern. He tried to keep work spread even between the men. He knew those with a family to feed, those fellas whose wives were living off food parcels from the nuns or kind friends. He would decide who was going to get work each and every day. And your dad. He was poor, Babby, he didn't have much money. But he was reliable, a wizard with the ropes, wouldn't balk at whatever cargo came in. Whether it was filthy carbon, or the bags of rubber for Dunlop tyres, he would get stuck in. But when he started working at the Boot Inn, he was making a few extra bob. What was me dad to do, Babby? He couldn't pick your dad over the other wretches who had nothing at all. If he was picked, they would argue that they needed the work more. He lost favour with some of the men and so gradually they turned their backs on him. That was when my father stopped choosing him ...'

'My mam always hated anything to do with the Boot Inn. But what about that night. What happened?'

'Well again, I weren't there and it's mostly gossip. But your dad was in his cups and my dad and a few of the fellas walked in and one of them started singing one of your dad's songs, mocking, like. And that was it. Like a cork popping. It kicked off and they started fighting. I remember looking out our window and someone had lit a bonfire on the waste ground by Grafton Street and the sky was lit up like it was the devil's hell. Blood red. Anyway, your dad hit his head on the corner of the table when he got punched and fell. Everyone knew that. And I remember me dad coming home, the Rozzers on his heels. He was bloodied, all right. They say he threw the punch, but they were brawling. Oh, the Mouse roared, that's for sure. All the years of choosing one fella over another, saying who should work or should not – it takes its toll. It wasn't just your dad who resented him, there were others. Many of them. The Rozzers took him away. But, by then, your pa was dying in the hospital. There's some say it was madness for my da to go to the Boot Inn, knowing as how your dad might be feeling. He was struggling because the wages there were nothing compared to what he'd been getting at the docks. Any road, my da ... well, he paid the price, all right ...'

'What d'you mean?'

'My dad. It's not like he's living the life of Reilly, like your mam says. He suffered too, Babby.'

'I thought he was living abroad. In Italy, Mam said. That's where you were supposed to have gone. To be with him.'

Callum shook his head.

'Well, she's got that wrong. I need to put her straight on that one. But never mind me dad. It's you I need to fix things with first. Because there's one more thing that I can tell you is true and there's no argument on this one. This is one truth, Babby, it wasn't *me*. It was me dad. He was there that night. And your dad – and they were all in it together. It was a fight and I have no details as to who threw the punch that took your dad down. But I know, me and me dad, we're two different people. And it wasn't the first time my father and yours had got into a brawl, friends though they'd once been. Men like that were born scrapping.'

'Why didn't you tell me, though? About your father?'

'It was only after that night at the hollas, when you mentioned the Boot Inn, that I put two and two together. That I realised you were Jack Delaney's daughter. And then I had to be sure. Mrs Reilly confirmed it.'

'The sisters tried to stop me seeing you. They wrote to my mother.'

'Well, they're a rum lot.'

'That's a nice way of putting it.'

'Any road, one thing this sorry affair did for me, though, if it's any consolation to you, Babby, is that I never want to be part of that world. And I never will, Babby. But you have to believe me: when I met you I had no idea Jack Delaney was your father. And when I found out I knew I had to leave Liverpool right away, I knew I would have to find out the whole story. And when I did, how could I tell you?'

'You could have tried.'

'I did. And I'll say it again. It's not my father you're looking at, it's me, *me* ...' As he said the words, he jabbed himself in the chest. 'Me, Babby, someone who raced across the field with a bucket of cowpats, the one who kissed you on the farm gate, the one who stood knee-deep in pigsswill and didn't care because he was with you. The one who loves you Babby. Please, please, please – you're not your mother and I'm not my father. This is our chance to start again and shouldn't we take it?'

She dropped her eyes, fiddled with her cuffs, for want of something to do. 'Say something,' he said. 'What's wrong with you? Are you crying? Please don't cry.'

Babby bowed her head. Tears were pricking her eyes in hot silent stabs and one of them fell with a plop on to her lap. She screwed one hand into the other and dug her nails hard into her palm, hoping that the pain might shock away her tears.

There was silence, now, apart from the sound of Babby's sniffling. Callum began scrabbling in his pocket and brought out a hanky. He was going to offer it to her, but instead he slumped forward, began crying silently into the crook of his arm. He gathered himself, blew his nose, put it back in his pocket.

Seeing him like that, she slid an arm around his waist from behind and rested her head on his shoulder.

'I'm sorry,' he said to her, raising his head, relieved at her touch. 'Do you love me still?'

She did love him, despite these dreadful revelations. She loved him, not only for the fact that he loved her, but for the fact that he didn't care what the world thought – it was what Babby thought that mattered to him.

'Of course, Cal. You didn't stop loving me when I fell pregnant, so why would it make any difference to me about what happened with our fathers?'

He twisted to her, put her head under his chin and spoke into her hair. 'How about me going to see your mother? Your Pat? I can explain.'

'No,' she answered. 'That would do no good. My mother will never come around to this ... this situation.'

'You sure?'

She rested her head against his shoulder, then lifted her face to look at his. 'They hate me for loving you. And there's nothing you can do about that.'

They went inside the pub, bloodied but not broken, and Florrie was there to meet them. She had pre-pared hot coffee with a dash of whiskey and when Babby started to make an apology for missing her shift, Florrie told her to shush.

'See the thing is,' said Callum. 'Babby ... Babby and me, well we are ... we are ...' It was as if he couldn't get the words out.

'Say it,' whispered Babby.

But Florrie, placing a hand on his arm, finished the sentence for him. 'You're having a baby,' she said. He dropped his eyes to the floor.

Babby sat with her chin resting on her knees which were drawn up to her chest. With a blanket around her shoulders, provided by Florrie, she sank deep into the chair. Tears welled in her eyes.

'Come on, love. There's no reason to cry,' said Florrie. She took a finger and gently tilted her chin up so that Babby was looking directly into her face. A single tear rolled down the girl's cheek. 'Why don't you tell Florrie what's the matter? Let's see if we can sort things out for you ...'

'Things?' said Babby, startled. 'No, no, I could never *ever.* And please don't tell me to go back to Saint Jude's – I could never do that, either. Callum is going to look after me. We're going to be married.'

'That's what I wanted to hear you say,' Florrie said, clapping her hands together and smiling. 'So, if you've made this decision, what's the matter?'

'It's my mother,' said Babby. 'Callum and I are closer than you would ever imagine, not just two people in love. We're bound together in another way, the very worst. There was a fight. At the Boot Inn. My dad and his.'

'Took me a bit of time to realise who Callum was at first. But don't you think everyone knows what happened? said Florrie. It's been the talk of Liverpool since it happened. Men fighting over a job. For a pittance. There were backhanders. Favours. Trouble was always brewing at the pens. And your dad, Callum, he always got the brunt of it. But it was never supposed to have ended the way it did. Your poor father dead, Babby, and Callum's dad in hospital to this day, not able to put two words together, and your mum devastated with the whole sorry business and drinking.'

Babby stopped. 'What do you mean, Callum's dad in hospital?'

Florrie faltered. 'Well, when I say hospital, it's not really a hospital is it, Callum? Saint Peter's Home for the Feeble-Minded. Sorry, Callum, love, have I spoken out of turn?'

Callum shook his head.

'What d'you mean?' asked Babby.

'It's one of the best kept secrets in Liverpool. But some nuns have a habit of talking. I know Sister Mary Joesph who runs the place. She could never have taken the vow of silence, that one. It would have killed her. She told me all about your da.'

'Your dad is in Saint Peter's? The asylum?' asked Babby.

Callum murmured a yes. His face emanated sadness. She could measure the desperation of his thoughts by the way he moved across the room to the window.

She sighed.

'So that's why you let everyone think he was in Italy?'

He shrugged sadly.

'I were ashamed. He got sick, really sick. Takes its toll when you live a hard life ...'

'And was it ... is it anything to do with me da ...?'

'Please don't, Babby ...'

No, this wasn't the time for him to explain. She would wait, say nothing more, ask no more questions. And they would speak about it when he was ready.

Later that night, the tears wouldn't stop flowing. But they were tears, not of sadness or joy, just a spilling out of everything Babby had been holding in for months and months. Babby supposed it was love that was making her do this. Whatever it was, it was overwhelming, so intense it hurt just to breathe. Florrie told her this was what happened when you were having a baby, you felt everything much more keenly. She had allowed them to stay in Babby's room – not a word to anyone, mind.

Babby talked to Callum into the early hours of the morning. How are we going to live? Callum? How

are we going to bring a baby into the world? We
don't know anything.

'There's only one thing we need to know, Babby.
That we love each other,' he said. 'And the rest we
can learn.'

He gave her a kiss that tasted sweet and good and
kind. And lying in bed with him that night, with the
blanket tucked around her body, beginning to doze,
skin against skin, each one of his breaths, like gossamer on her cheek, she felt safer than she had ever
felt in her life. And the strange thing was, despite
everything, she just wished Violet was here to be
part of it.

Chapter Thirty-seven

Callum stood up and the hinged seat of the tramcar slammed up behind him. When he stepped off and came out on to the pavement, he felt a rush of cold air. The lights in the city were coming on, dashes of colour against the smog of traffic fumes and coal fires. A few cars were parked on Netherfield Road, their roofs glowing a sickly yellow under the gas lights. Scrabbling in his pocket, he calmed himself down with a cigarette and then, placing his feet with great care to avoid cracks in the pavement, he set off towards Joseph Street. His eyes quickly adjusted to the smog as he made his way with the throngs of people coming back from the city to the tenement blocks and terraces.

Violet had fallen asleep in a chair, dead to the world. When she heard knocking at the door it was like a dim and distant dream. She struggled to her feet and went to answer the knocking. At first, she was confused when she opened the door and he reminded her who he was. Then, as he'd expected, she went to shut it in his face. He blocked it with his foot and begged her for just five minutes of her time. She replied saying that five minutes was too long after he had ruined her daughter, but he pleaded with her to let him come in. If it hadn't been for eagle-eyed Peggy, who was clearly enjoying the scene from her vantage point of the cab shelter, she would have sent him packing. She told him brusquely that he could come in and give his speech and then leave, but nothing would make her change her mind about him and Babby.

Stepping inside, Callum knew it would be pointless to cajole or entreat her. She padded aimlessly across the scuff-marked kitchen linoleum, worn smooth in the centre, the pattern visible only in the corners, the soles of her bare feet making squelching noises. There was a roll-top desk and she searched inside it, found what she was looking for – a bottle of gin, wrapped in an old nylon petticoat, and poured herself a glass. She sat down in the armchair, leaving Callum standing, his face half in shadow under the light of a wooden standard lamp.

'What have you got to say for yourself, then?'

'Nowt much about me. You know I love your Babby and I want to marry her. It's me dad I want to talk about.'

Violet bristled. She cradled the glass of gin in her lap.

'Your da? You've come all this way just to punish me?'

Her sentences came out in short, halting bursts. In between she took deep breaths, to try and calm her rage. When she picked up a cigarette, her hands were shaking so much she couldn't light it.

'No. Not to punish you. Just to set you straight. As to how things are – were – between my dad and your Jack.'

Violet tutted.

'You know they'd been pals since they were nippers. Paper boats on the boating lakes in Stanley Park, fishing in the River Alt, swimming in the Scaldies – me dad told me those stories. And I can't promise you I know what happened that night, no one does, but I know that when my dad left, Jack was a dead man. And so, in another way, was my dad ... But not being able to say sorry, that was the worst for him. And if we should be angry with anyone, it should be with the Rozzers. They were looking for someone to blame and Jack didn't have a voice to say what happened and I know that it's the one thing in my father's life that he would have changed. If he could have turned back the clock, if he had walked out of the Boot the minute before it kicked off, oh, he would have given anything for that. He never meant your Jack to come to harm that night. And I'm asking you, Violet, to please, please forgive my father.'

'Never!'

'Don't you think Jack would have? Da told me them days in the pen weren't always bad. Told me about when the two of them found a snake in that banana cargo from the West Indies. And they took the snake on the tramcar to the hospital. And Jack asking for dirt money when he came home covered in muck. And one time, the other foreman, Aga Khan, he was called, said because it was white muck – a sack of talcum powder it was, had split all over him – he wouldn't get a penny dirt money. Dirt money had to be the black stuff and he was white as a ghost, and my da kicked up a stink for your Jack and, in the end, they gave it him, and he bought everyone drinks at the Boot to celebrate their victory.'

'They might have been pals. But if your da hadn't stopped giving Jack work he would still be alive today!'

Callum felt a rush of blood to his cheeks.

'It was an accident. A stupid fight that got out of hand. You can't blame my father for being there.'

'He could have stopped it! It was his idea to bring his pals down to the Boot Inn! Just like if he had given Jack more work at the docks he might have given up playing that monstrous instrument and drinking all day, wasting his life away on music and booze!'

'Jack *wanted* to play at the Boot! He loved it! It was his passion! He would never have given it up! He was born to sing. Music was in his blood. He was a better man than those miserable creatures in the pen with only their brawn to make a crust. He had a soul. That's why me dad loved him. He was different to the rest of us. It was his life. Just like it's Babby's life!'

The mention of Babby's name sent Violet into a rage. She looked at him with fury in her eyes. Her whole body shook violently, her fists clenched, and her blood ran hot through her veins. Did he really think this would make any difference? That she would change her mind about him and her daughter? Ludicrous!

'Look, Violet. You lied to me. You lied to your daughter – about me trying to find her. And the letters ... But I'm prepared to forgive you, so why can't you do the same?'

'The letters? That wasn't me,' she snapped. 'That was Mrs Reilly and the nuns, thinking they were

doing the right thing by not passing Babby's letters on to you. You've no idea how these nuns take
control of any situation. You let them in – and then,
wallop, they have you. It's like they own your soul.
I can't do anything about that,' she cried out bitterly.
'I'm just not strong enough.'

'And the letter that someone wrote to Babby, pretending to be me? Saying it was over?'

'I suspect it was the nuns who wrote that as well.
Or our Pat. He was the one who turned you away
at our door. I admit, I didn't stop him. I'll take my
share of the blame. But can't you see that there's not
a soul who wouldn't think that the best thing was for
you and Babby to have the child adopted. I didn't
want you getting in the way of that! You're children,
both of you! Babies having a baby!'

Callum flinched.

'Will you give us your blessing? For the wedding?' he asked. It was the simplest of requests.

And when Violet said no, he could have shoved
his fist through the windowpane. He jumped up and
pushed his chair back sharply and it scraped across
the floor, making the sound of a squealing pig.

'Well, if that's the way it is, then that's the way
it'll stay. Won't change a fig though …' he said.

Violet stared ahead, sticking a cigarette in her
mouth, and sucking on it audibly.

Callum was about to leave.

'Wait. There is one more thing. That man? The one Babby found you with before you sent her to Anglesey? It was Rex Worrall, wasn't it? Your fancy man?' he asked.

Violet jolted.

'What of it?'

'What about Gladys, his sister?'

'Gladys doesn't care ...'

'And you so high and mighty about me and Babby, and you carrying on with Rex under our noses? That's why you didn't want her to work at the Boot Inn, isn't it? You didn't want to have to worry about Babby finding out from Gladys that Rex has a wife. She might have buggered off to Scotland because she couldn't stand Gladys, but he's still married. She'll never divorce him, so Florrie at the King's Arms told me.'

Violet turned puce with indignantion. 'No! It has nothing to do with Rex. You have no idea what kind of a place that is, what kind of a woman Gladys is. I never wanted that for Babby, *that's* why I sent her to Anglesey. It was her last chance. To get an education. To get out of this city.'

'And are you still ...well, carrying on with Rex? He was there at the Boot that night, wasn't he? Some say it was his fault for not calling the police soon enough, that he could have stopped it before it got out of hand ...'

'Now who's the judge and jury? He helped me after Jack died. Not only with the rent, finding me jobs! I don't know what Hannah and I would do without him!'

Callum expelled a long breath of air. 'It's time for all of us to end all of this, to stop telling lies, to stop being so concerned about what everyone thinks. What some people say is a wicked thing, is a fine thing to others. I have no truck with them that say you shouldn't step out with Rex Worrall, so let's put a stop to this, please.' He paused, but she didn't reply. 'There is a way, you know. If you don't feel shame, then you can't be shamed. You should try it. What crime have me and Babby committed? Loving someone? The only crime around herc is that two men could kill each other over a four-shilling job. So, what d'you say – will we not shake hands and forgive?'

Violet rose, puffed out her chest and jabbed the air with a finger. 'I will *never* forgive your father for what happened. My husband dead, and him living a life that is by right my Jack's!'

'And what life is that, then?' asked Callum, angrily.

'Who knows? But in Italy, I heard. Too ashamed to show his face in Liverpool. Left and not been seen since ... Living the bloody high life, no doubt. Well, you'll know all about that.'

Callum trembled. He knew he had to speak with a steady voice, for this was the most important thing of all.

'The reason my father has not been seen is not because he left Liverpool.'

Violet shrugged. She looked at him, her eyes cold, glassy, uncaring. Though there was a part of her that wanted him to continue, she didn't want to show it.

Callum paused, drew in breath, trying to calm himself.

'My father, after he was brought in by the coppers for questioning and then let go, because it's not a crime if a man hits his head on the corner of a table – well, he couldn't exactly remember what had happened, but when he went back to work, images of the fight kept coming back into his head. One day it was so bad he collapsed, fainted right away in front of all the lads. When he came to, he was like a dead person. He couldn't utter a single word. When he got home, he began to talk again, but he spoke in back-to-front sentences, didn't know the right words for things. He would call the butter dish a cradle, a bicycle, a chariot. Stuff like that. He forgot my name, talked about his mother as if she was alive, sitting in the next room. He'd had a hard life, Da, as a boy. Maybe it was the memories of those days that did for him, maybe it was the guilt and desperation of what had happened to your Jack – well, I don't know, but he slumped. Real bad. He visited the doctor, who said he was depressed, and they sent him to Rainhill hospital. And that was the beginning of the end. They put him on a ward for the mentally unstable. And my biggest fear was if people might say, "Where's your da? Cal? I heard he's in the Loony bin – the nuthouse." I would have hated that. I would have felt ashamed. So I told no one. Started the Italy rumour to keep gossip at bay ...'

Violet watched him gulp air and swallow. He's probably expecting me to place a hand on his trembling arm and say, 'Oh love, I had no idea', but why should I? she thought. It won't bring my Jack back.

'I remember thinking ...' he continued. 'It's over, Da – that was when I came to visit him. They had put him in a bed, strapped his arms to the sides of it. He looked like, well, like it wasn't him. Like it was some other chap that was wearing my da like he was a new suit of clothes. I've lost you to these people, whoever they are, Pops, I thought. And as if that wasn't enough, when he started to cause trouble, kick up a fuss, say he wanted to leave, he was given electroconvulsive therapy and injected with something – what was it? Imipramine. Yes. Terrible, that was. Seemed to make him wilder and angrier. He was straining in the bed, screaming at me to untie him, baring his teeth like a wild animal and snarling, twisting the sheets, tearing at them, plucking at the air. And all I could think of was that it was because of the fight that had got him to this sorry place, and why weren't they doing anything to help him? Then one day the doctors said to me, 'If we let him go home, he might do something really bad, like kill a little 'un. That would be on your head as well, Callum. You wouldn't want that, would you? This thing is only going one way.' I said I would be happy to take the risk, but the doctors just laughed at me. Said that it was out of the question. Which was when they told me that there was this operation.'

Violet stared ahead, blankly.

'They would get two nylon balls, put them into the scalp and then push rods through them into his brain, so that they could burn out the part that was making him violent. It sounded like Frankenstein or something. No bloody way did I want them them do that to him. I argued, of course. But they did it anyway. When I saw him after the first half of the operation, he looked like he was something out of a flaming horror film. He'd have given old Boris Karloff a run for his money, I reckon, with these strange lumps in his heads that were the balls. They pinned back his forehead, cut a flap of his skin, and opened him like he was a tin of pilchards. 'Don't worry we'll shave off the lumps in his skullholes when we're done,' they said, but I felt so bloody sick to see him like that and I begged them to stop. But they didn't.'

Callum waited for a response from Violet. There was none. Just silence and the soft tick, tick, tick of the clock.

'I asked them how, if they don't know where the mind actually is, they could find the right bits of the brain to burn? It's not like you can see people's thought, is it? They couldn't answer that. Dad was operated on for hours. Wide awake, he was, when they did it all. Can you imagine, Violet? A week later he was sent to Saint Peter's Home for the Feeble-Minded. Where he still is now. Italy?' he added bitterly with a hollow laugh. 'Hardly. Still has flashbacks to this day. Reliving that moment when your Jack crashed to the floor at the Boot Inn. The more drugs they gave him, the more they turned him into this kind of dead person . But maybe that's a blessing ...'

Violet turned her had away from the light. 'I think you'd better go now,' she said.

He nodded and walked towards the door, then looked over his shoulder. 'Who knows if my dad threw the first punch? But just because a man does one bad thing in his life, it doesn't mean he's not a good man.'

Shadows moved across the room. There was something in the breath that Violet let out, something that hinted at a darkness that came from the very depths of her soul.

'You can let yourself out,' she said.

Chapter Thirty-eight

She heard the door shut behind him, heard him sigh, heard the sound of his boots on the pavement. Standing, she moved across to the window, pushed the fraying curtain aside and watched him walk down the street, reduce to a silhouette, then disappear down the hill. She took a bottle, poured a neat gin into the coronation mug, took huge gulps, then stared into the bottom of it. Bewildered that she had finished it so quickly, she poured another, and another, and loathed herself for it, until she stumbled into the dresser, crashed down into a chair, and finally lost consciousness.

Two days later, Violet took the ten o'clock tramcar to the station. The train journey to Freshdale passed with her head gently vibrating against the window as she watched the outside rush past, grey turning green, then green turning to the powder yellow of the sand dunes, then yellow turning to the charcoal black of the spindly pine trees. Kathleen had had a friend who had worked at an asylum whose job was to take the dead bodies down to the mortuary. The dead body would be wrapped in a sheet and put in an open tin coffin and laid on the bottom of a trolley on a hidden shelf like a stretcher, with a sheet discreetly draped over a second shelf above; on top of this, sometimes a pot of tea and plates of biscuits were placed so that no one would guess that there was a person underneath as they rattled through the wards. They had laughed about it at the time, but today it seemed truly macabre. Please God, she thought, she wasn't going to see these things for herself.

She got off the train and set off down Virgin's Lane. In a dreadful revisiting, it was in the same road as the Mother and Baby Home where Babby had been sent and was run by the same order of nuns. Walking as fast as she could past the huge houses – priests' homes, Saint Sylvester's Orphanage, nursing homes, and the grim Saint Jude's, eventually she saw the building. Saint Peter's was like the others, but with a creaking cockerel weathervane, and there was no hint of what lay behind the wooden front doors. A thought came into her head that she puzzled over. Was Saint Peter's where many of the poor souls in this road ended up? Like the girls in the Mother and Baby Home who were considered not to have the strength of character to cope in the real world? Or the unruly children in the orphanage who were always in trouble, back and forth to the police, until they also were deemed too out of control not to be restrained. Did they all make their way down this cul-de-sac, never to find a way out? Outside the hospital there were dried-up flower beds with stunted rose bushes with black spots on their leaves, and plant pots of wilted geraniums by the front gates.

To push away thoughts of what desperate souls might be behind the grey nets, for it was too distressing to contemplate, she tried to lose herself by counting how many windows, how many steps up to the door. She noticed that the first impression was designed to keep people out: the closed curtains, the signs saying no visitors unless by appointment, the barbed wire running on top of the fencing, the thorny, prickly, forbidding shrubbery. But then she had a darker thought. Was this designed to keep people in?

Then, without warning, the front door opened, and a nun came down the steps and got into an Austin Ten car which was parked on the front drive. Violet shrank back against the wall. It was Sister Agnes from Saint Jude's! What the hell am I doing here? she said under her breath.

The car drove off. Steeling herself, she stepped out from the bushes and went up the steps. She pushed the bell and waited. Finally, she heard footsteps. The door opened and a nun wearing a veil, whose starched white coif framed a smooth face, nodded hello. 'You must be Mr Lynch's visitor?' she said.

Violet flinched. She felt the hairs on the back of her neck stand up stiffly. Nuns were not to be trusted, she thought, shaking hands with the nun, who introduced herself as Sister Michael.

'Follow me,' said the nun. She spoke in soft Irish tones, one of those sisters who said skissors instead of scissors and fillum instead of film. She didn't have the stern look of the nuns at Saint Jude's. She looked almost happy, as though she was living a useful and rewarding life. She had a smile that was serene and compassionate and her face was unlined. There were no bags under her eyes, no deep grooves between the eyebrows like those etched into Violet's face.

'My dear, please don't expect too much. Daniel is very sick. Each new year we can't quite believe he has survived but he is a fighter. Fiercely independent and determined, I'd say.'

Violet was led down the long corridor that smelled of beeswax and the criss-cross of the parquet floor stretched out in front of her in zig-zag patterns. When she was ushered in to a large room by a beady-eyed nurse dressed in white with white rubber shoes, she felt panicked. Beyond, through a half-open door, she caught the vacant stare of a patient, a young woman in a grey cotton shift, sitting in a bath chair, and she wondered if this was terrible mistake, coming here. A kind looking eighty-year-old nun, with the smile of a young girl, breezed in and led her through another room – the breakfast room, she told Violet. This was where the more independent patients were allowed to sit. Then they were into another corridor, with more rooms off it. This place really was a rabbit warren, a maze of despair, thought Violet, noticing names, written by hand, on cards stuck on the doors. Fathers, mothers, sisters, brothers, daughters, sons, no doubt. One was just a sad smudge. What had happened to the person whose name had been reduced to a smudge? she wondered. Death? They stopped outside a door with a brass name plate. Sister Mary Joseph, it said.

'Just wait a minute,' came the cry from beyond the door.

She could hear the wireless. The theme to *Music While You Work* was playing. There was a click as someone turned it off, followed by a pause. Then she heard a voice from beyond the door again, calling for them to enter.

'This is Daniel Lynch's visitor,' said the nun with the kind face.

'Ah, well now,' asked Sister Mary Joseph. She stuck out her hand and smiled and said, 'Pleasure to meet you. I believe he's expecting you ...'

Violet nodded, her eyes big, round, and worried.

She followed the nun out and into a large room with floor to ceiling windows and French doors looking out on to a rockery. There were armchairs lined up in rows and a wireless. Next to the wireless was a lectern and there was a man standing at the window, muttering something as he was flicking through a magazine. There was a second white-haired old man asleep in a chair. He stirred, looked straight at Violet and leered. 'Snow on top means fire down below! Hells ruddy bells! You're a little beauty.'

More patients now, all different ages, dressed uniformly in cream-coloured cotton loose clothing, seemed to appear like magic to look at her. Sister Mary Joseph shooed them away like flies.

'Get on with you,' she said. 'Don't worry, Violet. They're harmless.'

The nurses wore similar uniforms to the nuns and outside the windows of the French doors, on the veranda which looked on to a courtyard, they seemed like white birds, flapping and pecking about. One of them wheeled a patient, his head lolling, drooling as he took a nap. Was this Daniel Lynch?

'This way, please ...' said Sister Mary Joseph, ushering Violet to a curtained-off area. She explained that the men's ward was in a different wing to the women's ward but that in two weeks' time they would be having their annual dance where they would all come together in the ballroom and behave just like the outside world. She smiled. 'You know Daniel's son, Callum? He always comes to this. Always. He helps us with the rum punch. He's never missed it. Never. He's a good boy.' The nun touched her gently on her forearm. 'Now just a minute ...' The bunch of keys jangled at the nun's hip.

Violet fiddled with the collar on her coat as she waited.

'Ready now,' said Sister Mary Joseph, after unlocking the door. She took Violet through it, locked it again on the other side, and then led her through a secure ward with beds on either side. Patients with hollowed-out eyes followed ther progress. The nun walked briskly, shooed one, who lurched forward with a lolling uneven gait and a vacant smile, away.

'They try to get into the next ward,' she explained to a frightened Violet. 'Keep up now. We don't want them slipping through with us – or worse, getting caught between the two pass doors. Always a bit of a to-do when that happens. See, we need to separate the patients into their wards. They all have different categories. Category One won't do getting all mixed up with Category Two ... Then it really would be bedlam.' She laughed at her own joke.

Violet picked up her pace. She wondered what 'category' Daniel Lynch would be in.

'Well done,' said the nun. When they went through the door which had an oval glass window in it, she shut it quickly. Violet looked over her shoulder to see a group of three or four, who'd hoped to slip through with them, had gathered in a gaggle, sad faces pressed up against the glass forlornly. She shuddered.

Each room leading off the ward had names of the saints and martyrs. Campion, Southwell, Fisher. They arrived, finally, at one that was named Howard. It was hot and stuffy and the air felt thick and warm.

'Howard is where we'll find Mr Lynch.'

The mood here was different, more sombre. There were no patients wandering aimlessly around – they all seemed as if they had been sedated. Violet was led to a bed pushed up against the far wall. The man sitting on it had his back to them. His legs were over one side, a slipper dangling from one foot, the other bare, his back hunched over. She could just see the top of his head, wisps of his hair. It was going to grey and there was a lot less of it, but this was Daniel Lynch, all right. The nun went over to him. She examined his eyes closely, but perfunctorily, with what looked like a small pencil-like torch.

'Come on, lovely. You have a visitor,' she said, putting the torch away. Daniel Lynch raised his head and Violet approached the bed. His eyes turned to her and he reached out a hand, then frowned.

'Sheila?' he asked, squinting.

'I'll leave you two alone,' said the nun.

'Sheila, love, is that you?' A hopeful smile lit up his face.

Violet faltered. Sheila. Daniel's wife. He thought Violet was his wife.

'No. It's Violet. Jack's wife,' she stuttered.

Daniel Lynch nodded his head.

'Ah, the fella with the accordion. *Oh Danny Boy* ...' he sang softly, a smile playing across his lips. 'Sheila, you came. I knew you'd come.'

'Oh God,' Violet said. 'Oh God, Daniel, I'm so sorry ...' Her eyes filled with tears. 'I never wanted this ...'

Daniel exhaled a breath.

'Touch him if you want, dear,' said Sister Mary Joseph. 'Daniel's harmless. No one knows what a patient like this understands – and just because he looks like that, doesn't mean to say that he can't make sense of what you're saying. Only God knows what's in his head. He talks about an accordion a lot, sings all the old favourites. Don't you, Danny?'

Daniel Lynch sighed. ''Twas a Liverpool girl I loved ...' he murmured, then tapered off into nothing.

'Shall I leave you alone?' said the nun.

She left, busying herself with the patient opposite, and Violet sat on the chair beside Danny's bed. He was staring ahead vacantly.

'Danny...?' said Violet. His eyes swivelled, blinked away confusion, and for a moment, he was lucid, alive, staring deep into her soul.

'Yes, dear?'

'I'm so sorry. All this time. Blaming you. It was wrong.'

There was no way of knowing whether he had understood what she said. But when he reached out and grasped her hand, raised it to his discoloured cheek, she let it remain there for a moment. And then she took a handkerchief and wiped his mouth. He smiled slowly, reached out again, and touched a tendril of her hair.

'Our two children to be wed, Danny. And there is to be a child. A force for good if ever there was one ...'

Surrender. In that moment, Violet looked as though all the life had drained out of her, as if she wasn't

Violet, just a sad old woman with skin like paper and sunken eyes. This man that she had hated for so long, that she blamed for her husband's death. And here he was, his life destroyed by the same hand that had destroyed her husband. Drink, and poverty, and frustration. How she had dreamed she would make him pay. But now? To see him like this? All hate, recrimination, fell away in an instant. She felt foolish and ashamed.

She gathered up her belongings, the umbrella, coat, pushed her fingers into her shabby calfskin gloves, and left quietly.

'You've had enough time with him?' asked the sister.

'Yes,' she replied. 'For now.'

In a daze, she walked down Virgin's Lane to the station, tears streaming down her face. 'I'm so sorry,' she murmured. 'For such an awful thing. Such a stupid, wasteful thing. Oh Danny, I'm so very, very sorry.'

Chapter Thirty-nine

Callum sat at the table in the kitchen of the King's Arms, nervously tying and untying his tie. Babby looked at him and smiled worriedly. Her body curved into itself as she shifted in the chair. She smoothed out the checked tablecloth, pressed creases into the corners, her palms going sticky and hot with the fear of what was to come, Violet entered the room and for a moment the only sound was a whistling kettle on the stove. Callum took it off the heat.

'Can I sit down?' asked Violet, finally.

A stony-faced Callum pulled out a chair.

'Well then,' said Violet, with a tremulous smile. 'It looks like we've got a wedding to organise. And quickly.'

Babby jumped up and threw her arms around her so vigorously, Violet almost toppled off her chair.

Callum beamed. He could hardly believe it. 'Thank you, thank you, Mrs Delaney! I thought you would never speak to either of us again.'

'So did I. And I'm sorry for that. I was wrong to blame your father. Will you forgive me?'

'Nowt to forgive. I adore your Babby and that's all that matters.'

'She's my daughter. Maddening and bold and headstrong, but Callum, I do love her. There was never any doubt about that. And if you love her … well there's nothing else to say.'

'Will you bring Rex?' asked Callum.

She glanced at her daughter. 'Perhaps,' she replied.

The banns were read within the week. Father O'Casey had said he would do the ceremony on a Wednesday evening at dusk, but Babby had asked what was wrong with a Saturday morning and finally he had relented. Florrie provided the dress, brand new from Blacklers, which she had unpicked and re-stitched to hide her bump. It was ivory white and Empire line, the swell of her belly at four and a half months discreetly covered by a large bow and tiny pleats. There was also an organza stole and, to finish it off, she would be wearing long white kid gloves and an elegant Juliet cap veil that Violet had worn when she had married Jack. Violet had made

Hannah a bridesmaid's dress out of pale-blue chiffon with a white sash made out of Babby's old communion dress, which had come up looking good as new after she had washed it with Dolly Blue. She had bought herself a new frock that hugged her hips and showed off her tiny waist and Callum splashed out on a double-breasted suit from George Henry Lees and looked the business – like Errol Flynn, Violet had said. The Delaneys had done with shame. Finally, they had something to celebrate.

The morning of the wedding, Pat met Doris at her mother's house in Queen's Drive. 'Doris! Good news! The organist has agreed to play for the service.'

'Smashing,' said Doris, full of excitement about the tea dress with the sweeping net underskirt and the teardrop hat with a pearl-embellished birdcage veil that she had bought from TJ's.

Pat told her that Violet had suggested that they should also have the choir.

'How much will that cost?' asked Doris.

'A fortune, that's for sure. But can you imagine our Babby walking down the aisle in silence? She'll want music – and if she doesn't get it, she might even suggest playing the pub's flaming accordion.'

He smiled, and Doris smiled back. 'Can't have that, can we? Any road,' he added, 'Rex has offered to pay.'

'Has he, indeed?' replied Doris.

They arrived at Joseph Street with a good few hours to spare and discovered Hannah, flushed pink with happiness, standing on a stool in her dress and Violet, with a mouth full of pins, sewing a hem. Hannah's hair was pulled straight off her face and held by a rose flower crown – another of Florrie's miraculous creations – and Doris said she looked like Shirley Temple. Kathleen fussed around them, spreading a white linen tablecloth over the table, offering to make tea, searching in drawers and cupboards for sugar bowls and spoons.

Florrie arrived with jelly and butterfly cakes and put bottles of lemonade in the larder and beer on the cool step outside, ready for the drinking which would begin when they got back from the church. Her pepper-coloured wispy hair that usually sprouted from her head like gone-to-seed cornflowers, was coiled up into a French plait, and it was the first time anyone had seen her in a dress – the first time anyone had seen her ankles probably – and Pat declared she looked magnificent in the polka dot shirtwaister set off by a dusty pink bolero.

When Babby appeared in her petticoat and veil, looking more beautiful than she had ever looked before, her hair in perfect ringlets – the rags she had slept in the night before had done their work – tumbling about her shoulders, her skin dewy and fresh, Hannah yelped and clapped her hands together while Violet and Kathleen and Florrie fussed and clucked over her as though they would never stop. Babby and Violet hugged.

'You look beautiful, love,' said Violet, rearranging one of the curls of her hair and straightening her veil.

'Remember, the Queen of the May Procession, with the candles coming down the stairs?' Pat said, arranging the chairs so they were pushed up against the dresser, laughing.

'My veil caught fire,' said Babby. 'And Da threw a glass of water at me to put it out!'

'No, it didn't, love. You do exaggerate,' Violet said, with a smile.

'Wish Da was here today,' said Babby wistfully.

'We all do,' Violet said, sighing. 'But you know, he is in a way. He's part of you, love, always will be. Every time I look at you, I see him. Funny, it should be Pat. But it's not. It's you. Simple as that.'

'Look who's here!' cried Doris, when Peggy from the cab shelter arrived to take a look at Babby and ooh and ah over her.

'Would you like a sherry, Peg? Pat? Any takers?' asked Kathleen.

'Sounds grand. I'll get some more glasses,' answered Pat. Collar starched and gleaming white, he wore an Ascot necktie and, to top it off, a red carnation boutonnièrre.

'Violet? Fancy a cheeky tipple?' said Kathleen.

Violet looked at her. 'No thanks, love. I've given all that up for now.' Kathleen nodded and touched her sister's arm, and Violet knew all that the gesture contained. She was done with drinking. Not just for now. For good.

Suddenly Mary burst through the door, beaming.

'Greetings from Dublin!' she said.

'Frying Pan!' squealed Babby. And they fell into each other's arms, and kissed.

'Who's that?' whispered Doris to Pat.

'A girl from Saint Hilda's. Babby was very keen that we invited her. Took a bit of trouble to track her down, but we found her through Florrie.'

'Well, that's a turn up,' murmured Doris. 'Doesn't she look the business in that pretty green frock?'

'Hope you're going to give us a tune on your dad's old squeezebox later. We can't have a party without music,' shouted Kathleen across the room.

'Wait,' said Violet.

'Where are you going?' asked Babby as Violet went towards the cellar door, making her way past the assortment of chairs and stools and the chaise longue. She disappeared downstairs.

'Tah dah!' she said a minute later, coming back up into the room, struggling with what looked like an accordion case. Blowing the dust off it, she called Babby over.

'Open it,' she said. 'It was your dad's. He got this from his father. And his father got it from his. It's an heirloom, by rights, but it plays well, so your dad said. Just too precious for the Boot Inn.'

Babby looked at it in shock.

'Go on, love, open it,' Violet said, smiling.

Babby pushed the lock, which sprang open with a soft click. The accordion was Italian, a Trevani, with an intricate trellis and beautiful mother of pearl casing and keys.

'Your dad said he was saving it for you. To give to you on your wedding day or your eighteenth birthday, whichever came first ...There were so many times I nearly sold it. We've got Rex to thank for that. He always stopped me. Said it wasn't right, dug us out of a hole with a bit of money he had spare on more than one occasion.'

Babby's eyes filled with tears. 'I want to get to know Rex better, Mam. You don't need to hide him from us any more.'

'I'll make sure that changes,' whispered Violet. 'He's been good to Hannah. He's been good to us all. If it hadn't been for Rex who tracked down Callum and told him where to find you ... well ... I hardly dare think.' She gathered herself, brushed a tear away from her eye. 'Anyway, can't wait to hear you play later.'

There was a shout. 'Uncle Rex! He's here! He's here!' cried Hannah, sticking her head out of the open sash window, and waving.

'Oh my giddy aunt!' cried Doris.

'Did Callum persuade him?' said Kathleen.

'I don't know. Maybe that means he's finally told that sister of his, Gladys, where to stick it. Can't wait to see Violet's face!'

'Mam!' cried Hannah. 'Uncle Rex is walking up the street and he looks right posh, and lovely. Uncle Rex is coming!'

Violet steadied herself on a chair. 'I thought he said he wasn't going to. What's made him change his mind?'

'Who knows?' said Babby, coming up behind Violet. 'Just glad he's here.'

When he entered the door, he was welcomed as though he was already part of the family. Hannah rushed to meet him and he hugged her as he planted a warm kiss on top of her head and ruffled her hair. Then Violet led him by the hand – and Babby threw her arms around him, and greeted him like he was her second father.

Amongst the commotion of lost shoes and hairpins and hatpins, Babby took the accordion and quietly went upstairs. She placed it on the floor under the window and turned to her wedding dress, laid out on the bed. Babby had never seen anything as beautiful in her life. Holding it up against herself, she smoothed down the skirts and regarded herself in the mirror. She felt the swell of her belly, the child inside.

Shaking out her hair, she slipped the dress over her head. It felt tight across her breasts, but you would never have known she was pregnant. Florrie was a magician with a needle and thread. She tied the blue ribbon around her head, so that the shivering curls framed her face. Laughter floated up from downstairs where someone was telling a story, probably Pat. She listened to the noise. There was the sound of a car engine idling, the slamming of a car door, probably Rex setting off to the church with Florrie.

'Are we going to be late?' cried Hannah.

'They'll have to wait,' said Violet.

'Well, isn't this grand? Isn't this grand?' said Doris.

'I've forgotten my mantilla.' That was Kathleen, thought Babby. 'I can't go to church without my mantilla.'

Babby sat on the bed, slipped the accordion straps through her arms, and began playing a few chords. She felt a trickle of sweat on the nape of her neck as she pulled the bellows in and out. Softly she sang, ''Twas a Liverpool girl who loved me ...' The sound of the instrument was beautiful, not the harsh roaring sound she was used to, but delicate, tuneful and musical. After running her fingers over the keys a few times, she put the accordion down and rearranged her dress. This is it, she thought. No turning back now.

'Where's Mam?' she asked when she came downstairs into the parlour.

'She said we've still got time yet. She's gone for a fag in the back yard. She needed some air,' said Kathleen. 'Don't you look beautiful!'

'I'll go and get her,' said Babby, 'I'll be back in a minute.'

She found her mother outside, smoking a cigarette. Violet gasped when she saw her.

'My little girl,' she murmured.

'Mam, I might not always have liked you, and you me neither, that's for sure, but I have always loved you. You know that, don't you?' said Babby, grasping her hand.

'Oh, sweetheart,' said Violet. 'I do.'

And in that moment, all was forgiven, all was understood. The thread that they had thought needed to be snapped was the one that would hold them together.

Meanwhile at the church, which was a ten-minute walk down the hill from Joseph Street, people had started taking their places. At the altar, Callum, wide-eyed with nervousness, craned his neck to see Babby and Violet arriving.

'He looks a picture!' cried Violet when she saw Callum in his suit. She noticed Rex as he pushed his way down the pew past Florrie and flashed a smile at him.

Babby slipped her arm through Pat's as he prepared to walk her down the aisle. Looking at him, it occurred to her, he was becoming just like their father, calm-featured, kind-looking. Hannah following behind, carrying a bunch of posies, put on her most serious face, and pressed her lips together in studied concentration. Babby turned, winked, and Hannah's frown relaxed into a smile. Brilliant sunshine flooded into the church through the stained-glass windows and, when the organ began to play, the hairs on Callum's neck stood up stiffly as he sensed his precious Babby getting closer.

'I love you, Cal,' she whispered, as she took his hand.

'I love you too, Babby,' he said. 'You look so beautiful, like a flamin' work of art.'

And in that moment, she felt something moving inside her for the first time, just a tiny flutter, like a butterfly landing on her stomach, and she instinctively moving her hand to brush it off, with the realisation that this was no butterfly, this was her chld.

She turned to Callum and smiled that special smile, and the chorus of voices swelled to the music of Ave Maria, and Babby began to sing.

Later, as they spilled out on to the church steps, giddy and bursting with happiness, Babby looked at her mother. Who knew what lay ahead? She took note of the people who were gathered around. This was a day for the Delaneys, she thought. Instead of this baby pulling the rug up from under their lives and leaving them all with nothing, maybe, just maybe, with the help of Cal and Rex, and Violet and Pat and Hannah, the child would help rebuild this family.

Epilogue

Seven Years Later

'Mam! Mam!' There's a load of elephants coming out of Lime Street station!'

'Don't be so daft, Ted,' Babby replied.

She was scrubbing the front step with a lump of pumice stone and paused for a moment to wipe the sweat off her brow. She could feel moisture pooling on the nape of her neck, a trickle running down her back. She sat back on her heels and squinted up at her six-year-old son.

'I'm telling you. Elephants. Let's go and see if you don't believe it!' said Ted, hopping from foot to foot, excitement emanating from his engagingly snub-featured face.

'Elephants? What on earth are you talking about?' Rolling up her sleeves and shoving them up her arms, she sighed.

'Frankie says there's going to be ladies in their scanties wearing sparkly brassieres and chucking skinny sticks up in the air,' he cried.

'Ah,' said Babby, understanding. 'The circus, you mean?'

Word had already got around about how the Gallaghers had agreed to house some of the animal cages from the travelling circus in their stables at the dairy. There had been laughter and rumination over pints in pubs, and buckets on doorsteps, as to how that was going to work out if the beasts escaped, with lions roaming up and down Scottie Road and a hapless Johnny Gallagher chasing after them.

She dipped the pumice in the bucket of water, noticing her knuckles were reddening.

'Mam,' Ted said, tugging at her skirt. 'There's going to be a band and everything! Can I go?'

She thought for moment. Well, it would be the closest he would get to seeing the circus this side of Christmas. Or any Christmas, for that matter. There's no way they could afford to pay for a ticket at five bob each.

'Go. But mind you don't get trodden on by the elephants. Stand back off the pavement. Lime Street, you said?'

'Aye. Snorting and stomping and doing this ...'

He made a harrumphing noise and pressed his forearm against his nose, waving his hand back and forth.

She stopped, couldn't help smiling, undid the ties on her apron. 'Just wash your hands before you leave.'

Entering the parlour, she found Violet there, sorting through a pile of washing hanging on the clothes maiden.

'Mother. Please leave that. You don't need to do it.'

Her mother was finally beginning to show signs of her age. She was still only forty-seven, but the rouged cheeks and carmine red lipstick were starting to draw attention to her hardening features. And yet, standing there folding Cal's nightshirts, chest puffed out, Babby decided when it came to Violet, the flesh might be a little weaker, but the spirit was certainly not, and probably never would be.

'So. Aren't you going to ask me how I'm getting on at Muirhead Avenue?' said Violet.

'How is it?' asked Babby.

'Grand,' replied Violet. 'Oh love, Rex was right, it's wonderful! There's no gaps between the windows and the frames or loose floorboards blowing a draught up your skirts. And there's gardens at the front *and* the back, with a little passage down the side. We're going to plant roses. And it's so warm!'

'And the neighbours?' asked Babby, tentatively.

Violet glanced at Jenny. She held up her left hand, showed Babby the wedding ring. 'Recognise this?' she said, lowering her voice.

Babby gasped. 'From Saint Judes? You kept it?'

'You never know when these things might be useful. Don't know if we'd be able to pass off a curtain ring, but Woolies does the job just fine. Everyone thinks we're married,' she whispered to Babby, and winked.

'Nan,' said Jenny, 'Mam says you've gone to live in a right posh house where water comes out of the tap hot and you turn into a cabbage.'

'Cabbage?' asked Ted, wide-eyed with curiosity, coming into the room.

'Like a cabbage leaf,' said Jenny.

'Your mam's right. When you lie in the bath your fingers and toes start crinkling if you stay in too long. And another thing, you don't have an outside lavvy. It's in the house. And when you sit on the seat that's all toasty warm as well.'

'Wish we could have hot running water and I don't like the outside lav – it freezes my nuts off.'

'Ted! Where did you learn that kind of language?'

'Dad,' he answered, and grinned. 'He said, "that outside lav freezes your bloody nuts off".'

'The other day, when I was doing a wee, a spider fell down from the ceiling into my pants,' said Jenny.

Babby and Violet couldn't help laughing.

'Nan, she came running into the kitchen nearly in the nuddy,' said, Ted, grinning.

'Why are you laughing, Mam?' said Jenny.

'It was only a money spider. Brings you good luck. Makes you rich. That's what we need around here.'

Not long now. She had kept it from the children – they might explode with happiness if they knew about the letter from the Corporation that had arrived earlier that week, white and crisp, saying they were on the list for a maisonette in Bootle with a garden and heating and hot water. Two kids and a baby, all of them crammed in with Violet and Hannah, meant they were right at the top of that list. And the disrepair order on Joseph Street meant tight old Boughton hadn't been paid for months and there was not a damn thing he could do about it. Pat and Doris and their little boy, Jack, had never looked back since they went to the open spaces of Norris Green, but she would miss this place – the grime and the smoke stacks, the rail you had to grasp on to in order to steady yourself when walking down the hill, but most of all the people. The Gallaghers, and the pub, Peggy – and even Gladys.

'Maybe it was one of them poisonous spiders from one of them banana crates off the ships,' said Violet, as Ted shot towards the door.

'Mother!' said Babby, giving her an admonishing look as she hooked a finger under Ted's jacket, yanking him back.

'Mam! Can I go?'

Babby smiled. Then she said, 'Hey, Teddy. Why don't me and Jenny come with you? They're on their way to Stanley Park, so they'll be coming down Saint Domingo Road in half an hour. Mam, will you look after the baby?' she asked Violet. 'She's sleeping. We should be back before she wakes.'

'Of course, love,' Violet said.

'Let's swing by the docks and see if Dad's got a few coppers to spare. Payday today.'

Babby pulled Jenny along by her little hand that was curled up into a fist, and yelled at Ted to wait for them as he whooped and hollered, pushed his cowboy hat off his head, swung it by the elastic and raced off down the hill, shooting imaginary injuns.

'Stop at the tinnies!' cried Babby.

There was more and more corrugated iron these days – whole streets of tinned-up derelict houses waiting for demolition. They gave the place a desolate air and when they got to the dock road, even that felt empty.

'Mister, is me dad here?' Ted asked the man leaning on the front gate outside the yard, idly splitting a match.

'Callum your dad? You look just like him,' he replied, chucking the match into the gutter. 'Good fella. Lot of men pinning their hopes on him. They say he's the one who's going to make sure we see some changes round here.'

Babby nodded. If anyone could improve things, it was her Cal. Still so young, but he wasn't afraid to make demands of the bosses and he didn't care what anyone thought, despite those who said he should have stayed at Liverpool Assurance rather than taking the job at the docks, just to cause trouble.

'Should be coming off his shift.'

He shouted over his shoulder to a group of men with their billycans, walking towards the gate. 'You seen Cal?'

'Down at Bramley, supervising the guy ropes. But that were an hour ago.'

'Come on, Mam. We're going to miss the parade!' said Ted, tugging at her skirts.

'Oh no,' whined Jenny. 'I don't want to miss it.'

'Let's go,' said Babby, hoiking up her daughter with her arms, where she sat on the groove on her hip.

But suddenly, there he was, striding towards them, backlit by the sun, his silhouette blurred and golden around the edges, a little tired about the eyes, but still as beautiful as the first day she laid eyes on him. Fresh air suited him. 'Have you heard about the circus?' he cried, jogging over.

'I'm taking them down to see. They'll be coming through soon.'

'Here, sixpence for sweets, Ted. And save me a Flying Saucer,' he said, digging into his pockets, jangling change. 'I'll see you later, Babby. And remember – tonight, we're going dancing.'

'How could I forget that?' she said, as they exchanged a tender look. Her love for this man still pulled her up short, every time she thought of what life might have been without him. 'Been looking forward to it all week. All *month*. Hannah is staying in to babysit and we can get the six o'clock ferry.'

'Come *on*, Mam,' said Ted.

'See you later, Cal. Hey!' Babby cried, as they set off towards Saint Domingo Road.

They heard the roar of the crowd before they saw anything. It seemed as if the whole of Liverpool had come to have a look. There was the sound of someone banging a drum, whistles and tambourines. And

432

Ted was right – it was a parade and a half. There was a ringmaster with a pencilled-on moustache, wearing a tall hat and a red tailcoat, a whip curled about his forearm. Behind him followed a balloon seller, and behind them, six huge grey elephants with velvet drapes and feather-plumed caps, ears flapping gently, walking down the road, swaying back and forth. Sitting aloft on sequinned saddles on the elephant's backs were women with their hair piled up in chignons and curls. They looked serene and beautiful in chiffon harem trousers, diaphanous cloaks, and elaborate head dresses, as delightful and rare as tropical birds.

'It's the circus!' cried Ted. 'There's giant elephants. Look at the fat man! He's playing a funny trumpet that curls around his tummy, like a snake. Looks like he's going to explode!'

'Sousaphone, that's called.' Babby surprised herself as a memory streaked through her head of the nuns at Penrcath Farm. An education. Had *that* been the sister's gift to her?

'I can't see!' cried Ted .

'Push yourself forward. Hey, mister, move out of the way. I've two little 'uns here!' yelled Babby.

The man blocking the path, wearing a cloth cap, turned. He was with a small group, three other men and a woman, all of them with leaflets in their hands, two of them holding a banner above their heads with a shamrock on it. They had the complexion of the Irish – freckles, pale skin, red or dark hair. 'Jaysus! Can you give over barging into us?'

'Let these little 'uns through!' said Babby.

'Sure, a please would be nice, love!'

She smiled apologetically and set them off like wind-up toys, pushing them with a sharp shove – little scurrying weasels, darting between men's trousered legs and women's skirts, scouring, dipping in and out of the crowd. 'And mind you keep back from the blinking elephants!' she said, as an afterthought.

She had a moment where she worried it had been stupid to let them out of her sight. There were no barriers to stop the elephants crashing into the crowd, or misplacing a giant foot on to the pavement and squashing the onlookers. And when there was another huge roar, a clatter of drums and pipes, a cascading of sticks, screams, and people running, panic took hold of her.

'The elephant! It's loose! It's doing a runner!!'

'Ted!' she yelled. 'Jenny! My kids!'

And then suddenly the screams morphed into gales of reassuring laughter.

Someone cried, 'Where's the Elf and Safety when you need 'em? Some bugger'll catch it if that happens again! Did you see it stand up on its two back legs?' There were more guffaws.

'Mam!' she heard Ted cry, and relief flooded through her veins as she caught a glimpse of his red coat and Jenny's russet curls as a woman, clutching their hands, steered them towards her.

'Thanks so much,' Babby said to the woman. Then, 'Frying Pan! What are you doing here?' she yelped in surprise.

'I'm with that lot,' she answered, nodding toward the claque with the banners.

The children, bursting with the excitement around them, words tippling over words like dominoes, exclaimed, 'Did you see the elephant blowing his trunk?! He nearly crashed into us! How many lives have we got left now, Mam? Three? Two?'

'Ah,' said Babby. She recognised the leaflets in Mary's hand. Ireland's Freedom Fighters, she read on the green, white and gold sash that Mary wore.

'Wherever there's a crowd, we come along to try and spread the word, drum up a little support,' said Mary.

'Still at it then?' Babby said and smiled.

'Aye.' Mary was flushed pink to her ears. Her delicate green eyes sparkled and she smiled. 'These both your kids?' she asked.

Babby nodded. 'And a baby at home.'

'Swift work!'

Babby hesitated. 'What about you?'

'No. But I've got a fella. Not the same one as I had at Saint Jude's. That one turned out to be a right deadbeat. But my Eammon is top-notch.'

'But no kiddies yet?'

'No. And there won't be.'

'You don't mean that?'

'I do. Not ever.'

Babby faltered. 'And you're fine with that?'

She took Babby's hands, grasped her fingers. 'Ah love, I'm absolutely fine. I've got work to do. You've no idea. The fight gets harder. I've no time for that stuff.'

'But what about …?' Babby's question tailed off into nothing.

'My baby? I'm not afraid to say it, Babby. The nuns did me a favour. Honestly. I can't spend my life looking back. Why would I? I could cry a vale of tears, but what's the good of that? Never mind it would have been impossible to bring up a baby on me own, impossible because I never wanted to lose sight of *me*. Who *I* am. Kids do that to you, sometimes.' Mary took her hand, gripped it, and pressed a leaflet into the palm of it. 'Here, take this and read it.'

Babby folded it neatly, put it way in her pocket, then dropped her eyes, first to Jenny skittering in and out of the crowds, then to Ted, kicking the kerb-stone. Had kids done that to her? 'You sure you're OK?' she asked, once again.

'Right as rain,' Mary answered with a smile. 'Catholic's Honour. Cross my heart and hope to die,' she said making a small gesture – a glancing stroke with her forefinger, one, two, across her chest. And they kissed and said goodbye and swore that they would meet again, though they both knew that might never happen.

'Keep in touch.'

'I will. I'd best be off,' she said, nodding towards the small group of men, chanting the slogans on their banners. 'One Ireland! One Cause!'

Babby nodded and turned to go. But then she remembered she might have moved to Bootle by the end of the month. She should give Mary her new address. She turned back to find her. And felt her heart somersault.

There was Ted, still standing on the pavement, losing himself in a stupid game as he balanced on one foot and tossed a halfpenny in the air. And there was Mary, standing frozen to the spot, staring at Ted's perfectly formed face, as he watched the coin flip into the sun. It was the combination of Mary's expression, so sad and contemplative, and the tiny rise and fall of Ted's shoulders, that made Babby immediately look away. It was too much to bear. And as she hurried off, hoping that Ted would be bobbing through the crowds after her, she realised she hadn't believed a single word of what Mary had said.

'Let's go and tell Nan and Hannah about the elephants,' said Ted when he caught up and squirrelled under her arm. The three of them fell into a steady rhythm. And the elephants continued on, swaying gracefully in the sun, until the excitement, the cheering, and laughter, gradually diminished to a rhythmic throb and petered to a nothing.

When they got home, the baby was waking from her afternoon nap. Violet had left and Hannah had arrived home from the early shift at the Meccano factory and was taking off her coat.

'I'll see to her, Hannah,' said Babby. 'You put the kettle on.'

What she would do without Hannah? She would find room for her at the new house, to keep the promise she had made all those years ago.

Slipping off her shoes, she went upstairs, taking care not to tread on the loose, rotting board. This house had been threatening to swallow them up for years now. The baby was in her cot, struggling to stand on her chubby legs. She had a fist stuck in her mouth and was smiling.

'My little lamb,' said Babby.

She went over and lifted her out. The child twisted her face into her breasts and Babby kissed the top of her creamy head. She paused, remembering her father hugging her close and tight like this the last time she saw him. How far she had come and how precious these moments were.

She was overtaken by an irresistible impulse and, putting her baby back in the cot, she padded across the room and opened the lid of the wooden chest, knelt down and removed blankets, the old astrakhan coat.

The smell hit her first. That musky, familiar scent that hit the back of her throat and filled her nostrils. She sat on the chair, hauled the accordion on to her knee. As always, pulling open the bellows, it felt as if her father had noiselessly stepped into the room with her.

Time to bring music back into all of their lives. It was long overdue. Would she even have remembered how to play? She had been so busy with the children these past seven years she hadn't had time for much of anything. She began.

It was as easy as shelling peas.

And the strains of the music grew louder, sweeter, more joyful as the baby gurgled and chirrupped and clapped her hands with delight.

This was happiness – and Babby was ready to grab at it.

Acknowledgements

Thanks so much to my editor Gillian Greene at Ebury Press. Thank you also to my agent, Judith Murdoch, for her encouragement and advice, and to Trisha Ashley who told me my short story was in fact a novel, and who has supported me every step of this journey. Thank you to my husband Peter, for everything, and especially for talking to me at length about his job as a porter at Brookwood Asylum. Thank you to the life force in our home that is Louis and Joel, for putting up with their mother's dereliction of duty. Thanks to the indomitable Pat Scanlon who first shared her heart-stopping story over many cups of tea with me. And to my mum and dad for their constant and unending love. Without whom I would never have learned to play the piano accordion or have written this book.